Nob

Betrayed

D. Brennan

By

Dylan Brennan

Table of Contents

HOUSE WOODGAIRRD:

-KING EMANNAR WOODGAIRRD, son of Grimm

-His wife, ELIZELLA SLAIT, of House Slait

-their children:

-PRINCE VARN WOODGAIRRD, heir to the throne, 14

-PRINCESS JAIDE WOODGAIRRD, a 13-year-old girl

-PRINCESS DYANA WOODGAIRRD, a 10-year-old girl

-his siblings:

-STYVE WOODGAIRRD, former High Earl

-his wife, ASHLYH SLAIT, of House Slait

-his daughter, SARISA WOODGAIRRD, a 7-year-old girl

-KASE WOODGAIRRD, the forgotten younger brother

-his wife, ELA TYMBRENN, of House Tymbrenn

-his private council:

-SUPREME WITANEGEMOTE GREGORY

-LORD FRANCIS ASHFORD, tactician

-LORD STYVE WOODGAIRRD, Admiral of the Fleet

-LORD KASE WOODGAIRRD, Esteemed Lawmaker

-SIR KARRON WULL, Commander of the King's Guard

-LORD TOBAS, financer and messenger

-his court:

-SIR JARON CARNER, commander of the Kingsmen

-SIR KEGAN WYNE, a Wyne brother sworn to Prince Varn

-SIR ELDEN BRUNE, an executioner

-SIR JURAN HERQYS, known as The Exile

-RABBITHEAD, the jester

-ESQ. RUDD TYMBRENN, a squire to Emannar

-ESQ. SEAMUS TYMBRENN, a squire to Emannar

-SIR BRADYN BULWARK, an executioner

-his Guard:

-SIR KARRON WULL, Commander

-SIR STEPHYN TANNER, Lieutenant General

-SIR GARVY ORKWOOD

-SIR BYRRON VIKARIN

-SIR BRIDEN VIKARIN

-SIR DURAN DURRON

-SIR DIRRON RYGERT

HOUSE PARGION:

-SIMON PARGION, Lord of Bernstaplen

-His wife, LADY GWENDYS WAYNE, of House Wayne

-their children:

-DAMON PARGION, heir to Bernstaplen, age 17

-KRISTYNE PARGION, the older daughter, age 14

-ANNYTE PARGION, the younger daughter, age 11

-DAYRON PARGION, 9

-CORREN PARGION, 3

-DAMAN PARGION, Simon's self-declared 'half-child,' 15

-His ward, LAWRENCE MALVER, heir to House Malver

-his siblings:

-ALAVIN PARGION, deceased, died during The Stormholme Schism

-BRINNA PARGION, deceased, died during The Stormholme Schism

-CAMERN PARGION, his younger brother, hiding away in Lakewell

-his household:

-WITANEGEMOTE MORGAN, the House's Witanegemote

-JOHN BORRELL, his steward

-his daughter, KYRA BORRELL

-JAZE WYNE, Captain of House Pargion's guard

-His many guardsmen

-ODO WYNE, Simon's tactician of House Wyne,

-Elizabeth Wyne, his daughter

-PRIESTESS RONAYNE, hired as a teacher for Simon's daughters

-PRIEST NARISETTI, runs Bernstaplen's chapels and libraries

-HORSEMASTER SULLIVAN

-his son, STABLEMAN BUCKLEY

-KENNELMASTER RICHARDS

-STORYTELLER HICKMERE

-MOYA, the chef

-GERALD, the blacksmith

HOUSE SLAIT:

-ARVIN SLAIT, Lord of House Slait, rejected title of High Earl

-his wife, LADY LAENA OF HERESY, a commoner

-their children:

-ELIZELLA SLAIT, wife of King Emannar

-DONTIN SLAIT, known as the Veille, the sole son

-ASHLYH SLAIT, wife of Styve Woodgairrd

-SYLVINA SLAIT, the youngest daughter, 15

-his siblings:

-DREVYN SLAIT, his younger brother

-his wife PALINA OATWRIGHTT, deceased, died during The Stormholme Schism

-his son MANREL SLAIT, a member of Arvin's guard

-his son DALLAR SLAIT, a member of Arvin's guard

-BRIANEL SLAIT, his sister

-her husband, BYRRON VIKARIN, member of the King's Guard

-their son, GARVY VIKARIN, 4, named after Garvy Orkwood

-their daughter, MADELEINE VIKARIN, 12

-ARABELLE SLAIT, his sister, deceased

-his counsellor, WITANEGEMOTE ANKERSON

HOUSE WAYNE:

-MARVION WAYNE, Lord of House Wayne

-his wife, LADY SAEDE TANNER, of House Tanner

-their son, TYRAL WAYNE, 10, a feeble boy accused of treason

-their daughter, GWENDYS WAYNE, wife of Simon Pargion

-his counsellor, WITANEGEMOTE ADOM

-captain of his guard, CELIA FAEYRESON

-GYRARD, leader of La Perte Inconnue, a guild of assassins

-GOSFRIDUS, member of La Perte Inconnue

-MAUCOLYN, member of La Perte Inconnue

-SYMONNET, member of La Perte Inconnue

-KONDRAD, former bandit and air-headed advisor to Gwendys

-MAURICE, Marvion's beastmaster

HOUSE TANNER:

-DROMIN TANNER, Lord of House Tanner

-his wife, CLIARA MALVER, of House Malver

-their children:

-CLIARA TANNER, deceased, died in The Stormholme Schism

-STEPHYN TANNER, Lieutenant General of the King's Guard

-SONIYA TANNER, a young girl, 8

-DARLYNE TANNER, the youngest girl, 6

-his counsellor, WITANEGEMOTE ROCHE

-CONSEN DEGARRE, Captain of Dromin's Guard

-PRIEST BONIECKI, runs the chapels

-ANSELM SIMCOCK, Stephyn's former tutor

OTHER HOUSES:

HOUSE STUNN, led by RUGER STUNN and ALARINA STUNN

HOUSE MALVER, led by EDD MALVER and his heir LAWRENCE MALVER

HOUSE FOLER, led by DAVID FOLER and TERESSA FOLER

HOUSE NALLORT, led by JURAN NALLORT and GABRIN NALLORT

OUTSIDE OF THE GREAT KINGDOM:

HOUSE CANTELL, led by MARGAN CANTELL and IREYNE HEMLOCK

HOUSE MAGNAROK, led by AUSTER MAGNAROK and LILYANA HEMLOCK

HOUSE BATOUL, led by MAGNIV BATOUL and his heir MARZA BATOUL

HOUSE SQUDD, led by TIRIUS SQUDD and IREYNE HEMLOCK

HOUSE HEMLOCK, led by TRANIS HEMLOCK and ASTRIS HEMLOCK

HOUSE GRIMM, led by DRAN GRIMM, the last true Grimm

HOUSE READING, led by GARRAT READING and KIARA PICKERING, of no house

HOUSE MUBERRE:

-PATRICK I MUBERRE, Lord of House Muberre

-his wife, BARN MUBERRE

-their children:

-GREGOR MUBERRE, a thief-taker, heir to Tinquerebelle

-his wife, SUSANNE BAULDER, of House Baulder

-their son, ROBIN MUBERRE, the Silicon Swiper

-his Hund, MISSY

-members of his Take, ARON, MATY, and DANIEL

-TRISH MUBERRE, member of The Cobra Sisters

-TARR MUBERRE, member of The Cobra Sisters

-TEZ MUBERRE, member of The Cobra Sisters

-PATRICK II MUBERRE, her son, training to be a Witanegemote

-his siblings:

-CLEMENT MUBERRE, a travelling nobleman

-JOHNATHAN MUBERRE, a pirate

-RUTHERFORD MUBERRE, a convicted raider

HOUSE BAULDER:

-JOSEPH BAULDER, Lord of House Baulder

-his wife, ROSA BAULDER

-their children:

-SUSANNE BAULDER, married to Gregor Muberre

-REBECA BAULDER, lives in the estate

-ROZ BAULDER, fate unknown

-their household:

-SIR MAXIMILIEN ENGERAMUS, Captain of House Baulder's Guard

-WITANEGEMOTE JULIO, counsellor

Prologue: Ankerson

The Supreme Witanegemote has summoned me. I know of his plans.

I have arrived at Stormholme, where the King, the Queen, and all their children, his guard, and his household reside. The council meets here too, though little care to know what they discuss. The city of Stormholme is truly an extraordinary sight, built atop robust hills and magnificent pastures. It has a charm to it. The entire kingdom has a charm to it, as its description in the tales speaks true - majestic forests where the wild things hide, trade scattered around with the brave and the criminal, and influential architects have finely crafted stylistic and grand buildings and houses, making the working-class seem like they have money to spare. The serene skyline stretches with the fine addition of luxurious palaces for the King and his Noble Lords and a history that shines here more than anywhere; it is full of blood and tears, love and loss, pain and suffering. However, trade is at an all-time high in Stormholme. With 9 Great Houses, and several others sworn to the King, culture is rife. Too rife.

Culture leaves its mark - not only on architecture but on identity. A kingdom of small contrast to others has become a unique and blooming multicultural hub, which unites millions of citizens to this day. Hundreds of smithies, pubs, palaces, and barracks keep the fire of life alive and awaken each day to provide each citizen with the taste of escapism. This Great

Kingdom is the curiosity of the future, and culture shall bring it to heavenly heights.

But what did I know? I was just an insignificant Witanegemote, going to his superior.

It was dark as hell. I noticed a single comet flying by, a blaze of brilliant blue through the inky black, moving through the sky like the tip of the universe's brush; bold enough to light up a pair of eyes, respectful enough to leave the stars of the night in perfect form until it passed. I always believed there was something more beyond these blue walls. I didn't believe in omens. I didn't believe in gods. All I believed in was something bigger. And money. Definitely money. That was the code of every 27-year-old in the world these days.

I entered the council room. The Supreme Witanegemote was there, alone. Greed. Petulance. Determination. Such was to be expected from a man like this. Raised in a poor family loyal to House Cantell, outside of The Great Kingdom, he lived free of trouble until he was struck by the hand of fate. His father was arrested for treason, and the Supreme Witanegemote Maertin sentenced the man to death. Vengeance had devoured them.

"Ankerson, Good Lord! Thought you'd been slaughtered by the King's Guard already," Gregory smirked, like a devil welcoming his new slave to the underworld. His silver, oily head left an imprint of disgust in the hearts of all men.

"Better today than never," I replied with grit.

"I assume Lord Tobas has informed you?" he asked. His pointed beard trickled down his chin like a spider's web, each strand of facial hair drowning the other.

"Of what?"

"His Grace is looking for a new High Earl." This startled me. The High Earl was essentially the second-in-command of the entire kingdom. King Emannar had previously given this honour to his brother, Styve, but they were never close. Still, why would a man ever quit such a role unless they had died?

"Are you certain of this?" I responded.

"I am a Witanegemote. If I am not certain, I do not speak," he responded, slightly sombre. Witanegemotes were expected to spread wisdom, but now all they spread is corruption. Emannar has done well.

"What became of Styve?"

"Rumours fly around, none can be believed. Some say that Styve is dead, others say that Emannar demoted him, but Tobas believes that Styve has found another area where he can find a greater deal of power than he is eligible to receive as High Earl. If this is true, he must be a fool," Gregory stroked his pointed beard, and I noticed the twinkle on his bald head getting brighter.

"Is this why you called me here?" I wanted to leave, so I kept to the point. If we were here, alone for too long, the council would discover us, and someone would talk. Likely Ashford, I have never trusted Francis.

"You are a Slait Loyalist, and Emannar is displeased with Arvin's attempts to conquer his land. As a Slait Loyalist, you must prove your loyalty to His Grace or suffer the fate that Arvin will in due time. We will not be merciful," I took all of this in. Witanagemotes are designed to be loyal. Loyalty was the core of our creation. We are the wisdom-breathing, broken, malnourished underlings for our respective Noble Lord. We each serve one. I serve Arvin Slait, of House Slait. Arvin has a large and powerful house, the third most powerful at this time; the most powerful, of course, being Emannar's House Woodgairrd, and the second being House Pargion, led by Simon Pargion. Simon Pargion was in the running to be the High Earl, but as he lost to Emannar's brothers, he retreated to the North-West Corners of the Great Kingdom and has not been seen for a while.

"What must I do?" I begged for mercy, though I knew that whatever task they had would get me killed either way. My core is telling me to try.

"You must take Lady Laena of Heresy's life. War will not be accepted, but I will tell you my strategy," Gregory was willing to help me? I was almost flattered (never flatter a councillor. They take advantage of flattery). Gregory's head twinkle got even brighter.

Lady Laena of Heresy is Arvin's betrothed. She is as tall as two Gregories (in other words, average height). She has an angular face, a hooked nose, thin lips, and slanted blue eyes. Black hair, dyed with henna, is elbow-length, curled, and un-styled, and she has an unkempt beard growing. Arvin will kill her anyway when it is fully grown. Strong arms, a broad torso, and strong legs. She believed that being a woman was her greatest curse. I think birth was. Killing her would be no easy feat, but it was her or me.

I headed to Fort Hagueveil, where my Lord and his Lady reside, and entered their throne hall. Polished braziers attached to one side of each of the eight onyx columns light up the entire throne hall and cover the hall in warm oranges and dancing shadows. The paintings of angels and cherubs on the sloped ceiling dance in the flickering light while memorials look down upon the obsidian floor of this grand hall. A teal rug runs in a circle around the room, with two paths at the throne and the main entrance, while ribbon banners hang from the walls with burnished edges. Between each banner sits a shrine-like ornament covered in candles; they've all been lit and, in turn, illuminate the portraits of late rulers below them. Hefty windows are neighboured by curtains coloured the same teal as the banners. The curtains have been adorned with gilded linings and gold leaves. A striking throne of carved rock sits amidst two large statues and is adjoined by two similar but undecorated seats for the Lord's family, including Lady Laena and her children, except for her eldest daughter, Elizella, who has married Emannar against Arvin's wishes. The throne is covered in byzantine designs, and fixed on each of the rear legs is a crystal star. The light pillows are a light teal, and these too, have been adorned with emblazoned embroideries. Those wishing to witness Lord Slait can do so on the many modest yet comfortable marble benches, all of which are perfectly aligned in rows. Those of higher standing can instead take a seat in the stately mezzanines overlooking the throne. As one can see, Arvin loved himself.

I grabbed a tube full of amphetamines (produced in Grimmstone circa 86) and prepared a kind glass of water for the Lady. A sip would be enough to kill her, but the drugs perfectly blended in, and there was an unclear change in the extraordinary product's turbidity. I marched up to her seat and held the glass before the couple's eyes.

"Lady Laena," I nodded as my fingers clutched the finely-decorated glass of the chalice.

"Lady Laena of Heresy," she scolded, "You forget your place, Ankerson."

"He is a Witanegemote; he can be forgetful at times with his expansive memory," Arvin told her, "What do you want, Ankerson?"

"Seeing as you have chosen to continuously make your own decisions regardless of the King's cries for your assistance, I have thought it most beneficial to provide you with both with a well-earned period of relaxation. We can all do with one, can't we?" I made an excuse.

"I have no time to rest, Ankerson," he responded.

"Those who relax are those who fail," Laena agreed.

Arvin nodded as he looked at her, "Emannar Woodgairrd once sought to claim all that was mine when he led that damn rebellion against his father. Grimm gave me everything, and Emannar threatened to take it. Why should I put my faith in such a man?"

"You are the rightful High Earl. Styve Woodgairrd has forfeited his title for the chance to gain more. Secure his trust, and seize all that is his," I advised him.

"All that is Emannar's is all that I reject," Arvin waved dismissively.

"You reject too much," I told him, "Kings can still battle, as is your deepest passion. Emannar is simply too weak." This was a bore. All I needed was to give this woman her goddamn cup.

"You want my husband to take a most vulnerable position in society and then risk his life even further? You endanger this House, Ankerson," Laena scolded me.

"Indeed. Perhaps we should find the nearest jester and command him to teach you a few dances," Arvin hollered.

"Maybe he should sing of his stupidity as well," Laena cackled.

"That would go too far. He has served me too well for such a punishment," Arvin reprimanded her.

"Perhaps I have been foolish today," I sighed, "Lady Laena, will you share a cup with me? A cup in honour of the gods?"

Laena studied me, "Indeed."

I handed her the poisoned glass, and we toasted as Arvin examined the scene. I kept my own glass. This had to be done for the realm. For my King.

She kept her eyes on me, and her lips curled into a cruel smile, "I'm not sure you could even keep this water down, Ankerson. It seems...strong."

"I'm sure I can," I whispered.

"So be it," she laughed, took the cup, and drank for a while. There was only a drop left when she laid it on her armrest, "You have not had your drink yet. I insist."

My hands shook as I took the cup to my lips. How did she do it? Did I mix them up? I couldn't have. This was the only time today that I had held the glass in my hands. It was not the lethal one. The water was a thief of heat, taking what it didn't need. Icicles formed on the roof of my mouth. I ingested them and everything else.

"It seems you do have some power," Laena grinned evilly.

I blinked as I looked at Arvin, "I remember the Witanegemote before me. Gains, wasn't it? He served your father, and then he served you. Gregory told me what had happened to him. You weren't his Lord; you were his boy. The son he never had. He cared for you, he lived for you, and he loved you more than the rest. Better than Drevyn. Better than Brianel. You were the first one, the reject, the unloved. Drevyn was a better fighter, and Brianel was the looker - your father didn't even want his power in your hands. You had nothing but his love. You were the one who needed him the most. And how did you repay his love? You sold him as a slave to Teleos Magnarok and left him to die. He was skinned alive by Auster, and you didn't bat a damn eye-"

Then I coughed.

Then I bled.

I collapsed to the floor, a pulsating wave of blood erupting from my core. I shook my head in disappointment. Ashamed of him, ashamed of her, ashamed of the gods. I was going to die.

The glowing emerald in her enchanted necklace stuck out to me, and the last image in my mind was the reflection of my bloody hands in her golden eyes.

Dayron:

I love the Great Wood. It's a forest. Small, radiant, budding. Canopies are dominated by crab apple, oak, maple, and pear, their leaves and branches allowing for just enough light to pass down for a diversity of bushes to control the boulder-covered grounds below.

Thin branches, grasping onto trees in a warm hug, and an array of flowers claiming remnants of light, dispersed equally for each and every plant in the Wood. Without the flowers, this would be like any other Wood. Monotone.

A cacophony of animal sounds, mainly animals fleeing to other pastures through the Great Wood, brighten up the Wood every now and then and are out of sync with the occasional roar of the Griffin or Treant, scaring away any predators that would dare to enter.

Shame that it's going to be a hunting ground.

We're all here. Father, Damon, Daman, Corren, Lawrence Malver (Father's Ward), Jaze Wyne (captain of Father's guard), and John Borrell (Father's steward).

Why?

There's a traitor in my Wood.

Damon is the most eager to find the poacher. As the eldest son and heir to House Pargion, he'd do anything to kill a man. Any man. He wears a mop of black, straight hair. Father always demands him to make a ponytail of the ebony or clean the castle floors for eternity. That's what a mop would do. Glittering black eyes and stubble nearing the growth of a beard. Damon is 17, a grown man. A grown man without a scar.

Scars mark your status as a warrior, yet Father is the one with the scars. Daman has many too. Physical and mental scars. I wish to have none.

Daman will be the eldest when Damon dies. He has been on many campaigns against the Novak Warriors for 2 years - ever since he became a grown man. But his white, shoulder-length hair tells me that he is not of my blood and never will be.

I am 9, 4 years from becoming a grown man. Out of all of my family, I am the least likely ever to fight. Less likely than Annyte or Kristyne, even.

Corren is 5, only here because Mother cannot protect him at the moment. I wish she could.

Father and Damon have spent the last hour sawing through the trees, and Lawrence Malver handed me my blade. A long, broad, jagged blade made of ivory held by a grip wrapped in expensive, scarlet salmon leather. A razor-sharp point that could cut down five legions worth of soldiers without a scratch but with a waterfall of blood, caused by the puncturing of enemies to death, from ruthless speed and precision. The blade has a wide, slightly curved cross-guard, which tells me that the blade is both balanced and capable of protecting the owner's hands against any sliding sword. The cross-guard has an elaborate curl on each side, marking the House it belongs to. A large pommel is decorated with precious gems; no expense is spared for this gorgeous weapon. The blade itself is fairly simple. No markings, no decorations, and no engravings, but the blade will surely be decorated in battle. Victory.

This weapon is used by higher-ranked guards most of the time. An excellent weapon for the defence of the country. But I don't want it. I sheathe the blade and walk behind the warriors of the hunting group Father has established.

Jaze Wyne looked up and inhaled the scent of nature, then charged forward with suddenly bloodshot eyes. He had felt something—a change in the wind, perhaps. The Wynes are mostly tough as nails, with Kegan Wyne serving Emannar directly and Jaze leading Father's knights. There is a third, though I know not to speak of his cowardice. The warriors rush forward. Jaze has a hunter in custody. Daman has his throat, preventing him from any pathetic attempt at conversation, and he is thrust into a carriage. Stableman Buckley, the stout son of Father's Horsemaster, has been pulling the carriage, as horses are too precious for a mere poacher, unlike the one who rides them. The poacher takes one last look at every hunter who has searched for him, including me, as he is taken away by Buckley's might.

But why did we try so hard to find him? He was just a poacher. Even poachers have stories to tell. It could be the story of a hero, a protector of children, or a slave to greed. Was he a person or a walking corpse? Did his heart bear fruit or disease?

I'm sure he had a wife. I'm sure he had a child, maybe even children. And we've taken it all from him for slaying a monster on our ground.

Surely we're the monsters?

Pacifism has always been a good idea to me. Peace is always an option, and it is the option with the least bloodshed. Wish Father or my brothers would agree, even if they only agreed for a minor quarrel. There's never been peace in a Pargion war.

John has uncovered something from the poacher's cloak. An egg. They gave it to me, of course, to the pacifist. My egg was already going to hatch.

Out pops a gryphling. Its wing is damaged and bloody. I pull out a cloth from my arsenal of useful equipment and clean away the blood.

Despite its wound, the gryphling has a bonny bright soul and a joyful spirit, so in keeping with the leaves that danced all around it.

It smiled and chirped.

I had not heard anything all day until I heard that chirp. The chirp was weak and broken.

Like me.

Gwendys:

Nine broad, square towers surround the fort. They reach twice the height of the walls and are connected by enormous, vast walls made of light green stone. Rough windows are scattered generously around the walls in seemingly perfect symmetry, along with symmetric holes for archers and artillery. A great gate with thick metal doors and strong defences guards the only place with water within these hot, dry lands, and it's the only way in, at least without taking down the fort's walls. Various large houses are scattered outside the fort's gates; surprisingly, the rich are comfortable with living outside the gates as well. This fort has been improved and improved over the ages; some parts of the castle are clearly newer than others, the inhabitants are determined to keep their fort as modern as possible. I am one such inhabitant of the Fort Bernstaplen, and today, the gate shall open.

Simon, Damon, Daman, Dayron, Corren, and the guards all went to find a poacher. Simon always was extreme when it came to criminals. Sometimes he made me watch as a thief was justly executed. I always begged him to stop...

"Mum!" Damon called out to me, "We did it! We got the poacher!"

"Fascinating," I grimaced.

"What's wrong, mum? Oh, don't tell me..." he realised I was annoyed at Simon again.

"Yes."

"For God's sake, mum, he hasn't even done anything! He just took us to catch a poacher. What's wrong with that?" Damon complained.

"He's spending too much time with my children," I frowned.

"But we're not just your children. We're his too. He has just as much a right to be with us as you do," Damon responded.

I looked at him with disappointment, "Funny how you speak your mind when you're talking to the woman of the House, but when you're with your Father or any other damn Lord, you turn to a mouse. Do I not do enough to earn your silence? Now, leave me be."

Damon gave up and left me alone, slamming the door as he went. I wasn't the disappointed one; he was. But I wasn't going to acknowledge that before him. He'd relay it to Simon, the rat.

He was undeserving of my love.

They all were.

Eventually, the great gates of hell opened.

The great gate, with thick metal doors and strong defences that had been weakened for the moment, slowly reached out to close the gap between Simon and his House, and he walked across wearing his chosen set of armour for the day. This set had a pointed helm with a pointed, v-shaped opening, so I could see his cold eyes and his bleak mouth. A pointed nose guard protected his elongated nose. Attached to his forehead was an axe with the letters' Memento Mori' engraved on the handle.

The shoulders were rounded, fairly narrow, and relatively large, decorated with a fair skull on fire right in the middle of each. The upper arms were protected by round, layered metal rerebraces which sat under his pauldrons. The lower arms were emblazoned with vambraces which had a layer of chainmail covering the outer sides. The breastplate was made from squared metal sheets, covering everything from the neck to the upper legs. The upper legs were covered by another skirt of metal sheets reaching down to his knees, and the rest of the leg was protected by chainmail greaves and boots. Simon looked me dead in my eyes.

"Hello, Gwendys," he stated, sans emotion.

"Hello, dear," I responded. Was my response too timid? Too weak?

"Dayron has a new pet, and remember that you are to have no part in its upbringing. If Dayron does not kill, he will suffer the consequences of having no responsibility other than survival. If I find that you have a part, you will suffer all the same."

"I understand, my Lord," I was powerless, "May I see the beast?"

"Indeed you may, but do not touch the Gryphling," he had to spoil the surprise.

I took a peek and saw Dayron playing with the Gryphling. They were as innocent as each other. Dayron was a born pacifist. If only we could tell him the secret Simon forced us to hide from him. As I watched on with a blooming smile, a smile that hadn't bloomed for many hours, the King's Guard rode on by. Sir Karron Wull, the commander of the Guard, marched forward, with his second-in-command Sir Stephyn Tanner following behind, remaining on horseback.

"Lord Simon Pargion and Lady Gwendys Wayne, of House Pargion, we are here to deliver a message," Wull announced. He had aged since I last saw him. A blank union of facial hair had become darker yet paler, a solemn mixture of age and youth. His hair had greyed. Nearing 47, he was ageing. His life would be short from now, as far as I could see. Simon looked at him with frozen eyes.

"Sir Karron Wull, have you and your King's Guard forgotten how to respect a Lord? Please bow, all of you," Simon responded blankly, the sort of response I expected from such a man. Stephyn Tanner, followed by Duran Durrandon, the Vikarin twins, and the other members of the Guard, bowed in unison behind Karron Wull, a respected member of the King's Council who was being forced to bow to a Lord they were not loyal to. They rose, and Tanner read out Emannar's message,

"My closest friend Lord Simon Pargion,

I write to you today to inform you that Styve Woodgairrd, my chosen High Earl, has forfeited this role and some of his lands in an attempt to achieve power from another Kingdom in the North. My brother Kase, the members of my council, and the rest of the Noble Lords of the Great Houses are all ready to compete for the role. I know that you are against great amounts of attention, but if you participate, I can guarantee that you shall achieve the role. I hope you will consider this.

Best wishes,

His Grace, Emannar Woodgairrd."

Stephyn Tanner read that like a 500-year-old Ent who can barely move his tree lips. He should be marvelling in his presence. Even Emannar should be more respectful, the Supreme Witanegemote probably took a minute to mimic the King's great words.

"You have served your King well, knights, but I have no interest in becoming High Earl. The role of High Earl is for land-hungry imbeciles who care for money more than family. I shall not," Simon answered. It amuses me that he believes he cares for family more than money. Nobody would ever believe that. Not truly.

Karron Wull looked at him with disregard, "You would jeopardise the entire land so that you can have peace for a few months? Look around, Simon. The land is not safe anymore. The outsiders will invade any time now, and we won't be prepared for it if we do not have a High Earl. You have no choice in this, my friend."

"But I do, and I choose silence," Simon replied.

I couldn't take this stupidity anymore, so I spoke up, "Listen to Sir Wull, my Lord. If you do not help, one of these corrupt candidates shall receive the lands and titles befitting a High Earl, and the outsiders will maul us all. Your warrior children will never fight if they don't have time to live."

"Silence, woman," Simon ordered.

"Silence is all you want. But you can't keep silence," Stephyn Tanner mused.

Simon wanted to damn us all. He wanted to reprimand me for my disobedience. He wanted Karron Wull's sword hand dismembered and impaled with a chain to be linked to the roof of his throne. The other Lords of the Noble Houses, and the councillors too, would in no way be kind to House Pargion, and he knew that.

He looked up at Wull. "I accept your offer, Sir Wull," he said, with a forced smile breaking through the dawn.

'And Rakokh said, "There was a prince who claimed heirdom to the fortune of House Ashford, and he said to his father, "Father, give me what I shall be owed." And Lord Ashford provided him with a share of the fortune he was awaiting. Not many days later, the prince set off, and he journeyed close to Tinquerebelle when he encountered a succubus. It was not long before he fell to her charms, and he wasted his grand fortune in foolish love. When he finally dilapidated his fortune, she whittled his health down to its minimum and evaporated from his life.

Eventually, he chose to return to his father's lavish lifestyle and begged for forgiveness. He said, "I have drowned myself in sin, father, sin against our House and against my Lord. I beg, let me return to you." And his father said, "Begone, you egg! You have turned away from centuries of prosperity within House Ashford. You are no son of mine!"

And while the prince did soon bear a son in the countryside, he died of a pox a month before its birth."'

-Extract from Priestess Ronayne's edition of the Unitas.

Sylvina:

Mother and Father never told us stories. We found them ourselves.

There's one story that I like to remember from the Unitas. A Dryad, Hibiscae the Dryad, is on the run from the Demon Xargaron. She runs into a Wood, past the tall trees and the gathering flocks of birds chirping above her head, but she still hears the Demon calling her name. She cries for help. And cries. And cries. But they come closer.

The Treant listens. Nesterin, the kindest Treant in the Wood, awakes, listening to her cry. He whisks her inside of his bark with his silk vines, and she is safe. The demon thunders past without realising that the Dryad he has been searching for is by his side. Hibiscae is fearful and does not want ever to leave Nesterin's bark, so the Gods give her the power of a Nymph, and she becomes one with Nesterin. Xargaron never sees her again. Only in her dreams.

I believe that dreams tell the truth and only the truth. I've never had a dream that has nothing to do with my life. Sometimes the truth is sprinkled inside a world of lies, but it's always there and always will be there.

It's things like dreams and tales that keep me going while my life is on the line.

It's the Tymbrenns that want me dead. The three living Tymbrenns, as of now, are Ela Tymbrenn, wife of Kase Woodgairrd, and her cousins Seamus and Rudd, the King's squires. The last two are the ones who want me dead. Mother and Father care about their reputation with survival, so they have sent men to hole me up in Hagueveil and keep me alive until King Emannar orders their executions, as they shall be failures in his eyes.

I haven't been to Hagueveil since I was four-and-a-half, so this is all an extravagant holiday to me. Maybe if I'm here, I'll be alive for the next Festival of Miracles. Every Noble Lord and each of his children can ask for a miracle to happen, and it will come true. It has never failed to come true. Last year I asked for a ward to clear away the demons, like Xargaron. Xargaron is my greatest fear. I once had a dream about Xargaron. I was at home, which is a home off in the East near a large field, when the whole area was filled with mist. I found my way out the door and walked towards the embers of the grass, which were frolicking freely in that field when I noticed a blare in the mist, a clamour of metal, and a low growl. Like I was pushed with full force, I landed face-down on that colourless grass, inhaled the newfound dryness of the air, and realised the lack of taste on my tongue and ability to smell when my eyes met a towering beast of blood and gore. Five hungry eyes rested their gaze on my frail being with a paralysing ferocity, and another growl pierced its blood-stained lips in eerie triumph. Smouldering and smoking skin adorned a swollen head thick as leather. A constant snore escaped Xargaron's gnarled nostrils set within an obese nose. The swollen head sat atop a broad yet skeletal body. A giant scar crossed the entire body. He took joy in the cold terror that my pupils evoked. But it was still until it rushed forward. The biped monstrosity calmly carried its shadowed body with poised energy. The bloody lips broke into a menacing grin, and ten sharp fangs were unveiled as pools of blood dripped out of their sharp ends. Two meagre wings extend themselves fully. Jagged bones. Feathers of fire. They stretch upward, away from the beast. I can't look away from him, and he can't look away from me. He comes up to me, inspects me like I'm a broken plate, and then he consumes me. I have died.

Was I born to die?

Sir Kegan Wyne is opposite me, my personal escort. He notices my lack of enjoyment of the situation at hand.

"You bettah not be dreamin' 'bout them demons again, girl," his lack of an eye, ripped away from its socket in one battle five years ago, continued to unsettle me.

"There's no way for me to stop, sir. He will destroy me. He's destined to," I responded with an innocent beam.

"Shut the hell up, ya fairy," he grabbed me violently and spat at my cheek, "If a demon comes now, I'll kill 'im, so long as you shut up!"

Nobody ever believes me.

"I doubt you're up to the task," I pulled off another grin.

"What the hell did ye just say? Want me to pull yer 'eart outta ya right where you sit? 'Cause I'll do it, you betcha, try me!" He would never do such a thing. My end is his end. Unless he's feeling suicidal? He is simply the weaker version of Jaze Wyne. He is likely to embrace death.

"I'm listening, I'm listening. I'll let you keep your head on," I responded to his threat, knowing that he had no power in this situation, "But do you believe in any of the myths?"

"Praps until I lost m'eye and Emannar couldn't be asked to at least gimme a 'patch. Never gave a damn about him or any of his kids. Hope they rot in hell if you ask me. Before I lost m'eye, praps I did. Ain't all flowers and trees with legs in this world. It's tough. You gotta be tough, or you gonna be dead, ya 'ear?" There was contempt in Kegan's existent eye, and he stroked his mess of a brown beard, then swayed one side of his shoulder-length hair backwards. Was he being nice to me?

"Of course," I answered simply.

"Good, now you better listen," he suddenly looked as wise as Lord Tobas, "Them useless squires are sending some of Ela's men over 'ere to kill youse. Stay in there, and youse gonna live. The entire damn Guard is gonna be there, 'cept Stephyn 'cause 'e's useless as hell. If you need 'elp, send a raven to the council, and I'll come over, praps with Stephyn and The Exile. Got it?"

"I believe I do."

He suddenly smiled like a father, "Then go, yer daddy's lil 'ouse is 'ere. 'Ave fun sleepin' where they killed yer counsellor!" he broke into an uproarious cackle as I exited the simple carriage, and it carried on riding, back to Stormholme. I faced my father's fort with disgust.

31

Kegan Wyne was incorrect when he called Hagueveil my Father's 'lil 'ouse'. It's a fabulous place to live, and then you hear that our Witanegemote bled to death from a drug in his water on the Throne Room's carpets. Arvin and Laena, Father and Mother, were there to be escorted by Uncle Drevyn and my cousins. They passed by me, wearing dark and inconspicuous outfits to hide from the general crowd. Mother took a glance at me, but Fathcr did not look at me at all. Looking at me would strain his precious eyes too much, it seemed. My sisters had both been married off to Noble Lords - Ashlyh to the King's brother Styve and Elizella to King Emannar himself. And my brother Dontin, well, we don't talk about him. I'm a disgrace, but not the biggest disgrace.

I found my way to my old bedroom. Still has a manger in it, and it looks as though it has not been cared for since I was moved to my home at the age of 3 to live alone because I was spoiling Arvin's perfect creation. Pure white and gold became sienna brown and mud yellow. I am the daughter of a Noble Lord, yet I look as though I'm some smuggler's illegitimate child. And my ward never worked here. Xargaron was always watching me.

Sometimes I felt as if Xargaron was Mother and Father in some twisted conjoinment. They're just as evil as each other. But I must ward the demon off.

I must test the ward and see to it that it continues to function correctly. So I sleep.

I have a dream. I was at home when the whole area filled with mist. I found my way out the door and walked towards the embers of the grass, which were frolicking freely in that field when I noticed a blare in the mist, a clamour of metal, and a low growl.

Like I was pushed with full force, I landed face-down on that colourless grass, inhaled the newfound dryness of the air, and realised the lack of taste on my tongue and ability to smell when my eyes met a towering beast of blood and gore. Five hungry eyes rested their gaze on my frail being with a paralysing ferocity, and another growl pierced their blood-stained lips in eerie triumph. Smouldering and smoking skin adorned a swollen head thick as leather. A constant snore escaped their gnarled nostrils set within an obese nose. The swollen head sat atop a broad yet skeletal body. A giant scar crossed the entire body. They took joy in the cold terror that my pupils evoked. But it was still until it rushed forward.

The quadruped monstrosity calmly carried its shadowed body with poised energy. The bloody lips broke into a menacing grin, and ten sharp fangs were unveiled as pools of blood dripped out of their sharp ends. Two meagre wings extend themselves fully. Jagged bones. Feathers of fire. They stretch upward, away from the beast. I can't look away from them, but they can look away from me. They don't come up to me but inspect me like I'm a broken plate from afar, and then they consume me. I have died.

As I die, the Tymbrenns and their soldiers charge at Hagueveil, with Arvin and Mother safe, somewhere else.

Demons have existed all along.

'Saw the Stormholme Schism, did I. During the Schism, half the land was being plagued with a bad case of Death's Ulcers. Me nan got it. Nausea the first day, couldn't breathe painlessly the second, quarter-hourly urination the third. Some cases had an outbreak of skin bumps. All cases ended with the patient sneezing blood until they had no blood left. The cause of the disease was never found, so she continued to suffer.

Five days after she started sneezing, a doctor prescribed medicine, and it turned out to be a drug, making her sneeze more rapidly in constant hysteria.

She kept asking me, "Why me? Why was I chosen to suffer?" At the time, only 1 in 7 citizens contracted Death's Ulcers.

Me nan wanted to see me get a wife and fill her with a child or two. Surprisingly, met a girl, did I, on Giftsgiving Eve. Fell asleep in her bed and returned to me nan the next day.

On Giftsgiving Day, I returned home to find me nan had drowned in a pool of her own blood. The next

34

morn, the commonfolk found out that Emannar Woodgairrd was now their King.'

   -Told by a beggar named Barbara.

Simon:

I know what Gwendys thinks of me. She considers me to be a cold, selfish, careless man. She hates me because she thinks that she is the least of my priorities. In truth, she is my second. The first, of course, is my children. Damon has enough of a desire to be a warrior to make me proud, though he hasn't done much in the wars and conquests he has participated in. Daman is my favourite child, leading many successful attacks against the Novak Warriors of the East; he is younger than Damon yet has earned my pride the most. If only he was my son. Dayron is a pacifist - the one thing a man cannot be in these times. Kristyne is to be wedded to Varn when she comes of age, which is a year away, and Varn, son of Emannar, is a fit husband and could be a warrior king. Annyte is something else. Corren is too young to have a mind yet.

I hide many secrets from my wife and children so that they do not suffer the consequences of my care.

I had one reason for accepting Emannar's request: I could control what happened to them. I am on good terms with Emannar (few are), but I do not wish to befriend his council or a single one of his knights. Besides, there are many responsibilities with such a large kingdom...

The Great Kingdom is a colossal mass of land with a population of 14 million as of the last Proclamation Day. Bordered between the Cold Seas of the North, the Southern rivermen and the Novak Wasteland in the East, Emannar has transformed the Great Kingdom into something that lives off blacksmithing, wood-crafting and carpenting, though these all go into trade. The Great Kingdom itself is mainly covered in forests and has a rather calm climate, which has led to a localised population despite a large number of people. We live in rather large settlements, except for palaces that provide a fortified home for the Noble Lords.

We are not satisfied.

Emannar is coming on horseback. I see him riding in the distance. Above all else, the king was a man. I saw him in good times and bad, always weighed with the responsibility he accepted for others. He was brave on the inside, willing to see his flaws and work to be a better human being, kinder, and more empathic. He was brave on the outside, leading from the front regardless of personal cost. Everyone else had to see him flawless, the polished version to inspire such confidence, but not me. Everyone needs somebody to be a child with, to cry on, to tell their fears to. He was afraid of not being enough, of failing in sacred duty, of his purpose unfulfilled, weighty as it was. I can tell you that he was always enough for me, as a man, as a king. He never needed a crown, or fine things, or the hedonistic wants men can develop with greedy hearts. He never needed to ask for my love. It was his. One who nurtures needs love. One who leads needs solace. One with a brave heart needs a champion of their own, a protector to have faith in them when darkness is at their door. It takes a queen to stand by a king and a king to stand by a queen - equally loving, equally brave, equally duty bound as protectors in all ways. This is what Hickmere tells Corren before he shuts his eyes. Emannar approaches Bernstaplen's gates, remains on his horse, and looks down at me.

"Ah yes, Lord Simon Pargion. Kneel," he boomed with a dominant sneer in his tone. Behind him was the entire Council, ready to watch me pass the demanding tests of the High Earl. There was the cunning Lord Francis Ashford, the wise Supreme Witanegemote Gregory, the brave Sir Karron Wull, the devilish Lord Tobas, and Emannar's brothers Styve and Kase Woodgairrd. I kneeled so as to avoid execution for treason. I won't let myself die to this fool.

"Simon, each of these councillors have a test for you, as well as the other candidates. Complete them all, and you are eligible for the role of High Earl," he came down from his horse, "To begin, this is Sir Karron Wull's test."

Wull stepped forward, "I have prepared a Test of Might for you. You must defeat Garvy Orkwood, member of the King's Guard, in a duel. Succeed, and you have passed my test," he stepped backwards. Garvy Orkwood is a fierce warrior, and it would do me no pleasure to end his reputation, but it was what must be done. I unsheathed my blade and put on the same armour set I wore when I returned to Bernstaplen after The Stormholme Schism. Garvy wore no armour, only rags.

But Garvy Orkwood needed no armour to crush skulls while shielding his own.

Orkwood used brute force. I needed to be elegant with my sword. We faced each other and prepared for our duel right in front of the open metal gate of Bernstaplen.

Wull held a horn, ready to blow it, "On the sound of the horn, you may begin the duel."

He blew the horn, and Garvy lunged toward me. I speedily dodged backwards, barely missing the sharp edge of his cold silver blade. He was fast and lunged again. This time, I clashed blades with him, and I exerted a greater force on my blade, making him unsteady and weak. I took this opportunity to launch my leg at his gut, forcing him to the ground and loosening his blade from his trembling hand. Then I lunged and hit, winning the duel.

Karron Wull celebrated my victory, "You show might with your blade, Lord Pargion. More than these other councillors have, at any point. You have passed the Test of Might."

Tobas was the next, with a Test of Wit. He presented me with several political issues, and I needed to find a suitable solution to each. They were simple enough, ranging from shortages in wood to civilians disliking increases in tax. There was absolutely no reason for them to test me on this - any old fool could see the best solution to such trivial matters. I passed the Test of Wit, and Tobas stepped aside.

Then came the test of Francis Ashford, the Test of Coin, another trivial exam. I was expected to use money wisely to help with the construction of two monuments. The first was the

Fountain of Truth. First built a few decades ago, this fountain at the old town centre is here to act as a reminder of the struggles our last king, Emannar's late father Grimm, faced. It represents unity, and Hickmere tells Corren that if you toss a coin into it, you will find the truth behind your greatest dilemma. It was destroyed by Kegan Wyne in a protest against Emannar, and as a result, Emannar made Kegan a member of his court and gave him a higher societal status. Anything to end a protest, I suppose. The other was to be a mound in the marketplace, built to celebrate the failure of the Novak Empire to conquer the Great Kingdom thousands of years ago. The Fountain was more important, a symbol of goodwill in our society for many years, and so I told Francis to spend the majority of the budget on the Fountain and less on the mound.

Styve, The Supreme Witanegemote and Kase had merged their final Test together, the Test of Justice. They put several criminals on trial, and I was to judge them.

I rode with Styve to the prison.

"Good luck in there," he laughed, "I heard they bite."

He wasn't wrong. The walls felt closed in. I couldn't escape the endless darkness. This was what a wait for freedom was like. Sat in the corner of a chilled room for aeons, trying to soak all the blood out of your corpse and into the sharp corners that knife you. Three of every four walls were painted red, like a masterpiece of reflection.

Each man left for me to judge shivered in the darkness of their cell, knowing that the man before them could very well lead them to their death when the time came. Every hour of every day, the abusive guard patrolled the rusty wooden gates and explored the forest of madness. Every twelve hours of every day, he'd ring a little bell just to get a kick out of the madmen driving closer to the desire to add another speckle of blood on their cold stone floors. And then darkness fell in the real world, and a small crack formed. That was the great outdoors. The world outside.

It was time for them to walk the mile to hell. All of them - the eyeless man, the man carving out his cellmate's skull with his dagger nails, the man who had swiped a pair of scissors and was desperately trying to circumcise himself...

It was their time. Eventually, their corpses left the smell of burning flesh to plague the halls and reminded the rest that there was no escape from Hell's Gate. They would have suffocated anyway; the little oxygen in the room was the result of a thousand-year build-up. It was too hard to breathe through the rot. As I left, the walls began to close, coming closer with every step. The bell rang four times, and the guard patrolled again.

Eventually, I left, and I returned to my freedom, riding back to Bernstaplen.

I succeeded. I was now a candidate for Emannar's new High Earl.

"Congratulations are necessary. Completing the Tests is no simple task, especially with such a demanding council," Emannar applauded, and the council did the same.

"Wouldn't call it demanding," I spat, "It was almost like they wanted me to qualify."

Emannar sighed. "The results shall be revealed to-morrow. Good day," he boomed with his low voice as he turned his stallion around, and they rode off back to Stormholme.

If I become the High Earl, I must leave Bernstaplen for good until I lose the role. I will be with this council of sycophants and cretins and the unbearable King himself. I am allowed to bring two of my children with me. Daman will be fighting the Novaks, so he cannot be brought along. Damon is my heir and, as such, should be the one who guards Bernstaplen like he is its king. Someone will make the secret clear to Dayron too soon, and Corren is far too young to leave Bernstaplen. As a result, I shall bring my daughters, Kristyne and Annyte. Kristyne will be delighted to see Varn Woodgairrd, I am certain.

It was all too fast, too suspicious. Orkwood had the most embarrassing defeat of his life, and the councils never once expressed even a hint of pride or shock. My victory had been planned. Anyone could see it.

Of course, there was still the possibility that I would not end up as High Earl. That would be the dream result.

Daman:

I am simultaneously the favourite and the least-favourite child of Simon and Gwendys Pargion. I'd rather be dead than be that.

I'm my father's greatest warrior, but the furthest thing that he has from a true son; at least, that is what we are led to believe. Witanegemote Morgan linked a prophecy to me after Damon was born:

'The day the second one is born, you shall be reborn, but born he shall not be: a broken promise, a cursed age and a lifetime of sin await.'

We never knew what it meant. My birth parents were my true parents, but they listened to the 'wisdom' of their Witanegemote. Wisdom is what he is paid for. Wisdom is for fools, I say.

No promise was broken with my birth. At least, none that Simon or Gwendys can remember. I always suggested that perhaps Damon never wanted a brother, but Damon always wanted one, as far as Simon and Gwendys can remember.

I was not born in a cursed age. I was born in a golden age. Emannar's father, Grimm Woodgairrd, a corrupt and oppressive dictator, passed away, and the much more competent King Emannar took over, made House Grimm in his father's memory (full of loyalists who were willing to change their surname to fit their house), developed many new laws, changed the council to a more corrupt one and made every

Noble Lord have a thirst for power and dictatorship. A real golden age, eh?

My life has not been full of sin. Priest Narisetti and Priestess Ronayne worship several Gods, and some encourage sinning for the greater good, such as war. All my life, Simon has subjected me to training for war, and now I fight the Novaks at least twice a month, and I have brutally extinguished 212 Novak Clans in only two years, like Francis Ashford killing off all of his sister's potential suitors.

Prophecies are built on the truth, yet no part of the prophecy is true.

Or is it?

In an hour, the Vikarin twins, two members of the King's Guard, will march to the large metal gates of Bernstaplen, for the third damn time this week and, if all goes well, proclaim Emannar to be the new High Earl so he can be stuck in Stormholme and I don't need to see his cold, piercing eyes another day. So let's head to the Tavern!

There's a new Tavern in town. From the outside, it looks clean, enchanting and modest. Logs and hard wooden pillars make up most of the building's outer structure.

It's near impossible to see through the large, stained glass windows, but the passionate voices from within can be felt outside. As I enter the tavern through the heavy, metallic door, I seem to be welcomed by laughing voices and joyful music. The bartender is handling some customers but still manages to welcome me with a wink. It's as engaging inside as it is on the outside. Rounded, wooden beams support the upper floor and the chandeliers attached to them. The walls are clear of anything, though signs do show plenty of things used to hang on the walls, though they've probably been knocked off by customers who had too much to drink.

The tavern itself is packed. Locals seem to be the primary clientele here, which could be seen as the best sign you can get. Several long tables are occupied by happy, excited groups of people. Some are dancing on the table, while others cheer them on with clapping and yelling. The other, smaller tables are also occupied by people who are indulging in great food and drinks. While some do try to strike a conversation, others can barely speak a word between eating what must be delicious food. Even most of the stools at the bar are occupied, though nobody seems to mind more company. I did hear rumours about this tavern, supposedly, it's famous for something, but I can't remember what for. Though judging by the angelic voice who just started singing, it must be famous for this singer. I manage to find a seat and prepare for what will undoubtedly be a great evening...

Unfortunately, I needed to see my father (who doesn't think he is my father because his counsellor said so) fail to become important, so I bode my goodbyes and rushed out like a gryphon looking for some fresh earthworms.

I didn't have much time left since I was entranced by the mystical tavern. Priestess Ronayne had opened her chapel. 12 Gods and 6 Demi-Gods that we worship thrice a day. This was my first time seeing the chapel with my brain old enough to remember being there. Nobody had attended, of course. I entered.

For the most part, the forest was my church, for I needed to be able to see the heavens, feel the openness, experience the sunlight and let the birdsong be a salve to my mind. It was then my mind was free, then that I felt I was enough. I was one animal walking among many, all of us different yet connected. I guess it simply felt homely in a way that felt right, me quietly giving off my affections and nature giving back, nurturing a part that those stone walls left cold. As I became older, I softened in my feelings toward those steeple spires, toward those bells and windows of many hues. Just as a house needs love to be home, those walls of rock needed love to be a church. The day I felt that love, the day it flowed as easily as a natural breeze, and the light of the Son came from the eyes around. It felt right too. Dayron and I do our masses together. Better than this soil for false idols.

The Priestess was not present, but the priest was.

"Narisetti, where is the priestess?" I asked simply. Narisetti was from the Far East, a former trader who sold many spices to travellers. Rather do that than believe in the nonexistent, I say.

"Gone to Stormholme with Jaze Wyne to protect your sisters Kristyne and Annyte Pargion of House Pargion. May Rakokh bless their souls with goodwill," he responded, sounding like he was inciting a demonic ritual, though, then again, that was how he always sounded.

"I'm sure they'll survive, Narisetti," I assured him.

"You can never be certain, Daman, second son of Simon and Gwendys Pargion, of House Pargion. They, like us all, are sacrificial goats in the eye of Rakokh, ready to succumb to eternal peace in the Highlands unless we fail to believe, and then we rot in the pits of Magnar," he chanted, the poor demented soul.

"The pits of Magnar? The ones my grandfather Ebon Pargion tore apart many moons ago with you by his side? You surely don't believe we lack our father's strengths?" I questioned him.

"Well, who can be certain? People can die at the most unexpected times. Could be me, could be Ronayne...could be you, Daman," he smiled.

As he returned to his worship, I left the chapel to await the guards, but they were already there. Simon, Gwendys, and their children were looking at Byrron and Briden Vikarin, and Byrron was ready to announce Simon's failure.

"Lord Simon Pargion, it can now be confirmed that you are the newest High Earl of His Grace Emannar Woodgairrd, and we shall leave for Stormholme tomorrow. Congratulations," he announced.

I'd be happy for Simon if I could call him my father.

Gwendys:

My children are my children, and I love them. But Simon's children are Simon's children, and I hate them.

My children are the reason I have been forced to wed such a cold man until the day I die. I have no choice. Why, if I divorce, not only is it treasonous, and Simon would schedule my decapitation, but my Father Marvion Wayne would do the same, seeing no purpose for me, and Tyral would mock me to no end. There's only one choice with the life of love, and it's the one you don't want every single time.

If it were down to me, I would not even live in the Great Kingdom. I would like to live off in the South, living a peaceful life alone. Down in the South, there is no pressure to marry. I would be set free from the chains of marriage. It was most likely a dream that would stay as such, but dreams need not always mirror reality.

A lot can be said of Simon Pargion, but the fact that he is impatient and emotionless is merely the tip of the iceberg. To make matters worse, he is ignorant, difficult and pretentious, but in an odd way, I find that they're balanced by his habit of being perceptive and wise as well, without the need of his Witanegemote. However, perception is his greatest fear. Being too perceptive is what kills you in these times. So does being too wise. Even the best intentions have been soured because of his fears and his dishonesty, which I am one of many a witness to.

Fair is fair, though; Simon is not wholly evil. He is faithful, and he is wise, even if he shows it blankly and in small doses. He is not the full embodiment of doom and gloom - it cannot be said. Unfortunately, his ignorance spoils the fun we could have with those traits. I could be his wife, not his dog, but alas, I cannot control my superior.

Simon has already left today. I did not say my goodbyes, but the children did. His chosen two children to come with him to Stormholme were his daughters, Kristyne and Annyte, mostly so that Kristyne could meet his first choice for her husband, Emannar's son Varn Woodgairrd. I feel obligated to speak with my children. Perhaps comfort them, though they will not need it.

Damon is now the King of the Castle, and I can see the joy sprinkled across his delicate countenance. Perhaps now he'd receive the war scars he'd waited for his entire life to perfectly complement the scars he'd received from Simon abusing him for being worthless in battle. My son is a more gentle soul than he'll ever let on; a man must have his pride. He is courageous, astute and willing to think before he acts. He has balance, perseverance and intelligence. Some may think me biased, that he can't possibly be all those things, yet he is. Of my son, I am proud without reservation, and if that is a sin, then so be it.

Daman, the child of unknown blood, is off to fight the Novaks. I'd fight to welcome him as a true son, but the prophecy does not lie. He is not a child of mine or of Simon. The boy had eyes of pure mischief and a heart of gold; he had that way of moving that honest people do, with the spark of the child, the wit of the man, and a smile that went all the way through to his core.

Dayron, a boy of nine, will be the least involved in the war of my children. I wish we could tell him everything he needs to know about himself, but it is impossible, simply impossible. He was the chestnut and the acorn, the seed of everything good to come, my dark-haired boy. We could see the mighty goodness within him that branched out into all that he did at play. He was nature's child and our honour to raise.

Corren, a boy of five, has a bright future ahead of him. The boy is more fragile than the glass Ent that sits on my dresser at home. I think if I were to spin him too hard while teaching him to use a needle, his limbs might just snap. It's hard to get his attention under that mop of brown hair that dominates his narrow face. There are eyes in there somewhere. He has skin the same colour as my Father, that brown colour without the effort of trying to get a tanned look, not as white, like Mother or me. He holds himself like he's trying to take up even less space than he already does and his clothes look at least a size too small, only exaggerating his skinniness. He looks so lost. I wish I could change what would happen to him, but there's no avoiding it, I'm afraid. Good luck to him.

These are my children. My strong children. I just wish they were mine.

They shall be mine.

"M'lady wants a sword? Ever had proper training?" Gerald, Simon's blacksmith, questioned me.

"It's not a sword I want. I want a dagger. A sharp one," I spat.

"Alright," Gerald succumbed, "Give me some time, and I'll forge something for ya."

I took a moment to look around. On my right was a collection of letters he had been sent from his family.

'Dear beloved,

We've had to pull Timothe out of Lakewell today. He can't afford to pay the constant taxes, so he has returned to Bernstaplen and is setting up a tavern.

He hopes you will come back soon, my love.

Your Wife,

Clara.'

'Dear beloved,

Timothe's tavern was raided by takers today. Jaze Wyne accused him of unruly activities and sent the takers to steal his goods. He's closed the shop down today, and he lives with me now. Will you be visiting soon? We miss you.

Your Wife,

Clara.'

'Dear Gerald,

Timothe has given up. I found his body this morning, hanging off the bonsai in the garden.

Your son is dead, Gerald.

You could have prevented your son's death, but you didn't. Do you even remember us now? I have had to live without you for too long. Please...come back to me.

Kind Regards,

Clara.'

Clara sent another letter, but he had nailed an advert for his smithy over it, never to be seen.

On the other wall, he had formed a gallery of blades. Swords, daggers and crossbow bolts were kept on racks next to a storage unit for bows, greatswords and everything in between. Besides, that was a collection of vials of many poisons and potions, likely doused on the tips of weapons to give the wielder an edge in combat.

A hundred-year-old wheel continued to spin without purpose as it rested beside an infantile picture of a boy and a man holding hands, which had been collecting dust for decades.

'I'm waiting for you, daddy. Lots of love, Timothe.'

The fireplace, the poetry of the phoenix in confident gold flame, flickered with pride as the wood died. Gerald's Hund watched it eagerly, likely hoping to find the scraps of meat his master had scattered around for training.

Gerald went to a desk to pick up some bolts, then returned to his station, clutching the metal rod, and dipped it in the molten lava to fine-tune the edges of the dagger. He stuck a chisel into the rod and hammered it, swiping it across the blade to add a new layer of sharpness. He kept going until he eventually left the rod to bathe in a frozen basin of water, and smoke billowed out like a furnace.

"Ever taken an interest in blacksmithing?" he asked me.

"Never," I answered truthfully.

"I do mentoring now," he informed me, "I teach the intricacies of blacksmithing to the next generation. My son was my first student, but he had no interest in the craft. I had to go on without him."

He sharpened my dagger again while he spoke to me, and the chisel created an orb of sparks that he left to exist on the dagger for a while. Then he began to hammer it, and the flames roared every time until he caught the orb with the rod and doused it in the basin again.

"They say blacksmithing is a dying art," I mocked him.

"Blacksmithing is not a dying art," he laughed, "A revival of interest continues to grow as the knowledge is passed down. We still have our students. Humanity may evolve, but we will never truly escape the wonders of the flame."

He handed me the dagger. It was sharp and shiny. Glorious.

"You know what the payment is," he sighed, "Give me the coin."

I looked at the letters, "These letters...they're from your wife?"

He frowned, "Indeed. Leaving her is my biggest regret. But I can't go back now. It's too late. I am too involved in House Pargion to escape Bernstaplen."

"You are so loyal to Simon that you let your son die..." I realised.

"Indeed," he sighed, "If I could go back, I wouldn't make that mistake again."

"If you could, would you want to see him again?" I asked.

"I'd have to confront my guilt," he answered, "But it would be worth it. I may not be the one who hanged him on the Bonsai, but I am the true murderer."

"Doesn't seem like you'll ever speak to your son again..." I sighed.

He chuckled, "Thought that part was obvious."

"They wouldn't put you in the same sections of the afterlife," I spat.

He turned around to face me, "I know I'm going to hell. I'm just waiting for the day my journey ends."

"It could end any day," I replied.

"Any day," he repeated, "Damn your husband and his oaths."

"Yes," I agreed, clutching my dagger in my right palm, "Damn my husband."

Suddenly, he broke down into tears, "Timothe, my sweet boy..."

"Sweet boy," I echoed, "Grieve well in hell, Gerald."

"I shall," he cried.

Then I stabbed him. Repeatedly. Until he stopped his annoying wails.

I looked at Timothe's drawing of him and his father one last time.

Gerald's blood had stained it, and Timothe lost the radiant blue of his eyes.

'When the time comes that the rains return, the promised one shall bring a cursed age.'

'When the clouds roar with fury, the promised one shall deliver the end of peace.'

'It shall be then, when the seas turn to ice, the promised one shall send redemption and humility.'

'It shall be then, when the rivers are red, the promised one shall break a soul to mend a soul.'

-Prophecies engraved on the walls of the Witanegemote Citadel by Supreme Witanegemote Gregory, exactly one month before Emannar Woodgairrd's victory in the Stormholme Schism.

**Annyte:**

I'm a thief. I stole Damon's scars, and now I'm on the road to Stormholme.

It was Wyne who cut me. Kegan Wyne. It was not his fault, though - a Cantell invader carved his eye out of its socket, and as he was blinded by defeat, he flailed his blade around and cut my cheek. Now a long scar drips eagerly down from the top of my cheek to my chin. It has been there for five years.

I remember what it was like. Men howled in pain, clutching their grievous wounds as bows twanged, sending snakes of evil into the never-ending army. The Hagueveil walls stood high, defiantly in the face of such furious siege weapons, their proud backs straight. The siege towers lumbered on slowly at a snail's pace. "Fire!" King Grimm ordered suddenly as catapults unleashed waves of death, destroying siege weapons and burning men alike. The sun beat down on them furiously as the heat wave continued, unaffected by such chaos. Catapults and bows fired from both sides furiously, trying to gain the advantage. Rams battered at the gate as oil ran down with feet, and men ran in anguish as they were burnt from the magma substance; they screamed until they couldn't, and they rested in nothingness. The battle continued. And then age killed the battle.

My brothers never talk to me. Sometimes I feel like they're ashamed. I make them look like a failure because I was actually there, in action.

I looked out onto the battlefield later. The town was littered with corpses, weapons and blood. Red, blue and grey were the new colours of Grimmland, once the harmonious land of Grimm Woodgairrd, now the remnants of an unforgettable invasion. The air was once filled with the aroma of freshly baked bread and the sound of content people, but the war led it to hold a barrage of sounds of explosions, pathetic war cries and the screams of the wounded. No coming back from genocide. Armies engaged in war with miniature rebellions to regain control, power, and dominance, but there was no side to win. The battle lasted three years. The dead and wounded of one side lay in large groups across the town, and the faces of the futile fighters were hopeful, with nervous yet steady breathing and terror in their hearts. They pushed harder and harder on the enemy, to no avail. I had no way of knowing how to live or die. They fought courageously, with the hope of a small period of strength. Some succumbed to fatigue, barely able to stand, even lift an arm in defence. Some were unaffected, such as Damon, who was ignored by the conquerors and rebels like he was a lost child. We took a toll on nature. We took a toll on humanity. We were tragically evil. It will take a lifetime before we learn to make peace or give up and die. We caused gore. We spilt blood. We severed limbs and decapitated heads. Congratulations on the victory.

My brothers hate me, and I hate my brothers, but I hate my sister more than anyone else on this land. On Father's order, I managed to find a fat pig for Prince Varn (he loves his meat), and she stole a fatter pig just to sell it to Varn and appease him further. I assume that I should be flattered - she watches what I do and emulates it, making it better to make herself seem superior. I once tried to outplay her after she emulated me, and she crowed off to Father that I was copying everything she did, and Father ordered Jaze Wyne to beat me. I know she wants the power of Varn, so I do all that I can to spite her.

When I get a sword, I'll slit her throat.

The Vikarin twins have delivered us to the Stormborne Throne Hall, where we shall see Father's throne for the first and likely only time. I have seen the throne hall of Arvin Slait, and compared to his, this is a pathetic attempt at one. A dull, grey room with six chairs for the councillors, a throne for the King, and that was all. The Throne itself was nothing special. Carved of some 'fine' oak, crested with common jewels and decorated metals forming the Woodgairrd Coat of Arms. It's an impressive seat, sure, but it looks like a stool compared to the throne he should be taking. That throne is the one bathed in the blood of those who had fought for their kingdom and all the anger and wickedness in their hearts.

Kristyne looked at me in the carriage, "Annyte, any ideas?"

"Ideas for what?" I responded, half-listening.

"For dealing with Varn," she sighed.

"Jaze says his moustache is shorter than his wife's," I replied.

"Jaze doesn't have a wife," she told me.

"He does. He doesn't tell people he doesn't trust," I responded, grinning.

"What are you on about, girls?" Ronayne complained.

"Jaze Wyne. Does he have a wife?" Kristyne spoke up.

"Why would I know?" she chuckled, "I don't bother with brutes unless they come into my chapel and beg for a blessing."

"That's your problem," I told her, "If you don't bless them, you don't talk to them. You don't bless many people."

"Are you insulting the integrity of my faith, Annyte?"

There was no point in trying to argue with a zealot. "No, Priestess," I responded.

"I see, Annyte. You truly are becoming a fit royal," Ronayne smiled.

"I don't want to be royal."

I would rather be dead than be royal.

Eventually, the carriage stopped, and Juran Herqys, The Exile, welcomed us to Stormholme.

"Alright, ladies, get out," he smiled. He was the only black man in the court, an exiled prince from the Novak Empire. "Ever been to Stormholme?" We shook our heads. "Not a problem. Make your way to the castle, and they'll set up your chambers...somewhere around there."

I took a look at Stormholme. It was magnificent. The sun glaring down upon the thick cobblestone walls, free of moss. Stark, vivid shadows. The spiked standing stone of the portcullis looming like the twisted teeth of a demon. Horses bickering in the stables and the musty, damp air.

Here lived a King.

'Entry: Roc

This enormous bird of prey makes its home in only the deepest of forests (once seen in The Great Wood). It is known to leap upon its prey, which includes small creatures, humans, and beasts with magical enchantments. It attacks with its flaming tail, able to scorch even the least flammable of structures. Once landing with its massive feathered wings, it feasts on prey with its beak and talons. These days, the Roc has mostly fallen victim to near-extinction, and now variants of the species are generally exclusive to their biome.

Known Variants:

-Arctic Roc, a white variant of the Roc found in snowy landscapes. Its feathers have great insulation.

-Coastal Roc, a yellow variant found in sunnier landscapes such as Tinquerebelle. [EXTINCT SINCE THE HUNTS OF JOHNATHAN MUBERRE]

-Hill Roc, the standard variant, found in forests.'

-Entry from the Bestiary of Shaun Finneas Donnelly.

Dayron:

When I was six, Daman and I worshipped the Great Wood. We made up a god called The Son of the Forest and believed that if we cared deeply enough for the Great Wood and tended to it, we could receive his blessing and do anything. I was never sure if Daman truly believed in it or if he was fooling around with me, but I never stopped praising The Son. If any God is real, he is. I even formed a garden in the Wood. The Garden of the Gates...

It's a luxurious plot of moss-covered grass, enclosed by a variety of hedges and shrubs. A proud fountain reveals pools of water in the back left, offering a welcome to the creatures that reside here. The flowers and the plants, my pride and joy in my garden, are cared for weekly. They buzz with insects. The hedges and shrubs are higher than each Witanegemote, a unique trait of the garden. A path of stone twists around, offering a glimpse of the best spots to look at. Grass and plants creep and crawl their way beyond their own borders, sneakily trying to take just a little more land. The fountain is the main attraction. The flowers and plants have no hard time getting their equal shares of attention, and the hedges and shrubs are nothing to sneeze at, but the focus is the fountain.

I met The Son with this fountain.

I pray to him each night, oftentimes for forgiveness:

"Dearest Son, protector of souls, I come before ye to confess my sin. I once went astray, and my pride led me to attack in a

63

moment of weakness. I am truly sorry. Bring light to my darkened soul reminiscent of the evil I have done. Sanction me for my sins so I may strengthen my soul to ward off evil anew."

And other times, for aid:

"Holy Son, the redeemer of souls, witness me in my time of need. Touch my spirit so I might make the right choice. I ask this of you with open arms, o god of gods. Empower me with your holy mercy."

Appeasing the Son appeased the other Gods, the other Children of the Forest. He told me that I had appeased him.

All is good in my garden this year. All is good in this garden. My garden is secure, but it has not reached its full potential.

My garden must grow.

I ventured out, Grey behind me. My Griffin has remained loyal to me, and he chirps often. Though he is a hatchling, his chirps are louder than the sounds of nature swirling around us.

I petted him as I noticed a man hacking away at a tree in my garden.

"Grey, attack," I commanded with menace. My garden shall not be disturbed.

But Grey did more than attack. Grey pierces his skin with knife-like talons, and he lays on the floor, blood oozing from his thousands of cuts. He shouldn't have disturbed my garden. And then The Son appeared, froze time like it was water, and I looked at Him. There was a seriousness to the gaze of the lion he inhabited, a grace that begged you to call it Lord. Four proud paws trod proudly through the Great Wood, transforming the forests into savannas as they carried a heavenly burst of light through the landscape that erupted into clouds of joy. With each step, fluorescent streaks of green light flickered across his elegant skull, highlighting the exotic blue of the lion's irises. The mane – the mane flew through the clean air, billowing like smoke freeing itself from a chimney. A glimpse of goodness was flickering before me.

"Dayron Pargion. This blood has spoiled my garden. Do you wish to be exiled from your joy?" He said statically.

"I do not, but I do not wish my joy to be harmed, Dearest Son," I responded meekly, quivering at the lip.

"Then atone for your sins," He commanded. I genuflected and recited the Prayer for Forgiveness. His eyes dimmed.

"You have atoned. Listen, Dayron. This Gryphon is special. You may never realise why, but I will do my best to ensure that you do it in time. Now, they are coming," and like that, he faded from existence like he didn't belong on this human plane.

And that was when the Veille grabbed me and pinned me down.

'1. If youse steal my cow, I steal your milk.

2. If youse steal my horse, I steal your stable.

65

3. If youse steal my ox, I steal your left eyebrow.

4. If youse hurt my brothers, I congratulate you.

5. If youse lie to my face, I cut your tongue out.

These are the only five rules.

Think youse have what it takes?

Then come on down to La Perte Inconnue, where your greatest threat isn't the Sirenmen. It's me!'

-Text from a La Perte Inconnue recruitment poster, written by their leader Gyrard.

Dontin:

I wish there was another male Slait in the family. Why the only men left are my father and me, and I know no man who is fond of my father.

I have no family I can trust. I have no friends I can trust. I am alone in this world, and that does me just fine.

So, I just pinned a defenceless Pargion boy on the ground for trespass. Ought to do me good, knowing my reputation, both in society and with the law. This is the boy with the secret. It must be. I'll do Simon some good and keep the secret for him, I suppose. Won't say a word about his condition. I dragged the boy's defenceless body over to my cell and locked him in there. He'll only be in there for a little while. Just enough time for me to find out everything I need to know. The Pargion boy must have gone far in the Great Wood because while I am on the other side of it, I am still around 10 miles away from Bernstaplen. He must have had a good reason.

This house is my home, where the laughter happens, and I can rest at the end of the day. From the winding paths and roads, it is bricks and mortar topped with tile, the same as any other. Yet if you step inside, you'll feel it's so different, a place where the lungs choose to fill a little deeper and the heart beat a little steadier. These bricks were laid one at a time on a fine spring day. I let my eyes wander the roughness and how each is so very straight. This house was made with love, that's for sure. Bundles of it.

I only wish it had my name upon it. This is an old house of my sister Elizella and her husband, good old Emannar. Never thought that Emannar was a good fit for a king, especially since he loved hunting and slaying more than he ever did love politics. Just like me, he finds them dreadful. As dreadful as he finds me.

And Elizella is no different. She in no way deserves to be Queen Woodgairrd. Yes, it means that I receive the comfort of this home, but I'd rather she didn't have the ability to gloat about her achievements that I will never achieve. In fact, none of my sisters are tolerable. Ashlyh is wedded to Styve Woodgairrd, Emannar's cruel brother, and has just as many bees in her bonnet as Elizella. And Sylvina, well, she's always had her head in the clouds. She may be my favourite sister, but that doesn't mean that I like her or she likes me.

I have this brilliant house to myself, so I might as well make the most of it. I head to my private dining room to enjoy whatever meal has been laid out for me. However, calling it a dining room was somewhat misleading. It was a room. They ate in it. That was all. In it stood a cheap Northern table that rocked when you leant on it, two old white chairs from some working-class crafter and a pair of thread-bare orange curtains that let the heat escape in winter as easily as if they were not there at all. The opening of light in the centre of the room was bare and hung loosely from the ceiling it opened from, adding to the meagre ambience of the room. It was the kind of room you ate peasant dinner washed down with expired ale. Still, it is a dining room, and you eat in it.

There's a letter by Elizella's plate, and I am not one to fear knowing too much. Elizella is no threat to me anyway.

What kind of letter could this be? A council document? A request from the King or a member of his guard? Or something worse?

'We do not belong to one another.

Love has no possession.

We are not in love,

For love is not a cage.

We are not two halves,

For love makes us whole.

We see one another's imperfections,

Love is not blind.

Yet my love is your salvation,

And yours is mine,

Instead of open wounds,

We bare silvery scars,

Healed by acceptance and nurture.

This love we share,

It heals us both,

Granting the strength for us to be,

Who we were born to be.

-Stephyn Tanner.'

Stephyn Tanner, quite the romanticist. Who knew?

It seems that Elizella is having an affair with a member of her husband's guard. I'm not surprised; I would never put it past her.

My, this is rather intriguing. I have all the blackmail I need. But I need more than what I have. And there's only one man trustworthy enough who can collect every piece of information I could find to crush Elizella into the ground.

I finished my meal, downed my ale, and began the search for Lord Tobas. The only problem was the bumbling blockade before me - Consen Degarre. The Captain of House Tanner's Guard had agreed with Elizella to observe me. He was drunk as a bard.

"Consen, I must go. Keep an eye on the boy for me, will you?" I begged him.

"Ah, look, here's a brave one. Rolling out into the Sun, thinking facing hell gives him the eyes of Rakokh," he sputtered with a thick accent. He always had a thick accent when drunk.

"I'm not facing hell. I just need to go outside-"

"Hello, hello, hello, shut your trap. Everyone here says so."

"Consen-"

"No, no, no. You remind me of m'wife, you know? We were in love, you know. Then I had a tad, a teensy tad too much ale and may have slapped her once or twice, and she leaves me! She leaves me to rot with you! You just want to leave me to drink to death, you do!" he nearly tripped over the air below him.

"You aren't going to die, I'll send people over-"

"Last time I drank to death was when m'wife left. Found a few pretty maidens after she left. There was one, an Arian girl, she was beautiful, and she loved me too. Then I raped her," he spat.

"I'm sorry to hear that, Consen," I offered my condolences.

"Shut up, shut up, shut up! I want peace! Get out of here!" he slurred and then collapsed.

Well, I suppose it is time for me to go.

Now, where the hell is Lord Tobas?

Daman:

Before we head out to Novakia, I must check on my crew. It's the right thing to do these days when everyone wants to slit your throat. We were barely outside the Bernstaplen gates when we chose to leave. All I do is hope that this isn't the last time I see these steps. That's all I think about every time I do this. Everything was warm but quiet. Far too quiet.

I need to keep up my courage. Usually, I'd have enough courage to cut off the wrist of any stranger in sight, but today it all dissipates within me.

First was Fawkes, the youngest. He specialised in cannons and loved explosive missions. This quest could easily require blowing something up, so he was useful to us.

"Hello, Fawkes. Ready for tonight?" I faked excitement in my tone so as to not startle the maniacal being I had no choice but to converse with.

"Yes, sir. Must say, if I had a choice, I'd be one a yer reinforcements. Me sister died last week. Let's hope there's a to-morrow for us all, sir," he sounded like a beggar, and I'd help him to the best of my ability if I had a choice. None of us have a choice with warfare.

"There's nothing to be afraid of. Keep your courage in the stars, Fawkes. The more you focus, the more likely you are to survive through the night. I guarantee you that you will have your to-morrow," I assured him. I wish my words were true.

"Your words speak the truth, sir. I shall obey your commands," he suddenly sounded obedient and passive, unlike the Fawkes I knew. His face did not change a bit, and then I realised that he had been lying. Fawkes was no different to us men, except he had less of a want to be here than the rest of us but wanted to kill some Novaks far, far more.

You see, Fawkes was the descendant of the founder of House Grimm, a Noble House outside of The Great Kingdom made to honour Grimm Woodgairrd, but when his father was killed by Novaks, the succession went to his uncle, who cut Fawkes off from the Grimm lineage and killed his mother. Well, he can't get revenge on Dran Grimm because that won't do him any good in getting back the kingdom, so he thinks that if he deals with the Novaks, they'll listen to what he says, and Dran will put him back on.

It was likely what caused Fawkes's addiction. He used to be a generic prince with generic blonde hair and a generic muscular build. Now, he has ash for hair, eyes black as open pits that saw chaos and chaos only, and looked like the stem of a flower waiting to be flung far away by the wind.

After taking in his cruel lies, I grabbed him by the throat.

"Listen to me right now, you worm, if you lie to me one more goddamn time, I'll let 'em kill you, and then you're never gonna get family respect back, you're never gonna show Dran Grimm, your superior, that you are worth being heir, and you will die alone, a disappointment to everyone you represent. Do you hear me?" I threatened him, piercing his soul with heatwave eyes that burned his lies to ashes. I didn't actually care. I was just trying to scare him into caring.

"Yes, sir," he mumbled, "But...I haven't bloody lied!"

"Do you hear me?" I shouted, thrusting him against the cold sting of the metal case behind him with increasing pressure.

"Yes, sir!" he finally exclaimed, proving his loyalty.

Excellent. I released him and headed towards Aldo, a fine swordsman. He had the easiest life out of any of my men. He is the Duke of Guillemin, a Kingdom far off in the West, but has been temporarily exiled by the King while the King orders a genocide. He was a friend, I assume. But he was no friend to me. He had never been seen without a large set of silver armour on, a symbol of Guillemin. Nobody knew where his loyalties laid.

"The men are waiting for you, Daman," he told me, "They're ready for you to command."

"I'm well aware. We shall be departing soon, Aldo. Soon. I've never found it so hard for men to agree on a time to leave," I responded.

"In Guillemin, there's a set time. If you don't meet the set time with your preparations, you either come only with what you have prepared, or you don't come at all. Simple," he smiled, and I wanted to knock each of his teeth out then and there. How dare he compare The Great Kingdom to Guillemin.

"None of us will die, my friend. I can see it in the Sun. We are safe," he assured me. I care not for his assurance.

"We are hard to kill in the Great Kingdom. Can't say the same for Guillemin if they're all killing each other," I hollered in his face mockingly. He unsheathed his sword.

"Want me to prove that wrong? Remember your place in my Kingdom, fool," he shot a glare of death at me. I continued to holler.

"Your Kingdom? You truly are pathetic!" I raised my voice, and he turned around, knowing that he was fooling himself.

"Perhaps I am in your head, Pargion," he sheathed his blade, "Barrett is awaiting your command. I can't wait to use my sword again!" he flexed his muscles and marched away elegantly, and so I went to find Barrett.

Just before I did find Barrett, it was probably best to bid my family farewell. I stood at the door to Dayron's room for a moment and saw Mother crying there.

"Why are you here?" she asked.

"I'm here to say goodbye to Dayron," I explained.

"He's not here. He hasn't been here. I don't know where he is," she cried.

"He's probably at the Wood," I told her.

She looked at me coldly, "Leave."

"I don't care if you think I'm your 'half-child' for some reason. I want to see my brother," I resisted.

"Dayron wouldn't want to see you," she cried.

I took a step forward. In Novakia, I would be facing far greater dangers than Gwendys Wayne. "He'd want to see his brother."

"Get out of here."

"I'll send some of my men to do a quick sweep of the Wood before I leave. See if they find him," I resisted.

"I don't want to risk your men killing my boy," she scowled.

"Have it your way," I resigned and turned to leave.

"Daman," she said. I turned to look at her.

"Yes?" I replied.

"When someone next disappears, I hope it's you," she told me. I turned back around and returned to the yard.

Damon was there with his best friend, Lawrence Malver. "I've been looking for you," Damon called out, "I thought you'd left or something."

"He was wondering if you forgot about him," Lawrence cackled. Lawrence was the kind of person to laugh at a funeral.

"Leaving is hard. Well, mostly," I looked in the direction of Gwendys.

"What's wrong, half-child?" Lawrence mocked, "Mummy doesn't love you?"

"At least my mum is alive," I shot back.

"My mum died fighting for your family," he responded eerily.

"Yeah, Mother..." Damon sighed.

"She was kinder than usual," I assured him.

"That's different," Damon grinned. This was the problem with Damon. He was too submissive and couldn't detect a lie. Now he had to manage Bernstaplen, and he was going to struggle.

"I'll be back soon," I told him.

"Not soon enough," he sighed, and we embraced, "Good luck, brother."

"Good luck doing Father's job, brother," I laughed.

We broke off the embrace, and I left him standing there as I went to see Howard Barrett.

Howard Barrett was not someone people wanted to be around. He was mentally unstable, especially because his betrothed and her sisters were all slaughtered by Novaks which made him feel suicidal. He tried poisoning himself, but the Gods stopped him, removed the poison from the drink, and then he stopped believing. He tried stabbing himself, but the blade was too blunt. Shooting himself with an arrow almost worked, but it bounced right off his chest and pierced a rose that was his last memory of his wife-to-be. This was more revenge for him than for anyone else. He could avenge his wife and his backup wives by helping us.

"I thought you left without us at this rate, Pargion. They wouldn't let me out to get a breath of fresh air with my knife in hand. Not very kind, are they?" he questioned, with an eerie atmosphere echoing through the solitary confinement that was the room he was in. Every room felt like solitary confinement if he was in it.

"Did you kill someone?" I asked, somewhat petrified by this man.

"I wanted to," he answered, with a chilling grin, "I was ready for it. For a minute, I held my steel dagger behind the ugly back of the captain of your guard. Mr. Wyne's not very courteous nowadays, eh?"

"What were you trying to do? Shave his back?" I tried to bring a humourous tone to this awkward conversation.

"Lord knows he needs it," he cackled. I stifled a laugh just to satisfy him.

"I'm so close to killing Aldo and Fawkes today, I must say," I tried to find a topic that we'd both enjoy talking about.

"I have been since I knew them. I have a plot to kill everyone, boy. Even you," he cackled again. The room got far colder in his presence.

"I'd quite like to hear this plot, you know," I smiled. He didn't enjoy my smile.

"I'll slit your throat in your sleep, with this dagger, likely. A cold blade in the hands of a cold man is all the pain a man needs to become a legend. Satisfaction is at hand with this quest, boy, don't you see? I need this!" he begged. He was even less stable than before this conversation.

"I can see that. The edges of the dagger are sharp enough to mow through hair," I observed.

"I think Kegan Wyne might need that, you know. Maybe even big brother Damon. Let's hope I don't etch out a couple of chunks of his head," I hate how he cackles at the thought of pain.

"I hope you don't as well because there's no way in hell you're laying a finger on my family, you dog," I threatened, getting tense.

"I know that. I know that. Very well, do I know that" he said, now getting sickeningly poetic, "Name my blade. Name my blade. Elia, I shall name my blade. Elia. She truly was my Queen. All I must do is slaughter every one of them. For Elia."

"And slaughter them you shall. For Elia," I smiled. He looked like a pathetic underling for a demon, and then he unleashed another devilish grin.

That was the grin I remembered as we headed for the Novaks in a worn-down carriage.

I stayed up all night.

Sylvina:

They're breaking down the doors while I write. I must be ready to depart. The Tymbrenns have no reason to want to kill me. The only thing they need to do is appease the King, so they lose the status of squire and become full knights. Unless my death was the King's wish, perhaps to force Arvin to succumb to the throne. I doubt Father would care if I died to spite him, but if this was Emannar's plan, I would gladly volunteer.

The King's Guard had all arrived to protect me, except for Stephyn Tanner, for some reason. Probably off doing some campaign far away from here. Elizella, the Queen, sent him on many private campaigns. Seems like he's her favourite of the Guard. I wonder why...

Sir Byrron Vikarin burst through the door without a helmet.

"Sylvina, we happen to be holding them back for now, but this won't be the case for long. These Tymbrenn squires are sending double the amount of soldiers over in an attempt to slaughter us all. No casualties on our side as of yet. If matters grow in severity, I will inform you, and you must send a raven instantly. I suggest you prepare a batch of crumbs, so one flies over. I've known the outcome of this from the beginning," he demanded and then put on his hissing helm and shut the frail door with one mighty swing. Outside the wall, Tymbrenn loyalists were slayed in fives by members of the King's Guard. I knew the members solely by face, not by their armour. There was the Captain, Karron Wull, twins Byrron and Briden Vikarin,

Garvy Orkwood, Duran Durrandon and Dirron Rygert. I could see just as many King's Guard members as there should be today. The battle had already lasted an hour, and not a single of these fine warriors had fallen in battle.

I watched for two more hours of Tymbrenns suffering at the hands of the Guard when Byrron opened the door again.

"Do you have the raven, Sylvina?" he questioned. I had no crumbs to tempt a raven with.

"No crumbs, sir," I responded simply.

"I see. Take these. I slayed a Tymbrenn soldier who attempted to do the exact same thing," he pulled out a fair amount of crumbs and left them on the windowsill, which a raven would soon come for.

"Thank you, sir," I responded simply.

"Get to writing. You have a quill?" he remembered to ask all the right questions. One of the few honourable members of the Guard left, I suppose.

"Yes, sir," I answered simply.

"Good. Get to it. No time for hesitation," he responded, hurrying out the door.

I wrote my letter and addressed it to Kegan Wyne. It went like this:

'Sir Kegan Wyne,

Assistance is needed at Hagueveil. While the Tymbrenns are being pushed back, double the number of soldiers are marching to the gates. No members of the King's Guard have been felled yet, but without reinforcements, some shall. I suggest bringing 50 men, if you can, as well as Juran Herqys and Stephyn Tanner, if possible.

Kind Regards,

Sylvina Slait.'

I waited another 2 hours for a raven to arrive, and I felt insane.

Insanity was my curse. It was the thing I feared above all else. I'm cured. The strange thoughts that once sunk me into new realities with graceful ease, never leaving a trace or a clue they had taken hold, still come and go like they did before. Each is a florid daydream, not viewed like a play but lived in the first person. I'm always the main character, elevated and heroic, a delusion of grandeur, I suppose. I like them that way. It's much better than a mundane life. So if the thoughts still come, how is it I say I'm cured? A true delusion is a fixed false belief that gains traction. Like a carriage on the road, it carries a person in different directions, often erratic and toward disaster. Mine has become more like a glorious wonder, taking me to new fantastic views of life but unable to alter my direction or fundamental beliefs. So what once required attention no longer does. The delusions are no more than daydreams with an extra kick. I'm stone-cold sane. In fact, I'll wager I'm safer from insanity than anyone else. Others can still fall and still become lost in the mental maze, but I can't. Unless something that should come to save me never does.

And something came.

It was a murder of ravens. The branches, newly bereft of their leaves, were weighted down with birds so black they looked more like shadows or perhaps silhouettes cut from the dawn canopy above. As the day lightened, the ravens became so raucous that the noise of the war below was drowned out, and some Tymbrenn loyalists grew distracted and lost their heads. A murder for good causes is a perfect crime.

Now all to do is await the arrival of Kegan and The Exile. I always found war a trivial ordeal.

The war continues to rage on. Let's get some rest, shall we?

No, too risky. Xargaron is watching me. Always watching. He preys on my dreams for supper.

What is it that the Pargions say?

Memento Mori.

Simon:

I awoke in the Outpost my men had laid out for me at dusk when all was dark and misleading.

One servant woke me up. I knew not her name. I knew not a name of any servant of mine. As I woke up, I scattered outside of my post to see my stallion Reinhardt, Emannar and his horse Tybalt, ready for a prolonged journey. While fully armoured, except for his head only being defended by a royal crown that sits upon his head as a boat stuck on a stream in one place, entangled in the devilish roots of his hair, he did not want to fight. He wanted to talk.

"I assume you are prepared, High Earl. You must be," he commanded.

"In all ways", I moaned, "Shall I prepare the horse?"

"If you would rather walk, leave Reinhardt where he is," he roared, with exhaustion dripping like the sweat on his brow. Had he been practising? I cleared away the sleep in my eyes and mounted my stallion.

The thundering of hooves split the silence as a pair of stallions galloped through the bleak landscape. The wind wisped their manes into the air like flames; after all, they were both flame-coloured chestnuts. Reinhardt and Tybalt were their names. Their muscles rippled from under their freshly-groomed pelts and their powerful legs. They propelled them forward and kept them going as they powered over the land. My land. Reinhardt and Tybalt were both one of many marriage gifts Emannar and I received from our wives. The gift was better than the giver this time.

I was weak at controlling Reinhardt tonight, understandably. Tybalt and Emannar powered forward. Reinhardt tried his best, but without my command, he was weak, too. Communication is the foundation of riding your horse. Eventually, Emannar reined his steed near an abandoned bridge.

"Riding like a true warrior. I hate that goddamn carriage. Far too slow, breaks too often. Only use it because Elizella's too damn stubborn to ride," Emannar ranted.

"Sounds like you are begging for a divorce," I smirked.

"I will request one if it allows me to bear a level head for once in my life!" he chuckled heartily.

"Many of the Stormholme peasants would do any hit just for the payment. They'd do the perfect assassination for a bit of gold. Shame there's nobody to kill these days," I lamented.

"I've been receiving many complaints about the quality of life recently, so I put devising a new class system in the hands of Francis. You can probably guess if he's actually done it yet," he responded calmly.

"I doubt he's tried," I spat. I did not trust a single councillor, especially Francis Ashford. Ashford especially focused solely on personal gain. The Supreme Witanegemote Gregory used false lies and pretended wisdom for bias in court, Lord Tobas had too many messengers to know all that he knew, and Emannar's brothers were both fools. Sir Karron Wull had the highest probability of being trustworthy, but he was blinded by his love for war.

"Well, I did not bring you here to discuss thief-takers and the faults of my councillors. Some of my men found a messenger heading towards Elizella's old cottage. It was one of Tobas's men," he revealed darkly.

"Did you capture the man?" I inquired.

"They crippled his horse and held him for interrogation. Even after being beaten to death, he refused to give us the message and said that his lips were sealed by fate. I have sentenced him to the stocks. Should be a nice sight for the young ones, eh?"

"I have no interest in how you find it. I only care for the message. Why would he go to Elizella's cottage?" I asked with grinding teeth.

"Elizella lent the cottage to my brother-in-law, Dontin. They are likely cooperating," he answered.

"I'm assuming an interrogation is out of the question?" I questioned.

"Tobas is stubborn. He has no loyalties, no master. Doubt we'd get a word out. Dontin is the same, and Arvin would charge me down if I bothered," he responded and then changed his voice to a suspicious tone, "Do you remember Stephyn Tanner?"

"Wish I could forget him," I said bluntly. Stephyn Tanner was the upstart of the King's Guard. He had about ten slaves and no friends for very good reason.

"The entire King's Guard has been sent to protect Sylvina Slait - except for Stephyn. When Stephyn arrives with Sir Kegan Wyne and Juran Herqys, he shall force the Guard into submission and kill all who betray his commands. We will use this to lure Dontin out of hiding, and if he doesn't comply, we'll anger Arvin until Dontin is pressured into view," he explained. I had questions.

"Why bother with this note-passing? This is a minor thing to massacre for. Why bother?" I asked.

He spoke even more seriously this time. "Dontin has only ever longed for the deaths of his family, predominantly Elizella, Ashlyh and his parents. Elizella thinks that Tobas is conspiring with him. If I don't put my full force into this, I will be the one betrayed - and by my own damn wife.

"What about Sylvina? Could she be involved?" I suggested.

He shook his head, "Unlikely. Dontin and Sylvina may have been the kindest to each other, but I wouldn't call them close. Sylvina isn't one for politics. Also, she hasn't been around. Only came to Hagueveil when I ordered Kegan Wyne to escort her, a sirenman picked her up, and we told her parents that the squires were coming."

I changed the subject, "Last I remember, divorce was a thing in this Kingdom."

Emannar chuckled, "If only it were that simple, Simon, if only..."

"Well, I don't see why it isn't," I shrugged.

Emannar's face shifted into a frown. He looked over his shoulder and turned to face me again.

"Let's continue to ride, my friend," he faked ease and rode Tybalt away. Reinhardt and I followed.

Emannar, this sorry fool. Yes, he is right to think that Elizella could betray him...

But if Dontin is against him...

And Tobas...

And Elizella...

I'm sure he's already been betrayed.

'Betrayal is a conscious choice for cold indifference. When you betray someone, you're taking a personal gain over a loss that would have benefited another. You're shattering a million shards of positive outcomes as you break your vows, all the while trying to hold on to your humanity as you swing your vile words.

You can't be blamed for betrayal half of the time, however. Sometimes all you can do to survive is leave everything you know is secure for you. However, is it worth it? Betrayal backfires more than it succeeds. You can make yourself beyond saving. That was your choice. You chose your duty and failed. You took the only option of interest...and left with a new life, but not yourself.'

-A Discussion from Lord Tobas on betrayal.

Dontin:

I waited forever for the messenger when it dawned on me: he had been killed. What a shame.

I left for Stormholme on the same day I realised that he had died, riding alone through a short path I had discovered through the Great Wood. The Pargion boy will be fine rotting in that cell. Don't even care if he breaks free. He was just a boy taking a tour of the universe.

I found my way to Lord Tobas's chambers, and he was there sitting patiently as if he knew that I was coming. I don't like it when people know that I'm coming. He was reading a book, and I don't care to know which.

"Why do you read?" I asked.

He chuckled, placed a twig on one page and closed it, and said, "Entertainment is rare these days, my lord." He was a twig himself, with a couple of strands of hair making up his round head. His golden silks and velvets let me know that the only effective term to use for this man was vain.

"Yes, well, life can't be very entertaining when you're able to fail to send a competent messenger on your most important quest," I spat.

"Ah yes, that was a complication," Tobas smirked.

"You are what, thirty?" I asked.

"Thirty-seven, my lord, with 19 years spent perfecting my trade," he seemed full of himself, boastful.

"Not an accomplishment when you're worthless," I responded bitterly.

"Empty words, my lord, empty words," he grinned.

"What was the message?" I questioned.

"Well, if I'm worthless now, the message is likely worthless, isn't it? No reason to care, eh?" he chortled.

"Tell me the damn message, Tobas, or God knows I'll hand myself in, and we'll both be dead," I was growing in annoyance and tension, but Tobas still seemed amused, like his amusement of the day was to annoy me for eternity.

"I have begun my snoop around the town, and I have heard this - the Council are plotting Emannar's death," his face grew dark and sombre.

"A conspiracy? If the King found out."

"He will not. Everyone close to him is in on it. Even his dear, dear wife," he howled.

"Elizella is involved? And what of Stephyn Tanner?" I asked. This is deeper than I realised.

"Tanner has informed the rest of the King's Guard of the plan. Emannar's orders were to draw out Arvin Slait by taking Sylvina hostage, but instead, they're planning on waiting until

Emannar is alone or weak, and then he will be slain. Poor, poor man," he sorrowed.

"All I want is Elizella to fall, but it seems not a soul can be trusted who could give me what I need," I realised.

"No clue why you are surprised, Dontin," he seemed shocked, oddly shocked.

"Why is that?"

"When it comes to the upper-class, all is but a web of lies. You need to be the spider who spins it. That is how life works here," he dispersed wisely.

I thanked Tobas for the information and returned to the cottage. Perhaps if I can cause a civil war between the Noble Houses, I can find a weakness in Elizella's campaign. Well, there is, of course, Dayron, who could be all I need to cause an uproar between the Pargions and another Noble House.

Time to be the Veille, I suppose.

I returned to the Slait Cottage and found the cell.

Where in the living hell has the boy gone?

Gwendys:

In the ten hours I've been in bed, I must have woken up six times.

Not for that long each time, but enough to break my sleep into worrying chunks.

With every disturbance, there is a new nightmare.

I've resisted my husband, and he leaves without even a look at me.

My son has disappeared.

I lost my job and my role as a mother.

I failed it.

My world is burning, and I can't dowse it in a baptismal font.

I'm running for the carriage home, but it's pulling away already.

The girls are sliding on thin ice.

Then my bedroom lights up, and my mind moves faster than my five-year-old (Corren) can speak, like it's stuck, repeating, the voices getting louder every second.

I want to wash my brain in cold water.

Freeze the whole thing right out.

But I can't.

I'd take some ale or some drugs, but it would ruin my corpse now.

None of my duties have been done.

None of my duties will be done.

Blood pounds through my ears and feels on the verge of spilling out but never will.

The heart thuds in the chest, loosening itself from its veins and arteries.

Hands shake vigorously.

Feet tingle numbingly.

Vision blurs uncomfortably.

I need to get away.

To a safe place.

Damn Bernstaplen.

Damn Simon.

Damn my children.

Damn my House.

Damn my parents.

Damn my siblings.

I have no one.

Damn me.

Either way, I will ruin everything.

Damn the King.

Damn the council.

Ashford and Tobas are arriving to-morrow.

After that...

I run.

Nails dig into palms.

Breathing stiffens.

Stiffens.

Crying hurts.

Breathing hurts.

The chest grows tight.

Bile rises in the throat.

Stiffens...

Damn Simon.

Kristyne:

Father had left me and Annyte behind with Priestess Ronayne, mostly so I could talk to Varn, I believe.

"His Grace took him for a ride. It could be anything, likely something crucial. All kinds of things lurk on these lands, they say," the Priestess informed me.

"What kinds of things?" I asked.

"Dark things. A princess does not get curious, Kristyne. The Gods give you all your answers," she answered.

"If I have a question, it shall be answered, and if you call me a princess again, I'll tell Father you hit me," I warned. I loathe the Priestess. She has spent her entire life believing in false idols. But I must keep my beliefs to myself, or Father will exile me like the rest of them. And I'm not a princess.

The Priestess had none of it. "Don't try to intimidate me, Kristyne. The Gods have set your future in stone. I can't keep protecting you forever, so you should avoid asking questions," she answered calmly, "Where is Annyte today?"

"Somewhere," I sighed, "Misbehaving, probably."

"If you see her, send her to me so I can get her ready. Prince Varn would like to take both of you sailing. In Jaron Carner's ship too. A kind gesture, is it not?"

I wouldn't call it a kind gesture. Varn is intolerable. Abusive, even, so I've heard. I do not really know Varn yet, but I've no choice but to marry him. Why? Because Annyte is too young and Father will do anything for power. Maybe it's just so he doesn't have to see our faces as often as he does now and can just get drunk with Emannar every evening (then again, he does that anyway). "Yes, a kind gesture it is," I responded, lacking certainty, "And I'll tell Annyte what's happening if I see her, Priestess."

"Good, you are excused," she dismissed me.

I found Annyte by the docks, looking as ugly as always. Mud sprayed over her leather rags that she wore like a stray dog looking for a pack of mutton. She was a pathetic princess.

"You look like Kegan Wyne," I told her, "Priestess Ronayne says that Varn's waiting to take us sailing."

"No. I don't want to sail," she responded pathetically.

"Why not?" I questioned.

She looked at me with her dull eyes like I was the stupid one. "I don't want to see Varn, and I don't want to see you," she threatened, looking away.

"Don't be stupid," I snapped, "When I'm Queen, I'll get Varn to discipline you. You'll learn how to be a Lady."

"You can't teach your enemies," she grew annoyed.

"You can when you're King," I responded.

Jaron Carner and Kegan Wyne took us to Varn later that day. Jaron looked me dead in the eye and chuckled without either of us speaking a word to each other. I suppose he pitied scared little girls? Varn came out of one door on the ship. His right cheek was red raw, with the shape of a hand imprinted on it.

"Ah yes, Kristyne, my love, and your sister. How are you today?" he grinned. His voice had a rather high pitch, like an infant.

"Overjoyed, Prince Varn," I curtseyed in my blue dress, but Annyte remained still. "It is a pleasure to finally meet my future betrothed."

Varn kissed my hand, "I assure you; it delights me to finally witness your beauty." He looked at Annyte, "And how are you, child?"

"I'll be better when this is done," Annyte answered, and I looked at her with scorn.

I looked at Varn, "Let's get to sailing, shall we? Annyte is not the fondest of sailing, you see," I responded. He chuckled.

"Well, that shall change. Nothing is greater than sailing with Varn Woodgairrd," he assured us.

"I'm sure that is true, my Prince," I answered.

We were sailing for around an hour. He spent a while just picking a direction to travel in. I could tell that he was planning on turning around, going to the same spot, and acting like he was a magnificent navy general who knew the geography of the entire Kingdom. Everyone was so pathetic today. I decided to talk privately with Varn a little more.

"Do you always look like this?" Varn asked me.

"What do you mean?" I blushed.

"Your lovely blonde hair, paired with the elegance of that blue dress," Varn gazed at me, "Your parents aren't blonde."

"My aunt was," I told him, "I must have gotten it from her, somehow."

"I suppose among the Pargions, there is always one child who inherits the beauty," he smiled.

"You can say the same for the Woodgairrds. You look like the princes from the stories."

"My sisters were beautiful too," he sighed, "They just...discarded everything."

I grinned, "You can drop the act now. We don't have to pretend to love each other."

He laughed, "That is good to hear. N-not that you're not pretty, though. I just wanted to find love my own way."

"Some want their love handed to them, some want to find it, and some, like my sister, would rather die before they start it," I smiled. "Speaking of Annyte..."

"Let us find her," he stood up and pulled me up.

Then we saw the boy.

A boy. A mess of a boy. I didn't get a good look at him before Varn grabbed him and put a sword to his neck.

"Who the hell are you?" he questioned with his grip strengthening on the boy.

"Nobody you care about..." he managed to get out. Barely. Annyte saw the boy and rushed over.

"Leave him! He's ought to be scared. Don't touch him!" she yelled.

"Why not? I'll kill you too," Varn giggled, proceeding to slit the boy's throat. The boy lay dead on the floor as Annyte cried.

"You...you monster...you...I'll kill you!" she screamed, grabbing Varn's dagger and twisting it inward, leaving a large cut on his left shoulder, cutting through the rich fabrics he wore. Varn pushed Annyte to the ground with one hand and was about to slay her like the beast she was when I stole his blade and tossed it out to sea, leaving it to drown.

We all remained in silence for the rest of the sail. If we didn't kill each other, Jaron would, or Emannar would, or Father would. We had all made gargantuan mistakes.

But it's all Annyte's fault.

'I could recite all the reasons, and yet I still harboured all the pain, kept every scar on my wrists. I knew that every trauma of the past decade was

present in the room when either of my parents surrendered their self-control when their cannibalistic brains consumed the overbearing tasks of empathy and logic. Being mixed, as many a family is, can lead to trauma descending down many lines, damaging the brains of all future generations. And the slaves, the slaves, the worst part of being a Lord is the slaves. So many cultures and peoples used it as a means to an end. When I was a boy, I wanted to end this terrible cycle of pain for my children, but I never truly found out how. It took too long, and my inner desires finally came out when my parents started feasting on each other. I read all the books I could and met all the people who could have helped, but they could not cure me. I was immune to all cures. I lost my self-control, discarded empathy and logic.

However, I beg thee, Dear Reader, do not fear for my sanity. Despite my parents' devilish natures, I have learned to keep a level head in the discussion and keep my evils in my head. Brains can heal themselves over time. They simply require the right opportunity and environment to do so. Be your mind's role model. Give it hope, a chance and a small helping hand. A recipe to make the dysfunctional function and release the prison of your brokenness. Be well, Dear Reader.'

-Extract from the Memoirs of Francis Ashford

Simon:

"The children have returned, Lord Pargion."

I eyed John Borrell with cold eyes, knowing that he meant my disgraceful daughters and the King's son. "Good for them," I responded darkly.

"Varn has a large bloody cut on his chest, but the girls are in peak condition. Oh, and another thing," he grew cold and tense, "We found a boy's corpse."

This alarmed me. A corpse on a boat of three? "Who is the boy, Borrell?"

"I am sorry, Lord Pargion, but that we do not know. He could be an orphan, as no family recognised his face," he seemed sorrowful. He pitied the boy.

"Must have been a stowaway. If he died that easily to Varn, of all people, I could see why his family likely disowned him. Perhaps suicide. That would certainly be entertaining..." I replied.

"I'm sure it would be, sir," he whispered weakly, "Emannar and Elizella are being escorted to the Council today. Your daughters and Varn shall stand trial," Borrell informed me.

"How is your daughter, Kyra, sir?" I changed the subject, "Is she alright? She always was rather fond of Annyte, if I remember. Hated Kristyne, though. Despised her. How is she?"

"As far as I am aware, she is doing well, sir. She has befriended Jaide Woodgairrd and Darlyne Tanner quickly enough," he was terrified of me.

"Perfect. Now, get my damn daughters to the Council, or Kyra will become an orphan," I threatened, and he hurried out the room anxiously. Borrell was a good man, but I had no time to waste with these pathetic discussions. My daughters could die.

The entire Council was waiting in their chambers to hear this testimony, save for Ashford and Tobas, who were sent to meet Gwendys and the Supreme Witanagemote, who was holding a meeting for the members of his pathetic little cult. Just a check-up for both. A pathetic little check-up.

They came later. Emannar took his seat on the Throne like an obese goblin, and Elizella was next to him, grinning smugly.

Annyte stood in the centre of the room. Kristyne and Varn were behind her, held by knights like captives.

"Annyte," I bellowed. She looked at me and began bawling like a toddler.

"I'm sorry, Father. I'm sorry. I'm sorry, Father. I'm sorry," she repeated, each time gaining a more depressed tone in her voice.

"I know. Did you kill the boy? Did you harm Varn?" I questioned soothingly.

"No, I did not kill the boy. I defended him. Against Varn..." she cried harder.

Elizella stood up and howled, "How dare you accuse your superior! Wretched girl!"

Emannar snapped at Elizella instantly, "Shut your mouth, Slait. If you try to petrify this girl, I will ensure that Varn is the one punished. All you care about is your washed-up idea that Slaits are superior beings. Shut your mouth."

"No! You know very well what has happened, Emannar, and Simon does too! This girl attacked my son! Killed a boy and blamed it on him! She's a weasel! Tear her arm off!" she screamed.

"That's not what happened. Varn killed the boy because he was a stowaway. I defended him. I pushed his sword back at him. That's how it cut him," she screamed meekly.

"I believe Varn's word over yours. He's an angel. You're the ugliest weasel I've seen. And ugly weasels lie as an attempt to seem less like ugly weasels. This is a facade I will not give in to!" Elizella was trying to intimidate her into submission as Varn rushed forward, escaping captivity.

"Council, do not believe the weasel! She tried to kill me with my own blade! If it was not for Kristyne interfering, I would be dead!" that last part amused me.

"Kristyne interfering? How so?" I asked.

"She pushed Annyte backwards, and her dagger flew up and into the depths of the ocean," Varn responded with an arrogant grin.

Kristyne walked forward. She was still wearing that ward for protection. She now put it on without realising, I suppose. Gwendys gave it to her, saying that Priestess Ronayne had enchanted it to protect her from all harm of any kind and that my mother had ordered the ward's creation. It was the last memory of her grandmother. Her favourite.

It was time for the council's interrogation. Styve, Kase and Karron eyed her, and Karron was the one who spoke to her.

"Tell us what happened, will you, Kristyne? Your information is valuable to us," he asked calmingly.

"I didn't see," she insisted, "I didn't see anything happen. Could have been either of them."

Both Varn and Annyte flew at her, yelling. Annyte threw a few punches, even. Simon and Elizella dragged their children away to the side and ordered knights to hold them in place. This was painful to watch.

Elizella looked straight at Emannar, "Punish these girls for their lies. Now."

"Shut your mouth, Elizella. Look at these girls. They are young and weak. Do you believe they can handle a sword? They all deserve punishment. Now, pipe down, rat," Emannar spat and then looked at the council, "Any punishment ideas?"

Karron and Kase both shrugged, but Styve spoke up, "For Annyte, I suggest a severe whipping and constraints to her chambers for a week. For Varn, I suggest the same, as well as a 10% cut on his inheritance upon Emannar's death, and for Kristyne, in an attempt to make her talk, crush that ward of hers," he smiled like a cruel goat.

Kristyne cried, and so did Annyte, surprisingly. "No!" they screamed in unison.

Elizella grinned at Styve's decision like a child, "How about Simon does it?"

"What?" I responded with confusion and a hint of terror. Emannar shook and looked at me.

"Elizella, I said shut your mouth..."

"It's the council's decision, isn't it? Ask them."

Styve was the first to answer, "I like that idea. Karron?"

Karron looked at me humbly and shook his head, "It does not seem just." Styve and Elizella grimaced, and all eyes went to Kase Woodgairrd.

"Well," he responded, "I'm not quite sure..."

"Yes, you are, Kase. You know you are," Styve said through gritted teeth. He then grabbed Kase's shoulder with a gripping intensity. Karron was too honourable to stop him.

"Well...yes, I am. It sounds like a good idea," the King's youngest brother answered meekly. He was afraid of Styve. For a good reason.

Emannar, mourning what I now had to do, concluded the session, "Alright then, it is settled. Elden Brune, please take the ward and place it before Simon. Bradyn Bulwark, please fetch an axe for him to break it open."

The executioners did so, and they handed me Bulwark's axe. Upon the handle of aged old oak was a blade of sharpest steel. It had been fashioned in a time when an axe could be anything, from a homely firewood maker to something for defence, but this, this was for an offence.

The ward had many emeralds circled around it. I analysed every glinting green gem that sparkled with the reflection of the beautiful blue river that flowed endlessly through them. One last glance, I thought to myself. I watched them shine off the sun. Indeed, they did. They shone and glowed, waving me goodbye and luck.

I saw my mother, looking like she was the day I was born, mouthing 'disgrace' at me as I plunged the axe through the ward, shattering it. Ending my daughter's protection as she screamed with hate at my cold, dead heart.

I am my mother's disgrace, but all I can do is think about it, not act on it.

Memento Mori.

Dayron:

I was a warrior.

Me and Damon, and Daman, and Corren.

We were dressed like warriors, in chainmail, ready for combat, blades and shields in our hands.

It was noon.

We were before a mighty beast.

A gryphon.

But this wasn't Grey. It was something special.

Something...evil.

Then I saw Grey fly up behind me.

He was half my size now.

He nuzzled the beast.

Befriended it.

And then Damon plunged his sword into the gryphon.

And so did Daman.

And so did Corren.

And all I could do was watch as it was slaughtered before me.

Then Grey attacked.

I called him back and tried to get him to stop, but they kept swiping at him and missing as he flew around and wounded them all severely.

And then the world shook.

Blurred.

Up and down, swapped places.

They didn't breathe.

I didn't breathe.

The light was emitted from the gryphon's corpse and blinded us all.

Ensnared us in the roots of our bloodthirsty natures.

We all choke.

Unbearable, long-lasting pain, as we all choke.

I scream for help.

There is no help.

Then it stops.

Silence.

Then all descends into madness.

They speak to me, but I can't hear them.

Just like I haven't for years.

I've heard Grey, though, and the Witanegemotes, but not them.

There is some music.

Soothing music.

Sounds like a lute.

It is John Borrell.

I can't capture how good the music is with words.

Then he destroys the guitar.

Mischief is etched in every corner of his cruel, 61-year-old mush.

Then the lute transforms.

Into Kyra, his daughter.

Kyra is lying there, dying, and he doesn't move.

Then they disintegrate from view.

And I bawl, like an infant, I cry.

I'm still crying as I wake up.

The dream stayed with me throughout the day.

I was unsettled.

I had had the same dream the day before.

I needed answers, but Dontin will be searching for me.

He would understand.

Would he?

It's a crisp morning in The Great Wood.

I can find home.

And so I do.

I need to find answers.

The answers that Witanegemote Morgan can give me.

Gwendys:

"They will be here within an hour," Jaze Wyne told me, with the flock of other guards behind him.

I looked at him seriously, "You have done well to prepare Bernstaplen, Jaze. You and each guard shall be rewarded double the gold. Consider it a token of gratitude from House Pargion."

Jaze looked down at me from his stallion and shook his head modestly, "I need none of your gratitude, Lady Wayne. My service to Lord Simon is all the gratitude I need, and, likely, the same goes for my men. If you must show your gratitude, please redirect it to my brothers. Odo has been having issues tending to his daughter's wounds after the Cantell raid, and Kegan needs the motivation to end his alcoholism. Their lives are worse and more dire than mine, I assure you."

"I shall pay you double in addition to this, please, sir."

"Your wish is my command," he responded, smiling humbly, "I've sent two men to check on your Stablemaster and Kennelmaster. Sullivan is considering retiring, as his horses are few, his pay is low, and his son is dying. The Kennelmaster Richards has found work in House Ruttiger and will leave for Rutt once this visit is over. Do we let them leave or execute them for treason now?"

I didn't think about this very much, "The Kennelmaster must die. Send a guard to inspect the actions of the

Stablemaster. If he, too, commits treason, execute him as well. Otherwise, let him live."

My panic attack the previous day made me uneasy. Francis Ashford and Lord Tobas were two of the most untrustworthy people in Stormholme, to my knowledge. Simon sent me a raven telling me to trust them as much as they can be trusted. So, about as much as Simon.

The bile was still high and stiff in my throat. I had not fully recovered, especially since I had done very little resting last night. Not much could have been done about it. I have had these moments frequently ever since I realised who Simon was. I regret doing everything I could not but do. Luck for the next life?

I listened as Jaze spoke with Damon. Damon had always taken the Wyne brothers as his idols. "Lord Wyne, it is wonderful to see you so joyful. When is your next fabled conquest, may I ask?" he questioned meekly.

Jaze looked at him solemnly with his golden helm. "My conquest days are behind me, Damon. I am not a Knight, not a Sir, certainly not a Lord. If you want another fabled conquest, perhaps you should do one yourself. Maybe kill Arvin Slait on the way, do me some justice," he responded, roaring with sickening laughter.

Damon looked better than most days. He looked a shade brighter than usual, which applied even to his ebony mop of hair. Perhaps he was going to collect his scars from Ashford or

Tobas? Not the best idea for the public eye or the council's approval, but it would be hilarious. And terrifying.

"You look well, Damon. How are you?" I asked soothingly.

"Fine, I suppose, Mam. Miss the girls, though. Annyte ' especially. She was always willing to watch me fight. Saw me like an idol. I liked being her idol," he answered sorrowfully.

"And now she's gone and been whipped by the King's damn executioners and is being locked in a grey hellhole for a week." I disapproved of Annyte's actions, but Kristyne did far worse things. Libel, they called it. Defamation of the perfect Queen Elizella's perfect, rosy-faced little boy. To hell with her and her boy.

"I must be on my leave. Enjoy your pleasant little encounter," Jaze sneered, with all the hate of Hell in him being directed to the thought of these councillors.

As Jaze left, they arrived.

Francis Ashford spoke to me first, "Gwendys. Dear Gwendys. How are you these days?"

"Why are you and Tobas here, Ashford?"

"Men, prepare a fine meal for Lady Wayne here," he gestured at his guards dismissively, "We have found details of an invasion. And a complicated twist to it. If our presence has angered you, dear Gwendys, I apologise. It was never my intent," he smiled. His smile dripped with cynicism. He was always cynical since his youth as a working-class labourer for

Father Marvion Wayne. Now he was this, and this let him be more cynical than ever.

"How do you know about this invasion you speak of?" I questioned.

"Lord Tobas finds all. He shall speak when I let him. How are you, Gwendys? I have not seen you for some time," he answered cynically.

"Where was this invasion?" I asked.

"Hagueveil. Sound familiar to you? That's right. It's the Fortress of Arvin and Lady Laena. Emannar told them to pack their bags and rush off to the South, but they left their daughter Sylvina there. The whimsical one. Emannar has sent his entire King's Guard there to defend her," he answered.

"From who?"

"His brother-in-law's trained esquires. Rudd and Seamus, the Tymbrenn twins. When the King's Guard starts to get pushed back, The Exile, Kegan Wyne and Stephyn Tanner are to enter the fray with a band of new knights. Only, there's a catch to it all. These men are there to force the King's Guard into submission, and together they will all take the child hostage. And yet, that is not what they plan. Once Emannar gets what he wants from this hostage situation, they will turn their blades to him, and our beloved King will be dead. Alas, a complicated situation," he explained.

"I see," I responded simply.

Tobas then dismounted his horse. "I shall be the one to speak now, Ashford. Shut your mouth for a moment, will you?" he giggled. Francis mounted his stallion again.

"Good morning, Tobas."

"Good morning, Lady Wayne. A pleasure to see you again," he responded, "I have heard about your son's disappearance. It's a cruel world, isn't it? I hope he is safe, for your sake."

"Thank you, Tobas."

"There is, ahem, one minor detail that Ashford forgot to mention. 'Tis the reason why we arranged this meeting with you."

"What is this detail?"

"The betrayal of the Guard to kill Emannar has been orchestrated by a man of no affiliation with our brave men. We have our suspects," he explained.

"Who are your suspects?"

"Arvin Slait himself, as he harbours a hatred for his children, Lawrence Malver, Dromin Tanner...all of Dontin's enemies, truly. But one sticks out, and you will not enjoy the sound of this," he continued.

"Who?"

"Before I explain, promise me that you will aid us with our espionage and distraction of this potential evil while we prove either his innocence or guilt. Promise it," he insisted like a toddler.

"Then I will promise it," I responded, caring not for his youthful games.

"Your brother," he responded, to my shock, "Your brother, heir to Minbury, Lord Tyral Wayne."

Daman:

The hooves of the horses danced to the song of war as we arrived in Novak lands.

Our armour was bronze. Bronze like the faith of the Pargions. 'Memento Mori', Simon always said. As the strongest of us men, Aldo rode in front, the symbol of Guillemin emblazoned on his helm (a golden mistletoe). Fawkes stumbled in behind. This was his first riding experience, poor boy. All he wanted to do was win this day. Barrett was northeast of Fawkes, riding his horse viciously, making his horse stagger pathetically. Fawkes chuckled at sight, and Barrett looked over his left shoulder to pierce his eyes through the boy's soul.

"Have you found yourself a topic of humour, boy? I need something to laugh about, you know. Care to share?" he asked with a chilling smirk.

Fawkes shook his hand with a sense of inferiority and whimpered, "No, sir, no sir..."

Howard hollered with a cruel delight and plunged his dagger into Fawkes's wrist. Aldo and I stopped our horses.

"Enough of this," Aldo exclaimed, cutting into Howard's soul, leaving a stinging mark on his fragile skin.

Fawkes cried like an infant, "'e put a knife in me wrist! A knife!"

"Not a knife, boy, a dagger. A Novak Dagger, if you must know. And if it weren't for these two, this dagger would be cracking your skull open and forcing it down your horse's throat. Sound fun?" Barrett looked at me then, "What's your verdict, Pargion? Am I the one to blame?"

They both need to be here for their own sake, "No one is to blame here. Fawkes is guilty by causation, and Howard is guilty by assault. Best not to speak of this again, do you understand?" The lack of response told me clearly that they understood, and we continued to ride.

Aldo turned to me, "You have made a wise decision, Daman. Make more of those and one day you could be as wise as the Duke of Guillemin," he gloated.

"That's an easy feat to accomplish, seeing as the Duke of Guillemin has a brain made of rocks," I spat lightly. He guffawed.

"Believe what you choose to believe, Pargion."

"A Pargion I am not," and we stifled another band of laughter.

After another half-hour of riding, we approached the marked Novak camp. We readied our armour and weapons for what could become the bloodiest battle of our lives and sent Aldo further ahead, as he was the sole one to speak the Novak tongue. We continued riding, but slowly and cautiously now when Aldo skidded to a halt in his tracks as he noticed a Novak gazing directly at us.

"Cano, kladholk! Cano!" he exclaimed, "Oidkakolk rao aidkako! Fail aidkakolk! Karr dho aidkakolk!"

Aldo turned around swiftly to translate, "'Come, brothers! Come! Outsiders lie outside! Four outsiders! Kill the outsiders!'" as around fifty Novak soldiers came out of five tents like a horde and chanted "Karr dho aidkakolk! Karr dho aidkakolk!" and they surrounded us with their spears and shields. There was no point in attacking now.

Aldo attempted to reason with them, as he later explained, "Wo nouv avai va huln. Wha ak avail Chaod?"

They understood, and one Novak stepped forward, speaking to us and then to his men, "Mo, Balog Novak Gabor. Kladholk, ruav kavv avail kkoulk, vo huxo u dhuvdo ad koudo vadh dhoko nov."

Aldo translated again, "They call him Balog Novak Gabor, and he's telling the others to try for peace with us for now," and then he looked back at him, "Yail koakro huxo kavo avkikdadok da dva ad ail nov. Muav vo nuko kikd dhoko avkikdadok?"

"Yai nuav vad karr nav nov, aidkakol."

"Thak ak ivkolkduvkukro, kid kolhukk avai vairk vuvd da houl dhoal kdalaok?"

"Addokdukro."

Aldo looked back at us, "Go on, Fawkes and Howard. Tell your story, and I'll translate. He won't let you do justice otherwise."

Fawkes detailed his life first, "I am Fawkes Podde, once Fawkes Grimm, and my uncle, the head of House Grimm, has cut me off from all inheritance and titles after my father's death. He has harboured a long hatred for Novaks since they killed Grimm Woodgairrd, a King who inspired the House's creation. If I could kill a Novak, I could dream of earning my inheritance back and gain his approval." Aldo translated, and Gabor nodded comprehensively.

Howard Barrett was next to speak, "I am Howard Barrett. My wife, Liya, and her sisters Darlyne and Marlbough were slaughtered by Novaks, and my entire life, I have wanted to seize one of your men and carve out holes in his sickening little skull. Perhaps feed his eyes and tongue to a stray cat as well."

There was no way that Aldo translated that exactly as Barrett said it, as again, Chief Balog nodded comprehensively.

"I khurr kaxo avai khordol dal davakhd, uvk da-nallav vo duv vokadaudo," the Novak Chief responded, and Aldo prepared to translate.

"They shall give us shelter for the night, and we shall negotiate to-morrow. Sounds fair to me, eh?"

We all nodded in agreement, though Barrett took a while to make his decision. I can sympathise with him in that regard. Why would he trust the men who killed his wife?

"Wo uddokd avail dolnk," Aldo replied in the Novak tongue.

We were given four rugs to sleep on, in a tent, with ten Novaks around us emitting the scent of rotten manticores. Reminded me of the stenches of the Horsemaster and the Kennelmaster, or perhaps the aroma of the King's Guard, but I'm not quite sure. Our throats were dry, and we were freezing like hell in the Novak Desert. Somehow, Fawkes managed to sleep soundly through the biting pain, and Aldo fell to a slumber shortly after him. Howard stayed up all night, juggling two daggers maniacally. He was a perfect juggler, I must say. Could be a Jester, and I wouldn't know better.

Sometimes, my life is like a tautology. You know, a tautology, the term in the English language? Hickmere taught me about it. Every moment is just another word in the sentence that will all lead to the same meaning, and then the next sentence starts another tautological cycle. One word is part of the definition of another word. One of these words is useless and can be removed, but it could be either of those words. The words won't change the meaning unless every word is different.

I dreamed of home that night. Of Simon and Mother, of Damon, and Dayron, and Corren, and Kristyne and Annyte, of Uncle Camern, of Witanegemote Morgan and Storyteller Hickmere and Horsemaster Sullivan and Kennelmaster Richards. I wonder if Simon is enjoying being High Earl. I wonder how Mother is dealing with being alone at Bernstaplen. How's the King? How's the Queen? How's the Council? How are the Woodgairrds, and the Slaits, and the Waynes, and the Tanners, and all the others, even the Stanes, the Folers, the

Nallorts, the Malvers? That reminds me, how's Lawrence, Simon's former Ward? Hope he likes being with his family again. I miss them all.

Then the tent set on fire, and Chief Balog Novak Gabor rushed through it, riding a vicious manticore. It let out a massive roar to awaken us, and then he pulled us on as he rode away, seemingly leaving his other people to die. He explained to Aldo later that another Novak Tribe had learned that they had given shelter to outsiders, so the Novak Leader ordered an assault with anarchy. All would die except for us.

This could scupper our plans rather easily, or aid them significantly, as we now knew to trust this powerful Novak Chief.

But who knows for now? It's just another word in the sentence.

Simon:

Tired, hungry, and short-tempered, I entered the Council Room for the first time. All I could do at that time was dream. Dream of my highest priority being acting as the dominant Noble Lord of House Pargion, seeing my children until the day I die, seeing Gwendys go mad...

Those days are the best days.

Gregory was the one who called for this meeting. Just an introduction for me to the councillors, nothing too serious. 'The most serious thing about Gregory was his incurable baldness,' Emannar told me. John Borrell came to my chambers sometime after I woke to escort me.

Borrell bowed, "It is time for the introductory council meeting imposed by the Supreme Witanegemote Gregory, Lord Pargion."

"I'm well aware, Borrell. I suggest you shut your mouth and escort me," I snapped.

Borrell frowned. "Simon, I simply refuse to escort the Noble Lord of House Pargion to an official council meeting, which His Grace the King and Her Grace the Queen will be attending, in his bedwear."

"Damn your refusal."

"Damn your stubbornness, Simon," he exclaimed with a vicious fury. It was a fury I had not expected to see in such a kind soul. This, shockingly, motivated me to change into something that was more, ahem, socially acceptable to wear in public. Borrell later met me again outside of my chambers, and he began the ride.

"While I serve on this council of Emannar's, ensure that my daughters are safe and sane, and send a raven to Gwendys asking her how everyone is at Bernstaplen. It would please me to know that they are on task," I asked demandingly.

"Of course, Simon, that's only what you've demanded of me for the past week," Borrell spat again. He seemed to be in a fragile mood today, and I did not care for it.

"Remember your place, John, or I will ask for a new steward at this council meeting. Wouldn't that be a shame for Kyra? Knowing that her father was a victim of struggling poverty because he was a staggering fool?" I responded darkly.

"All you do is conjure torture these days, Simon, and I have had enough. You cannot behead me if I am not a member of your House. I am merely a friend. They'll see. An innocent friend."

"An innocent friend who knows nothing about the law these days, it seems," I replied loathingly. I never realised that such a knowledgeable man knew so little about the truth of the world around him.

There was a hateful silence as he rode to the council chambers, and I dismounted his mule to see four of the six councillors awaiting my arrival. I hadn't taken a proper look at the chambers when I was here to deal with my daughters' escapades. The chamber was stunning, likely greater than anything Arvin or the Magnaroks could produce, with detailed paintings depicting great wars and political rivalries, fantastic beasts and their cruel slayers. A tapestry of a demon hung over Emannar's throne, which he was not currently sitting in. Another mistake Borrell made, I suppose. Gregory, the one who decided for this proper introduction to occur, was the first to greet me.

"Ah yes, of course, Lord Pargion himself! How've you been, lad?" he asked me kindly.

"I have been well, Witanegemote. How is your crumbling cult?" I answered mockingly.

"Ah, just splendid. What with the atheists, those with false idols, and the many religions of me own Witanegemotes, we're doing mighty fine, aren't we?" he roared with an uncomfortable volume.

"I can tell by your insanity," I quipped, making him frown hilariously.

In order to cut off Gregory's rant about my quip, Kase Woodgairrd was the next to speak to me, "It is...good that you are safe, Lord Pargion," he observed meekly, "It rather depressed me to see how painful it was to bring your eldest daughter to tears. Let us pray for all three of the children's recoveries."

"Of course, but to which of our 70 gods?" Gregory cut in uproariously, "I'm not so insane as to be blinded to basic logic. Believe me, Simon!"

I dismissed Gregory's pathetic hollering, "It is good to see that you are safe as well, Kase. I'm sure all of the 70 gods will help them recover. The recovery has already begun. I firmly believe it."

"And I firmly believe that ye pray to the wrong people!" Gregory cut in again.

Styve Woodgairrd, Kase's older brother, grabbed Gregory viciously, "Hush, Witanegemote, or we will unanimously vote you off the council. Hm, perhaps my horse master would be a better fit? He has a larger brain, after all..."

"Believe me, Styve, if one's place in society revolved around brains, you'd be some peasant's farmer," Gregory grinned.

Styve dismissed Gregory's wisecrack and looked at me, "At last, we finally meet, Lord Pargion. I once knew your brother, Camern, very well."

"I am aware. You're the one who cut off his left thumb," I responded. Styve was my least favourite councillor. Gregory was an annoyance, Tobas and Ashford were untrustworthy, and Karron and Kase were somewhat submissive, but they had not laid a finger on my last surviving brother.

"Indeed I am," Styve grinned cruelly.

Karron Wull remained at his seat, "Lord Pargion. What a pleasure it is to see you today."

"And to you as well, Sir Wull. How have the days been treating you?"

"Well enough for a man with as many years as me, Simon. I'm afraid I find these political squabbles rather tiring, but I have all the energy out there on the battlefront. My men are my brothers, and that is all I need these days. Now, where is that damn King?" he rambled.

"That's my brother you speak of, Wull. If you want to end up like Camern's thumb, keep damning him. See how it goes for you," Styve responded icily.

"Will there be any duties for today?" I asked, attempting to avoid the rambles of this council.

"We are simply waiting for the King to arrive. Tobas and Ashford should be around soon as well, after their recent visit to Gwendys Wayne," Karron answered.

"You sent two councillors to visit my wife without informing me?" I questioned.

"Not our decision, Simon. His Grace's," Karron answered humbly.

"What was the purpose of the visit?"

"To inform her about the prime suspect for initiating the plot," Styve smiled.

"Prime suspect? Of what plot?"

"Tyral Wayne is thought to be plotting treason against Emannar. He's supposedly turned my King's Guard against him, and they will assemble at Hagueveil, where they are sheltering the Slait girl," Karron summarised.

"Despicable."

"Believe me, Simon, this is the start of the despicability. All will grow far worse from here. The Gods foresee it. Here's to keeping our heads intact while the world burns, lads!" Gregory roared, with all the councillors chanting 'Hip-Hip!' and bursting into the laughter of drunkards in unison.

What truly scared me was the truth of his words.

'In the deepest waters of the grim ice lakes of Cal Dunn lies what remains of the Seraphim, Rutherford Muberre's ship, which had last been reported as in the custody of Rutherford's nephew Robin 115 years ago (the Muberres possess an immortality gem, affecting every family member). She's falling into more and more pieces; three now, and there's far more damage than that. The cold waters help preserve what remains of her, but she's in the company of various mermaids and sirens who see her as their home now. They're a calm bunch in the safety of her waters, a new crew ready for new adventures, but she won't budge.

The Seraphim remains an impressive sight. It's a show of defiance against the chaotic nature of life. She has fallen over on one side, and her absent pieces leave a fading memory of what once was. Crates, chests, and barrels, scattered along the ocean floor, some on the nearby shores and half-buried in the sand. Rutherford's glistening treasures can be seen through dark cracks in the wood. Various bones and slices of human meat can be seen floating in the sea and sticking out of the sand, likely belonging to the crew, but it's impossible to tell without investigating. The Seraphim belonged to a raider, a cruel man who slayed men and raped women. It's best left in a state of rest.'

-Report from deceased knight Sir Benedict Sagard.

Dontin:

"Definitely want to return to that little cottage of yours?" the leader of l'Inconnue asked me.

"More than definitely," I answered, "I need to complete some minor ordeals and straighten my line of chores. It's all a bore, really, but it must be done."

"Aye, I understand," responded Gyrard, taking another bite of mutton, "La Perte has its fair share of ordeals, I tell youse. But nothing minor. We get hits from men and women alike across the damn globe. It pays well, but the blood on our hands, it lessens the value."

I took a succulent bite of mutton, "Perhaps we should trade jobs. Blood and gold? Count me in." La Perte Inconnue, as a whole, chuckled at that. It was not that I wanted them here, though. I was here to see Laena. I suppose Laena had better things to do than see her son after six months, so she brought a guild of assassins to feast with me and stalled the time while she made her great escape.

Mother's Witanegemote, Emmott, was by the door and looked far from amused, "I'm sure Lady Laena would cut off every strip of her hair with the sharpest blade if it meant forging a hit on you, Veille."

"She'd do the same to make you realise your place, Emmott. Or just to shut you up. You and your pretty white cloak," I joked, and my audience of assassins roared with a burst of laughter that, judging by the brilliant look on his mush, Emmott found uncouth.

"Silence or I will tell Lady Laena that you make a fool of her Witanegemote," he demanded pathetically.

"She'd agree and get a new one. Youse have no wisdom to give, Emmott. 'Tis but the truth," Gyrard responded with an unexpected seriousness.

"And you are an assassin befriending a future hit. Shall we just go and get a new one, then?" Emmott ranted. He came over to the table with a timid strength, but his mouth was stronger than his arms.

"Go ahead. I'll be fine. Youse'll be some cannibal's pet pig in three weeks, and then he'll cut youse open and serve youse on his plate with some cow's haunch," I could not but cry gold, and nor could the entire guild.

Suddenly, the strength in his upper lip vanished, and he stormed out of the room like an infant who had not gotten his way. "Victory has been attained, lads!" I bellowed. The guild chanted 'Victory, Victory, Victory!' and Gyrard said, "Cheers!" as we held a toast and downed our drinks.

I had never laughed so loud throughout my cold, dead life, "To Dontin goes the last wedge of meat," Gyrard said victoriously, handing me some hare's leg.

"Thank you kindly, Gyrard. This has been one hell of a meal," I admitted.

"Youse must be brave to annoy the Witanegemote," he responded.

"He is of no worth to me or my House. He knows not his place in House Slait," I took a bite out of the leg.

"He has more of a place than you may know, Dontin," Gosfridus, known as The Paladin, warned me, "Rumour has it that the Supreme Witanegemote has made a council for 'em all. They share news and falsify their beliefs in secret so as to manipulate the nobles."

"Witanegemote Emmott may be part of that council, but he doesn't possess half the brain needed to make good use of the membership. I doubt Gregory does either," I responded quickly, grinning.

"Peasants knowing about the council would do more for the public eye than we could, though," Gyrard interjected sadly, "Because they'd trust the 'wisdom-givers' of the kingdom to make good choices and keep them visible. The growth of thief-takers these days renders us invisible. Assassin guilds were once the apple of their eyes, I tell youse. Now they look for men who guarantee no loyalties to be their dashing heroes."

"Better honour than approval," I reassured him.

"But is it?" Symonnet, the Cavalier, mused, "I can tell that the peasants want to overthrow Emannar. Even Emannar wants to overthrow Emannar. When the day comes that the Great Revolt finally comes to fruition, and those we have been of upmost loyalty to their King fall below our cobble roads, what honour do we have without the commoners' approval? We shall rot like the rest of them, with our heads below the ground as we suffer in the cells we have feared for so long."

"Symonnet, when it comes to honour, there is no safety. Those who attempt honour are the ones with their heads below the ground. Life is a mystery, left in the hands of the gods, and honour is their chosen punishment," responded Gyrard darkly.

"There are many different concepts when it comes to honour," I added, "The Novaks believe that honour is fair fights. For us, it is obeying your Lord. Some of the Lone Houses outside ours believe that honour is not for the upper class but for the peasants between themselves. Approval links to honour, Symonnet. If our concepts of honour are broken, our concepts of approval break all the same."

"That is something I can agree with, for now," Symonnet responded, and I swear I saw his eyes turn a demonic purple for a millisecond.

Gosfridus and the others had been watching this for a while, smugly.

"And I thought religion was the biggest load of garbage," he cracked, and we all bellowed again.

"I suppose it's better to acknowledge all the blaring issues with society rather than commit to it," I stated, "More beer, please," and Maucolyn, the Large, filled my tankard.

"Ye possess a large stomach. I can tell," Maucolyn told me.

"Oh, yes, it is quite large, larger than his brain," Mother screamed from the door that Witanegemote Emmott left, "You told Emmott that he was worthless?!"

"Well, he is, Laena. You know it. You're just too weak and afraid to admit it," I responded honestly.

"I am more man than you have and ever shall be," she scolded through gritted teeth.

"And yet you find the Witanegemot scary. Afraid it will be under your bed kissing Father's feet?" I grinned, and La Perte Inconnue bellowed again, this time right in Laena's face.

Laena grew more annoyed. She was past fifty but had not grown a single strand of grey hair. And yet, here she was, acting like an older hag than any witch I had ever heard of. "Do not disrespect your Father," she demanded.

"The Father who has abused and tormented me throughout my lifespan, alongside his cruel accomplice, his witch of a wife? Oh, of course, I'll be a submissive little sheep to you both," I snapped.

"Damn you," Laena whispered, looking defeated.

"'Damn failures for parents,' the peasants say. I suppose you must be one they damn," I responded, grinning victoriously, as she hurried back into her chambers like a weasel.

After everything serious had evaporated into vapours, Emmott returned reluctantly to sort out his mistress's affairs, "I have informed Arvin of the conspiracy that you have discovered. He plans to draw out the truth, if it is the truth you speak of, and punish Elizella swiftly and justly when the time comes," he informed me.

"So it won't, in truth, be swift or just," I realised.

"Indeed."

Gyrard turned to me, "Should Her Grace or Stephyn Tanner find out about this, many a guild will be after your head, Dontin. I shall provide some men to ensure your safety."

"If you insist, Gyrard. Five should be enough. Oh, and I forgot to ask, how is Aldo? Still fooling the other knights with the illusion of the Duke of Guillemin?" I asked.

"As far as we know, he has kept to the charade. He's doing our hit from the Superior Novak. He's already signalled them to one massacre of a rebel camp, but the chief and the knights escaped. He's to bring them over and then kill the knights himself. The only thing that has ever put Aldo off a hit is being exiled from Guillemin. Daman Pargion, Fawkes Grimm and Howard Barrett shall all be dead soon," he explained.

"I must say I don't agree with killing them, Gyrard," I confessed, "Daman and Fawkes are only boys, and Howard is a grieving nut. Why must you kill them?"

"It's what we get paid to do," Gyrard responded bluntly, "Youse don't seem to grasp how lucky youse are, Slait. Your eldest sister is the damn Queen. Your elder sister is married to Styve Woodgairrd, an heir to the throne, and your younger sister is a tree whisperer. Not to mention that your Father is the Head of a Noble House, and your Mother is the heir to the lands of Heresy. But us? We get breadcrumbs for status. We must do all that we can to survive. Even if it means killing a couple of children and a widower."

"Whatever you say," I yawned.

La Perte ignored the yawn and prepared to finish their meal. Maucolyn put out the fire that he had laid out to the left of the tables. "We sent Aldo because Daman knew nothing about him. Daman was the most likely to recognise a liar, but if he had not seen Aldo before, he was less likely to suspect any odd behaviour. Daman is as cunning as a viper, but vipers don't know every poison. We picked the deadliest one."

"Sounds wise," I yawned again.

Gosfridus turned to me, "If you don't mind me asking, what became of Witanegemote Ankerson? He was always here to clean my tankard after every use. To be fair, I haven't been here in near ten years.

"Laena and Arvin realised that he planned to poison them, so they wore magic wards that prevented their death and tricked him into suicide," I explained.

"Who told them that he was to poison them?"

"That's what I don't know," I answered.

But I planned to find out.

'I could love you as no other has. In a way, you'll always crave it. I could be the lover of your dreams. If I ever need to walk away, if I ever become less than you desire, less than what you touch with excitement and joy, less than the one whose voice has the power to soothe you, the one you could walk next to with pride, then I will.

It feels these days that there are no standards for lovers or husbands, but you deserve the world, my love. I shall be a true lover to you. The poetic kind who loves with the soul, for them, there are standards.

For those with standards form a bond beyond marriage, beyond mortality, beyond reason. So be my lover for always. Be my poem. Be my song. The one I long to touch and keep safe. The one who stands together with me, both my shield and my heart, in the real meaning of love, accepting the costs.'

-A love letter from an unknown suitor, found on Brinna Pargion's corpse after the Stormholme Schism.

Annyte:

They were still watching me. I could tell.

John Borrell came in with supper like an oversized weasel, briskly handing me a bowl of spoiled porridge and a loaf of bread gone hard. Delicious. Father would be on his way soon to deal with me. John kindly allowed me to be left to my own devices until he arrived, but as I tried to walk out the door, he grabbed me weakly.

"Annyte, please be seated," I sat down on the floor, "I'm afraid the reports tell me that Lord Pargion is on his way. Make your way to your chambers immediately. I have let you have your fun."

"Have you? You could have let me out at any time, John. But you came ten minutes before Father and let me out five minutes later. Were you wasting my time? Do you need a new horse? Or are you just incompetent?" I rebelled.

"I did my best to let you enjoy some time alone, Annyte, and I will not have you act like a self-entitled little obnoxity. Now, go to your chambers at once," he commanded. He always did have a short temper when forced to be in charge.

Father was holding a feast for family and friends, and John was preparing everything so that Father could do as little as he ever did. Father arrived after my hour of isolation when every one of value had arrived. I had been allowed to sit at the right end of my table, next to my chambers, so I could run if I got bored. Father was to my left, and opposite him was John,

140

Priestess Ronayne, Alizia Grissall, Kristyne's pathetic companion, and Kristyne herself, as far away from me as possible on this table.

John looked at Simon, "How was your council meeting, milord? They say that they never make their members tire."

"That's the fattest lie I've ever heard. This council meeting was the last thing I hoped for whilst being the wretched High Earl," he looked exhausted.

"Would you like some solitude once this feast is done and dusted?" asked Borrell.

"It would need to be a long period of solitude to satisfy me," Simon turned to Kristyne, "Kristyne, I have considered allowing you to see Varn in Stormholme whenever you wish."

"Whenever?" she whispered in awe, "Please, Father, please. It would be amazing to see!"

"I guarantee nothing, Kristyne. They would need to find your chambers and handpick some guards for you. I have suggested Kegan Wyne for his reliability and The Exile for his skill with a sword, but their availability is not something I control. The Tymbrenn attack on the King's Guard is more important than your holiday," he expanded, "And you, Annyte, you shall stay here."

"I don't want to stay here."

"You have no choice. I command it."

"Why do you command it?"

"As justice for your treason and assault of Prince Varn."

"He deserved it!"

Priestess Ronayne banged on the table, John Borrell shot me a glare of sympathetic death, and Simon boomed, "No matter how you feel, you must obey, Annyte!"

"Why is that?" I hissed, and Simon waved his hand in dismissal to everyone around. Priestess Ronayne dragged the miserable girls to another table, and Borrell nodded and marched away humbly.

"Look, Annyte, I think we need to talk," Father said with comfort.

"I don't think we do," I shrugged and looked away.

"I know you prefer killing animals over wedding princes, but it's the harsh truth of the world, I'm afraid."

"It's a truth I don't want to accept."

"Too bad. I don't suppose your opinion matters, in truth," he accepted.

"It should."

He stood up and took something from a case nearby, "How about this?" he handed me a beautiful bow, "I'll let you use this in your free time, but when you must be around, you will be?"

"Give me the bow," I responded, shocked.

"This is Jaron Carner's bow," Father explained, "It has been his steady partner all these years, safe at his side, flying arrows straight and true, right on target. It gave him ease of trespassing through the lushest forests. It was a part of him, and now, a part of you."

"Why do you have this?" I asked.

"I have my ways," he smiled for once, "I can find someone to help you practise with it, and Priestess Ronayne shall go with them."

"No, please," I begged, "I hate her."

"The Priestess is simply doing her job, however difficult you have made it for her. She has been forced to make you and Kristyne fit to be noblewomen."

"I don't want to be a noblewoman."

"I should snap this bow," he threatened, so I became silent, "Emannar demanded I lectured you because his wife told him to. Why did you injure Varn?"

"He just...he just killed that random boy. He didn't even say a word. It just...seemed so evil. I hate them all. I hate the King. I hate the Queen. I hate Varn, I hate Kristyne. I don't want to be a noblewoman," I explained timidly.

"I need to explain something to you, Annyte. In this world, people never care about your insides. Your outsides are all that matter. Who you are, your birthright, your gender and race, and so on. Your personality isn't what wins you money. It's who your father is and whether you're a white male or not. A lucky few have made it, but they have lost all respect in doing so, their souls tarnished by the evils of society. Do not be them, just accept it," Father mused. He coldly stated, "Memento Mori," and then moved to another table as he gave me my bow.

I waited for nobody to be putting their eyes on me, which only took half a minute, and rushed out the door to find some hunting partners. Juran Herqys, The Exile, grabbed me by the shoulder as I rushed into him.

"Where are you going with a bow, Anny?" he asked.

"Father gave me a bow, so I can go hunting!" I exclaimed.

"You've got this, kiddo! Let me know what you do, and if you need a hunting partner, anytime!" he smiled.

"Ok, Juran!" I replied and ran off, giddy, like an infant.

I found a nearby hunting ground and snuck in. I noticed an innocent deer feasting on some grass, drew my bow, and released it. The deer toppled over, and I went to collect my arrow and perhaps find a place to store the corpse so I could skin it for hiding.

I went over and saw that the deer had two arrows in its stomach, and yet I only fired one.

"Hello," a girl said.

I turned right to see them.

Jaide and Dyana Woodgairrd. Madeleine Vikarin. Soniya and Darlyne Tanner. The forgotten daughters. Like me.

Incognitae.

'It is dawn as the stallions tremble from the wreckage of Stormholme. Half of us are awake. Half asleep. Our eyes are bleary. Our reactions are slowing, and tiredness coursing through our veins just the same as our blood. It takes forever, it seems, for the Saviour to rebirth our society, for King Emannar to roar our Kingdom back into life. Once it does, I'm sure, a funny feeling will come – not excitement, although we are excited. We shall feel relief, albeit some fear, some grieving for the ones we have had to leave behind. The future is unknown. All we can do is pray for things to be better where we are heading for, we cannot know what is on the other end, at the fortress the horses shall stop at, their hooves cooling in the wind. Some of us will cry, and some collapse with sickness while our children are held close and loved with our fading strength.

For what else is there to care about than the children? What else? And though the land is famine and the roads are pitted and coarse with rocks, soon our feet shall kiss the smooth marble of our destination. Will there be flowers and love? Will there be bread and a nice warm bed? With our lives in motion, this no-man's-land takes form in our myriad of manifestations, every one of us unique, with our destinations unknown. Pray for our health.'

-Diary entry taken from a refugee, who was slain by Styve Woodgairrd's men hours later.

Sylvina:

"Lots of blood on these Slait fields," Byrron remarked, rushing me through the chambers that the Tymbrenns would conquer last. Above these eerie catacombs were the piles of rotting corpses and Tymbrenn-sworn flesh. The rest of the King's Guard were up above, holding them back as they breached the doors of Hagueveil whilst hiding the fact that Stephyn Tanner, Kegan Wyne and Juran Herqys were riding on their stallions to save me. Their rescue meant that I could go back to The Fountain, perhaps discover its purpose, and perhaps cast away any chance that Xargaron could return, even though I firmly believe that he already has.

"Xargaron's blood," I responded.

"Come back to Earth for now," Byrron replied, "Even if that demon that haunted your dreams is back, he'd be waiting for the perfect moment. He's not only out to kill you. He's out to feast on the bones of many a man. There are hundreds of demons out there, Sylvina, but remember their key principle - 'A Feast of Souls requires souls.' They must possess someone to be able to attack. And it will not be the Tymbrenns. Rudd and Seamus are far too weak to destroy the Kingdom."

This made me realise that I could not trust anyone, and I looked into Byrron's dark eyes with fear in my heart and stepped backwards, "Let's not consider who may or may not be evil, let's just wait here until they arrive."

"Of course," Byrron responded humbly.

147

I then heard one man scream in terror, and something fell to the ground and splatter, spoiling Father's golden floorboards, and hopefully, his chair would be next.

Stephyn Tanner had called for a Pincer Ambush to kill off this wave of Tymbrenn reinforcements, and then he would pick one Defensive Strategy from The Omniscium to hold them off until it was safe to take me away. Juran Herqys would release a flare to signal their attack, and then the King's Guard would fall back and feign surrender as Stephyn and Juran, the most competent knights of them all, would begin to flank them and crush the current wave. It was an ingenious strategy that only Stephyn would bother to claim was his own idea. I was miserable. I wish I could just return to The Fountain and complete my quest, but now I had to wait for this puffed-up hog and someone who was exiled for entertainment and his skin colour. But that's off the table now.

I could hear Dontin laughing at my state of mind. And Elizella. And Ashlyh, all laughing, "Look where it's gotten you. Look where you are now. Look at that. You're gonna die because you're unhinged, deranged. Look where it's gotten you now."

I don't want to hear the complaints of The Three Brats. I just want peace. The type of peace that Stephyn Tanner would never give to a Slait girl.

"Go back up there," I told Byrron, "Tell your Guard to swear an oath to me, to kill Stephyn and Juran if they come anywhere near me. Tell them it is my command."

Byrron chuckled, giving me comfort, "You sound like your sister."

"Which one? The brat or the brat?"

He chuckled again, "Both."

"Well, I am not my sisters. I am me," I stated as I hurried to the Gateway. The Gateway was where we would go if Stephyn's plan failed, as I knew it would, as he was the last person to help any Slait. I'd need to lower both ropes before it slowly descended into an open state, and I could hurry out and scramble for safety. It was an old bridge, The Gateway. It had freed many a tortured Slait, with its pathways hideous and bloodied, chafing any bare feet that tread upon it. But what was a splinter to survival?

It could cure nightmares. I had another one last night. I was in a midnight scene, stuck in the void, wrapped in malevolent darkness. And He was there. Xargaron looked different, with scaled green claws and a manticore-esque structure which was punctured with blood, sweat and tears of victims. Victims like me. Eyes of fire, a breath of air; the voice of the void, a power unfair.

I fell asleep eventually to have another one of such dreams. The world was pitch black. The further I went into it, the more the flames covering me burned into my flesh, leaving a stinging mark. The longer I live bringing knowledge of the supernatural to the Kingdom, the more I shall linger in the void. I am the beast of society now. The stakeholder. I call others to listen to me. Follow me. I do my best to avoid neverending loneliness. All I want are some human friends, but those I can trust are those who do not listen. I have no power or control if I have no partner in power or control. I failed. I give out the joy of inflicting pain, the love of influence, the power of power, and the ability to lack care as we face impending doom. I can save those who need saving, but now I need to rely on knights to save me. I use the knives that cut open your indifferent heads and remove the powers of your minds. Make you strong with no voice to tell you otherwise, and listen to me. I can make you fit to be king, mighty, crushing enemies with your proud guise. Remove the lies of right and wrong. Only what can and can't be done. Close the door to humanity. Make you a beast like me.

I'm the one to forge beasts.

Then, unexplainably, the Gateway opened, and The Exile was there.

"Sylvina Slait?" he asked me timidly.

"Yes?" I asked.

"We're here to rescue you. It's just me and Stephyn, though. Kegan had his duties reassigned by His Grace, so he couldn't come-"

"I don't care who's here and who isn't. I just want freedom," I cut in.

"That's the thing. Stephyn's following the orders of Cathedra, and that means that if he sees you, you won't get your freedom, I'm afraid," he looked genuinely sad for me.

"I expected as much. He has never respected the Slait bloodline. No Tanner ever has," I responded, sans emotion, "But who is Cathedra?"

"Someone who has organised this whole thing. The Council is suspecting Tyral Wayne for some reason, but Stephyn assures me that it's not him. He's leaving it up in the air, a mystery."

"And the Council haven't bothered to ask?"

"The Council want it to happen," Juran responded, "Cathedra wants to overthrow Emannar, or at least kill him while they manipulate his son. Now, I should like to free you from this hellhole."

"Gladly," I responded, and he grabbed me as we ran through The Gateway, and he placed me on his plump horse.

We rode for a while up to the ruins of Tinquerebelle, the old fortress of House Muberre when a single arrow punctured his steed's heart, and I collapsed on the floor in tears.

Xargaron was still here. He always was.

Dayron:

I heard that Mother took Corren to the countryside. That's what Morgan told me.

I looked out across the fair fields. Four hectares of thick spring grass were wet under the early morning dew. Ankle-deep, undulating, thick and tangled as a horse's mane. Steel water trough, lined with green algae, filled with a bucket from the faucet every morning. Wooden fence, post and rail, five bar gate. Beech trees lined the fence to the north, and overhanging boughs provided dappled shade for the horses in summer, standing, flicking flies away with their tails. Corren adored these fields, as far as I could tell. I could never hear his screams of joy frolicking through them like a giddy lamb. Usually, Morgan would talk to me over the joy, giving me wisdom and keeping me calm.

Morgan never let me go there, on my parents' command. I wanted to be next to him, laughing and crying in the joy of the garden. My tears cannot fall. The Son tells me that Damon shall receive neverending scars once his ashes are cremated, Daman's heirdom shall never be recognised, and my Father shall one day pass. I shall be Lord Pargion before the sun sets one final time.

"When can I go?" I asked the Witanegemote, "When?"

"The time is not quite ripe," he responded mystically, "You shall get your moment."

"I don't want to wait for my moment," I cried, "Your prophecies have been ruining our lives. First, you ruined Damon, then Daman, and most recently me. You're just waiting for your chance to leap on Corren with your prophecies."

"My prophecies? I'm afraid they are not mine, Dayron. The Witanegemot have discovered them among the stars of the true Gods. Ignore your falsified beliefs in The Son and The Daughter. They do not, and shall never, hold domain over fate," he explained, unnaturally sorrowful.

I had thought Morgan to be the wisest Witanegemote. He was a greater inspiration for my life than my own parents, mostly because ever since I had a working memory, they have not spoken a word to me. Avoided me. Now, I realise that he is a sorrier fool than the King's Jesters. "I don't care who made the prophecies, they ruined my life, and that's all I care about."

"They have told me your prophecy. It all starts with your reluctance to listen, I tell you," he smiled childishly, and I dismissed him. He had no answers for me.

I thought that my dismissal could escape his rambling, but it did nothing as he stood stationary, "I ought to tell you more about your prophecy, but it would ruin some aspects," he said.

"I don't want to know my prophecy, Morgan. I want to be treated like a normal child," I complained, getting more annoyed by the sentence.

"What, in truth, is normality?" Morgan mused, "So many warped visions of the truth of what is and is not original, and for what? All it does is create hope for what does not fixate on one view. All is normal, and so your argument fails."

"You have tortured me my entire life. Yours is the failed argument. Your meddlings in society have failed. When I become Lord because of your prophecies, I shall execute you first," I confessed.

"Go ahead," Morgan replied, "The Witanegemot was first forged by Jat of Inarra, who came to power in the Year 128, thousands of years ago. There came a night that King Jat realised how significant the stars and the prophecies were. We were but a group of activists. We spread peace and love, and guidance. Jat gave us what we wanted, and we have never once failed to show the truth. The Supreme Witanegemote is the man who can guide all. If you wish to ignore, then you succumb to the evil that shall befall you. Is this what you want?"

"Well, no..." I responded, "But there is no evil to befall."

Morgan grinned in triumph, "Can you ever be certain?" he changed the subject, "This dream of yours fits the prophecy. Think about it. But now, come, Damon wishes to see you."

"Why?"

"A message has been addressed to all Pargion siblings, sent by Daman," Morgan explained.

Morgan escorted me. Damon was seated on the Pargion throne, Corren to his left, waiting for me to take the right.

Lawrence Malver and Jaze Wyne were to guard the three of us in case the letter called for an ambush.

Damon grabbed the letter and opened it. He seemed shocked and gave it to me.

"Dear House Pargion,

If you are reading this, the Novaks have likely killed me by now. Aldo, Howard, Fawkes and I had managed to come to an agreement with one Novak Leader, Balog Novak Gabor, and we took shelter in one of his many settlements. But this was treason discovered, and the Novaks retaliated. They burned down the settlements and slaughtered Novak men. We have been escorted by Gabor to a modest camp in Novak Lands, and we require reinforcements. Please send some as soon as possible, at our request.

In case of death, please do the following: pray for Damon to get the scars he desires from a victory in battle, tell Dayron the truth, do your best to make peace between Kristyne and Annyte, and between Mother and Father, and forget my birthright. I do not die a Pargion. I die a soldier for King Emannar.

Kind Regards,

Daman Pargion."

As I looked in anger at Morgan's troubled expression, I chased him as he hurried out the door, but Lawrence threw the leather end of his blade at me and knocked me down.

Simon:

"We still haven't fully recovered from Styve forfeiting the role of High Earl yet," the Supreme Witanegemote confessed, "He's not the most agreeable of the Council. I'd rather he was killed in battle or was fired from the role. He simply disappeared without explanation, and it caused great economic losses. Ruined him too, so he came back when he realised."

"I see," I responded, letting him continue.

"You do not seem the most...educated on our history, my Lord," Gregory observed.

"Not interested in your education," I waved in dismissal.

"Well, you shall be," Gregory grinned sheepishly, "Please take a seat," I took a seat, "Would you like a drink? Some bread? Nourishment shall be needed to keep you interested, I expect. This may take hours."

"I do not have hours. I want to know the location of Tyral Wayne."

"He likely resides at his home, the Stronghold at Minbury. We are still searching, my Lord," Gregory sounded disobedient. I care not for his obedience, but the history could be useful during the council meetings, especially to combat the wits of Styve and Ashford.

"If I must," I eventually gave in. Some water would be rather nice for now, in this exhausting heat. I think it's Summer. The King abandoned Sundials because the Witanegemotes proved their inaccuracy, so nobody could even keep track of time anymore without counting the seconds in their weak minds. A servant came by and dropped a glass of water and some bread for us to share. Gregory called him 'Gavin K'. He was an import from Batoulia.

"I can tell that you are not used to the Stormholme Summers. Compared to Stormholme, Bernstaplen is a neverending December, some say. Here's to the forthcoming succession of House Pargion, I suppose. Might let me breathe again," he chuckled.

"Would it let you grow your hair back?" I responded bitterly. I had no interest in royalty. I was here because it was my duty to be here, and that was it.

He grinned with pain, "There's no hair to grow back. Upon becoming Supreme Witanegemote, they gave me The Pigment. One symptom, I'm afraid, is permanently having a rather shiny head. The other symptoms were heightened senses, delicate skin, increased superstition and undying obedience."

"To whom?"

"To the Gods."

"Sounds bearable enough," I shrugged.

Gregory sighed, "Sounds it, doesn't it? But alas, I miss the normal taste and smells of food, I miss when the melons and the peaches tasted and smelled like melons and peaches and not like a pile of triangular rocks on my pathetic tongue. Whispers are exclaims of anger. I am forced to see all that is possible when I wish to be blinded. I wish to touch a brick and not all the mould between the hills of its texture. I wish to be a normal man doing my duty. The Pigment has ruined many a man's life, but the Council refuse to cast it away. I beg of you, help me to let them see the light. The Gods would never want the most devout of their followers to suffer in such a way."

"Talk to me about history, not your wishes," I replied. Gregory dismissed 'Gavin K' sorrowfully and turned back to me.

"Of course, High Earl. I have served on the Council for donkey's years, but my memory clouds. The Council of Grimm Woodgairrd consisted of the lords of every house. There was Dromin Tanner, Marvion Wayne, Ebon Pargion, Arvin Slait and Margan Cantell, among others, and myself as Supreme Witanegemote. Upon his death, Emannar disbanded this type of council and instead organised it into departments that each member would deal with. I do not know the details of the others' work, as it was enveloped in secrecy. Edd Malver was a controversial choice for High Earl, I must say, especially as he used rather...machiavellian methods. He crushed Cliara Tanner and her rebels, throwing forgiveness out the nearest window, and he only quit the role because he had a corrupt lust for gold and power, which he was able to expand further. While he served, his men decimated hundreds. Ebon Pargion was Emannar's other initial choice for High Earl until his betrayal and death during The Stormholme Schism. Your father's death was a shame to us all," Gregory described.

"He was the one who made Emannar King. He gave up the role of High Earl for justice. And look what that led to, with Styve Woodgairrd on the council..."

"Truly, I tell you, I did advise Emannar against keeping his brothers so close. Siblings are always in these types of squabbles," Gregory lamented at his failure, "When Ebon found him, just a small abandoned son, he saw his virtues. Emannar could have been righteous with Ebon's help. Then Ebon died, and all went to hell."

"I know about enough about my father, Gregory," I replied, "Is there anyone whose history I ought to know?"

"Thousands," Gregory laughed, "How about I tell you your history, Simon Pargion?"

"What do you mean?" I was intrigued.

"Us Witanegemotes have our prophecies," he smiled, "When you were selected for the role, I looked to the stars. Do you want my riddles?"

"Not a fan of riddles," I sighed, "But go on."

"You shall serve many Kings," he grinned.

"Must be living a while then if I'm to outlive Emannar," I chuckled.

"You shall die in arms you have never truly known," he continued.

"Whose arms?" I asked, and he shrugged.

"Finally, beware the ones you love," he concluded.

"Not many to beware then," I shrugged.

"You seem satisfied?" he questioned.

"If there's one thing I don't trust on this Earth, it's you and your riddles. I doubt every word you speak," I answered truthfully.

"That...that is a shame, my Earl," he sighed, "It is a shame that you refrain from accepting your true destiny."

"Well, never really cared much for destiny," I looked at him seriously, "Are you even certain of Tyral's destiny?"

Gregory frowned, "Tyral Wayne is the true culprit. There is no other man who I believe has the popularity and wisdom to lead the soldiers into treason."

"My brother-in-law is the most innocent lad I have ever met," I responded, "He's just a boy."

"And I am the most innocent council member, but I can still be a threat," Gregory grinned.

That was the greatest truth Gregory had ever said.

'In the absence of truth, comfort is a delusion.' - **Supreme Witanegemote Gregory.**

'Truth is treason in an empire of lies.' – **Priest Narisetti.**

Daman:

Fawkes and I were testing some harvested Novak gunpowders when the Chief came in. "This could be useful in the greater battlefields, methinks. A cannon loaded with this could kill a hundred with a single shot," Fawkes observed.

"Where'd you learn so much about gunpowder, Fawkes?" I asked.

"Did a turn in Jonathan Wilde's gang of thief-takers. You know how his men found a stash of those rare weapons that fire metals and puncture the skin? Got to tinker around with those and learn how they work. I did more with it than them, I tell you. Some of them were inhaling their gunpowder like a drug. It was sickening," he explained.

"When did you decide it was time to give that lifestyle up?"

"We were just doing our jobs, capturing criminals and delivering them. Then one of our mates got done for making a deal with a gang and delivering fake goods to Magniv Batoul. Jon took us all on a jailbreak. It was awful. He was massacring the men and raping some of the women, only the pretty ones...it was when he ordered me to kill a man that I decided to quit. Rounded up some Sirenmen that he was bribing, and they testified. They sent him to the same prison he was assaulted. Took a swig of Laud, and he never woke up, but Emannar decided to just take his corpse to Elden and Bradyn and let them do their thing. Wherever you looked, there was nothing but hollowing and huzzahs, as if it had been upon a triumph. Tickets were sold in advance. They didn't bury him. They tossed his carcass off a cliff," Fawkes continued.

"You did the right thing, Fawkes," I assured him, "Did they seem innocent before that?"

"Like your typical thief-takers. Egotistical but lawful. They just went mad with a vengeance."

"And the other men?"

"My mate Charles succeeded him for a week, then the Mamba came calling," he trembled upon the mention of The Mamba.

"You were in The Mamba's gang? Heard he stopped them from going to Takes," I continued.

"Yeah. After my example, The Mamba learned not to be fond of outsiders," he chuckled.

Aldo, behind us, watching with a suave smile, turned to the Chief, "Daman omd Fawkes ora ubkarqems aeuir simvuvdark kur sraer ikak, ek aeui com occavs kicr, ker."

Balog frowned, "English, is what you call?" The Chief seemed worn down and exhausted. His leather torso was thrashed, just like our scarred chainmail. He had lost a stone from all the riding and dragging, and sweat dripped from his stern unibrow. Chief Balog Novak Gabor was in his worst ever condition.

"Yes, English," Aldo responded, surprised by Balog's reaction, "The Great Kingdom English."

I had worked out by now that Aldo knew more languages than he let on. He was unnaturally surprised by Balog's reaction, likely because he knew not that Balog could speak our language to some extent.

Howard came in later with the hides of a boar he skinned in the wild. He had removed all blood and guts from the hides, and they were clean save for one small pool around where its ribs were. "Not that many animals around, huh? Didn't get that many animals to slaughter today. What a shame, what a shame. Are leather and poverty all you have around here, Chief?"

Chief Gabor sighed with agitation and collected his armour. The armour was shiny but, in some places, rusted. There were still cuts, scrapes and dents from when it was used. It was never polished but kept in a glass cage, so it wouldn't rust anymore. That is until he cracked it and put it on.

"Trouble coming," he said, wiping the blood from cracking the cage off his wrist with his sword and then sheathing it, "Must survive. All survive, to win." He turned to Fawkes, "Boy. Use gunpowder well. Have little," and then to Aldo, "Guillemin boy, hard fight for you," as Aldo's countenance reddened, he turned to Howard, "Kill them for wife," and then finally to me, "Kill them for rights. There is a camp near. We take camps one by one, and when friends come we begin to kill all. Attack camp tomorrow. I scout, ready," and he left the hut to go scouting.

Howard looked at us, "We're not really doing that, are we?" We collectively agreed to follow the Chief, which Howard realised, "This is gonna be uglier than the Queen's moustache. To hell with this!" and for once, we shared emotions, as he was absolutely correct.

Aldo stepped forward, "Perhaps we should train. Who shall be our target practice?" his eyes surfed around for a volunteer, but we all looked directly at him, and he frowned with pain.

The fight did not last very long, as the three of us overpowered him speedily enough, and one cut that Howard swept across his lower back bled uncontrollably, so we ceased to battle. "On your feet," I told Aldo, "We'll stop now. This was never the best of ideas, to begin with. On your feet." But he never once moved, and he stayed on the ground as he bled out, and Fawkes tried to force him up, but Aldo was too heavy. Then Howard assisted, but still, the armour, despite its rust and fractures, was greater than all our strength combined, and Aldo started to wail in pain.

"On your feet," I said, "On your feet." But he didn't budge.

And he didn't budge.

And he didn't budge.

I thought he was dead until I heard him whimper a small plea for help.

The Chief came in later to help him up and clean his wounds and told us to get ready for the raid of the nearest camp.

Memento Mori, Memento Mori, Memento Mori...

'To brew the Empathetic Elixir, gather the following ingredients:

-2 handfuls of dragon salt

-3 pinches of any grounded herb

-5 tablespoons of shimmerer

-3 tablespoons of Arctic Ginger

-3 heaps of Rain Chervil'

-Ingredients for a potion that forced empathy into its consumers.

Tyral:

"Everyone seems to want your head now, sire," Adom told me, "Nowhere can be safe for you now."

"I would never want to kill His Grace. Please tell them that I would never!" I begged politely.

"I have done my best, my Lord, but the Witanegemot will not believe me. They are fond of their prophecies. They're sending knights from every corner of the Kingdom to Minbury, and there are only two outcomes to be offered: Your Father Lord Marvion surrenders you for execution and Minbury remains without you, or the Stronghold is besieged, and the House becomes extinct, save for your sister Gwendys. The Kingdom has been rather susceptible to the cruel works of the Gods as of late. Your sisters' children all have their own dooms. Nobody seems to know why they simply sprout, fresh from the Earth, and give many the worst fates."

"I don't wanna die," I pleaded.

Father looked at me with cold eyes, "If you cannot convince me of your innocence, Tyral, then I shall be rid of you. My allegiance is to the King, to the Kingdom, and then to my family. There will be no exceptions."

Tears were welling up in my eyes, "Who could have done this? Father, I am, but ten, why would I want to end His Grace? You know I look ever so much up to Kings. You know I do!"

"And I am aware. But the Witanegemot has never once failed a prophecy. If you have not yet, you shall soon. For that, you cannot be trusted, my son," Father frowned sadly.

The Captain of Our Guard, Celia, cut in, "The Witanegemot themselves could not convince you of Tyral's innocence once they've said that he's guilty once. You're so pathetic when it comes to listening to those bats, Marvion. I need more men to defend the Stronghold."

"How many more, Faeyreson?" Father asked, ignoring Celia's wisdom.

"As many as I will need, Marvion," she grinned, "At least fifty, though, if you need your answer that badly."

Marvion clapped his hands and shouted, "Woman!" and Mother came down.

"Yes, dear?" she whispered. She came down the stairs whimsically, focusing her attention on Marvion.

"Your brother Stephyn may be around soon, Saede. Your presence will weaken him, perhaps make him easier to kill," Father said.

"That is, if he comes," Celia cut in.

"Even if he doesn't, no true Knight would want to instantly kill a Lady, no less a Lady of the Noble House Tanner," he turned to Adom, "Adom, go with Celia and motivate our soldiers for war while I search for reinforcements. If this castle is besieged, even for a second, I will execute you two myself."

168

"Hope you enjoy it," Celia grinned.

Adom frowned at Celia and looked at Father, "My thanks, Lord Wayne. We shall do our best to use your fine troops wisely."

Celia hit his shoulder, "Shut the hell up and help me win the war!" and they ran off to the barracks.

While they left, Marvion turned to me, "I am not helping Tyral Wayne with this, you hear? I am helping my son because I prefer him. Saede?" he looked at Mother, "Be my little lookout, dear. If you see men marching towards us, ring the Bell. Understand?" Mother nodded meekly and ran upstairs like she was honoured to only ring a bell!

"Father, you must believe me. How can I make you believe me?" I begged.

"I don't believe that you can," he gritted his teeth and marched past me, shoving me against a wall.

An hour later, Celia came to collect Father and me with an announcement, "I could not collect 50 knights, so I found something better. Dontin Slait has arrived with La Perte, the assassins' guild. One of these assassins would do better than a hundred knights."

"And Dontin is not the fondest of his sister and her royal husband," Father mused, "He has no reason to betray us. I can accept it for now. Bring them in." And they came in.

"The peasants love little quarrels like this one, Marv! I heard of your situation and did not fret to pay you a visit. We are certain of Tyral's innocence, and we shall help you fight for it," Dontin exclaimed.

"Please let them stay, Father, please!" I begged, and Father nodded.

"Good ol' Marv," Dontin joked, and one assassin came forward.

"Good day, Lord Wayne. I am Gyrard, leader of La Perte Inconnue, and we are here to serve youse until youse are all safe. We have uncovered a safe house on the coast of Hagueveil. As youse will know, Hagueveil is currently where the Tymbrenn squires are sending useless men to fend off the most powerful knights in the Kingdom. Hold the foes off of Minbury for some time, then retreat through the back gates until youse reach Hagueveil. The King's Guard will mistake them for Tymbrenn soldiers and help us kill them off. The Tymbrenn attack is merely a ploy for Arvin Slait to submit to the King, so helping the King's Guard may help youse secure an alliance with Arvin Slait and keep your House safe," Gyrard explained.

"I enjoy the sound of your plan, Gyrard. Dontin, escort Tyral to the safehouse at once," Father responded.

"Of course, Marv. Come on, boy, you shall be safe at once!" Dontin exclaimed.

As we rode, Dontin spoke to me.

"You are lucky that your sister is not with us, Tyral," Dontin said.

"I hate her. She hated me," I cried.

"Do not fret. I likely hate my own sisters twice as much as you ever will. Remember when Gwendys had that fit of insanity and tried to kill your brother-in-law? That was a wild ride, I can imagine," Dontin joked.

"Yes, it was," I whimpered timidly.

"Besides, your innocence can be proven. Witanegemote Emmott has let me know that the Witanegemot have been hiding the truth of this prophecy," Dontin explained.

"What?" I asked, shocked.

"It is not necessarily you, just a Wayne, that will cause the King's demise one day. They simply saw you as the only plausible option. Your parents have faithfully served the throne for tens of years, and Gwendys is married to the High Earl. That left you."

"But I would never! It must be one of them!" I screamed.

"Your mind may alter in the future. It is only known as the day Emannar dies. There is no death date."

I nodded weakly as Dontin came off his horse and entered the safe house alone, knife in hand. I waited 10 minutes before realising that something was wrong, as he had vanished and had not made a sound in doing so, so I opened the door.

Dontin was lying on the floor with bloody bubbles flowing out of his wretched mouth, but the sight of it was cut short when Gwendys put her dagger into my side and let me sleep as consciousness faded from her hostages.

Gwendys:

"It is not too late to fix this mistake, your Lady. The King's appeal will do nothing to put you in a better light," Jaze Wyne commented on my actions.

"There is no mistake to fix," I snarled. I seemed the ugliest I had ever been in my hand mirror. Perhaps it was because the visor was cracked, and there was nothing separating the bridge of my mouth from the centres of my pupils. The stress had broken me into the wrinkles of a hundred-year-old corpse, from the looks of things. My hair greyed and stuck together from the moisture of the damp and humid rain. It all reminded me of the endless days of torture I had endured when Simon and I were in our youths. And after all, he did to me, he had only gotten colder and more bitter over the years, but he was still as evil as he ever was. I did not for a second even think to trust Jaze or any one of the Pargion guards. They had greater loyalties than to me.

I still felt the pain of those cruel hands against the frail cheek of me in my 20s. His hand was cold and hard, and it stung like a wasp around the imprint it had left for decades. Our marriage had no symbol more fitting than that imprint.

"Your infant brother and his companion are sleeping well in their cells," Jaze complained, "Too well. They are hostages, not civilians. It discomforts me. I patched their wounds up, and they're alive."

"I do not care if it discomforts you," I told him, "Get my father on my side at once."

"A fine Stronghold you have at Minbury," Jaze responded, "It would be rather fun to visit...but not in these trying times. I'd rather not risk it. We shall stick to the shadows like their assassins. Perhaps their assassins will even take the gold we shall offer. Besiege the castle, and we shall return Dontin to them. We shall send a thief-taker to deliver the message. I have recommended The Mamba already."

"Do not put your trust in him," I warned Jaze.

"I don't," Jaze responded, riding off.

Next, I turned to my advisor Kondrad, a member of a gang of bandits that I had swept off the streets. I wasn't going to trust Morgan with this, so I found someone new.

"Kondrad, what would you suggest?" I asked him.

"Well, to be quite frank, Gwendys, I don't even know what I'm doing here. Who is this boy?" he questioned, grinning ear to ear. When I tightened my grip on the dagger, he learned to silence himself.

I turned to my prisoners as Tyral was already beginning to wake.

His eyes were weary as he woke, "G-Gwendys?"

"Hello, brother," I knelt down to look at him threateningly.

"Where am I?"

"In the cell that I have laid out for you."

"Cell?"

"I'm sorry, Tyral. But the King is the only one who can break off my marriage to Simon, and he wants your head for my happiness. Dontin is an additional incentive. The head of The Queen's greatest foe shall earn her praise as well," I explained.

"Don't be so stupid," Tyral was angrier than he had ever been, all of a sudden, "The King and Queen will never help you. They're too close to Simon, and they don't care if you're happy. You are nothing to them. All I need to do is say that you helped me with the treason and then betrayed me, and you'll be done for. And I'll do it. I hate you more than Father, more than Mother. If you'd give my life for your happiness, I'll give your life for mine." He was on the verge of tears...

"You wouldn't," I frowned, realising that my plan was already crumbling.

"I would. Would you rather die or be happy?" he asked.

"That's the thing, Tyral," I answered, "I don't know."

I looked at the dagger one more time. It was a magnificent instrument. But it was just a tool. A tool for my noble defence. A tool for my evil, cold-hearted deeds and desires. It releases the high fruit from the trees, but I still have to climb up and then collect them at the bottom.

The dagger doesn't matter. The heart that wields it does. A broken wielder is a broken dagger.

Later that day, I found Jaze again at the barracks.

"I assume you are ready?" he asked me.

"You assume correctly," I nodded.

"Give me a moment, and I will prepare the training grounds," he pointed at me, and I waited for a while.

Then we began.

I was on the grounds every night while I was safe. Learning to put one foot in front of the other as a stance, pushing myself harder, choosing to do one more duel than Jaze ever asked for – more control than I had ever felt. The grounds gave me a soul. I made my own label. I was a knight, a swordsman, a mercenary, a member of the King's Guard and not the Lady being abused by her drunken husband at every wrong turn he took... Looking back, I see him for what he was. A sad man with a sad existence. A small life, that only felt bigger when he unleashed his dominance over his frail bride.

I will go further than him. With my dagger's help, I will make him submit.

Because I can be great.

I can be as strong as I want.

I can be wise.

Why can't I be?

I've been through hell and back, and I'm not going to take a breath now.

No, I'm going to adapt, and I'm going to overcome.

What else am I going to do?

Look at me now!

Sweat is consuming my organs.

Dust devours my strides.

I'm exhilarated!

I'm so strong and wise!

Nothing can stop me now.

'Entry: Bersander

Bersanders are reptiles the size of triceratops, with four legs, two arms and a short but mighty tail. They have thin but coarse skin covered in large but smooth scales, which are usually either purple, light bronze, dark grey or light emerald, or a combination of these colours in rare cases. They live in darker areas and are near extinction these days. They are herbivores and have relatively small mouths, but their teeth and large tongue are ideal for consuming plants.

These creatures are diurnal and rely on their taste buds and sense of smell to get around. They do have gorgeous eyes but poor eyesight. They have thin noses and tiny, near-non-existent ears. Their heads are long and narrow in comparison to their bodies.

They make sounds ranging from low-pitched roars to high-pitched chirps and have a wide range of sounds they can make to indicate discoveries, dangers and affection.

These creatures are calm but very territorial. They mate once every 18 months. Which with such a long lifespan is to be expected.'

-Entry from the Bestiary of Shaun Finneas Donnelly.

Kristyne:

I had said my goodbyes to Alizia and the Priestess by the time that my guard arrived: Kegan Wyne. Most of the members of the King's court were scary enough, but solely due to their commitment and cruelty. Jaron Carner will happily accept assassinations, Elden Brune conquers nations without reason, The Exile had committed treason long ago, Bradyn Bulwark was a renowned executioner, and the Tymbrenn squires would do anything to join the council one day. They were unpredictable schemers, controlling tyrants, piling wound upon wound until the Kingdom bled fire, a fire that would only leave all that is bitter and cold once extinguished.

Kegan Wyne is stranger. He's a living enigma. All people know is that he despises his brothers for reasons unknown, he has a slurred accent even though he was from the Highlands, and he was a fine warrior. He has reasons to be bitter but inspires by his bitterness. The stress he imposes rolls back out of our ears rather than sinking into our flesh, putting out hate like a candle. He was the best of the guards I could have had, I suppose.

He shook his head to ward away some flies like a mutt and grabbed my wrist, "Yer Prince wants ye in 'is chambers," he boomed.

"Can I finish my gruel first?" I asked dryly.

His grip tightened, "Cut the questions. Yer his lil mouse. Ye do whatever 'e tells ye to do. Clear?" he whispered, tossing pools of phlegm onto my face.

"Yes, sir," I obeyed, cleaning my face.

He took me to Varn, but it didn't feel like he was taking me, more like he was delivering me. Within a minute, I was locked in Varn's chambers, and Kegan was taking guard outside. I looked up from the floor to see Varn grinning devilishly.

"My princess," he smiled, "Nice to see you today."

"Leave me alone. I needed some time away from my family. Otherwise, I would not be here," I confessed bitterly and shuffled over to a seat.

"Sweet Kristyne," he said, "Nobody will lay a finger on you here unless you disobey a command. And besides, I have bigger matters on my hands than you, my lady. The Council say that your uncle desires the slaying of my father, but I believe that it is the Council themselves. They all seem to have motives. I intend to prove their guilt, and I have decided that you will help me."

"Why would I help you? If Emannar's dead, I don't have to marry you," I smirked.

"Because he will die before then. I know he will," he stated eerily, "But if all you want is to prevent the marriage, I must ensure that the Council is either circumvented or killed to stop it from going forward. And that's all you really want, don't you?"

"Not much goes my way these days," I lamented.

"I can tell," he chuckled menacingly, "Now, the Supreme Witanegemote is the grandest issue. He has the power to manipulate the beliefs of anyone in the country. Tyral Wayne's assassination is his current ploy. If someone else could kill my Father, I would have reason to crush the Witanegemot where it stands after the coronation. But who to ask? Or perhaps, someone could kill Tyral Wayne to prove him wrong, which your Mother seems rather close to doing, wouldn't you agree? And then there's Karron Wull, the commander of the King's Guard. He possesses no power over me, and he is ageing. I can easily send him away, dismissing the cause as concern for his age. Tobas and Ashford are rather unpopular. I'd even believe that all would believe me if I had them executed for treason. Emannar let Styve off easy, something that not a soul agreed with, and his death would prove rather popular. Kase can be threatened into submission or perhaps suicide, yes. Do you find weaknesses in my strategies?"

I did not get a word out of his rambling, so I cracked a joke, "I think you should repeat your strategies into the tip of Karron's blade. Might be fun for you." I smiled innocently.

"That would not do," he suddenly grew worried, "All I want is to achieve my one goal, and I shall go to any lengths to ensure it is achieved."

"What would the goal be?" I asked curiously.

"Rights for the unfortunate, those who have befallen the same unfortunate circumstances like me, and become a man like me," he responded strangely.

"Right, and what kind of man is a man like you?" I asked again.

"Like the Nallorts. Not right," he started crying.

"You're not right?" I was shocked. No Prince had ever been not right, not in history.

"Yes, curse the gods," he was bawling like Corren when his chair toppled over.

"You must be the first gay prince," I admitted to him.

"I am, god damn it!" he wailed.

"When did you realise?" I asked him.

"My experiences with females made me blind to the gender," he confessed, "My mother ignores me, my sisters ran off without me..."

I had never felt sympathy for Varn Woodgairrd. He had done cruel things, fractured the relationship between me and my sister, and constantly jabbed at my humanity. But now, it was all a facade. Only the Nallorts had ever proclaimed that they were not right and benefitted from it, becoming a wealthy house. He would not be so lucky while his Father and the Council reigned.

"How can I help?"

Tyral:

When I next woke up, Dontin was gone. Vanished. Without a trace.

I looked around my cell. I had thought that my jail cell was real for so long that I never even checked to see if the walls were there. I heard screams from other cells, and they stopped me from even touching the gate. Then, the next day when the brilliant sunlight shone in, I stood and put my hand on the bars. With a prayer to the gods, I pushed with all my might, and after a bit of pain, the cell was behind me, and I was safe. From the outside, it was tiny, pathetic, like me. After so long, stuck in the depressing dark, I stood up and let the light cover my skin, my posh black hair flowing in a heavy wind. Upon the walls written in stone were the words "fear" and "guilt." Words my mind had written for me. I threw my head toward the sky with relief. All I had to do was conquer those bullies all along, conquer them and be free.

I was free.

When I actually woke up, Dontin was gone. Vanished. Without a trace. That was the only truth told in my dream.

The year was still 2000. I think.

In this jail cell, I only know when it is daylight by the small window of light that penetrates the source of air on top. I wish it was a little bigger. I'm so skinny I could fit into a sandwich, maybe be some dog's next bone. Perhaps someone did make it out of a royal cell one day. I'd like to think so. The only other way out is the door, thick oak, new and strong. It's out of place against the stone walls, but that's common now. As the ways of Karn Turgen, the Conqueror, decay, it is replaced by the methods of centuries earlier. Once, this prison was a punishment, a place where your mind was treated like a tool for future wisdom. Now it's just a place to rot. Whatever your "crime", there is only one outcome- you're here until you are dead. Rumour has it that once your relatives stop visiting, they take you out to the fields for a shallow grave. My relatives would never visit, though. They're not cruel, just busy, but the priests and the Witanegemot and the Council are. If you dig it yourself, they kill you fast and let you die in the lie of peace; otherwise, they won't waste their fine swords on you.

No matter what you do, you're worthless when you are going to die.

Might as well shut your eyes and wait for it.

Then the door opened.

"Youse seem rather afraid, Tyral," the lead assassin noticed, "Maucolyn and Symonnet are gonna take youse far away from here. Youse are gonna be safe, trust us. Where's the man himself?"

"I don't know," I responded, "He was gone while I fell asleep."

Maucolyn frowned, "Then I'm afraid he's dead or on trial. The Queen, she's not gonna be the nicest to 'im. But maybe, just maybe, a trial."

Symonnet looked at him with no expression, "You can hope, but do not expect it."

"Just get on your horses and get around this boy's sister and her soldiers. He needs to be safe, do youse get me? I'll pay youse all double for his safety," the leader commanded, and they nodded in obedience.

"We'll see you on the other side, Gyrard," Maucolyn assured him, and they took me to their horses, and I was mounted on the back of Maucolyn's.

"How did you find me?" I asked curiously.

"Your Father's planning to knock some sense into your sister's head," Maucolyn answered, "He sent us after you. But us assassins, we have our ways."

"Weren't there four of you?"

"Yes, there were," Symonnet lamented, "Gosfridus was struck down whilst helping us. Gyrard was there too, only just managed to get out in time. The Captain of the Pargion Guard is the culprit. One of the Wynes. He has no honour and never did." He seemed uncharacteristically agitated, he foamed at the mouth a bit, and his eyes turned a bit more purple.

"Why are you helping me? You're the leaders in a guild of assassins. Shouldn't you have a target to kill?" I asked.

"We do. I'll tell you another day. We're near the Pargion camp. Be silent now," Maucolyn whispered.

I could hear Jaze talking to some other guard in the camp, barely making out the words, "Heard that Marvion's somehow left the Stronghold," the other said.

"Yeah, by some miracle," Jaze responded.

"How's Gwendys going to feel?" the other asked.

"He'll show up. Until then, she doesn't need to know. She's enough of a kook right now as is," Jaze answered.

Suddenly, Symonnet howled, "Jaze Wyne! Murderer of Gosfridus The Paladin! The Gods say that you shall suffer for your crimes!" and he ran off to face them. Maucolyn and his horse were motionless, watching with a weird pride.

Jaze exclaimed, "Blow the damn horn! This is one of them assassins. We're compromised!" the other knight blew some horn, and Gwendys came down in a rage with two bodyguards.

"Your men cannot save you!" Symonnet cried, and as he twisted his head, Jaze's right hand snapped and disintegrated, and he fell to the ground in pain. Gwendys raged forwards with a dagger in her hand.

"Who sent you?" she screamed, holding the dagger at Symonnet's throat.

"The true God did..." Symonnet said blankly, chuckling.

"Who sent you?" she howled again, even louder, holding the dagger with a stronger grip.

"Take your blade off him, daughter," demanded a familiar voice, and Father stepped out of the shadows, blood staining his sword and armour, but his hand was not on his blade. He walked past Jaze's wounded body and pierced Gwendys's soul with his eyes.

"I cannot. He will bring his own upon me instead," Gwendys whimpered, welling with tears.

"Move your blade away from him, Gwendys," Father repeated.

"No!" she screamed.

"Be calm, Gwendys. Drop the blade on the ground. This man is part of La Perte Inconnue. He is an assassin. His only option is to be here. I know what you went through with Simon. Forced to do so much for your life and everything else you love. That is what happens to men like these, forced to kill to survive. I will give him another hit, a greater hit, with double the gold. Blood for gold is the life of the assassin, not the life of the lady. Now, drop the blade, sweet daughter. Drop it, Gwendys," Father pleaded.

Gwendys screamed for a second, collected herself, and broke down into more tears, "I want you to leave, Father! I want you to leave! You ruined my life, marrying me off to that man! You ruined my life! Leave! Leave! Leave!" she screamed like I did before this situation made me a bit more mature.

Symonnet laughed again, "In the future, specify what you mean by leave."

Gwendys looked at him with a lack of understanding, "What?" As she was distracted by his prophecy, Jaze picked up his sword again with his left hand and cut Father down with a single strike, and he fell to the ground, bleeding. My Father was dying before me, and I couldn't do anything. I wanted to scream and run to him, smack Gwendys across the face, whack Symonnet's head against the ground and stab Jaze with his own sword, but if I tried to get off the horse, Maucolyn would bear-hug me until the pain was all gone. As I saw blood spill out of my Father's mouth, he quickly whispered, "Avenge the Waynes," and succumbed to his wounds.

As soon as this ended, Symonnet unsheathed his blade and struck another blow, this time on Jaze's chest, and sprinted like a jaguar to his horse but toppled over and was wrestled by Gwendys, and Maucolyn continued our ride to safety.

I was safe.

Not that I wanted to be.

'Death is a tragedy for the young, but a rite of passage for the old.' – **Priestess Ronayne.**

Dontin:

Jaron Carner was skinning a dead horse for me, the sole meal I would have before Elizella found any way possible to get me dead for treason. She had taken me from Gwendys's hands to beat me, starve me and send me to a trial before the council. But the council would not aid her. They would be reasonable. But these horse guts wouldn't exactly reason with my stomach, would they?

"This is all you're gonna get, Veille. Enjoy it, you mutt," Jaron grumbled. He was a stiff old man, formerly the executioner but now Emannar's prized military tactician, conquering lands with luck rather than brain cells.

"I'll enjoy it when I get out of here," I responded, "Horse guts aren't the most delicious delicacies in the Great Kingdom. Slait stomachs aren't very fond of them. You should see Ashlyh's face when she's eating meat."

"Don't disrespect the Queen's sister," Jaron threatened.

"If you can't disrespect the Queen's sister, you can't disrespect the Queen's brother either, but here we are, Jaron," I grinned.

"Do you take yourself for a respectful individual, helping traitors in their plots to overthrow the monarchy? Only the Veille would do that."

"Elizella gave me the nickname Veille when I turned eighteen. Means Eve, doesn't it? Which means living. She was calling me that as a threat, do you realise? You threaten the King's brother-in-law, Jaron. I have not yet been found guilty, so you too are treasonous," I responded, and he scowled but didn't respond.

I scattered over to the back of my cell, and Jaron walked away bitterly.

The council would see me soon.

And they did. They sent for me eventually. I entered the council chambers, which were as unkempt as usual, and before me sat Ashford, Tobas, Gregory, Karron, Styve, Kase, Simon, Elizella and Emannar. The 'Royal' Council.

"Dontin Slait," Tobas bellowed, "We swear to treat you justly and fairly, with your rights in mind. Swear an oath to no treachery and trickery in court, as we have."

"I don't need to. We all know what the outcome of all this shall be in the end. Just call me guilty and be done with it," I rasped. My throat was dry from all the conversation.

Styve was the next to speak, "Dearest brother-in-law, I hope your courtesies have not been misplaced. Lord Tobas calls for swearing of an oath. Do it." He misplaces his status, it seems. "Do not make the mistakes nobody wants you to make. You have had a part in protecting a traitor you very much knew was a traitor. As such-"

"A traitor-to-be," I cut in, "Or, at least, that's what Gregory and his little prophecies believe. If he actually does something evil, I won't continue to assist him. You have my word." I bowed, smiling.

"You're word is less valuable than my prophecies these days," Gregory responded, "And much less trustworthy."

"Get him killed," Elizella hissed in Emannar's ear.

"Shut up, woman," Emannar grumbled back, which made me guffaw.

"This is a rather friendly council," I chuckled.

"Enough games," Simon stated, "All those in favour of condemning Dontin to death, raise your hands." Styve and Elizella were the only ones who raised their hands immediately.

"It appears the rest must be convinced," Styve observed, "Even the King himself." He shot a dirty look at Emannar for not raising his hand.

"Witanegemotes are selected for religion and honour," Gregory explained, "Therefore, I would be convinced by a trial, and a trial only."

"A trial..." Francis repeated, "That could be accepted. What kind of Trial do you call for, Dontin?"

"I call for a Trial by Ordeal," I called out, "A trial...of Cold Water."

"This can be arranged," Tobas giggled, "Let's see what Elizella thinks of this one.

"All in favour of giving him the trial, raise your hand," Gregory stated, and he, Tobas and Francis raised their hands.

Styve spat, "So it's down to Simon, Emannar and Kase. You know what to do, don't you, Kase? This man is evil, isn't he? Be a wise man and condemn him." Styve then grabbed Kase's shoulder and dug his nails into his flesh.

"Yes, sir," Kase whimpered.

Elizella cackled, "Well, that's three votes for condemning Dontin and three for the trial. Emannar, you must agree with me. Think of all the torment he has put me through!"

Emannar looked at Simon instead, "Simon?"

Simon kept his thoughts to himself for a bit and then stared into the deepest pits of my soul, "A Trial."

Elizella begged, "Emannar, please make it a tie! If it's a tie, one of them will change their mind, I know it! I know it! Please!"

"Shut up, woman," Emannar waved dismissively and turned to me, "Grimm Woodgairrd condemned people to death. Dran Grimm condemns people to death. But I am not my father. I am not Dran Grimm. I am Emannar Woodgairrd. I have sworn to be just, and I shall be. Let a trial determine your fate. By Cold Water, if you shall."

Elizella cried, and Styve scowled while Gregory raised and grinned giddily, "I shall connect the rope to Lake Saviour."

Half an hour later, it was ready for me.

Nobody has ever survived the Trials in Lake Saviour. It was like it was cursed out of sheer irony.

Looking through the waters of the lake was like peering through the perfect glass, unsmudged by the sticky prints of small children who trespassed. The stones at the bottom were as many shades of brown and grey as there are on a thief-taker's emblem, likely more. After a few minutes of looking, I could notice some that were more reddish or closer to white. The water at the point I stood had a current. It was where the glacial melt water entered from the mountain peak that stood still white-capped behind me. The earthen path stretched wide to my left and right, making a complete loop around the edge just behind the trees that grew directly on the bank.

Might as well take it all in if I'm going to drown in it anyway.

There was no sound at all as they tied my arms and legs with ropes, and Gregory pushed me straight in.

I had to survive for a minute to be innocent. When I was in that water, I felt free to move, even though I couldn't move a muscle. It was like the water had no atoms like there was nothing stopping me from flowing with the highest ease. It was impossible to guess the lake's depth. It could be ten feet or forty feet. But it was freezing, so I was fairly deep down.

Maybe I should just let myself drift off and die. It's not like the gods ever wanted me to live, and they wouldn't now.

Farewell, Great Kingdom. The Veille has reached dusk.

As I was about to give in and let my lungs fill with salt water, I was pulled up for some reason. Had my innocence been proven? I looked up when the water was cleared from my eyes and stared at the giddy face of Tobas.

"You're welcome for the gills I slipped on your head," he giggled, "An old friend gave them to me."

"Why did you help me?" I asked, short of breath.

"Because my friend is a witch. And she foresees something that the Witanegemotes hide from their superiors," he explained.

"What do they hide?"

"Tyral Wayne is not the one who shall plot to end the King. He is the catalyst. The fuse that lights off the cannonball."

"Who might this cannonball be?" I pleaded for answers.

"His sister, Gwendys Wayne. She shall start a scramble for the crown that shall change the lives of all forever," he giggled.

Though I didn't want to believe it, it would explain a lot.

Annyte:

Mother told me something about loneliness.

"They say once you have mastered being alone, you are ready for the company of others, but that doesn't make it easy," she told me, "When everyone's life journey separates from your own when the only heart beating in the house belongs to you, it is never something the average human could take. For there are days when the brain becomes the coldest of blazes. Perhaps that is what others call panic, but when you are alone, who are you going to cry out to for help? The good news is that in time, after many unpleasant days, you are better than you were. Then you find joy again, or maybe it finds you. After that, your journey can change, and take on new and exciting adventures...I wish I could wave the stick of some old bearded mage for you who are alone, but there are some things you must learn the hard way, Annyte. Like me."

Like us. Incognitae.

Jaide recognised me first, with a look of familiarity that I shared, and while no words were spoken, they led me to their current lair, a cave in the woods.

To enter the cave was to become wrapped in chilling blackness. The lack of light meant the lack of its warming touch. Underneath us, the loose stones shifted, twisting my ankle one way and another, and the noise of those disturbed rocks echoed off the dense stone walls. Ahead was the sound of water dripping into a river. But without even a match to cast light into the blackness, there was no way to tell how deep it was or if my next step would take me into its frigid depths and die. As afraid as I was, I believed that this would be a good place to lay low, away from all the stupid noble people, and instead with a trusted group of people like me.

"How long have you been here?" Jaide asked me.

"Probably ten minutes," I responded, "Father just gave me a bow."

"Nice bow," Madeleine admired it. I thought of naming it. Maybe rain, so I can rain down arrows in its name...

I nodded in thanks and laid down on the cold stone. Dyana turned to me, "Do you often feel forgotten?"

"What do you mean?" I replied.

She looked broken, more broken than the others, "Like..." she tried to find the best words, "Like you're lost. Lost since before the Kingdom became the shadow of what it was, the autumn before the winter. You can't find a sign of someone, anyone, to just bring you home, keep you warm, keep you safe. So you, you take in every single detail, breathe in the Earth like you need it to function. You need it desperately. You have no home, and you need these breadcrumbs of detail to fuel you. Because you're dead. You're alive, so you can rot. And the less they care, the more you believe in it. You can try to find your way back to the light of the remembered, back in their cold, cold arms, but you will never. You've had your chance. You're lost forever."

"Dunno about all that stuff you said after 'like you're lost', but my parents don't really like me, so I'm gonna agree with you," I tried to grin, and she frowned.

Soniya started laughing, "Don't go scaring her off like that! She'll be running from you, you freak!" She slapped Dyana's back with a fit of giggles, making Dyana grit her teeth in annoyance.

"I'm gonna go hunt. Does anyone want to come and help me?" Dyana asked.

"I'll come, Dyana," Darlyne spoke up and shot a dirty glare at Soniya as she rose and followed Dyana out of the cave.

Soniya looked at the opening where they exited, and her face turned bitter, "They need to lighten themselves up."

"You were wrong to do that," Jaide scowled.

"No, I'm not. I'm just trying to keep our heads up. If all we think about is death, all we'll do is die. Looks like you need to see that too, Jaide," she countered.

"I agree with Jaide. They'll get over it in time," I spoke up.

Soniya laughed, "No, we need to make them get over it. Actually, do something with our lives, and exhilarate them! They'll get over it when we leave the woods, believe me."

"If anyone finds us in these woods, we'll get hanged for poaching and trespass. I'll be safe, Dyana'll be safe, but the rest of you won't, believe me," Jaide threatened.

"You worry too much," Soniya mocked.

Jaide snapped, scowled and drew a knife to Soniya's throat, "And you worry too little, Soniya Tanner. Our families are enemies, so maybe I should keep to what they want me to keep to."

Soniya chuckled, "Then you're a bigger fool than the rest of us."

"Let her go, Jaide. There is no point," I rebelled.

They looked each other deeply in the eyes, and then Jaide loosened her grip, putting her blade back in her holster and beginning to relax.

"There's no use in conflict, Jaide. You should know that," I advised.

"You should be against that idea yourself, Annyte. After all, my father has plans for your sister, or so I've heard," she revealed.

"What?"

"He's gotten Varn to manipulate her. False sense of security. Then he's gonna trick her and take her hostage. All houses need to submit to the King one last time. My Father trusts no one. But one thing is certain: if your Father doesn't show undying loyalty, Kristyne will die," Jaide sighed.

"Where did you find that out?" I questioned her.

"It was always the plan," she sighed, "Never trust your King until the day you die."

'She only ever loved me for my strengths. To be loved solely for one's strengths is a torment. For when you struggle to be strong, when you fail to be admirable, your lover isolates you. They lock you behind a mask, hiding that which they find a repellent. Yet, in the end, it wasn't her that broke me. It was my need to feel superior; that deformed ego we cradled together. My desire to be the wind beneath her wings and not a free-soaring sparrow any longer.

She was a capital offence. So, I thank my men for swiftly casting her away, for destroying the one who destroyed me, because now I can make different choices. I can choose to love one who nurtures. One who provides emotional warmth. Nothing comes closer than warmth. For when you are warm, righteous and just, it is time to drop your mask and find your true happiness.'

-Extract from the Memoirs of Francis Ashford.

Tobas:

They call me the biggest spider in the village, spinning thousands of webs, the epitome of egotism. It is but a mask I wear. All I will do, all I have ever done, is for my Kingdom. And that must be why I just betrayed my King to save the life of Dontin Slait.

"Where the hell are we supposed to be going?" Dontin dared to ask. After all the work I went through to save his ugly rear, I expected him to learn against asking too many questions.

"Wherever the wind takes us," I replied, "We need to find you a place of sanctuary, somewhere Elizella won't search for her hideous brother and her foolish councillor. Does that suit the Veille?"

"If it doesn't, the Veille will wait for bed-time to make his judgement," Dontin sneered childishly.

"Who sleeps these days," I remarked brusquely.

"I still don't quite understand how you gave me gills. I haven't seen you since this ordeal began. Did you carve them out of some raw salmon and slip them on me in my lack of conscience?"

"Another damn question," I scowled.

"A question that needs an answer," he retorted.

I sighed, "A while ago, a good deal of months by now, Francis broke off some engagement he had with a peasant girl he encountered in Batoulia. He was afraid of the public realising such a scandal, as she was underage and poor, so he offered Sir Ashburne Ventren a life's worth of pensives (the outdated currency of Batoulia, no longer used) if he stole her away to a far-off land and wedded her, but he would only receive the pensives if the girl was satisfied with being his wife. He tried his best and spent all his fortunes on giving her gifts and gold and jewellery, but she would not take it. Eventually, he gave her all he had, but he did not have her desire: Francis. After a year of being worthless in her eyes, Ashburne grew mad, and he hit her. Several times, with a cold, stinging silver glove. She could not take it anymore, so while he slept, she released his blade from its sheath and tore away at his flesh. She bawled with every stab as he cowered in pain and cried for any help, but she never stopped trying to end him. Eventually, it worked, and she was the sole owner of his inheritance until the landowners realised what had truly occurred that day. When they realised, she was thrown out, exiled from the land, and left homeless. She had no friends to run to, no Francis to help her anymore, and no family to support her because Batoulia was so far away. She resorted to becoming a slave."

"After being a slave for a week to Molker Novak Jensen, he sold her to the Novak Cov'Soem, Jokak Novak Borrazo. Jokak made her the personal assistant of his nephew, Lido Novak Lacraruik. He cut off two fingers and whipped her daily, and she pleaded Jokak to transfer her to another role, but he refused as Lido enjoyed tormenting her too much. Eventually, Lido was jailed for bribing a taker, and Jokak saw no use left for the girl. Even poorer than before, she made her way down the Sienna Sea and found a Witanegemote Society outpost. Ankerson was present, holding dominion over it, and she came to him to ask for help. Seeing no way to help her, he refused and instead returned her to Stormholme, where she encountered Elden Brune. Brune found her situation laughable and delivered her back to Francis just for kicks. Francis gave her some more money to support herself and ensured that she had a place to stay outside of Stormholme, but without his love, she grew mad, and so she strutted over to the Lake of Fantasies and dived in. The Gods did not help her."

"She died?" Dontin seemed interested in this story.

"No. Her skin reacted to the lake like acid. The left side of her body was that of her 15-year-old self but paler than she had ever been. The left side was too delicate to make contact with anything. If it did, it tore away like a dog at meat. The right side was that of her 70-year-old self, but darker than she would have ever been. The right side was too rough to touch anything without crushing it purely by friction. She was a split soul, half-young, half-old. She could not be seen by anyone. They could easily kill her. So she stole away to a cavern not too far from Stormholme, and she possesses a horizon-like view of all she despises. A priestess dead by now taught her the arts of witchcraft, and now she practices it."

"So you sought her out, and she gave you the gills?" Dontin put two and two together.

"I met a traveller from an antique land who mentioned horrible witches in the area. As always, I initially visited to clear out the superstition, but I found her there, waiting for someone. I was not the first of her clients. She told me that someone else had met her a few days before. He was a client of the priestess who taught her around 15 years ago. She would not tell me the terms of their agreement."

"I care not about the other man," Dontin grew impatient, "What did you ask of her?"

"She came up to me and told me all that I needed to worry about to keep the balance in the Kingdom. I hadn't even said a word. She knew just from looking me in the eye. The first statement was that I needed to ensure that you survived the trial, and she planted gills in you to do so."

"The gills are within me? I thought they were false," Dontin placed his hands over his gills like a toddler.

"The second was that I must not have any major involvement past that. The fate of the Kingdom is not something in our control anymore, Dontin. All we can do is sit back and enjoy the bloodshed like the commoners do," I sighed.

"Nonsense, the witch fed you a pack of lies," Dontin scowled.

"Go ahead then. Do whatever you want to do. See how meaningless your actions truly are," I warned him.

"I'll take that chance," Dontin scowled again, and he rode off with his horse's thundering hooves.

Perhaps he would have stayed if I had told him the third statement.

Wisdom is a strange concept. They say we exchange beauty for wisdom as we age, and so perhaps wisdom is the root of all societal narcissism. We live in a philosophically poor culture. We lack what we need to be wise. We cling to the ephemeral. So, in truth, can we ever call ourselves wise?

Byrron:

This damn battle at Hagueveil has been going on for too long. But now, it is time to end it.

The war had been raging for what seemed like decades outside - chaotic, inevitable, the end of the line for many men, one last stop before the Gods welcomed them. I had to enter the front leagues now. The Tymbrenn squires had chased after some other distraction, and now the men left were good men, honourable men serving their leaders, and that almost made me want to surrender. Almost.

"Who dares oppose the Tymbrenns?" a voice called out.

"Byrron Vikarin does." I stepped forward, and so did the man who called out to us.

What a scene this all was. Packed with soldiers, slayers, and scum. The most honourable of the lot of them was my opponent, who dared to lead the charge and risk his life against me. He drew out a broadsword, and I unsheathed my rapier.

This whole ordeal was insane. Every man here knew it too. Not because of all the swords, not because of all the blood, but because of the blinding loyalty. It was like they wanted to die for a lost cause. I may lack honour, but they are slaves to it.

Both blades were pink and intimate in the warm light of the sunset. He approached me, eyes poking through his jade set of bulky armour. He was from the Highlands, it seemed. Had the skin tone for it, olive and rough as it was.

One of them blew a horn, and we were off. The others cowered backwards, watching and waiting for a potential failure or a certain victory. I cracked a smile and made eye contact with the opponent - judging by how widely his eyes opened. I had weakened him with my stares. He advanced. He advanced. He charged at me, blade upwards and hilt towards me, likely for a downward strike that would pierce my armour. He threw the swing and then threw one to his right as I sidestepped the first. I parried it briskly with my rapier and threw a light jab to his back in his moment of disorience, leaving a dent in the back. He had not yet recovered, so I continued, forcing him backwards, backwards, backwards...but he had not yet fallen.

Another strike from him. I blocked it but didn't parry, so he only staggered. I poked at his chest plate and broke off another emerald chunk.

Three more swings. He sidestepped two of mine, but the third found flesh. I had hit the bare chunk on his back again, and he was bleeding out. And now, as they accepted our victory, the other men charged for us like a pack of wolves.

Briden cut down two spearmen who charged at me and covered my back while we talked.

"Mum used to say that the King was too far up his castle. She was being kind to him," he hollered.

"She was an old bat, but she got a lot right," I admitted, impaling another swordsman.

"Stormholme is really strong now. Almost too strong and higher than Johnathan Muberre," he chuckled, raining down arrows upon five archers.

"Like Father did, Emannar matched strength with the huge and immovable. Armies and castles," Garvy Orkwood mused, who came to our aid briefly.

"He once had a point. Grimm Woodgairrd's armies were destroyed by a lack of confidence and direction. To be a true leader, he had to be huge and immovable, standing firm, like a castle," I explained, snatching the shield off of a corpse to help myself.

"Think about a waterfall. The rocks in it are huge and immovable, but it yields water. It doesn't have to be a castle or an army because we can find it anywhere," that was the most inspirational thing Briden has ever said.

"Waterfall rocks don't give us honour," I countered.

"Our honour died with our father," Briden scowled.

I looked at my brother. The most honourable man here, yes, but it was stained by our Father's death. That, and his role in it. I looked back at the man in the jade armour I fought. He was still alive. I raised my sword and smiled another time, not looking him in the eye out of respect and pain, and brought it down for the last strike of his life.

Stephyn Tanner's men came then, chanting and blowing vicious horns that poisoned minds. They enacted the pincer, cutting down the men in the middle with worrying ease, and left the other 10 to the rest of us. As we cut them down, I saw Stephyn's blade accidentally jab Duran Durron in the back, piercing his armour and leaving a bleeding cut.

"Sorry for that, lad. Get up now," Stephyn helped him up, grinning, and then looked at me with spite. "What are you looking at?" he sputtered.

"I'm not looking at anything. I'm studying," I smiled.

"Not everyone can accept you being an observer," he jested.

"They can accept me being a killer, and that is what I will be," and that got the message across to him.

"I am here to pick up the girl and take her to a safe house. Where is she?" he asked tiresomely.

"Inside, last saw her in the cellar," I wanted him out of here faster than he did, "Briden, take him inside, but keep your sword trained on him." I grinned.

Briden nodded and took him in a patrol position towards the cellar. Stephyn seemed alright, I suppose, but he was too proud. The proud do not endure. They fall in the end like the rest of us.

Several minutes later, Stephyn rushed out and grabbed me, "Where - where the hell is she- she's disappeared - has she?" there was blood-curdling in his mouth.

"Not us," I was honest, not that he'd accept that answer, "Do you have any ideas?"

He looked at his horse and sighed, "It's the damn Exile. He was supposed to be with me, damn it. I need to find them, I will find them-"

"Calm yourself, or he might retaliate. He was exiled for a reason."

"I don't give a damn. If I did or will cross any lines, I have and always will be on the right side of it. I know little, but I know that" he really was that brainwashed by the praise from society. It was almost pitiable. He rode off not long after.

Briden sighed, "What a piece of work he is."

"Indeed," I responded.

"Promise me, right now, that even though I've crossed many lines, you'll never oppose or cross them with me," he suddenly begged.

"Briden, look. The path ahead for us may never even be reached. We may be doomed to cross too many lines to see a bright future. But I will walk the path with you. Always. Until I die," I convinced him.

"And also, never get revenge on those who have made us suffer. Our honour will suffer regardless of the blood we shed," he asked of me.

I smiled, "Why, Briden, the wounds they deal our souls will never heal. There is no such thing as revenge. Only punishments. Our punishments."

Tobas:

I slept on my begrudged horse that eve. It was surprisingly comforting, resting my prestigious countenance on a saddle rough as hell which laid itself on such a mule, neighing and whining like an infant being bludgeoned with a piece of mud.

"Vete somnum te muera mulica," I whispered in the horse's ear. He obeyed and snoozed like a baby immediately. I could now rest in peace.

I dreamed of terror. The apparition came as an ambassador for a God far away, came to speak of pain that those who knew could not tell, to break men out of their peaceful comas. For too long, her master had been locked in prison while we made him suffer, and a resurgence of love was beyond reach. No joy of a voice, no suggestion of a smile, only the seriousness of a messenger visiting the mortal.

She took the form of a treant, emerging into such a wonder from a pixie of light. All but the treant was void.

"What are you?" I asked.

"A treant. The grand poem of the living world, a beauty that encourages the spirit to dance through words, to make our odes to its branches that spread like the false idols you worship. The producer of the kiss for the sense with the moving leaves, the thousand green hues and the soft whisper of the wind," it answered.

"Why are you here, ghost?"

"One shall not refer to this entity as 'you' or 'me,'" it answered, "This entity is no more than a distortion of light, a fragment of all that is seen but unrecognised. The woods bow, and the beasts cower. As quickly as it comes, it leaves without a speck that marks its presence. Nor shall one refer to this entity as 'ghost.' What do you believe is a ghost, Tobas?"

Pathetic superstitions, I thought, but not the answer I'd give a precognitious being like this, "Ghosts frighten me. They...they could be real, and if they are, they would be menaces. More menacing than any apparition could be. I remember when I was a small child, a boy, dressed for The Oath of Supremacy. I encountered a little girl on my way there. I thought her some farmer's girl and exchanged pleasantries with her kindly, but her face shifted about five times in one conversation. I pretended to lack observance for a while, thinking myself blind or mentally troubled, but eventually, I had to question. She looked at me blankly, as if she had been overcome with dementia, and randomly formed a bleak smile. I blinked once, and she had vanished. I wish...for the sake of my mind...there was a rational explanation, with the slightest bit of sense, that I could happily go with, but this is all that makes sense in hindsight. Perhaps she was never really there, or she had somewhere urgent to go, but it was the Stormholme town square. There was nowhere to go."

The treant frowned, "You lie."

I became startled and stuttered, "M-messenger, I would not dream of such a thing. Such a story, s-such a detailed story, and you listen to not a word?"

"If you do not lie, describe the girl to me," the treant bellowed.

I stuttered harder, "W-well, she was pretty, rather pretty, I suppose at the time. Brown hair, yes, brown hair and browner eyes. Her hair was braided, yes. Very long..."

The treant had none of it, "You fool. You lie to the messenger. Perhaps you do not deserve the message."

I shot a bitter glare, "I suppose now I must even earn information in my dreams. What do you propose?"

"Listen to your witch partner. Follow her sentences, for they have been fed to her brain by the true God."

"Ah yes, the true God that the world knows nothing about. Tell me about this God, and prove that you too do not lie," I jeered.

"He is one who shall not be named. He has not been so cruel as to hide his presence from the whole Kingdom. Messengers lie, devils within the walls, some spreading their messages like pathogenous flies, and others keeping it to themselves who risk passing the thin line of mercy He grants all."

"You lie, treant. I know the religions of all in the Kingdom, and none will believe in your unreal deity," I jeered again, thinking myself triumphant.

"The religion has not been made official, why would they record it? True belief is not shown on a piece of paper." I was losing again.

"Tell me the damn message," I grew bored.

"You'll know when you awake," the treant laughed.

The treant faded suspiciously, and I turned to notice a woman in my view – the witch.

She was stirring a cauldron of blood.

"Here's a man's arm," she cackled, "How was he? He lived a life of bitterness and knew no love."

Her stomach was stained with blood. She reached her hand into the mixture to take a taste with her finger.

"My Lady," I called out.

"Come, Tobas," she giggled, "And taste humanity."

I gulped, "Of course, my Lady." I approached the cauldron, and she stuck her bloody finger in my mouth. I tasted the substance (it was wretched), and she continued stirring.

"Delicious, my Lady," I assured her falsely.

"Look inside humanity," she pointed at the mixture, "What do you see?"

I looked at the dismembered limbs and organs floating in the stream of blood, "A spectacle, my Lady. A feast for the eyes..."

She pulled the ladle out of the cauldron and dipped it on a nearby flower, which wilted and crumbled before me.

"Do you see what humanity does to my children, Tobas?" she cried.

"It is truly a shame, my Lady," I sighed.

"Bear you not humanity, Tobas?" she pointed at me.

"Indeed, my Lady," I quivered, "Humanity can be shameful."

"Your taste lingers on my tongue," she told me, "Why shouldn't I remove it?"

"Because without humanity," I looked at her, regaining my strength, "You have nothing."

Suddenly, the woman evaporated with a piercing cry; the world was a swirl of galactic dust, and as I gravitated towards it, I became aware of everything.

All the answers.

All the answers that the world needed.

Sylvina:

Juran rushed me through the labyrinthine ruins of Tinquerebelle, its gates forged by emerald pups, rushing on the spot to uncertainty, trembling like the wreckage round them.

House Muberre never needed gates for this fort. It was the furthest thing from a fort around, with no proper walls and seemingly no proper buildings either. Yet it was there, the elegant wolves looking prideful despite being unseen by men for tens of years, throwing long shadows of shade over the driest grass in town. There was a lynx on the side closest to the cliff it overlooked, I think. I didn't get to see it properly after Juran cut its head off as a diversion.

"I can hear them," he whispered desperately in my ear and pointed to an enclosed area with a fairly small hole in it. I could fit through, but he and they wouldn't. I scrambled over and squeezed through. It was a tight fit, but I made it through. It was a dent in the wall or something, in between two hallways and pitch black save for the entry point.

"Where the bloody hell did she go?" I heard a growl from the other side. I signalled to Juran that they were coming, and, for some odd reason, he sheathed his blade.

"What-" I whispered. The Tymbrenns would not take his presence very lightly. A 'brunner' known as The Exile? They would kill him even if they thought him to be innocent. That was the sadness of it all. What was he exiled for? Rebellion, or so they've told in the stories. Why did they exile him? Not because he was a rebel, but because of his skin colour, and that was the truth of it all. His death would've been a deterrent for those who wanted change, who needed change. It was horrible, and it is horrible.

"Find the lass!" a squire scowled.

"No lass here," Juran announced foolishly. Was he trying to die? He knew nothing about his opponents.

"The Exile! Find and kill the brunner!" a Tymbrenn, the first to speak, spat. It seemed like there were at least two people with him.

"Don't need to find me, I'll find you," Herqys promised.

"Charge him!" the second Tymbrenn exclaimed.

After their boots clanked messily, like a three-legged horse doing a sprint, they found him. Rudd was wearing an opal helm with a feather at the peak and a spear for impaling 'brunners.' Seamus wielded the Blade of Storms, which pulsed electricity through its stone-cold steel. He was outnumbered and outbladed.

"Are you ready to die, Exile?" Seamus grinned.

"Not the most fascinating prospect to me, I must say," his expression was blank.

"You know what I want to do to your corpse," Rudd unsheathed his sword and pointed it at Juran's heart, grinning.

"Tickle it a bit?" he smiled.

"Don't joke with my honour," Rudd whined.

"It's fragile enough. Doubt joking with your honour is going to do much," he laughed harder.

"Enough!" Seamus separated Rudd and Juran, "We shall have a Showdown, like the King's Guard do in the battles. To your ends." They both nodded and obeyed.

Juran was on the left, Rudd on the right. Juran approached...

Rudd approached...

Juran unsheathed his blade, letting the gold dazzle in the darkness. Juran approached...

Rudd gripped his spear into an offensive position. Rudd approached...

"On the first swing," Seamus called out.

They stared at each other intently for a moment, anticipating the other's first strike.

Rudd pulled his spear backwards and threw the first strike when Stephyn Tanner tackled him, and Rudd's skin made contact with Stephyn's sword.

Rudd screamed with anguish and bled while Stephyn spat some of the blood curdling out of his mouth at Seamus, blinding him. Seamus waved his sword around in a futile manner and then collapsed.

Stephyn hollered with victory and looked down to see that Juran now only had one hand. There was a pool of blood swimming around the limestone, his snapped arteries spilling out straight.

"You damn fool..." Stephyn looked down at him.

"Thanks for cutting my hand off," Juran snapped back.

"I'll cut the other off if I have to," Stephyn grew tense, "Where's the girl?"

"Down through that hole," he nudged his head in my direction.

"Hold them off. I'll get her out," he ordered.

Juran obeyed, "If anyone hurts her, I'll kill you in the next life, mark my words."

"Don't have to. Gods will think you're so perfect I won't be able to see you from Hell."

Stephyn pulled me out of the hole, hoisted me over his shoulder, covered my mouth and ran off.

Seamus wiped the blood off of his face and got up. Rudd recovered, and they charged at Juran. Juran fought them with one hand, and he was winning for a while, almost killing Seamus at one point but was merciful. Stephyn put me down but kept my mouth covered, and by the time we left, and I could look back, Rudd raised his spear victoriously above Juran's corpse and stabbed him one last time.

But I knew what had really happened. He was coming for me, taking away all who could actually help me, starting with Juran.

Xargaron was breaking my shields.

Dayron:

The crunch of the snow falling was killing my ears. Lawrence Malver opened my mouth vigorously with his sweaty palms and filled it with Tonique. Tonique was normally used by interrogators to open the victims' minds and get them to speak by heightening their senses severely. I had no clue why they would use it on me.

"Are you ready?" Damon asked me, twitching.

"I don't understand why I have to come," I responded.

"Didn't want to put you through this, brother, but Daman needs our help. Grey would be very helpful, and he only listens to you. Could you call him over? Please?" Damon had been pressured by Lawrence to bring a beast with him. It was obvious. I whistled, and Grey flew over, chirping gently.

"Let's ride," I nodded, and Damon started riding. Grey rested himself on my shoulder, but I was told to take the rear, so I waited for Lawrence and Odo Wyne, brother of Jaze, who had stayed behind, to take off. Lawrence went second, and Odo third.

"Go," I whispered to my horse, and it started forward. Grey flew eagerly behind me, chirping gleefully and flapping his wings like a soldier. He was smarter than any gryphon should be. Gryphons were merciless, bloody creatures in myths, legends and life, but Grey was a gentle child who preferred tickling the enemy over eating them.

We rode for a while until we reached Malvus, the residence of Lawrence and his father Edd, and Lawrence dismounted to run up to some girl and smiled like there was a joke that even he didn't understand. "Ah yes, Lady Delilah," he grinned and looked at Damon, "Useful spy Daddy keeps. Not the best at keeping her mouth shut though. She wails like a sirenman when her feet are tired."

"Why should I care?" Damon asked like a curious puppy.

"It's a spy. Could be anywhere," Lawrence sniggered, making Damon unnerved.

"Hey, don't make me paranoid like that," Damon countered weakly.

"It's good to be paranoid," Odo agreed, "I'm paranoid that my girl might kick it."

"You can drop the act here, Odo," Lawrence assured him, "Nobody here will know or will care that your daughter is dead, and seeing as she's not anyway, drop it. It's not like Damon or Dayron are going to tell anyone, are you lads?"

Damon puffed his chest out and acted tough, "O-Only if you make me," and Lawrence and Odo chuckled in unison.

Lawrence approached me and patted me on the head, "How about you, little boy? You gonna tell on me?"

I looked at him blankly and dismissively. Grey fired off some warning chirps.

"Thought not," Odo looked at me with disappointment. Lawrence mounted his horse again, and so we continued riding, but Damon fell behind a bit to talk to me.

"You were brave to do that, Dayron," he told me.

"Why do you talk to that fool?" I asked.

"Lawrence? He's more useful than he looks," he assured me. He seemed like the best of them when talking to someone who couldn't be a threat. When they could be, he was a timid little mouse.

"Can I go ahead of you? Seems like you need the protection," I joked. He laughed, but looked ashamed of himself when he was done.

"Go ahead."

Odo looked back at us, "Welcome back to the plane of the living, Pargions. We shall go at a faster pace now, so be ready."

Damon kicked my horse, and it thundered forwards, hooves clacking in the forest, "Riding! This is riding!" I laughed. This was great, however painful it was.

"I'd go faster if I could pass you," Damon joked.

"I doubt you could, Damon. Baby brother here has twice your skill and half your experience. You should be worried that he won't take your titles," Lawrence jested. He was an idiot.

"Could say the same about you," I defended Damon and pointed at Lawrence. Damon patted me on the back, and Lawrence looked bitter.

"Well, we'll see if you can," he muttered, and as he slowed down, we did too. Damon nudged his horse a bit closer to mine.

"I need to tell you something, Dayron," he told me, "A messenger from Tobas gave me some information on what's going on in Stormholme." He sounded really sad and even more scared.

"What did they say? Is Mother coming home? Is Father?" I begged to know.

"It was a report on current events from Father. They thought that Uncle Tyral was plotting to betray King Emannar," he informed me.

"Why would Uncle Tyral do that?" I asked.

"Because he probably hasn't. Anyway, when Mother left with Jaze and his knights, they went to make Minbury submit and hand over Tyral to appeal to the King," Damon continued.

"Why would Mother want to hurt Uncle Tyral?" I next asked.

"So that the King will protect her," he responded.

"From who? Bad men?" I next asked.

"Yes. Bad men like Father," he answered sadly and looked away for a bit to wipe tears from his eyes.

"What has Father done?"

"Bad things. I'd rather not tell you," Damon continued, "Anyways, Celia and Pap held them off for a while and Mother's forces fell back. But, the camp they were at was attacked by an assassin that Pap hired to protect Tyral. He stabbed Jaze's knee."

"He killed Jaze?" the pain was swelling up. Jaze used to chase me through fields and make me laugh and smile when Father wasn't around, and there were no wars.

"No. Jaze survived because Pap arrived alone to talk to Mother. While they talked and Pap tried to convince Mother against killing Tyral, Jaze picked up his sword and cut him down," he couldn't stop the tears, "Pap is dead, Dayron. Killed by Jaze."

I cried even harder than Damon when he said that, "Jaze killed Pap? Why would he do that? Why?" I begged to know.

"I couldn't tell you, Dayron. I really wish I could. Because of this, Emannar has labelled Jaze guilty of murder, and they want to execute him. But Mother won't give him up. Father is afraid that if she doesn't let them take Jaze, they'll take her too," he then grabbed me tightly, like a brother, "I promise you, Dayron, when this is all done, I will not let anyone forget how foolish they are being. Not Mother, not Jaze, not the assassin, not even Father. I will give Pap justice, I promise you."

"How are you gonna do that?" I asked.

"Lawrence thinks we should get all the Pargions together," Damon told me, "And then we defend Bernstaplen. If Mother fights us, we fight back. And if Jaze is still there, we do everything we can to get him killed."

Lawrence looked back, losing his smile, "You must."

"Only Lords and Heirs can let you make your own decisions," I reminded them.

"If your Mummy does attack, she loses her heirdom, and Damon becomes heir. He can do whatever he wants. Would also be the case if your Daddy dies."

"Those things won't happen! They won't!" I yelled at him.

"I really hope they don't, not just for you all, but for the Kingdom as well," Odo sighed, "Imagine what would happen if the public discovered this ordeal. The Kingdom would be in an awful state."

"Who cares about the public," Damon rebelled, "We need to focus on our family."

"Where are we going again?" I asked.

"Into Novak territory. We're getting Daman back," he explained again.

"Mother wouldn't be very happy with that," I reminded him.

"Mother, let my grandfather die. Why would I care?" Damon smiled like a devil and rode ahead of me.

'The duty of a Sirenman is to patrol their designated neighbourhood and search for criminal activities. They are known for 'wailing,' a high-pitched cry they make either when they have discovered a criminal activity or when it is the break of dawn, and it is time for the workers of the neighbourhood to awaken.

All Sirenmen are trained in the usage of a shortbow. Their fine shortbows are constructed from the skin of an onyx, heated up in a furnace. The strings are fabricated from a bear's gut (a rare material these days, as bears have evolved to a new digestive system which does not contain a gastrointestinal tract). The limbs are decorated with ornate gold and end in narrow points shaped like snake heads (the Sirenman insignia is an arctic viper). The handle is wrapped in hide and decorated with intricate threadwork. The wide quiver is made from woven fabric. In the hands of a capable Sirenman, a shortbow can fire arrows up to 114 metres away while still retaining lethal power.'

-Sirenman Recruitment Details

Dontin:

"Food for the Lord?" a merchant on the road asked me. He was drinking a thick tomato soup with the appearance of dried-up mud.

It didn't matter if I starved to death doing it. I had an ugly business to attend to. It would get me killed anyway, but I'd rather die fulfillingly than get poisoned by some ruffian on the road. "I'd rather fry up your fingers and feed them to your wife, my friend. I doubt she'd recognise you, and I doubt she exists," I responded, and when he didn't react, I continued, "Maybe it would also suffice to find some desperate slaves. They'd beg for some good cannibalism, washed down with a bit of wine to refine the taste. They aren't that picky. Nor am I."

"It's not poison, my Lord. And I won't charge you. These journeys can be days long and tiring for many men twice your size. I merely offer hospitality," he laid the soup on my saddle, "It would depress your horse if it spilt, my Lord."

"Hospitality?" I laughed in his face," they said hospitality was being the Queen's brother and getting all the benefits. Instead, it's being the Veille and having some wrinkle-faced dog laugh in my face while he carries out his employer's mission."

He reached up for the plate and pulled it back to him. "I am no servant, my Lord. The Queen is a vile hag in the commoners' eyes. The whole Council treats men unjustly, and we see through it."

"I see through your deception. Were these lies given to you in a book?" I spat.

"Yes, in a book. There is no other lie," he responded ominously.

I eyed him evilly and tipped the soup over with one hand, "What did she offer you, heh?"

He shook his head, "I am never the offered, only the offering, my Lord." He pulled out a cloth to clean up the soup.

"Was it money, land, sex? Look at you. You'd take whatever you can get, by the look of it," I looked him up and down.

"I accept what I have. It is all I need," he looked down sadly.

"You pathetic, worthless cretin," I cried with rage, "I hope you die of a goddamn pox with the rest of 'em! Good night!" and I rode off furiously.

"When I have suffered like I have, and you have not, my Lord, it is hard to call me the cretin," I heard him whisper as I rode off. I had far better uses of my time than that fool.

"Forget it then," I scowled through gritted teeth, "I'll kill you myself one day, I swear on the names of whatever pathetic Gods there are on this damn planet!" and I rode further, for about a mile, when I arrived at Stormholme.

Perhaps if I had learned the art of keeping my mouth shut and my correct opinions to myself. Before I entered, I waited and thought. Who do I find? Emannar or Elizella would have me killed, and most of the councillors would hand me in. I suppose I could find a member of the court. But I swear, if I see the executioners or that twit Jaron Carner, I come back tomorrow. I stared out at the night sky. I waited until night because it would cover my entry - no watchmen on patrol or the cranks they call takers with their fancy swordbreakers.

The wind was here to bite me though, with its sharp fangs. This horse was boneless and full of chills, miserably weak, and would die regardless of what they did to it. During the normal hours, four hooves away would be four thieves and an animal abuser, ready to rip your sacks away and kill all you owned while you basked in the sunlight and breathed fresh air in your last moments. No fools lurk at night, but when the occasional buffoon chooses to, you're as good as dead. I should ride out during the normal hours more and see what glories befall me.

"Fabulous riding, my Lord," the merchant spoke in my head, "Maybe when you grow up, you'll be less of a cretin and a big enough boy to ride a man's horse." I grit my teeth.

"Veille!" a voice welcomed me, "How the hell are you!" I turned around to regretfully see Jaron Carner's smug face.

"Just about to leave, Jaron. Took a wrong turn, I'm afraid," I responded.

"How'd you get shorter?" he jested with a devilish grin.

"Being in a cell does some wonders for your weight, and I'll prove it by being out of here in a hurry. Now, good night," I rushed to my horse, but he launched onto me.

"No, you're gonna do whatever you're here to do, and now, otherwise I'll twat ya, and we'll see how it goes from there," he threatened.

I gave up, "I'm here to tell Simon not to do whatever he plans on doing," I confessed.

"Right. And why's that?" he asked again.

"Tobas told me that some witch wants us two to have no involvement and let things play out as they should-"

"And you want to risk everyone's lives to prove her delusional because you're a desperate, pathetic rat, scrambling for any hope that you still have a shot at any Tom, Dick or Harry cowering submissively and kissing your kneecaps, fulfilling your dream that you matter, when you don't, nobody gives a damn about the entire class, so stop being pathetic and turn your horse around, get out of here and let us all die as we should!" he ranted.

"No, look. Simon will only let Emannar react if she attacks their children at Bernstaplen. But the eldest is Damon, and I met Damon a couple of years back when I actually had muscles of my own. All Damon cares about is victory, even if it's a victory against the family. He knows better than the others about the history between Simon and Gwendys, what he's done to her. He'd kill her without hesitation. It's not Gwendys Simon needs to worry about, no no, it's their children," I explained my thoughts.

Jaron loosened his grip on me, "I see. Well, it's a damn shame, really, because Styve just saw Simon out of this place a couple of hours ago."

I was shocked, "Where is he going?"

"With Emannar and Kase. To see her," Jaron grinned.

"Well then, I'd hope you know what I want you to do," I stood up and started walking.

"I have no goddamn idea. What?" Jaron asked.

"Get the army ready. We're going to war," I told him.

Simon:

Emannar Woodgairrd, Kase Woodgairrd and Simon Pargion marched on horseback, the land suffering from Gwendys' engrossment in a library of blood. My friends rode with me in my head. Jaze Wyne, still morally stable, with his brother Odo having a healthy daughter; John Borrell being my faithful friend as always; Morgan before he gave in to Gregory's half-truths; my brother Camern too, and of course, the fallen Alavin and Brinna Pargion riding their Silvermanes. The last two were greyed and misty, echoes in my mind. Like their lives. Alavin had been betrayed and slain by Grimm Woodgairrd when he was carrying out espionage. Brinna was hunted by Grimm's sister Dhalisa soon after, the other spy. Emannar gave them a proper funeral once Grimm Woodgairrd was dead, and since then, we have become true friends.

7 of us. With Emannar and Kase, we had 9. 9 against most single threats would be enough. But not the threat of conscience.

I turned to Emannar, "I would like to thank you again for the magnificent funeral you gave my brother and sister."

He nodded, "They served me well in the Schism. They deserved the right funeral."

"I remember that funeral," Kase looked up to the sky, "So many roses...it was fabulous."

Each rose represented a fallen soldier. While the funeral focused on Alavin and Brinna, it included every late lord and lady who had lost their lives conquering the hierarchy.

Emannar chuckled, "You have no idea how long it took to gather the roses. I assigned Kegan to the job."

"Was he painful to listen to?"

"Very much so, and I tell you what, it was absolutely hilarious," we laughed in unison.

"I wish I did more during the rebellion. All I did was lead one assault on House Magnarok, and more men died than necessary. My Father was a war hero, and my siblings were useful spies, but I was nothing but a warrior," I frowned.

"Even Teleos Magnarok found you hard to break," Kase acknowledged.

"It doesn't matter if you're hard to break if there's nothing to be opened," I disagreed.

"Teleos Magnarok," Emannar added, "He lost because you wouldn't give in."

"We should have tried to draw Teleos to our side. Lord Auster is a psychopath now, and Lilyana is too shy to pipe up," I frowned again.

"Draw Teleos Magnarok to our side? Preposterous!" Emannar exclaimed.

"Why?" Kase asked like an inquisitive pup.

"There was no cracking that egg of a head, only frying," Emannar dismissed the idea.

Kase was restless, "Are we there yet?"

"No, Kase. We'll hear the horn. Be careful, though. It might shake you more than Styve's punches," Emannar treated him like a child.

"Styve's punches? How do you-"

"Styve Woodgairrd abuses anyone he has more power than. I know that for a fact. He tried it with my wife, and now there's a giant slash mark on his right hand. You need to stand up to him, Kase," Emannar advised him.

"But how? He'd kill me!" he screamed.

"If he tries to hurt you at all, Kase, I'll take away his heirdom and give it to you. He'll be as useless as Rabbithead after that," Emannar grinned.

Gwendys came out of the tent as Emannar finished his sentence. Behind her was a trio of knights escorting dragging Jaze and the member of La Perte that assaulted them to us.

"You," Gwendys refused to look at me.

"I promise you, Gwendys, we won't bring you harm," I assured her.

"You will," she persisted.

"Only if you don't give us these criminals. We will make them suffer," Emannar promised.

234

"You won't," she persisted.

Kase groaned with boredom. He was such a child.

Jaze looked up at Emannar, "Your Grace, I only acted in defence of my Queen."

"By killing her father?" Emannar retorted.

"Symonnet cut off my hand and struck my chest violently, sir. My aim was off," he sighed.

"I doubt that," Emannar looked down at him.

Gwendys looked at him furiously, "Your laws prove that Symonnet deserves a harsher fate, Emannar! Jaze's hand fell like dust on the floor when he cut it! It's witchcraft!"

"That's a serious accusation. I'll have Matthias Hopkins look into it when these two are in our custody," Emannar responded.

Gwendys got on her knees, "Don't take Jaze away from me, Your Grace. My best knight, my strongest knight...I'll die out here alone."

"You won't be alone, Gwendys. You'll be home again, with your husband and your children surrounding you with love," Emannar promised.

She looked at me with evil in her soul, "With him? I'll be safe with him?" she looked back at him, "I'll never be safe with him. He's a monster! Domestic abuser! He'll kill me one day. What will you do then? Caring for your precious friend because of your pathetic honour, is that it? You don't give a damn about the Kingdom. You never even gave it a goddamn name!"

I stepped forward angrily, "I know what I did to you in my drunkenness, Gwendys, but ever since I've given you the world, and you just kept taking! You used me for gifts! You don't deserve protection, you deserve to suffer, and I see that now!"

Kase screamed, "Calm down!"

Gwendys looked at him and cackled, "Oh please, like you're ever calm! You're brother looks like a goat, and he treats you like a lapdog because that's all you are, mindless and obedient, an excuse for a human being! He could leave you bleeding in a field of weeds because you spoke a second too early, and you'd think it to be your fault!"

Kase stuttered, "N-no, I'm not that stupid!"

"Silence," Emannar bellowed softly, "If you hand the criminals over and come quietly, Gwendys, I'll supply you with many knights to ensure your protection from your beast of a husband. Do we have a deal?"

"No. No. No, we don't!" she cried, "Your whole army couldn't protect me from his evils. Not a whole army! Kill him, Emannar! Kill him right now! Besides, it's not like my children would give a damn-"

That's when I struck her.

She clutched the bruise and cried, "See! See! He's abusive! Doesn't love me or my children! Claimed that Daman isn't our boy! Called Dayron deaf just to keep him naive! Kept Damon out of any battle he'd easily survive just to make him suffer! What's next, doing the same to my daughters? Cutting off one of Corren's legs and making him think he can walk?"

"I may have hurt you in the past, but don't ever bring my children into this! I have loved my children fittingly. Damon was on a high horse that I need to trim! Daman is spoiled! Dayron needed to learn life the hard way because the easy way sure as hell didn't work out for the first two! And don't act like you've done nothing to them! They all prefer me over you, and you know it! Except for Corren because you've taught him nothing about this cruel world!" I fired back.

"He's three years old!" she protested.

"Three years of learning nothing!" I spat.

"Both of you, both of you, both of you, shut the hell up!" I thought Emannar had exclaimed this, but when we looked at them, it was actually Kase.

Emannar was surprised, "What do you think you're doing-?"

"Face it. You're both bad parents! There's no such thing as a healthy family in this Kingdom. Look at us, the royal family, the prestigious Woodgairrds. I had to kill my Father, get abused by one brother and be yelled at by another even though he's as scared of Styve as I am!" Kase shouted.

"Why the hell would I be scared of Styve?" Emannar seemed almost amused.

"Don't pretend. If you wanted to help me, you'd have already done something. You're a bigger laughing stock than our father, and that's pretty difficult, you know!" Kase responded.

"Maybe you're right," Emannar reclined.

"Forget your family struggles. This is domestic abuse we speak of," Gwendys responded with stubbornness, "This means war, Simon."

"I see," I responded simply to the denouncement of war, and she reentered her tent with the prisoners in front.

Emannar was extremely bitter, "Look what you've done now, you fool. Did you ever think for a damn second that you could start a war? Gwendys is a psychopath, you idiot!"

"Why would you send your council to search for me as the next High Earl if you can't even see the wisdom behind my choices?"

"Why?" he was amused again, "Because I expected there to be wisdom behind them. You have failed your role, Simon. Accept responsibility for this, get your head in the game and do some good for once. We have a war to plan, and you better plan it correctly. If you ever fail as horribly as you have, here again, I promise you, I'll deliver Gwendys your head and give the role to Auster Magnarok."

Gwendys:

I took a moment just to sit outside and recollect myself.

There was a single lone hut nearby, tending to the villagers. Wrapping them in a cold embrace, like they were sickly and needed a cure. The only cure for idleness is work, and they are very, very ill. They looked so happy, suffering there. It was almost warm, like my children and I were. But Simon was always cold.

"My Lady," Jaze bowed behind me, "Should I execute the prisoner now? I have an itch on my right finger an axe could easily scratch."

"If you're up to cutting off your own head," I sneered, "Emannar was right. I should have handed you over."

"Then Simon would have been right, and you don't want that, do you?" Jaze seemed amused, but he wasn't wrong. I needed him dead, bleeding on the ground, in the palm of my hand to prove his worthlessness.

"No, I never did," I admitted.

I looked out again. A peasant man came out of the hut, but his wife and daughter stopped him. He hugged his daughter, kissed his wife, and departed with a smile. Their besotten bliss would be broken as a carriage rammed forward, probably to escort him to his workplace, and he stepped in. They waved one more time, smiling ear to half-ear (there was an equilateral triangle of blood in the daughter's left ear), and he shed a tear as he waved again. The carriage startled forward, horses neighing and snorting as they set up their victim.

The highway robbers were near. The Black Dogs? The Wolverines? The Posse? The Crimson Mamba. Víboro Siniestro and his Take.

The grandest heist of their lives. An escape to the outdoors. An end to poverty. It all began with Siniestro's breath turning from quiet and regular to a pant of readiness. The man behind him was sucking air like it was too hard to multitask, both breathing and riding. Then, deaf to all surroundings, Siniestro whipped his flintlock out, twirled it between two fingers, and knocked on the carriage. A woman opened the door, probably a proprietor of a business or the driver's wife, and immediately surrendered. The family man I saw earlier did the same, and the driver put his horses on the brakes. The change of mood was now irreversible.

"I think you'll find that I am a simple man, travellers. These are dangerous roads and dangerous times to be out and about, so I'll be rather quick. Luke Sicarius! I know you're in there, old chum! Oh, the bounty the Magnaroks have put on your head..." he fiddled with his gun again, "I have an obligation to bring you in. But I have a better idea," he looked at his crew, "Men! Take everything on the carriage! If Sicarius tries to get in our way, sedate him, and for the others, shoot them dead. I'm gonna get double the money for stealing the carriage too. That's what I really want," he smirked.

The driver just froze in place. He had seconds before they stole everything he cared about. Years ago, when he was a good and strong man, he could have held them off long enough to escape, but not anymore. As frail as flesh. The Mamba liked them like that. That's why they shot him when he was too stiff to move out of their seat.

As the shot penetrated his chest, Sicarius, the family man, gritted his teeth and tackled a thief. An explosive mess - pummelling, hitting, kicking, biting him. The robber was probably dead by the time The Mamba shot him in the leg.

"He won't be a problem now," he blew on the tip of his flintlock, "Leave the woman in the carriage when you deliver her to The Client. That psychopath will find the best way to make her suffer." He looked down at Sicarius and poked the tip of his flintlock at his right cheek. "What's the matter, Luke? You look like you're about to die. Auster doesn't want that to happen, though. No, no, he's taking something from The List for you. The, well, special treatment, if you will." Two men drove the carriage off, while a third and a fourth held the woman in the carriage hostage. The Mamba glared at the men standing still. "What the hell are you doing? One of you boys hogtie this filth and follow behind the carriage. Don't let him sway you - he may be persuasive, but I can be punishing. I don't like to be punishing. Now, hurry the hell up."

"I'll make you pay for this, Jonathan! I just...I just told my daughter that I'd be back soon. You - you really want to leave my little girl fatherless? Please. Don't do this," Sicarius begged.

Siniestro looked directly at him for a second. Two pairs of cruel eyes met. Then The Mamba chuckled evilly, "Of course! Your little girl! Brianelle! What are we gonna do about Brianelle? Oh, I know! Leave it to Auster, seeing as you're begging so badly for a worse punishment!"

Sicarius collapsed with fear, "No! Please! Auster'll crush her!"

Siniestro lowered himself to Sicarius' level, "I'll advise him against it, and then we'll be dying together. Just hope that your family doesn't pop up in that twisted, twisted mind of his. That's all you can hope for, Luke. I'm deeply sorry." The Mamba rose and whistled, "Hogtie him." While one of the two robbers hogtied him, the other kept his head buried in the dirt so he couldn't cry for help. A minute later, Sicarius was taken away. Siniestro stood still and then looked at the driver's corpse, left to rot in the dirt.

He took his wide, flat-crowned hat off and held it to his chest to pay respects, "You were in the wrong place at the wrong time, sir. I am deeply, truly sorry. Now, we can't leave you on the road for the watchmen to find us." He lifted the body and threw it violently into a heap of long grass, not too far away.

"That's better," he clapped his hands and chuckled again, "One more respect to pay."

He knocked on the door of Sicarius' family. The mother opened the door, and The Mamba knelt down.

"My darling Valletta, I come bearing awful tidings. Rumour has it that Auster Magnarok has seized your husband, and he is choosing from The List. I am sorry for your loss," he seemed woeful, almost truly woeful.

"So I assume you want your payment?" she looked at him sternly, but they couldn't keep it in, and they both broke into laughter.

"It's even better because he was begging me not to deliver him to Auster, to prevent his daughter from being fatherless! I told him it wouldn't happen, never elaborated on why," The Mamba tried to compose himself.

"Because she has a new father?" Valletta asked, smiling.

"Because she has a new father!" they kissed as he stuck his flintlock into her chest and pulled the trigger. It was a mess. Blood everywhere on the road. Nobody was tough enough to defend the woman. They wouldn't be.

"But no, mother," he finished and shot her in the head again. He disposed of this body in the tall grass as well and entered the house to pay the child a visit.

I wanted to kill him. To send my entire legion after him and make him suffer dearly. It was in my power. But not now.

Dontin, La Perte Inconnue, Jaron Carner and a whole squadron of knights were marching in their hundreds.

Blood pumping through their veins.

Hatred etched in every corner of their eyes.

That look of vengeance.

They were going to attack me.

'Eventually, found the cure to Death's Ulcers, did Emannar. Huge plant, they called it the Paviflora. Only found within the darkest caves in early summers. It had thick, needle leaves, sometimes large bronze flowers. They thought it to be poisonous until the day Morgan chose to commit to being a Witanegemote, and his final experiment was testing the effects of Paviflora on those with the Ulcers. They were cured.

It was too late to save anyone, though. For the Paviflora were sentient. They evolved and became truly poisonous. Science had failed us.

Died over the month, we failed to realise; thousands did.'

-Tale from a beggar named Barbara.

Daman:

Chief Gabor gave us two different tasks: Aldo and Fawkes went to steal supplies from an outpost, while the Chief, Howard and I raided and conquered another.

I rode a white horse. 'Cosmos', the Chief named him. The rain beat down on my sweaty brow, piercing my adrenaline rush with pure depression. The forest cried, too, for the trees were being violently swept away by the barricades of wind, struggling to cling to existence. There were some gentle tulips before me, turning a shade of teal as a punishment from the downpours.

Howard's wrists were twitching with fear while they gripped the reins of his browner steed. The Chief's horse was the natural shade of the Novak stallions - black and beautiful. We weren't far from the outpost.

The Chief pushed off, and we followed suit. We subconsciously agreed to keep quiet until either we were dead or the outpost was ours. Hooves thundered towards the front gates, but as Howard and I readied our bows, the Chief broke off the trio and headed off to a side-road. He planned a diversion.

Howard and I paused our horses at the gates. Two archers, each on separate towers, interrogated us.

"Ssosa aeuir bikemakk rara," the Novaks demanded?

"Wa vuird reda su sroda kvecak, sros ek orr," Howard responded, fully translating his thoughts. The Chief and Aldo had entrusted Howard with knowledge of the Novak tongue. He had nothing else to do.

They nodded, and they opened the gates.

I shot the right one dead with a single arrow from my bow, and Howard did the same with the left one in perfect synchronicity. It made the whole scene cooler that I was on Howard's left. It reminded me of the tale Jaze told me of when he and Kegan stabbed each other's opponents in a gladiator pit. Sure, they were thrown out for cheating after that, but it was still one of the best things they did together and one of the last.

It was kind of peaceful, watching them bleed out and fall off the tower to crush any chances of survival. They seemed peaceful.

We powered through the gates to another archer tower and a soldier cloaked in armour, wielding a spear. I looked at Howard, and we both nodded. I swept to the left and rode across the coastline, letting Cosmos play in the water for a couple of seconds. While he fired a quick arrow right through the archer's heart, I leapt off my horse and plunged my blade into the spearman's neck. Wouldn't kill him though, as only a small area of flesh was exposed to outsiders, and he tried to strike back at me. I stabbed him on the right side of his neck after parrying the spear, and then he collapsed.

Then the cavalry came.

About ten Novak men approached: four with swords and shields, three with spears and three archers in the back. They attempted to make us submit - to take us in peacefully.

Howard dropped to his knees, "If you're gonna kill me, kill me! I had a bride! I could have been someone! Now I'm doing this! Take your strike!" he was pleading for death...

A shadow emerged from the silence of the foliage.

The Chief. He vaulted off a hill and buried his sword in a spearman's back. He turned his head towards the archers - they tried to fire at him, but he deflected every shot they fired and swept through them eagerly. I tried to help - backstabbed one of the swordsmen while they gawped at his skill - but he needed no assistance. He had killed four, and he could kill five more. One spearman made his move, but it was swiftly parried, and he was swept off his feet and given a merciful death. Howard picked up his bow, surprisingly, and fired at two swordsmen, piercing their skulls. One swordsman and one spearman remained. With Howard's arrows and our swords combined, they fell in seconds.

It was not over. Some men maintained their stance in their camp, tending to the food and the fire.

"Should we each take different corners, Chief? Take them by surprise?" I asked.

"No," Howard argued, "I just made myself look pathetic. She wouldn't want that. I need to redeem myself."

The Chief didn't argue, and Howard ran towards them. He cowered in a bush and pulled out a wind chime. A wind chime? Had he gone mad? He tossed it at the ground, and its ringing sound drew some of the men over to it. While it rang, he climbed up the roof of a hut and, by the sound of things, stabbed an archer with his dagger. The group turned back around to investigate the sound of steel against the flesh, and as soon as he did, he threw one of Fawkes' gunpowder contraptions right at them. No man caught in the blast was left to live.

He signalled at us, beckoning us to come over. I was in awe, and so was the Chief.

"That-that was incredible, Howard-" I expressed my admiration, but he cut me off.

"Up there," he pointed up the hill, "There are a couple left."

The Chief started rushing up the hill, and we followed closely. Two men were tending to a campfire. The Chief sank two daggers into one while I ran up and cut the other across the back. Howard looked up, and two archers were on two more towers, guarding another set of gates. Howard decided to settle this, climbing up one tower's ladder, throwing a dagger into the archer on the opposite tower and cutting through the one on his.

A bigger man, bigger than any we had already fought, heard the commotion, saw us and ran at us. The Chief held still and whistled. Suddenly, three horses pressed through acres of long grass and trampled him before he came close.

One man remained, as we could see him walking off, blind to the fact that everyone he worked with was dead. Howard found it funny, so he ran at him with his horse, threw a contraption Fawkes made which stuck to the enemy, leapt off his horse and stabbed the swordsman, then kicked him backwards to leave him to detonate.

It was a rather loud detonation, though, as two legions of soldiers on horses entered the outpost. One half found us and began a chase, so we mounted our horses and stole away to the mountains. Howard fired arrows at a couple of them to push them back, and eventually, they gave up the chase and fell back to safety.

"Wait," the Chief held his hand up as we reached new heights, "Idea."

The Chief grabbed his bow and knelt down. He positioned his left hand up in the air, wrapping his thumb against his little finger and flickering the middle three. It only became apparent that he was checking the direction of the wind when he fired a single arrow up in the air. It landed in the outpost.

On their stash of gunpowder.

The whole place burst into flames, one explosion producing a chain reaction of others that echoed through the outpost. Survival was improbable and impossible. The Chief had just slayed legions of Novaks with one arrow.

Howard was confused, "I thought you wanted to take this place over? You just...you just blew the whole damn thing into flames! Did you forget?"

The Chief shook his head, "Idea."

"Idea?" he asked.

"Better idea."

"Spit it out," Howard demanded, though it still came out frail.

"Friend. General. Hajdu Novak Szilveszter. Much money. Good place. Fight is good price. Good price," he responded in muddled English.

The Chief went to bed in his tent. Aldo and Fawkes had not returned. They had to survive. We just pulled off the most incredible mission ever, and so they had to survive. We just murdered hundreds, but we would be nothing without them.

Howard looked at the fire silently.

"Your bride. What was she like?" I asked him.

"Everything I wanted. I...I remember when her grandfather died. I was there. The day after he died, we chanted 'Good mourning', like it was fun to remember, like we took comfort in his death. We all stood by him. His...corpse. But, of course, there were rough edges. Demons came back...those who watched him die called him a noble sacrifice for their sake and acted like they'd keep him in their thoughts and prayers. And her family, they acted like by loving his memory, everything could be wholesome and wonderful, and there would be no need for revenge. Her family was full of cowards; none of them was willing to see that he was murdered, not sacrificed. They...they killed him, the gods didn't do anything! Couldn't they see that? They...they never did. They still don't. Eventually, I worked out why."

"Why?"

"They were responsible. Her father sent his father out there. He was already a dying man, and he sent him to fight because he was too scared. So he locked the truth in prison and warped their love for him into joy. Celebration of his life. They did the same with her when she was slain."

"I'm sorry to hear that," I offered my condolences.

"Spare your sympathy. I know what death is like now. Everything is recycled. One thing's particle waste becomes another thing's particle treasure. Everyone moves on too fast, they grow to love the treasure, and they discard the waste. They know that everything they grew to love will transfer to someone else, so they spend a lifetime looking for those things and leave the person to erode."

"Those are misguided views," his words were frighteningly true.

"I wish they were. Look at me, Pargion," he grabbed me tightly, "I've heard the stories, the tales they tell of you. I have no idea who you are. Or where you truly are. Or what the gods want you to be. Or what the gods plan for you. All I know is that I will see you again tomorrow because we have survived today. And I know you are special. I can feel your future through the air. It calls your name. You're going to be somebody great! So, whether I become someone else or I get recycled, I'm okay with whatever happens. I'll be seeing my bride, and you'll still be somewhere. So will the Chief, Aldo, and Fawkes. You'll still be somewhere. I don't fear death. So that's all that matters to me."

"You're forgetting one thing, Howard Barrett," I told him.

"What would that be, Daman?" he smiled weakly.

"We're brothers in this."

His smile shifted into a frown of pity.

'We approach a new season! Few clouds, moderate winds operating in the north-west! Gloomier skies in the south-east! Slight showers! Lightning! High winds in the north-east! Colder than it has been, I tell you!

Tomorrow, tomorrow! The clouds start tomorrow! Many clouds! Moderate winds begin! Drastic warmth to prepare for future coldness!

The afternoon, the afternoon! Heavy showers, rain! Skies go gloomy! Winds go high! The sun shall die in our arms! Heavy snowfall in the south!

The world shall bleed!'

-Transcript of a Sirenman's weather announcement during the morning crow.

Dontin:

Commoner ideals on what makes a 'hero' are happy tales told by ill-advised common fools. Perhaps, if I had the right talents, I could be a hero. A rather happy camper, always riding on a fat horse, on the battlefield saving lives. Commoners love their knights, and so they do not love their heroes. They have never loved their true heroes.

I could never be a hero. I'm a dark man, an archangel serving the gods. But only the evil gods would want me. I am not built to save. I am built to outwit, to cripple and to kill. And so, here I am, surrounded by gents designed for murder, killing a child's kidnappers and the civilian terrorisers within their walls. Masters of the ambush because we can do every task with clean efficiency and emerge unscathed.

Why do we do it? For what we get when we win the war. Land, titles, and a sizeable stack of money to seize.

This war's gimmicks seemed to be right out of the same dust-collecting book - dehumanisation of captives, destabilised and mentally-ill rulers, antagonisation from the attackers, cold hard revenge - it was right there, all of it, practically begging for war. It helped that Gwendys was only holding one castle to her name (Minbury), and she ruled it just like Auster Magnarok ruled. Following his strategy never helped anyone but him.

It's human nature to think of ourselves as wise. To think ourselves prudent. To think that each war is unique and needs its own approach. It's done so much, to the extent that we train our children to be like us, future war criminals. We aspire for them to cut off heads. We trade their humanity for slavery. We know what we want them to become, so we whip them until they become it.

This wouldn't be some large battle. Gwendys would run off with Jaze and Symonnet soon enough, and then Minbury would be ours for the taking. And then, taking a castle would become taking a kingdom. That's how it goes.

Under the chill of the mist embedding the fields, Maucolyn bumbled his way over to me. He held a hefty musket in his hands, an overweight battle-axe on his back. Tyral was following suit. His helmet was too large for his head. Gyrard, off in the distance, ignited an arrow of his to be used as a means of commencing the battle. Jaron laid his sword at his feet on the damp grass of the Wayne Fortress and lowered the cannons.

"More likely to thunk Jaze in his ugly face like this," he murmured as I observed.

They gave me the shortest of any of them besides Tyral, the greatsword. It's over a hundred damn pounds, but at least it has the range to slay about five soldiers in front of me and maybe twenty-five if I did a little spin. I would rather have a musket though. My own mini-cannon, last put into production by Dran Grimm. Only men who served with him or stole from those men have muskets. Or any gunpowder machine. Gunpowder is now in the hands of Fawkes, an erratic addict who probably drinks it after crushing it between two and a half boulders.

A greatsword can reach enemy hiding places with a wide, repetitive path to follow under its master's commands. But a musket, a musket is a free spirit. It can kill whoever it wants to kill. Though, I'd rather use a big metal stick than be plagued by the acrid stench of stale gunpowder, breaking my nostrils apart.

Then Gyrard fired the arrow, and we heard a poor blind soul scream as he burned alive. How pathetic.

Gwendys stepped out from her perch at the summit of Minbury, "You should not have come. This fort stands strong. We will kill you all!"

Maucolyn looked at me, "My knowledge of Minbury is a little rusty, actually. I don't know where anything is; castles are pains, but to hazard a guess, take the front and then push them back until you get the back. That's my kind of strategy."

"I'll handle Gwendys and Jaze. You and Jaron focus on everyone else. Gyrard can find Symonnet," I responded.

"Define 'focus'," he joked.

Archers started to rain down arrows.

Jaron called out, "Aright! Let's have this down quick as!"

So they charged. I stayed back for a minute, surveying the fortress. She had kept it rather well. It'll be useful for getting Tyral lost.

The doors collapsed quickly. Wood. Who designs a powerful fortress for a leading house, and they choose a wooden door?

Once the door collapsed, I charged in with the others.

Half of us went left to the Gatehouse, while another half went right to the courtyard.

I didn't even need to cut any men down to capture the Gatehouse. Jaron left a man for each cannon and darted over to lay down the flag of La Perte. That was when Jaze emerged at the perch.

He looked skinny. Boneless, even. He wore the helmet of House Wayne and carried four spears - one in his right hand, three stashed on his back.

"Some killer gear this Jaze has," Gyrard came up to me, sweating rivers, "Maybe I'll fetch a new sword for meself. Could use a new toothpick."

"Pick your damn teeth later. We have a fort to take!" I shouted back.

"Of course, sir, I'll bite him 'til 'e bleeds!" Gyrard cackled as he killed two soldiers.

I made my way to the courtyard. It was rather satisfying to see Jaron's friends making a path for me. I could just walk through this place, and it would become mine. The courtyard was just outside the main castle, where Jaze and Symonnet were.

As we captured it, Jaze commanded his bodyguard, "Bring out the prisoner. Just like we planned. This part of the fort will remain ours."

Tyral ran up to me, smiling like a toddler with a new toy, "I like this! I killed someone!"

"Congratulations," I grinned at him for half a second, "Once this one's yours again, you'll need a bodyguard. I think Maucolyn or Gyrard might throw their hats in the ring for that."

"I'm not picking them," he smirked, "Only the best, here at Minbury."

I laughed, then turned away.

What have I done? This army's power should be more limited than this. Why have we won?

I attempted to find my way to the keep when Gyrard stopped me.

"Symonnet is in there. I'm coming with youse," he stated, and I nodded.

"Just don't snuff Wyne for me. Killing Jaze will send a message throughout the Kingdom. That message comes from Dontin Slait and Tyral Wayne. Nobody else."

"Of course."

We entered the keep surrounded by the uncomfortable sound of heavy boots on damp cobblestone. There was Jaze, seated on Marvion Wayne's throne, with Symonnet in chains and a single bodyguard beside him. As we approached, he rose from the throne and pointed his sword at me.

He looked at his bodyguard, "You can take the assassin, Lanz. I want Dontin." Lanz rushed at Gyrard and was stabbed through the chest. By Jaze. Jaze jerked his sword out of Lanz's chest and left him there to bleed out. I wasn't surprised. He had tried the same technique before.

"This fort belongs to Tyral Wayne now," I called out, unphased by Jaze's attempt.

"Can't do anything without people crying treason now," he frowned.

"Wouldn't be the first time they were correct," I responded.

"You know, I thought I recognised that voice on the battlefield. Talking to the boy. The one prophesied to slay our King," Jaze simpered.

"Ah yes, I forgot that we have so much to catch up on. Where do I start? Everyone wants your head because you felled Marvion Wayne, remember that?"

Jaze looked at the ground, "I didn't break any oath killing Marvion, despite what Emannar tells them. I am pledged to House Pargion. Marvion Wayne is not a Pargion by blood, and he kept his hand on his sword while approaching Gwendys. I was protecting my Lady."

"You failed."

"I know I failed. Gwendys has relieved me of my oath. I serve no one," he wept.

"So now, anyone can kill youse, and it's fair game," Gyrard spoke up.

"I remember how I got to be here. Kegan, Odo and I were captured by slavers. Then sold to cannibals. We were eaten alive. Then The Woman brought us all back. Odo's brains, my brawn, Kegan's ugliness, we managed to rise the ranks. We have our places in society. Now, I have no place."

"Well, it's been nice catching up and all, but Gyrard and I came by to tell you that Minbury is Tyral's now," I reminded him.

"Well, he's welcome to it. I don't give a damn about Gwendys, and I sure as hell don't want it. Take Symonnet. I'm done with the games. I have brothers to find, and then I'm leaving this Kingdom at the first opportunity," Jaze began to run out the same way Gwendys did.

"One fault with that plan, Jaze," he turned back to look at me talk, "You can't be done with the game until you've stopped playing. And you never stop playing."

"You're not wrong. Well then, what can I do?"

"Youse can join us. We don't play, and we get along fine," Gyrard offered. What was he doing? Was he a fool?

"Be an assassin, eh? Worth a try," Jaze smiled.

"This is an absolutely terrible idea, but if you're going to be a good boy now, Jaze, go and fetch Tyral. He has a speech to make," I commanded.

"Of course."

He brought Tyral up eventually. The boy stood at the perch of Minbury, the three of us at his side, as he spoke to his followers.

"We fought, and we suffered. But we stand. There is a new evil. My sister. But there is a new good: you! In the days ahead, there will be more battles to win, more castles to claim. We will not fall. We will not fail until we disrupt the balance. We eradicate evil. Starting today, Minbury belongs to Tyral Wayne! Minbury belongs to you!" it was a short but effective speech. I didn't realise that Tyral actually had a knack for speechmaking. The crowd erupted into cheers.

I didn't join them, though. I was too busy wondering where Gwendys was. And when she would return.

'Soon, Grimm Woodgairrd began to fear his subjects. The revolting peasants would soon revolt if they weren't given a more decaying state of mind. One worry was not enough -they needed many to be too weak to fight against him! And so, he cut all food supplies, so it was the fashion for them to be thinner than ever, so their own corpses would be their greatest threats. But the upper-classmen could still revolt, so he saw to it that poorer peasants were driven from their cottages to compete with the nobles

for the most basic of wages. The Kingdom tore itself apart, and Grimm was pleased.

The Kingdom was too broken to fix itself. From time to time, groups of peasants would unite in an attempt to find peace, but they all collapsed in disaster. Grimm kept them loyal with the threat of an overseas enemy conquering their land without his exceptional military prowess. Upon that cold gilded throne, he laughed at us all. I'd love to tell you the peasants finally deduced the game he was playing and found peace under his rule, but this story is not one with a happy ending.'

-The Witanegemote Chronicles, published by Gregory.

Simon:

"You're quite certain that Jaze Wyne lives?" Emannar questioned the spy who came before him. It was the King's royal hearing after our journey to see Gwendys. Gregory ran the tips of his fingers through a dark-grey beard beside him while Francis Ashford combed his hair, and Tobas fidgeted in his seat. Kase and Styve had gone on a personal excursion with Kegan Wyne, Elden Brune and Bradyn Bulwark, and Karron was aiding the King's Guard with the capture of Sylvina Slait. Any excuse to escape the King.

The spy was a peasant. Kneeling to his King. Covered in bloody rags. Confident but afraid. Afraid of us.

"He lives, Your Grace. He lives without a doubt. Under Tyral Wayne's wing, Your Grace," he confirmed.

I wanted to tell him to ease up. I wanted to tell him to shut up. It was better to stay silent. We already knew that Tyral was being aided by Dontin Slait and a guild of assassins he befriended, but if they had the numbers to level Minbury, someone else had to have helped the enemy. Francis had already called for a strategy to weaken their alliance, something he claimed was only for the King's ears until the plan commenced.

"It is said that Gwendys has relieved Jaze's oath, and so he has betrayed his former Lady to resort to a life with La Perte Inconnue," the spy continued.

"The guild of assassins? Why would he do that?" Emannar demanded answers.

Francis spoke up, "One moment, sir, never listen to a man on his knees. To ensure that he continues with the truth, and the truth only, he must be using both feet to lift himself. Ensures that the truth must spout out and past the lies."

"Whatever," Emannar never looked at Francis, "Tell me everything as you stand."

The spy looked confused, "I have told you all that I know, Your Grace, that I can confirm to be true. However - there are rumours."

"We know how to sort between truths and half-truths," I continued, "We bear some great knowledge and some great ways to gain knowledge. Tell us the rumours."

"Some say...some say Jaron Carner was spotted on the battlefield, next to two of the assassins and Dontin. A maiden here in Stormholme tells me that she saw Jaron and Dontin discussing armies hours before the raid and that Jaron left to fetch many knights at different Takes in the city. That's where the men came from," the spy was stuttering. Calling a member of the King's court treasonous? He trod on thin ice.

"A maiden, eh? Where is this maiden?" Francis inquired.

"An unfortunate fate has befallen her, Lord Ashford. A horse rode her down this morning, very unfortunate-"

There was the sound of Emannar's hand being brought down on his lap.

"I've heard enough from this...this blubbering fool! Throw him in the dungeons! Keep him there until our executioners return!" he demanded.

"Do not be so rash, Emannar," I held my hand up, signalling to the men who grabbed the spy that they should pause, "What was the maiden's name?"

The spy looked defeated, "I know no names, Lord Pargion." Fantastic.

"Ah, this is pathetic!" Gregory scowled, "Listen to His Grace. Throw him in the dungeons."

"I agree with Simon, do not be so rash," Tobas was the one to agree with me, "How cruel can you men be? Carry out an investigation into Jaron Carner," he looked at Emannar, "Your Grace, can you not see the suspicion there is that Carner has attended neither your brother's excursion nor this hearing?"

"He has not," Emannar was listening.

"So, Your Grace, where is he? Getting drunk? Or helping the enemy?"

Emannar resigned, "You might be right, Tobas. Hire a thief-taker for it. Pay them for how little they harm him."

"It shall be done, Your Majesty," Tobas accepted, and he left the room in a hurry.

Ashford looked at the spy, "What proof do you have besides your rumours? Any solid evidence? Or is it all just...waffle?"

I spat at him, "Only fools would ask for that. Jaron Carner is a fool, but not that big of a fool. Why would he bring anything that gave it away?"

"How many men were there?" Francis changed the subject.

"Hundreds, Lord Ashford. Hundreds and hundreds. An army of drunkards and killers, they say," the spy answered.

"Well, sir, I think you'll find every army is an army of drunkards and killers," Francis grinned cynically.

"Mainly ones of lower-classmen," Gregory frowned.

"Or my knights," Emannar continued.

"Jaron Carner!" the spy shouted, growing impatient, "You don't doubt it. You just refuse to believe it, councillors. Jaron Carner has committed treason!"

"I think he's right, Emannar," Francis looked at the King.

Emannar sat in silence for a moment. Then he looked up at Gregory, "You are a wise man, Gregory. What say you?"

Gregory stopped his fingers and looked up, "With all due respect to this peasant, he cannot know that Tyral's accomplice was Jaron Carner. Many a man can pose for another."

"Unless you know them well enough," the spy spoke up, "Mister Carner has always had a fascination for cannons. He was spotted readying two and firing them."

"Then I agree with Simon and Tobas," Gregory concluded.

"Damn it," the King growled.

Francis smiled cunningly, "I think we should have a vote. Who votes for the investigation into Jaron Carner?" Gregory, Tobas, Francis and I raised our hands.

The King looked surprised, "Even you are against me, Francis? Why?"

"You need a wiser court, Your Grace. Now, escort this spy to safety, as we have decided," Francis responded, and two knights dragged him outside.

The loud bang of the wooden door was never heard, as Kase and Styve had just returned from their excursion. Kegan Wyne, Bradyn Bulwark and Elden Brune remained at their side. They had a prisoner.

Laena of Heresy. Dontin's mother.

"What in gods' name is the meaning of all this? Unhand me!" she screamed and then looked at Emannar, "Your Grace. Why am I here?"

"Ask Francis," he gestured nonchalantly towards Ashford.

"Vengeance, my Lady," Francis was dripping with cynicism, "You shall be our means of justice. Dontin Slait has allied himself with the enemy. He has slaughtered our people and charred our walls. Capital Punishment will not restore the Kingdom's displaced honour, only grant us short-term happiness. We cannot give back to those affected by their homes or their crops, nor can we resurrect the dead. So we shall give them the most justice we can by humiliating the Veille. You shall be our hostage. If he surrenders, he loses his life. If he doesn't, you will take his place as the sacrifice, and he shall be scorned for life and will be crushed mercilessly. But there shall be one more twist: if he doesn't surrender, he will be abducted and forced to be the one who executes you."

How could he be so cruel? The council would not agree with this plan.

"Who votes for this plan of mine?" Francis looked at us.

I was the only one who didn't raise my hand.

'Democracy had been deleted. The sacrifice of all who died for the present day had been dishonoured. King Grimm Woodgairrd had lost all control of his kingdom.'

-Said by Shaun Finneas Donnelly during the Stormholme Schism.

Kristyne:

Priestess Ronayne watched over Alizia and I as we discussed the news, "Would you kill Dontin like they're going to do?"

"Dontin Slait tried to kill Jaze. There's no way I'd help him," I responded, shocked that she didn't see my answer as obvious.

There was a knock on the door. Priestess Ronayne begged us to be silent as she tiptoed over and looked through the peephole. It must have been a friendly face, for she opened the door with one big pull. A woman stood there.

"What are you?" the Priestess didn't break eye contact, "Some kind of prostitute?"

"A messenger, priestess," the woman was polite, "Prince Varn Woodgairrd would like to see the Pargion girl."

"Why?" the Priestess was suspicious.

"Messengers don't know more than their message, priestess," the woman smiled and walked away.

Ronayne looked back at me, "Kristyne! They want to see ya. Don't be too long now." I got up, said goodbye to Alizia, and walked out of the room. The messenger took me to Varn, who was not alone. He was currently in conversation with Francis Ashford.

"Make something clear to me, Varn," Francis seemed cold, "Are you sure that you want us to directly attack Dontin? It seems like suicide, and after all the atrocities? He deserves more suffering than death can grant him."

"Oh, I'm not quite sure, Francis," Varn spat, "I think that if I wasn't sure, I wouldn't be telling you now, would I? And besides, he attacked our trusted allies. He deserves to die!"

"Are you sure that you aren't doing this to please Kristyne?" he questioned in a mocking tone.

"I've never cared about that girl's opinion. I just want my uncle to suffer," he kept his eyes on Francis like a raw steak thrown amongst a pack of wolves. Francis spotted me and left us immediately.

"What do you want?" I asked at the sound of the door closing behind me.

"I know you want me to get Dontin killed, but it's getting increasingly hard. Francis is stubborn as hell when he has a new idea."

"I don't care how hard it is. I want him dead," I responded through grit teeth.

"It's not that easy, dear. Life isn't a slave. It's a whole mansion full of picky masters," he sighed.

"Who's leading the charge to find him?" I asked.

"Sirs Duran Durron and Dirron Rygert," he responded with absolute certainty.

"Awfully old," I grew depressed.

"What does their age have to do with anything?" Varn seethed.

"It would be funny if the person who killed him was young," I responded. Alizia's favourite member of the Guard was Stephyn Tanner, but it didn't seem like he would be doing the job. It never made sense to me anyway - he was more than double her age. He was way too old for her.

"I suppose so, but I can't get the younger members of the guard to act right now, I'm afraid," he told me. I didn't respond. "Oh, and my men are investigating your sister's disappearance. She'll be torn when she finds out about The Exile." I forgot about Juran, to be honest. He was a bad role model for Annyte.

"I don't know how Annyte feels about anything. She's weird," I admitted to Varn, and he laughed.

"Would you like to know what we know or not?" he got annoyed.

I nod.

"As you are aware, my father is trying to get my grandfather Arvin to submit to him, but Arvin won't do that. My father planned an attack, but Arvin expected it, so he and his wife stole away to another continent. However, Francis managed to abduct Laena on the way there. They left Sylvina at their castle, and my dad sent the King's guard to kill all of the knights there and take her hostage. But Herqys saw through this, and he didn't see it as just. He tried to ride Sylvina away to Tinquerebelle, the old fortress of House Muberre, but Rudd and

271

Seamus found them. They overpowered and killed Juran, but unfortunately, Seamus is slowly dying from his injuries. Stephyn picked Sylvina up and should be riding her back here soon. But the war is not over," he explained.

I noticed some food on the table next to him, a small bloom of summer strawberries and cream adorning a plate, "Can I take a cake?"

"Go ahead, you child," he smirked. I ate one.

"Thanks," I grinned.

"My pleasure, whatever. My father will be arriving soon. He says he has a new plan, and I think that if you're here to hear it, then he'll still think that I'm right," Varn laughed.

"The world's first not-right King, eh?" I raised an eyebrow, "Sounds different."

"Nobody will call me that because nobody will know," he frowned.

"That's going to be a hard secret to keep," I smirked.

"It's easy when you're the Prince," he told me.

The messenger from earlier arrives again, "His Grace will be here shortly. He would like to ensure that Kristyne feels she is properly dressed."

"This should be good," I say.

Moments later, Emannar bumbled in.

"My son! My daughter-to-be!" he hugged both of us in one mighty embrace.

"Hello, Father! What is your reason for requesting us?" Varn asked, oddly polite. He knew how to suck up.

Emannar frowned and sat down, "Sit next to me, children." We sat down.

"Is this about my mother?" I asked. If it was, I could be in danger.

"No. Well, partially. She's involved, but she's not the reason I'm talking to you two," Emannar looked like he was about to cry. It was surprising to see the King like this.

"Your Father is...growing increasingly reluctant to follow what we do around here. Despite her hatred for him, he still harbours feelings for her. He doesn't want his wife to die. Or your mother. We're trying to get her to turn to our side, but she's gone mad. If only your father hadn't..." he stopped, and I wanted to know why.

"Hadn't? Hadn't what?" I asked.

"Hadn't abused her for years. You were too young to remember," he tried to avoid telling me the details. I could see Varn in the corner of my eye telling me to push him for answers.

"What did he do?" I demanded to know.

"Your father was a bit of an alcoholic. We went to a lot of pubs and the like back in the day. I didn't know anything about what life was like at home, but he never talked much about Gwendys, so I knew something was a bit off," he expanded, "So I made an excuse to stay in their guest room. There were nights I'd lay in the guest bedroom, listening to the sounds of brawls. I could hear Gwendys screaming for help and Simon shouting like a drunkard. I peered over the corner, and I could see Gwendys. She was doing well, hiding her purple ribs and purpler bruises. I couldn't stand it, so I resorted to leaving your father with Witanegemote Morgan for rehabilitation. We learned that your mother was being abused for years under the influence of alcohol."

I started bawling like a baby. Was my father hitting my mother for years? Punching her? Injuring her? What if he was punching some of my siblings too, and they never mentioned it? What if he was hitting Daman or Dayron? He always bullies those two. What if he was hitting Annyte?

Emannar realised that I was brimming with tears, and he tried to comfort me, "But listen to me right now, Kristyne. Your father is not an evil man. He just needed help. He was addicted. He's safe now. And you don't know what he always said about his children in the rehabilitation sessions."

"He had children during these sessions? How long has he been doing them?" I asked, wiping a tear from my cheek.

"He stopped three years ago. But he was full of praises for all of you. He knew that Damon would be his heir, and he would achieve everything that he wanted to achieve someday. He had the highest of hopes for Daman and knew that he was the most like him out of his children, so he pushed him for that success. He knew Dayron would unlock something special because he was such a special boy. He loved talking about Corren's dreams. But he talked the most about you and your sister. I remember everything he said about you," he looked up to the ceiling in remembrance.

"What did he say?" I asked.

"He called you a snapshot of the best times of his life. Every day he didn't see you, he could picture your chestnut hair blowing in the winds of Bernstaplen. He could picture your youthful face. He said he didn't care if someone considered you to be no-one because to him, you are the world itself, and without you, your sister, or your mother, he cannot enjoy life as he does. He said that there was nothing that he would not do to keep you safe from all harm. He vowed to be there when you fall and stand back when you reach for the stars."

I couldn't stop crying. Varn tried to comfort me, but it was no use.

Francis rushed in with a legion of knights.

"Is it time, Your Grace?" he asked Emannar.

Emannar looked at me with sad eyes, "I'm so sorry, Kristyne. But we have no other option."

The legion of knights suddenly directed their swords towards me. I felt so weak, like a hostage. Varn tried to get them to take their hands off me, but two guards seized him as well.

"Your parents love each other too much, Kristyne. It is too dangerous for this kingdom. Our only option is to make them submit. And at this point, they'll only submit if we kidnap one of their children. You're the only one we can obtain. I'm so sorry, Kristyne. But we have no choice but to arrest you on the grounds of treason. Your parents will come around, and then this will all be over. Take her to the dungeons," he waved dismissively, and they dragged me out.

"No! No! Please! You can't do this. They haven't done anything wrong! NO!" I pleaded as I was taken to prison.

It was time for me to starve.

'Prince Emannar had been born to King Grimm Woodgairrd and a prostitute on a starlit night, amid the warmth of a season-late summer. Some may say it was a blessing to be born in the conditions he did, for the brilliance of the light seemed to shine through his mind, and the summer's warmth seemed to fill the holes in his heart with morality. Cold days seemed much warmer after he was born, like his baby skin was absorbing all the ice. His youthful sounds had a gravity to them as if he had all the time in the world to make you matter.

And as he grew to see his kingdom's state of decay, there was no person who ever held the future in their eyes the way he did. For in all that gentle yet formal spirit, there was a warrior, waiting to break out and decimate armies, ready to make any sacrifice to save the lives of others, to guard them no matter what price they requested.

Within three years of Emannar's birth, Styve Woodgairrd came next, delivered by a different prostitute, on a mundane night, amid the warmth of a season-late winter. The days remained cold.'

-Extract from The Witanegemote Chronicles.

Simon:

I woke up suddenly, my eyes in a higher definition than they had ever been, taking in every ray of light, every wave of sound. There was more noise than usual. The odd bird chirped every five seconds, and the floorboards creaked like there was an invisible man treading on them. I was dressed like usual, with a bowl of gruel on my bedside table. And then I heard it. The sounds of protest.

I took a look outside and the crowd, being held back by a group of knights.

"Free the girl!" an old woman with auburn hair cried before being struck across the face with a shield.

Girl? What girl? I headed to the dungeons.

The dungeons were dark. The dungeons were empty. The dungeons were cold. None of the cells had been used in some time because Emannar was hoping to save them for Gwendys and her men. Fluorescent lights flickered as the devils in the walls screamed out in pain. Lifeless shadows curled up in the corners, whispering demented secrets to demented men. Inside these dungeons, there would be a demented girl.

That demented girl was my daughter. Her hair darkened by ash, her youthful face going frail from the tears. But she wasn't the only one - they had Alizia and Ronayne too.

"Who did this to you, Kristyne?" I asked, shocked.

"The King. His Court. Varn. They all did this," she was crying. I wanted to reach through the iron bars and comfort her, but that was a crime.

"What did he do to you?" I growled. This was the last damn straw. It was time to confront him.

"I was...talking to Varn," it was hard for her to speak through the tears, "When he came in. He told me that you weren't listening to their decisions. He expected you...to help mother. He called me the last option, and they dragged me down here."

"He's using you to get me to submit. Probably to get Gwendys to submit as well," I realised.

"You aren't going to, are you?" she asked me. I thought that meant she wanted me not to.

"There's no way in hell that I'm going to submit," I told her. But that made her lash out. She ran into the bars and punched me right in the face. I couldn't believe it. "What was that for?" I looked at her.

"He told me what you did. To Mother. For years! He told me about the sessions," she ran back to Ronayne and carried on crying.

"Kristyne, I..." I would have finished if I could have. There was no justification for what I did to Gwendys for so long. There was nothing I could say to make Kristyne trust me again. I walked out, depressed. Then, my depression turned to anger. I made my way to Emannar's chambers. Varn was outside, trying to bash the door in. Upon the sight of him, I grabbed him and spat in his face.

"What do you think you're doing?" he whined, "I am your Prince!"

"I know what you did to my daughter, you little worm! Where is your father?" I yelled at him.

"I-in there!" he pointed towards the chambers. I let go of him, and he lost his footing, falling to the ground. I was about to burst the door open when he exclaimed, "Wait! Look, I'm not against you in this. I would never go against my wife-to-be. I think what my father did was unjust. I will help you negotiate her arrest. No blood needs to be spilt, I assure you."

I would have listened to him, but I was so tired and annoyed that I couldn't be bothered. I thrust the door open and saw Emannar.

"Simon! What's the matter?" Emannar was clearly faking a smile. He knew that I knew. I pinned him against the wall.

"What the hell do you think you're doing?" I shouted like a man with sleep deprivation, "Putting my daughter in a jail cell? Release her, or I'll kill ya!"

"It wasn't my decision to make, Simon," he looked frantic, "It was the Council's decision! They all voted to imprison Kristyne, except for me and Tobas. It was Styve that proposed the idea!"

"Styve?" I questioned. He would always blame his brothers. I didn't believe him.

Elizella walked into his chambers and saw me on the verge of killing him.

"What the hell? Unhand him, you drunk!" she whacked me with her handbag.

"I will when my daughter can walk free!" I spat at her.

"How dare you!" she shrieked, "Guards!"

A messenger girl who was with Elizella suddenly ran over to a group of knights. They came over, beat me and arrested me.

By the time I could take in my surroundings again, I was exiled.

I did all that I could do. I waited by the roadside for a traveller. After about an hour, some old brown-skinned man with a wrinkled face arrived in a carriage. I paid him seven shillings.

"What is the destination, sir?" he whipped his horses to ready them for a long journey.

"Minbury. The stronghold. Now!" he could tell how impatient I was today.

"Are you sure, sir? The King advises against going to Minbury at this time. Calls it unsafe," he was pleading for his own safety.

"I don't care about your damn safety," I shot back, "Get me to Minbury!"

The traveller kicked his fat horses, and they powered forward. It was a good ride until he stopped to take a breath. He was going too slow, so I stole one of his horses and rode off alone. I could feel the heat of the summer sun beating down on my back. The leather reins rubbed soon-to-be blisters between my fingers. I knew I should have grabbed my gloves. The horse beneath me was just as done with this earth as I was. His neck was lathered in thick sweat, curling the short, stiff hairs of his summer coat. Foam leaked from the corners of his mouth from working with the copper snaffle. Just once, I need you, stallion. I gave him a pat on the neck and picked up the reins - trotting off. His wimpy mane bounced with his stride. He had never even had enough to braid. I shifted my weight to my outside hip and dug my heel into his right side. He picked up the lead in perfect rhythm, tucking his head in and bounding towards the low fence.

Eventually, we made it inside Minbury. There was nobody around except for a group of guards at the gate. I dismissed the horse, letting it run free, and snuck around, approaching the castle's keep where they would be. I stood by a post that ran up to the peak of the keep and put all my strength into climbing up it. I nearly fell and died when I made it.

I could hear voices downstairs. Marvion's throne used to be just below the peak, with the peak being where he could inspect his enemies. There was a staircase by the entrance to the throne room that took you to the peak, so I found it and went down silently.

I could hear them.

"What's our next move? Do we attack Gwendys again?" a man whose voice I recognised asked.

"I think we need to wait, see what happens," the boy I was looking for responded.

"Good idea. Let's find supplies, repel attacks and lay low," the man agreed with his idea.

Eventually, I made it all the way to the bottom and peered around the corner. There were hundreds of knights, and I could see Jaze in a corner as well, next to Jaron Carner. Dontin was at the front, kneeling before him. I stepped out, and Jaron spotted me. The knights suddenly all turned to face me.

Jaron shouted, "Trespasser!" and the men advanced toward me.

Tyral held his hand out and halted them, "Wait! It's my brother-in-law!"

I walked toward them so they could see my face.

"Oh my god..." Jaze hid his face, ashamed. If he was with them, I could forgive him.

Dontin looked right at me, "It's Simon Pargion. Simon Pargion is here!"

Sylvina:

The countryside lay before me like a divine fingerprint, curving and changing, no two parts the same. In all the world, this view was unique. Such is the way of the organic world. The dip and sway of the land, the patterns and species of flora, the ever-changing sky and wind. Every day was a new snapshot in time, for even this one place, this view from one fine oak tree on a hill could never be exactly the same two days in a row. Little by little, the seasons would bring changes. Riverlike minds meandered back to the far away Stormholme, their home. It had its rhythms, too: the start and end of the year, the adoration of summer and the winter. Yet the countryside had a way of reminding me that I wasn't apart from nature but a part of nature. Often on these travels, I'd reach out to touch the bark of the trees as I passed or feel the softness of new leaves. But I can't do that when I'm on the run.

The war horse galloped onward despite the danger and the blasts, four hooves meeting earth in full valour. In each noble breath upon the field where goodness made its stand, the stallion towered above the tallest strands of grass, full calm in its soul, bravery enough to fill the verses of any song you could think of. Any song from centuries ago and any song from centuries to come. It rode on hallowed ground as strongly as the mightiest oak tree. It was a shame that it was overworked, a slave to its rider, Stephyn Tanner.

Stephyn Tanner. I'm not sure Stephyn Tanner ever agreed to anything. He just went for it at the moment that he felt like it. Never a yes, maybe a maybe. But he always seemed to come through. Sometimes. A possibility. He was the kind of person to never take an order but always do what he was ordered to do. He never made jokes, but you still hated his jokes. He never danced, but his moves gave humanity pleasure. Sometimes. He was the kind of man to ask me if I was alright when I was running away from a dead body and two men covered in blood.

"Are we there yet?" I asked persistently.

"We're in the middle of a goddamn field. Does it look like we're there yet?" he retorted.

"Xargaron clouds all eyes," I responded.

Stephyn skidded the horse to a halt and looked at me, "For the last time, will you shut up about demons? How the hell are you the Queen's sister?"

"I was born this way," I responded, waving my hand through the tall grass.

"There's a steadiness to your soul. A steadiness I don't like," he continued to ride.

"It's good to be steady. The world often disappoints," I responded.

"We could be in the middle of a goddamn storm, and you wouldn't even feel the wind change," he spat on the ground.

"The wind doesn't need to change for there to be a storm," I pointed out.

"Do the gods pay you to talk? Shut up," he yelled.

"There are no gods. Only demons."

"Life sure makes it seem like it," he looked back at his horse as he rode.

"You could do with some counselling. Might give you a more positive outlook on life," I grinned as he looked back at me, full of rage.

At first, he seethed with rage, but then he calmed himself, "There is no positive outlook on life."

I decided to reveal what I knew, "I would have to disagree with you there, Sir Tanner. And I'm sure you do as well, considering how happy you were to have an affair with my sister."

He stopped the horse and looked at me, more afraid than angered now, "How-"

"How do I know?" I answered, "The wind gave me a feeling."

"Don't test me, fairy," he looked at me, "Who the hell told you? How many people know?"

"Well. It really depends on what you count as a person," I smiled at him, "Because if anything counts, then the wind knows, the grass knows-"

"I will drag you to the ones who want you dead, you hear me! Now, who the hell told you?" if you asked me if he sounded angry, afraid or tired, I would say all of the above.

"Fine then," I confessed, "I heard my dad talking about it."

"How the hell does your dad know?"

"I don't know. He's been trying to cause the King's downfall for years. It's like a game of Trinz. If he plays correctly, it'll benefit everyone. If he doesn't, everyone suffers," I shrugged.

He continued to ride, "Listen, good. You're gonna tell your dad never to mention the affair to anyone. If he refuses, I'll get permission from Emannar to go up there and kill him myself. See if he refuses then."

"I'll consider it," I responded, half-listening.

"The sun's setting," he pointed out.

The sun set in the sky, as fresh colours brushed upon an artist's canvas, as if those rays were destined to create a great work of art - one given to those capturing moments in the soul. The orange-gold stretched far and wide, the colour of hearths and tangerines. Reflecting the dawn, the promise of the rising sun coming after the velvety night has had its say, and the land has rested once more. But we would not rest for another hour.

"Are we there yet?" I asked again.

"How about you look ahead? I can see the fort from here. Why the hell did you want to go to Bernstaplen though?" he asked.

"I'm not an idiot, Stephyn. You want to hand me to the King so that my dad will submit. The Tymbrenns were being used for his greater plan. I worked it out. But you want the Queen for yourself, don't you? You want Emannar to lose, don't you? So you can be with her," I spelt it out, and he gulped.

"Don't tell me what I think, girl," he responded.

Basically, I was correct.

"Ever been to Bernstaplen?" I asked.

"Not a place I've ever been interested in going to," he responded, his voice shaking.

"You sound afraid of a heap of bricks," I pointed out bluntly.

"A heap of bricks will topple you and kill you if it gets the chance," he countered. Now he was talking in riddles.

"I'm going to let you in and then head back to Hagueveil. They'll find it suspicious if I go back alone and the rest of the men turn up a week later," Stephyn told me. I got off the horse and walked in myself. As soon as they saw me, the knights pointed their swords at me.

There was a stableman by the gate who saw me. He ran inside and called Damon over.

"Thank you, Buckley," Damon Pargion dismissed the stableman and turned to me, "What does a Slait want with us during these times? Have my parents done something stupid again?"

"Probably. I wouldn't know about it," I answered bluntly.

"Well, er, what do you want then?" he stuttered. With Damon's conversations, it was always the same, I'd heard. It was like he wrote down the first thing he'd say and practised it for centuries, and then he struggled to continue the conversation.

"I want to stay here. I can't go back to Stormholme or Hagueveil. It's not safe for me. Your place is probably the safest place right now," I answered honestly.

"Get Morgan over here. I have no idea how to respond to this," Damon asked a guard.

"Morgan and Dayron are doing the Sission, Damon," the guard responded.

"Aw yeah, forgot about that. Well, what would you do? Would you let her stay here?" Damon asked the guard for his opinion.

"She doesn't seem dangerous. Everyone knows that she poses no threat. She's just weird, sir," he answered.

"So let her stay? Thank you. You just made my life way easier," Damon thanked the guard.

"If your guard told you it would be wise to kill yourself, would you do it?" I asked.

"Honestly? Probably. My brain isn't, well, amazing," he admitted to himself. I laughed.

"So I can stay?" I asked.

"Yeah, sure, why not," he shrugged.

"Amazing. How is everything going with your parents?" I asked. I didn't actually care. I was just being formal.

"I have no idea," he responded. At least he was honest.

A man came over to Damon with a message, "My Lord. We have just received word from Emannar. It's about your father."

Damon's eyes widened, "What is it?"

"Emannar's men have taken Kristyne hostage as an attempt to make Gwendys submit. In response, Simon has quit the council. He's made an alliance with Tyral Wayne, my Lord," the man explained.

Damon looked at the man, "Send a message to my father. Tell him I'm gonna help him." The man nodded and walked away.

I stared at him, "Trying to overthrow the King. That's going to work out well."

Damon whispered to me as he walked away, "If you're going to leave this place, I'd leave now."

I smiled at him, "I have my own bones to pick with the royals. I'll stay where I am."

Simon:

Dontin sat down next to me, "Word has come."

"What is the word?" I looked at him urgently.

"They'll consider it," I sighed with relief as he said that. Dontin continued, "Tyral's managed to get Emannar to send his new High Earl over here. We're redirecting all the knights to the throne room in case he tries anything funny."

"Who is the new High Earl?"

"Emannar said that he told you who your replacement would be," Dontin looked confused. Then it clicked. No goddamn way...

"He's hired Auster Magnarok?" I stared at him, shocked.

"I'm afraid so," Dontin sighed, "He really has gone insane." Jaze was in the corner, readying his spear. He hadn't even looked at me once since I arrived. I was not ashamed of Jaze. All he wanted was to defend his oath. "What's it like," Dontin asked me, "Being in Minbury again?"

"When the Pargions were united," I answered, "Bernstaplen was our home, but Minbury was our fortress. A cocoon for our children because Minbury was never attacked. Then Gwendys went mad, and you attacked."

"I apologise for the damages, but it was justified," Dontin sighed again and then looked at Jaze, "Jaze! You gonna say hello?"

Jaze came over to us reluctantly, "Hello, my Lord."

I stared coldly at him, "You killed Marvion Wayne. You broke your oath."

"My Lord, I will take any punishment for the murder, but I broke no oath. Marvion kept his hand on his blade while talking to Gwendys, and I have no oath sworn to Marvion Wayne. Only his daughter," Jaze begged for mercy. He knew that I could convince Tyral to kill him.

"You broke your oath to Gwendys. You abandoned her," I pointed out.

"The King wanted my head more than he wanted Gwendys's at the time," Jaze disagreed, "If I didn't leave, we would have both died." He gave up, "Oh, it's no use, Simon. I broke my oath to Gwendys. I broke my oath to her children. I broke my oath to the Par-"

"But you never broke your oath to me," I pointed out and reached my hand out for a handshake. He froze for a second and then shook it.

"Thank you, my Lord," he seemed near crying, "I will not forget your mercy."

"Don't," I warned him, "Do you know why Ebon Pargion survived for so long, Jaze?"

"Why?"

"Because our family lived together. And not just the father, mother and child. The knights, the storyteller, the stablemen. The whole family stayed together until the father and mother died. That's how we survived. Interdependence. We were at the castle. We were the heartbeats. But for us to be the heartbeats now, we have to stay together. You're with us until death, Jaze. Believe that," I made that up on the spot.

Jaze nodded and walked back to his post. Dontin looked at me, "You made that up, you sly git. I could tell you stuttered a bit."

"I might have," I smiled.

Suddenly, a bony man with an obese horn walked in and blew it, "Ladies and gentlemen, I present to you, Auster Magnarok!" he announced.

Then Auster walked in.

Not even the ever-present darkness of the throne room could conceal the way Auster's pale face (imagine a face the colour of paper) wore eyes that visibly widened with desire for the man he desperately wanted to talk to or kill. He rarely said anything nice, and even rarer still in a confident and unwavering voice. He always sounded like a depressed adolescent boy with his soul ripped from his flesh. He always had thin red lips. Nobody knew if his lips were naturally red or if they went red from the blood he spilt. People did know that his hair wasn't pitch black though - he just dipped it in tar every morning.

"Good morning, sirs," he stated, void of emotion, "How are you today?"

Tyral looked at him, "Just fine, my Lord."

"I have no interest in being your lord, Tyral Wayne," he stated again.

"Then what do you have interest in?" Dontin asked, not really caring but having an obligation to care.

"I have an interest in doing my job. Which is why I am here," Auster answered.

"What does Emannar want from us?" I asked.

"To utterly crush the evil from the Kingdom. With this alliance, we double the chance of making Gwendys Wayne submit to Emannar Woodgairrd. Oh, and if you refuse, I have some new tricks with my daggers that I have been practising. I'll aim for the child," talking about killing Tyral made him laugh. He had the kind of laugh that turned your skeleton to stone.

"If you find it funny to talk about killing a child, you truly are evil," Tyral spoke up innocently. Auster stopped laughing instantly and looked at Tyral coldly.

"Do you like myths, Tyral Wayne? It is no accident that the reptile, the snake, symbolises evil in myths. These creatures do not require love to raise their young. Snakes do not learn to love. They learn to survive. I could be a snake. My parents did not use love to raise me. I did not learn to love. I learned to survive. I have a reptilian brain if you will. But like a disease, a reptilian brain can spread. From person to person. And soon, the reptilian brain dominates a family. A street. A region. A city. A country. A world. And soon, we are all driven into a hellish dystopia. Where the most cut-throat, the most immoral, and the most reptilian are victorious. We will hang our heads low but lift them higher than ever. We will hand our children over to a system run by the very worst we can offer. But here's the thing - that's the perfect world to me," Auster rambled.

"Who the hell hit you as a child?" Dontin asked, and the crowd started laughing at him. Auster showed no sign of shame.

"It wasn't my childhood that truly scarred me, Dontin Slait. It was my love. My darling Lilyana gave me a son, but she is afraid of marrying me," Auster looked at the man with the horn, "Bring my love in."

They brought in Auster's greatest prisoner.

Lilyana's emotions were not easily hidden on her innocent face. Her pain was evident in how her eyebrows creased and her lips curved downwards. But her eyes truly showed her soul. A deep pool of restless gold, an ocean of hopeless grief. I could see something that Auster couldn't take control of her passion. Her passion for life. Her passion for escaping him.

Auster put his arms around Lilyana, "My love. How are you today?"

"Better now, my love," she stated through tears. She was trying so hard not to bawl. She would not let a Magnarok break her.

"That is good. What do you think we should do with these traitors, my love? Shall I show them the tricks I practised on you?" Auster whispered in her ear.

"Whatever you want, my love."

"Well, I want to kill them all, but I can't do that, can I? The King will be after me."

"Let them live for now then, my love. You can kill them later," she never moved.

"You know best, my love," he kissed Lilyana on the cheek and looked at us, "Well, I suppose you have been saved. I will tell Emannar Woodgairrd to allow for the alliance. But remember something. If you cross me or my darling, I will bring you unimaginable pain and distress. I will take pleasure in it. I don't play by the same rule book as society. I will play the game with you. And I will win with ease. No morals. No restraints."

"So you think that we'll all be sheep while you're a wolf?" Dontin questioned in a mocking tone.

"If you want to be wolves, be wolves. I don't care. I can be a lion," and with that, Auster and Lilyana Magnarok left Minbury.

Dontin looked at me, genuinely afraid, "Well, at least we have the alliance."

Daman:

Anticipation. It's the sugar of life, isn't it? A looking glass for life. Or death. Who knows? It's just a fraction of a moment between when your eyes smile, and your mouth follows. Or when you frown and cry. An exquisite feeling.

I looked at Howard. He was fidgeting with anxiety. The Chief had spoken - today was the final battle against the Novaks. He had located his rival.

Howard looked at Fawkes and I, "Are you sure this will make us heroes? There are many ways to become a hero. Perhaps a hero at an inn, giving shelter. Or a hero building homes, cooking meals..."

"Where's your spirit, mate?" Fawkes asked him, "You're pickin' the easy way out."

"Alright, look, I'm scared," Howard admitted, "I am scared. So scared. I've been here many times, and yes, we win a lot, but right now, these forces have us out-manned. Please, please, open your eyes and see what's coming. Some of us will not survive. We may all die today."

"What happened to you wanting to die? For your wife?" Fawkes sounded like he was mocking Howard, but he was serious.

"I want to die more than anyone, but the truth is I'm terrified," he admitted.

"Of death?" Fawkes pushed him.

"Of pain. I can't deal with it," he told us.

"Right. You can't deal with it," Fawkes repeated.

The Chief came over. He was wearing some traditional Novak sash. We didn't learn much about Novak culture during our time in the region - we learned the most on our first day, and that was about it.

"We ready," he confirmed. Fawkes and I were going on foot, beginning the battle stealthily. Once we destroyed the flag in the centre, they would begin the attack.

It was cold in the desert. Snow danced in the light, a ballet conducted by the gentle wind. As Fawkes watched, his eyes grew a bit wider. The newly clothed trees rose as white fairytale beings in the wintry landscape, for the grey clouds had bequeathed a bounty of snow. Heaven's sunlit glitter came to bring our world to a new shine.

"I've got a couple of new tricks I wanna try," Fawkes told me, "Lemme at 'em."

"Do whatever you want," I responded. There was a group of four tribesmen beneath the snowy cliff we laid upon, and some suppressed explosives would do us good.

"Right," he laid the bombs out before dropping them, "Put these babies on." He handed me some heavy boots, "They'll let you get the drop on 'em. I call this one the firecracker."

"What does it do?"

"It cracks," he looked down at them and dropped it behind them. The men turned around to investigate and saw the pop of the bomb. He waited for the group of four to look up at us, and that's when I dropped down onto one of them, sticking my blade in his head. I was about to engage in a duel with two of the swordsmen when Fawkes threw a wallop of dirt at each of them, blinding them as I killed them. The fourth man, an archer, had cleared the dirt from his eyes and was on the verge of blowing a horn so everyone would find us when I stabbed his throat and let him bleed out. Fawkes fastened his heavy boots on and dropped down. The oddly heavy boots were oddly silent when it came to the crunch of snow.

"I fashioned some grappling hooks out of a rope and a dagger," Fawkes handed me one and pointed up at a post, "This should pull us up there, and then we can reach the top of this vantage point. There's an archer on the level below." He used his grappling hook to reach the post and used his right leg to push himself backwards and onto the ledge. He severed the rope on the grappling hook. It was for one-time use. It was my turn now, and I made it up with equal success. I jumped down before Fawkes and inserted my sword into the archer's heart.

There was a hug of houses in the layers of white that together made a village. The village homes were stamped in the valley as if placed by a careful collector. It was a shame the Novaks had desecrated it. I snuck past a snow-covered boulder to cut open a man's neck while Fawkes headed to the right to light some carts loaded with gunpowder. We ran back to the vantage point and let them explode. Not only did the explosives kill about 10 of their men, but they also burnt the flag to a crisp, signalling the attack. We heard Chief Gabor's famed war cry and noticed Howard and Aldo bumbling behind them. While the focus was drawn onto them, we continued our stealthy approach.

A tribesman was drinking his beer next to another gunpowder cart when he heard the cry. He almost spotted me when he turned his head, but Fawkes fired an arrow at a wind chime, which rang loudly and attracted his attention elsewhere. I ran up to the man and cut him down while Fawkes fired an arrow at another man in the area, piercing the silver shine of his chestplate.

We moved up to close in on a house that some men were defending with their lives. As I snuck up to the door, I could hear a man breathing unsteadily. Taking a risk, I plunged my sword through the door, making contact with flesh, and pulled the body backwards, ultimately crushing the fine creation. A man saw the broken door and spotted me, but Fawkes let another arrow fly at his skull.

Silently, I opened the door and swiftly closed it as I entered the building. A tribesman was taking a swig of wine. Fawkes cautioned me and approached the man himself.

"I like wine too," Fawkes joked as he slit the man's throat with a wind chime and poured the wine on the wound.

"That was brutal," I admitted.

"Nothing's bru'al in war," he told me.

"Wru sra rarr ora aeui svu?" some Novak tribesmen asked behind us. He was oddly innocent, and Fawkes solved the problem by stabbing him.

Leaving the house, we walked up the elegant stone steps and led another silent leap onto the building below. There was a trapdoor. I crouched through the building and made my way up and inside, collecting a Novak banner. The Chief told us to loot any sign of Novak culture for his own memories. I then carried out another door-kill on the man guarding the building. I was about to leap down to the next level when Fawkes stopped me.

"Lotsa guys down there," he observed, "Lemme at 'em. Alone." I was reluctant at first, but I nodded. He pulled out a second grappling gun that he kept for this moment and fired it at a tree, making it to an area surrounded by populous tents. He pulled his bow out and shot two men in the head. One man spotted him, so he ran inside a tent. I can assume that he survived the encounter with ease, as there was not a sound coming from inside, and he came out briskly enough. He fired a killing blow at another tribesman and made it inside another tent. He came out a while later with a Novak banner on his back. After this, he climbed up the third tent and fired an arrow at someone drinking wine. He then trod upon a slackline forged from rope and made it onto the top of the final tent, where some men surrounded a fire. They left the fire to investigate the screams of dying men when Fawkes threw a bomb down to exterminate them all. I heard a two-note whistle, signalling me to come over.

"It's a bit of a trek to the next guy," he pointed at an archer in a watchtower. We vaulted over a fence and climbed up a boulder to reach the tower. Fawkes pulled out another firecracker. "When I throw this, climb up the tower and kill the archer. Quickly," he told me, and he threw it. I quickly vaulted over the fence around the watchtower and stabbed the archer while he dealt with two men below us, cutting one's shoulder open and stabbing the other one's back.

"You see the bridge with the lilies?" he pointed at it, so I nodded. Let's drop down into the field of lilies. Down with the lillies was another banner. I took it.

"There are some grooves in the rock there," I pointed at them, "It'll help us climb up." We made our way up swiftly, spotting a tent. As we climbed up it, Fawkes dropped the wind chime, making an enemy investigate the ringing and firing an arrow at their larynx. He then threw a bomb at two men by a fire, the sound of the explosion nearly invisible in comparison with the sounds of war. After kicking a man off a bridge, we dived back into some lilies and beheaded a group admiring some skins. Fawkes even kicked a man off a cliff and threw a bomb to attach to him.

"Sticky Bomb, I call it. It sticks," he explained.

We walked past a red tree when a man spotted me.

"Looking for me?" he shouted, drawing attention to us. We approached each other. One. Two. Three. He struck. I countered. I killed. Two men who were alerted to us came over next, who I both killed in one strike, pumped with the adrenaline the standoff had granted me. Then they loaded the cannons. A cannonball flew for me, practically clutching my face, when someone fired an arrow at it, ruining the angle and missing me. I looked to my right and saw Balog Novak Gabor. He gestured us towards the cannons and continued to kill men. Fawkes and I climbed up some more grooves up to those manning the cannons. Fawkes threw a bomb at the ground that exuded smoke, and we crushed them with ease. Fawkes collected another banner and came over to the cannon.

"I think I'm at my best with these," Fawkes looked at me, "Some good figh'ing out there."

"You did well too," I admitted to him, "May you live." We shook hands.

"May I live," he grinned at me.

"You see that cart?" he pointed at one loaded with gunpowder. I nodded. "Watch this," he pulled out an arrow with a red coating and readied his bow for firing. "Aim the cannon at it and fire," he told me. I did, and as the cart fell, he fired an arrow at it, creating a glorious blaze for the huts below. I dropped down and defended our position. Randomly, everything went silent except for the Chief's screams.

We were told not to investigate if it was silent, so I stood still. After some time, a man cloaked in gold armour approached, with Howard and Aldo in chains behind him. He was looking for a duel. For a moment we stood, giving in to the wind and the silence. He unsheathed his sword and displayed it to the crowd of tribesmen watching. I waited a few seconds to emphasise how unimpressed I was and then unsheathed mine. The duel had begun. He rushed at me, but I fired six brief strikes at his shield, consuming his ability to hold the shield. I stopped for a moment, faking the need to catch my breath, and then fired a breezy counter through his chest after he tried to strike me. This left a large cut in his flesh, making him immobile. I used his lack of mobility to embed his skin with marks from my blade. After a lot of strikes, we clashed swords, and he tried to club me over the head with his shield. I side-stepped the attempt, and he lunged for me again. I side-stepped too late. He left a large cut on my leg, and the pain was seething. The pain also gave me an adrenaline rush - I stabbed him three more times, eating his stamina. I tried again, but he blocked the attack with his shield and cut my side. I dodged backwards as he tried to club me again and clashed swords with him again. This angered him, and he tried to kick me backwards. Anticipating it by the way his leg thrusted upwards, I dodged the kick and cut his side and then his chin. Then he clashed swords with me again as a block. He got a few body hits on me, and they hurt like hell, but when he lunged again, I swept to the side briskly and cut his back open. I lunged at him again, and he copied my move, but I parried his attempt and cut across his stomach. He blocked my attack once more, but I swiped upwards again and disarmed him of his shield. I prepared myself for another side-step, but he anticipated this and cut my knee open. Unable to move, I fell to the ground. This was it for me.

My life flashed before my eyes as the Chief appeared and challenged his former rival.

"Duskrem! Foca aeuir sria reqor, mus srek buae! Foca ka!" the Chief cried.

"I occavs aeuir daosr kamsamca," General Duskrem replied.

They started the duel at opposite ends of the field and unsheathed their swords in the fashion that I had. The Chief immediately parried Duskrem's first strike, and the Chief cut his stomach. Now, Balog let Duskrem attack again, and the Chief cut into his stomach again, sidestepping with ease. In the middle of Duskrem's next attack, the Chief did a spin and cut across his chest during it and then clashed swords with Duskrem. Gabor parried the next attack and cut his chest again. Unpredictably, the Chief fired three brisk strikes at Duskrem and crushed the man's ability to move with one of his legs. In Duskrem's brief moment of weakness, Gabor continued to destroy him. As a form of mockery, Balog let him recover and then plunged his sword into Duskrem's chest at the peak of his recovery, making the general fall to his knees. Balog Novak Gabor, our Chief, held his sword above his rival and was about to strike when one of Duskrem's accomplices put a sword through his heart.

I had no time to process that Balog Novak Gabor was dead. I just watched Fawkes fire a cannonball at Duskrem's head to kill him and then further cannonballs at the men holding Aldo and Howard. I ran away with them as Fawkes continued to crush them with cannonballs. Then it dawned on me. My mission was done here.

It was time to go home.

Simon:

"Are you ready to speak with the council?" Dontin looked at me.

"There's no way in hell that I'm ready," I admitted.

It had been a three-day journey ever since we were ready to make the hike. Dontin and I had to present our reasons for the alliance to the council. Emannar slouched on his throne, with his wife beside him. Styve and Kase took up the chairs that Emannar's children used at all other times. Gregory, Francis, Karron and Tobas took four wooden chairs at the side, while Auster had Lilyana in a tight embrace on two other chairs.

"I'm speaking first," Dontin looked at me, "And I sure as hell wish I wasn't."

Dontin walked out to persuade them, "Your Grace. The Council. How are you today?"

Styve spat, "We've been doing well ever since you ransacked a Noble House."

"You've done your fair share of ransacking too, Styve, you hypocrite," Dontin countered. This was a bad start, "Let me just give my goddamn statement."

Styve opened his mouth to argue, but Emannar silenced him, "Speak."

Dontin nodded and began his speech, "As a well-established member of the communities of Stormholme and Hagueveil, I would like to raise several points in defence of my most recent actions and bring them to the attention of the High Council this evening. Just to do a quick briefing of my actions, I would like to bring to attention the traumatic experiences that I have had to deal with as a result of the nobility of this kingdom. For instance, this biased remark that Styve Woodgairrd has just made to me and the years and years of torment that I have been subjected to by my father, Arvin Slait and my sister Elizella Woodgairrd. If it were not for the harsh treatment of me in the first place and the nickname 'Veille' I have had to get used to, I would not have done what I did, and I most certainly would not be facing the council for it. The first point I would like to bring to your attention is that of the election of Simon Pargion. This was a High Earl I once approved of. The Pargions had not been represented in court for some time. But then Gwendys Wayne attacked Minbury. Despite our initial predictions, she was victorious. Marvion Wayne was dead. It was even more troubling to me that La Perte Inconnue, an assassins' guild and close friends of mine, were present at the battle. In fact, one of them was killed by Gwendys's men, and another has been kept in chains to this day. I led a strong political campaign, using words before I ever used actions, and she supported her actions by claiming that they were nothing more than a guild of assassins and they deserved to suffer, of which I have sufficient evidence in the form of Lord Tobas, who was present when she made these claims. She then went on to publicly shame Simon Pargion and disregard all the good word of this council. Gwendys Wayne did contradict herself as well by pinning all of her actions on the distress given to her by Simon. While this distress is certainly true, and Simon has done some unforgivable things, these were years ago, and Simon has attended rehabilitation for years. It seems like an excuse. With concerns growing in recent months, I took it upon myself to forge a team and take Minbury back for the kingdom. I was aided by Gyrard and Maucolyn of La Perte Inconnue, as well as Jaron Carner, a member of the King's Royal Court. We were successful, and we drove Gwendys out of a large piece of her power, letting Tyral Wayne, who has been falsely accused by the Supreme Witanegemote on many grounds, rule the castle. Unexpectedly, this led Simon Pargion to join me for reasons he can disclose. Soon after, we requested an alliance with His Grace, Emannar Woodgairrd, and High Earl Auster Magnarok kindly permitted us to attend this council hearing," Dontin summarised.

The council thought about his words. Then it was my turn. I came up and eyed my enemies, then prepared to speak my mind.

"In addition to Dontin Slait's arguments, comments and accusations, I'd like to ask the council and, in particular, the Supreme Witanegemote whether this will be given due care and attention and be properly discussed, without the false accusations and poor actions that have been taken as of late, because as Dontin alluded to, there has been more attention put on making me submit than making Gwendys submit. Nothing's been done, and nothing's been said. It has been ignored. Please do not ignore that. It should be focused on more. My wife's mental health is at stake, and she may be plotting to kill any one of us. Secondly, I have received a few interesting pieces of information from talking with Dontin's men, which I would like to bring to awareness. Jaze Wyne, murderer of Marvion Wayne, a brutal war criminal with nothing left to gain, has publicly testified to Gwendys's guilt. Tyral Wayne, a mere boy, falsely accused by the Witanegemot, has testified against his own sister. Thirdly, during excursions with Emannar and Kase to see Gwendys, she displayed clear hatred for me. Her anger is wholly directed at me. At the end of the day, my wife has committed treason, and what has happened? My daughter has been imprisoned, and I have quit. Nothing useful has been done. Come on, there's double standards here. I don't want a cover-up. I want my wife stabilised. Are you going to do anything about these serious attacks, or are we going to continue to sit around like ducks while we lose everything around us?" I finished my speech and sat down next to Dontin as the council quarrelled.

Tobas spoke first, his vote being the most obvious, "Naturally, the issues that have been raised are of grave concern, and I have been on the receiving end of some attitude from Gwendys Wayne. The alliance Simon and Dontin propose, firstly, who forged it? Two men that have been humiliated and abused for years by members of this council," he shot a dirty look at Emannar and Elizella, "Secondly, as punishment for the Supreme Witanegemote's poor treatment of Tyral Wayne, I believe that he should write a letter to Gwendys Wayne and deliver it himself, declaring war," Gregory widened his eyes, "I would like to mention that I have spent a short time as a councillor, but I have still displayed more wisdom than some of my more senior councillors. I vote for the alliance," There was healthy applause around the room.

Kase spoke up next, also likely in our defence, "I must support what Tobas has said. When I had my first encounter with Gwendys Wayne, I must admit that it was a horrible encounter. I had a feeling that her words were not aimed at me but at the council in general. I personally believe that as a council, we have a duty to oppose those who oppose us. I am concerned that the behaviour of this council recently has been dreadful, and I'm not letting my brother's controlling antics get in the way. The King's job is to listen to his subjects, and he's failed to even do that! I have always been treated badly by this council, to the point where I can't be bothered to follow the crowd anymore. I vote for the alliance," the applause was only healthy from Tobas. Everyone was giving him dirty looks, except for Gregory, who chose to speak next.

"You two are right," Gregory spoke up, "I have failed recently. My thought pools have not been as accurate as necessary. It's down to the King to fix these problems, and the King has failed to fix them. Three votes for the alliance now," Gregory nodded.

Styve raised his hand to punch Kase but withdrew it and looked at the King, "Well, I, for one, Emannar, completely distrust these men, and I am ashamed that these three councillors have chosen to assist their corrupted desires. Emannar Woodgairrd is one of the most respected kings the kingdom has ever seen and should receive full support from all. Let's hope that this council is going to see that. I vote against the alliance," he grinned evilly, and the King, Queen and Auster clapped.

Francis spoke next, "I have little to add, but I would like to make a proposal. I propose that if Gwendys continues to exhibit malice towards any of us, we arrest her and make Simon carry out the execution," he cackled, "I vote against the alliance anyway." Elizella started laughing when he suggested I kill my wife. I prayed that they wouldn't decide on it.

Karron looked at me next, "Let's now come to Dontin's side of the story. I think we all know about the abuse that Elizella has given him, so I'll skip over that. Dontin is absolutely infuriated with Gwendys because of her murder and imprisonment of two close friends of his. This can be likened to Simon's infuriation because of Emannar's imprisonment of his daughter, which, as I said, was an awful idea and should never have been passed. I think this whole meeting is just a product of bias from our royals. I vote that we free Kristyne, and I also vote for the alliance."

Elizella simply voted, "I vote against the alliance. I'd rather they all wasted away under stacks of dirt."

Emannar sighed, "I admit, I have behaved dreadfully. My wife has behaved dreadfully. I have asked her to apologise, and I have asked myself to apologise, and I've asked Simon to apologise, which he has failed to do. You talk about wrongdoings, but no wrong has been done. Anyone not fuelled by anger would have forgiven our actions. I do not approve of the tantrums of these men. As well as this, Gwendys has not yet acted. We would be doing nothing with this alliance anyway. I vote against the alliance."

The vote was 4-4, but a councillor had not yet voted. All eyes turned to Auster and his wife.

He whispered in Lilyana's ear, "I'll tell them what we agreed on, my love." He kissed her cheek and then looked at us, "I can clearly see that these men have been dehumanised by the councillors. Everyone gets dehumanised every now and then, Simon Pargion, everyone. It can be of your race, your gender, your age, your education, your beliefs...your decisions. But here's the rub: teaching us to dehumanise induces psychopathy into us. It takes normal folks and makes them stop caring if others live or die. You can't be born crazy. You just can't be. Those twisted gods give us the bane of existence. They give us a soul. They give us rules. Morals. We are supposed to fight back, stay noble, be kind and be brave. The only other option is to give in to our inklings of crazy. Break free from the boundaries. Open our eyes. Once you do that, you stop being the damsel in distress. Nobody can save you, and you sure as hell don't save others. You become your own angel of sorts. We're born to learn the rules, to follow everything as it is laid out for us. But the power of insanity is creative. It's flexible. That's how we win. That's how we always win. And I sure as hell want to win. We could be wolves, but we can be lions. To be a lion, you have to ignore authority. To be a lion, you have to get power and take risks. Therefore, my love and I vote for the alliance," he cackled and then kissed Lilyana again, to her discomfort.

Emannar bashed his hand on the armrest of the throne in anger, "Damn it, Auster!"

"What's the problem, sir? I voted for the better option," he grinned.

"I can't change what option we decide on, but I can add conditions," Emannar smiled, "I will follow what Karron suggested and free Kristyne. But, I will also follow what Francis suggested and make Simon execute Gwendys if she cannot be helped."

Elizella looked startled, "You're going through with this?"

"I have to, woman, so shut up," he demanded, "Bring Varn in here."

Varn was dragged in soon after.

"What do you want?" he looked like he had been crying for a while. I assumed it was for Kristyne.

"Take the keys for the dungeons. Free your bride," he dismissed Varn, and Varn looked overwhelmed with joy. I hoped to see my daughter outside of a cell again before this was all over.

Dontin laughed in Elizella's face, "Oh, dear sister, I can see your face reddening with fumes. Are you going to throw another tantrum because you didn't get your way?"

Elizella looked bitter, "Shut up."

Emannar looked at Elizella with anger, "Damn it, Elizella! If you hadn't let your goddamn bias get in the way, we could have gotten Karron on our side! I should never have attempted the kidnapping of your sister for you!"

"Sister?" Dontin looked angry now, "Sylvina? What have you done to Sylvina?"

Elizella tried to get Emannar to stop talking, but he dismissed her, "Elizella wanted to punish her parents for not being loyal to us. I decided to kidnap Sylvina in an attempt to get them to submit. But I sent the Tymbrenn squires after them - they nearly killed her."

"You chose the only sister I ever loved to suffer? What about Ashlyh? She's just as bad as your goddamn wife," Dontin ranted.

"Sylvina is alive. Stephyn Tanner is bringing her here," Emannar revealed.

"You put her in the hands of your wife's secret lover?" Dontin snapped. Oh no.

"Secret...lover?" Emannar looked at Elizella with a fury, "What do you have to say about this, woman?"

"Don't believe anything the Veille says," she dismissed Dontin's claims, but she wouldn't look at Emannar, which gave it away.

"If you don't believe me, I have a love letter from Stephyn to Elizella kept on my person. It claims that they have had relations before. And it was written during your reign," Dontin was grinning the hardest I've ever seen a man grin. He loved the pain!

Emannar read the letter. Elizella tried to snatch it away, but Emannar shook her off.

"Ashford!" he ordered Francis to come over, "Send a message to the High Priest. Tell him I want a divorce."

"Yes, sire, but the documentation may take months to complete," Francis cautioned him.

"I don't care how long it takes, I don't want this woman in my life anymore," Emannar wouldn't even look at her.

"Emann-" her sentence was cut off by Emannar smacking her.

"Get out of my castle," he uttered.

Dontin looked at me, smiling like the Sun, "This was a fun day, wasn't it?"

'I love you. I would defend you with my life despite insurmountable odds. I would comfort you in your most painful times. I would dance for you and rejoice with you in your happiest hours. I would never betray you. I am never gonna give you up. I will find my fire when you are threatened, doing everything necessary for your protection – waging war even. I shall forgive you when you err. I am yours, and you are mine, into eternity. I will never abandon you. I will never endanger you. I will make your foes rot in hell. Love is a concept for lions. Be brave, my lovely wife, and know that I am here.'

-Words spoken by Emannar Woodgairrd to Elizella Slait on their wedding day.

Annyte:

When I want to be, I'm fast. I've been fast ever since I first ran. I first ran chasing a dog around the castle. A white dog, fluffy, with black eyes and an adorable little head who enjoyed belly rubs. I don't remember much about it. Just that I was fast.

But here, in this jungle, I can't move without a plant touching my skin. Everything I loved about this forest a couple of days ago was raising my heart rate unsafely and killing my ability to be logical. It's been hard to find our way back to Kristyne to free her, but we're nearly there. I hope.

The sheer density of the foliage had made me feel cosy, like in all this space, I could still be more at home than I ever was at home. The thousands of noises had crashed over me as refreshing as any waterfall, overriding my senses and setting my brain to the same chemical soup it was in when I joined Incognitae. I doubt there'd be a fortress behind the waterfall when we can hear nothing. We had wandered too far. We were too close but not close enough. Everything was too identical. The noises were rapping at the door of the jungle like thieves, banging for entrance so they could cut your head open. Cooperation is dead. My eyes are wide open, and I'm moving at the most pointless speeds. I don't want to see endless shades of blue and green. I want to see a human being that isn't one of us. I don't want to be flailing my arms around searching for something that isn't a vine or a deer's antler. Even the warm air, the refreshing warm air, has come to feel like rotting soup in my nose. I want to run back home all the way, but I don't know which direction to take.

"Shhh!" Jaide urged me to be still, "Look!" I looked at it.

The deer glanced with such sweet and gentle eyes that it gives you a revelation. This must be why nobles call each other 'dear.' For in that moment of dark soulful eyes is a natural, vulnerable honesty. The antlers grew upon the deer as if in poetic salute to the trees. But I don't want to be a deer. I want to be the panther eating the deer. Jaide fired the arrow and shot the deer dead.

"We can use the antlers for a fire if we need a fire," Jaide told everyone, snapping the antlers off.

"We won't need a fire. We'll be out of here before we do," Madeleine persisted. Nobody believed her, but it was fun to dream.

"We should never have come here," I grabbed a stick and threw it at the ground.

"Well, we're getting closer," Soniya pointed out towards a swamp, "When we came in, there was marshland."

Ahead the forest, trees are thinner, a clearing perhaps, or a glade? As we draw closer, we can see that it is neither. The firm ground gives way to a marsh of tall reeds, the soil submersed in water. The autumn sunlight falls directly onto a tree trunk, likely felled for just this purpose, a bridge. There is no hand rail, nothing to steady oneself. The drop isn't dangerous. Just one hell of a messy landing. With one careful boot, I test the bark. It's damp with a smattering of moss. Likely, the sun rays keep the worst of it off. It isn't too slippery, but it's no concrete sidewalk. It has a girth of about three arm spans, yet the top is still curved. Time to take a deep breath and just go - eyes on my feet and the next half metre of the tree, arms raised like a tightrope walker. Steady. Steady. One footfall at a time until the other bank appears.

"We made this bridge, Soniya!" Darlyne giggled, "We made it!"

"I know we did, Darlyne," Soniya smiled.

"Let's get home," Dyana looked at Jaide, "I want to go home."

"We're going home, sis," Jaide smiled at her.

Madeleine came over to me, "I'm glad I don't have a sister. It would be too annoying to look after them. Let's stick together, huh?" I nodded.

I looked back at the marsh and saw a crocodile. The crocodile lay motionless in the marshland with a mouth gaping posture. Its still body was basking in the sun. And the reptile predator's tough and scaly skin was absorbing the sun's strength. It looked like a still statue, but suddenly at a flashing speed, it crawled towards us, the prey. Before the prey could hardly see anything, the long snouts tried to snap Dyana's leg off. I briskly stabbed the crocodile's nose three times with a dagger that Jaide gave me while the other girls pulled Dyana free. When the crocodile gave up, we turned around. Dyana's leg was soaking with blood.

"we need to get you to a healer," Jaide pressed on as Dyana screamed. The length of the scream was what made my blood curdle the most. She was in so much pain.

Jaide picked her up and ran briskly, "We're going to save you, Dyana!"

We joined the chase, even though she didn't know where she was going. We had no idea where we were going. We just kept running. Until we found something. Darkness. Night had fallen. In that darkness, under a crumbling curtain of vines, laid the eggs. Without any detectable noise, the shells were pushed from the inside until they cracked and oozed clear liquid. No one witnessed the birth of the mambas, two feet in length. Nobody witnessed the snakes yawning, showing their black mouths and fangs. Nobody saw the dangerous poisons. They slithered in, and then I was bitten.

The pain took over a portion of my brain as if dealing with it was energy expenditure enough without the effort of new thoughts. It stole the part of me I most wanted to share with the others, my light and laughter, my generous heart. It was the sort of pain that burned as if some invisible flame were held against my skin. The emotions of loss are that way, right? Death, abandonment or betrayal, they all led here.

Jaide fired tons of arrows at the mambas, and Madeleine decapitated a couple.

"Are you alright?" Madeleine picked me up. I was trying so hard not to shriek with pain. It likely wouldn't kill me - the snake was just born, so the poisons likely hadn't developed to fatality. At least, I would hope for that.

"Wait, guys!" Soniya diverted our attention to a building. One of those inns that they have when you go past a town's borders. Stormholme!

While they dragged me over, my vision shifted between blurry and normal. Dyana was screaming so badly. It made me want to scream, too, as loud as I could. But that would double the pressure on them. I don't want to double it.

We found the castle easily enough after we wasted hours letting our wounds heal. A tower of rock amid the jolly green grass, a fine accompaniment to the gorgeous foliage.

They formed a stack and pushed me up and through a window. I was in someone's chambers. Not Kristyne's chambers. I found an escape to the halls and stole out into the darkened labyrinth drawing attention to the throne room, the centre. The ceiling was gaping like an empty void over my head, and the silvery slants of moonlight were piercing through the windows, casting an eerie cross-hatched spotlight on one of the bedrooms. Kristyne always loved moonlight. She was probably in that one. I gave the other rooms no more than a sideward glance to ensure that nobody was there, slipping past with no sound but the whisper of fabric and the slight scuff of a soft shoe on marble.

I peered through the peephole, and Kristyne was there. I opened the door, hushed her and whispered.

"Kristyne! Emannar and Varn are going to use you! I'm with Incognitae. We're here to take you home!" I whispered.

Kristyne frowned, "Oh, you mean the imprisonment? They already did that. Father found out and convinced them to free me. Speaking of which, everyone has been looking for you. Where have you been?" she asked me.

"I've been talking to Incognitae," I whispered.

"What's Incognitae?" she continued to ask questions.

"Bunch of girls like me who everyone hates. Varn's sisters are with me. They know what he's gonna do. They might have taken you out of the dungeons, but they're still going to use you," I persisted.

She shook her head, "I don't believe you, Annyte." What?

"Why not?"

"You're always making up dumb excuses so you can travel. Why should I believe you?" she was as air-headed as ever.

"Because they're all right outside! Why would they all be outside if this wasn't dangerous-" she hushed me.

"I hear footsteps. It's probably Varn. Get under the bed," she hurried me, and I slid under like grease.

Varn opened the door to look at her, "Well, this has been an eventful day. Never expected my mother to be gay, but here we are. We did good out there. They didn't suspect a thing."

"Your parents are getting a divorce, and you're thinking about yourself?" she asked.

"That's the fifth time my father has said that. Stephyn Tanner is the fifth man she's had an affair with. She always finds some way to wriggle out of it and hold on to her power. But believe me, I will never forgive my mother. When I am King, I will rob her of all her land and titles, like she robbed me of a mother. All I will need is a wife. Or a husband if they let me announce myself as not right. We'll just have to see," Varn left briskly.

I came out from under the bed, "What's been happening? I feel like I have missed a lot."

"To put it simply, Annyte, one of our parents, is going to die. And no, I'm not going with you because we need someone here to know which one," she cried with me.

"One of our parents? Which?" I demanded to know.

She looked at me, "One. Or both."

Auster Magnarok's Witanegemote once said, "Auster, you are a genius. Destined for greatness. Your wisdom is greater than we knew wisdom could be. And yet, you fail to focus on your Sissions. If you listen to them, you won't be alone anymore."

"Your sessions are too boring, too repetitive. You mean to tell me you aren't offering this to selected children from other Great Houses? You're not giving us hope, you're trapping us in a cage. You've been trapping us since the Stormholme Schism, perhaps earlier. We need to evolve as a society, and for that, we need to do away with people like you," Auster responded.

Kristyne:

My encounter with Annyte has made me decidedly aware of how little I can trust anyone in Stormholme, so I'm writing everything I see for the day down just so I can remember.

I woke up and chose a simple black dress, my face red and puffy from all the crying. Alizia was sent home yesterday, so I had to spend my time in the company of Priestess Ronayne.

"Another simple day today," she looked at me while we ate our gruel, "Don't expect much to happen." She looked at me, almost offended when I didn't respond, "What's the matter, Kristyne? You look like you've been crying all night. Did Varn do something? I swear, if he did something-" I banged on the table.

"I want to talk to John Borrell," I demanded.

"John Borrell's making his way back to Bernstaplen, I'm afraid. Simon dismissed him for his own safety. I'll be next, I tell you," she sighed.

"Please don't go without me," I begged.

"I'm not in control of that, Kristyne," she sighed again.

Two maids came in just before we finished cleaning the room, sweeping the floors and everything else. I don't think they actually looked at us once, except for when they delivered us our lunch, a three-course meal. Some kind of thick pottage, a fat slab of venison, a deceased boar soaked in all blood, salmon, pike, exotic carvings of exotic birds and some lemon cake. It may seem like a large list, but it was nothing compared to the banquet at tea time.

The maids cleared the table for us, and I grabbed one just before they left, "Can I speak with Auster Magnarok?" Ronayne dropped her holy book.

The maid smiled at me, "I will tell him to arrive shortly, my Lady." She walked away before Ronayne could tell her to stop.

"Talk? To Auster Magnarok? Have you lost your mind?" she insulted me.

"He won't hurt me if he cares to survive. And that is something he does care to do," I smiled at her. It relieved some of her anxiety, but she was still drumming her fingers along the table.

Another maid came back to us sometime after, "Lord Magnarok will see you, my Lady. But you must come to him alone." She escorted me there, despite Ronayne's protests.

He sat on a throne bathed in the blood of those who had fought for it and all the anger and wickedness in their hearts. His wife sat on a stool beside him too.

"Kristyne Pargion. You wanted to see me?" he didn't smile.

"I want to know what you're going to do to my parents," I kept my face straight. He couldn't break me.

"To be honest with you, if there is some kind of plot, I have no part in it. I haven't earned their trust yet. I will eventually. I shall make sure of it," he answered.

"Don't lie to me," I persisted.

"I wish I was lying to you, sweet child. I came into this role expecting hell. I suppose I have earned hell. To be quite frank, Emannar Woodgairrd has no reason to trust me. He doesn't. He just wanted to prove a point to your father," he elaborated.

"I don't believe you." He wasn't going to break me. He wasn't.

"My father almost disowned me, you know. Much like Dran Grimm disowned his own son. Want to know why? I killed lots and lots of girls. Young, pretty girls. Girls your age," he laughed.

"Why are you laughing?" I asked, full of anger.

"Because..." he continued, "I knew I shouldn't have killed all those pretty girls, but each one had been so deliciously sweet. I made their blood run until their flesh was ghostly and cold. Their deaths brought me such exquisite pleasure. Why? They were special to me. I had chosen them to die. They were the prettiest ones in the land. Then, I encountered the most beautiful girl I had ever seen," he looked at Lilyana and grinned sadistically, "I couldn't bring myself to kill her, so for the first time, I tried true conversation. And it worked. She bore me a son. She loves me. But my father scolded me when he found out I was wedding a peasant girl. He was brutal. He locked me away in a coffin for a month and a half while a Witanegemote read sermons to me idly. He beat my precious Lilyana. And he killed my son! He cut him open like he was skinning a pig. When the month and a half was over, I laughed. I punched my hand up to let them know that I lived, but no sound came out, and my limbs froze together. I could feel my heart beating. It was slow. It was cold. Over time, I felt another heartbeat. The heartbeat was in my palms. The heart I ripped out of my father's chest. Eventually, I found my darling again. Now I'm here, the happiest I've ever been. But their eyes see what I did. They remember. They will always remember," he rambled. I felt more like sleeping than crying now.

"I don't care. You're lying to me," I remained stable. He frowned.

"But I'm not. You know that. Don't you?" he looked at Lilyana, "My love, do I ever lie to you?"

Lilyana didn't look at him, "You have never lied to me, my love."

"And I will never," he smiled, satisfied, "Although I don't know much, there is a way for you to learn more. All the secrets are passed in Elizella's chambers. Maybe you can hide under her bed and see who comes around. But first, the banquet is starting any second now. I implore you, don't miss it. I hear they're feeding us plums stewed in rose-water tonight."

I hurried down to the banquet hall and sat down next to Priestess Ronayne.

"Did he hurt you?" she asked me.

"Do I look hurt?" I snapped back.

"He could have hurt you. He's a psychopath, I tell you," she assured me. They delivered us our food shortly.

A civet of hare, a quarter of a stag. Five stuffed turkeys, two loins of veal. Dishes covered with a Novak spice, sugar plums and pomegranate seeds. Two enormous pies for each person, the King's treat. A whole deer. A gosling. Three capons, six chickens, ten pigeons, and two rabbits. A stuffing made from a crispy veal, two pounds of fat, 26 eggs soaked in saffron and flavoured with cloves. A sturgeon cooked in parsley and one of Putrick Muberre's famed spices. A kid, two goslings, twelve chickens, twelve pigeons, seven rabbits, and two herons. A white and red jelly. Cream covered with fennel seeds, cream covering slices of cheese, and cream-covered strawberries. Plums stewed in rose-water, like Auster promised. Wines in vogue. Water in vogue. A feast!

I slipped out of the meal a bit early and hid under Elizella's bed, waiting for anyone to enter. The first group to come in was Elizella and councillor Francis Ashford.

"Can I see him?" Elizella begged Francis.

"I doubt His Grace will allow that, my Lady. With the news of the affair and divorce breaking out, everyone will be using their eyes as Stephyn returns. You will have to be rather secretive about it," Francis advised.

"They can't reprimand me if we're getting a divorce. I can see whoever I want now," she argued.

330

"But that is the thing. You're not divorced yet. Legally, you are still the Queen and the wife of Emannar Woodgairrd," he disagreed.

"I don't want to be anyone's wife anymore," she yelled, "I just want to be happy again!"

"It's not that simple, my Queen," he sighed.

"Why can't it be simple?" she cried.

"Believe me. I wish it was," Francis faked sympathy.

She looked at him with tears, "Get out. Send Stephyn in here when he arrives."

A horn had been blowing for a while now, and it was likely to signal Stephyn's arrival. They both left, and a few minutes later, Stephyn and Elizella came in. They waited for the sound of the door closing and then kissed.

"They know! They all know! Somebody told my wretch brother!" Elizella screamed.

"And somebody told your wretch sister, and I know who! Your goddamn father found out! He wants to use it against us! Who the hell did you tell?" Stephyn grabbed her violently.

"I didn't tell anyone, my love, I swear!" she yelled defensively.

"Then how did your father find out?" Stephyn spat on her.

"My father uses magic. He has for a long time. It's slowly decaying him, though. He'll be dead soon enough," she grinned, and they laughed together.

"Well, we better hope that he decays faster," he warned her and left the room. Eventually, Elizella did as well, and that's when I went back to my chambers.

Eventually, the horns sounded again, and Priestess Ronayne rushed back into my room.

"It's a miracle!" she shouted, "Daman's coming back to Bernstaplen! He's alive!"

'Marvion raised his chestnut brows at me, "There's no room for naivety in these times, Ebon. In a world with the deadly blades that we possess, we can't have a naïve swordsman. It would be suicide sending those men out on the field. You're just a monster hunter, you don't know how to fight a real man. So, I suggest you learn how to cut one open, or every league of our army will disintegrate in a matter of minutes.'

-Extract from an anonymous diary entry, confirmed to be during the Stormholme Schism.

Daman:

I was still tying the horses to posts when Damon started to recognise their faces.

"Howard Barrett," he pointed at Howard, "Fawkes Grimm. Aldo Brousseau. Where's my brother?" he asked. He hadn't seen me yet, so he probably thought that I was dead but didn't want it to be true. I walked over to the group, and then he spotted me, "Dearest brother!" We embraced, "How are you? Did the harsh Novak deserts treat you well?"

"It's good to be home," I told him, "But there were problems with the Novaks. They hate each other more than we realised. A chief we befriended, Balog Novak Gabor, he didn't make it."

"Sorry to hear it," Damon sighed, "Why do people find it so easy to get in bloody battles? I just want one victory. Against anyone. But they always ignore me. If I do slay someone, it never matters because they weren't going for me anyway. Wh-"

"What?"

"You're bleeding," he pointed at my wounds from the duel with Duskrem. Some of the cuts hadn't healed yet. They hurt like hell until we started our ride back, and then Aldo patched me up with some of his medical remedies.

"Only a cut. If it was going to kill me, I'd be dead," I assured him.

"Are you sure?"

"Certain." I was ignoring the slight sting. I had felt greater pain, "Who else is here? Is Dayron here?"

"Dayron's doing a session with Morgan right now. Talk to him later. The session is important, apparently," Damon told me.

"Yeah, probably teaching him how to be useless like all the other Witanegemotes," someone joked. It was Lawrence Malver, Damon's childhood friend. I never trusted him, but he had done a lot for my brother.

"Name one useless Witanegemote," Damon looked at him.

"You want a useless one? Try Putrick II of House Muberre. He hasn't even attended half of the sessions," Lawrence erupted into laughter.

"That is pretty funny. How did they accept a Witanegemote that lazy?" Damon laughed with him but stopped when he noticed my frown.

"You're a good brother, Damon, but your sense of humour is oddly childish," I admitted. That made him frown.

"We do have one problem," Damon confessed, "Storyteller Hickmere has caught pox. She is dying."

I remembered a story that Hickmere told me once when I was seven.

"Tell me a story," I asked her.

"No," she responded.

"It's your job to tell stories. You're a storyteller," I demanded a story.

"When the Gnolls were released to the world, the box they were kept in was opened. It was their door to the world. We kept hope not that the Gnolls would be killed but that the box would be woven into myths and legends to keep our children forever safe," she advised me.

"There are still Gnolls in the world," I told her.

"And there are still myths and legends being told," she responded, "They are the boots of valiant souls. Do you want to be a valiant soul, Daman?"

"Yes," my eyes twinkled, and she chuckled.

"All it takes is a valiant soul. Valiant souls end the armies and inspire men and women to listen to their hearts and take a stand. If you want to be a valiant soul, Daman, be one."

The candle she held flickered, briefly showing her face. There was no laughter in her eyes or a smile twitching at her lips. She looked skeletal. Deranged. Her eyes looked like lakes of ink, entangling themselves with the yellow of the flame to make her look like an exotic demon.

"I will be one," I assured her.

"Oh, Daman, you probably want me to give you an update on everything here," Damon brought me back to reality.

"What's been going on? How are Mother and Father?" I asked.

"That's what I didn't want to answer," Damon fell silent.

Lawrence spoke up, "Turns out that your dad had been beating your mum for years. Your mum went insane, killed your uncle, and took Minbury for herself. In response, your uncle Tyral took Minbury back, and the King exiled your dad. Your dad united with Tyral to make a treaty with the King, but it's not going so well. If they can't help your mum, then your parents will duel to the death."

What the hell?

"Where are my sisters?" I asked next.

"Kristyne was imprisoned but is free now, and Annyte's whereabouts are currently unknown," Damon spoke up. This was getting worse.

"We need to go to Stormholme! We need to stop this madness!" I was about to rush out, but someone grabbed me. I looked behind me, and it was Corren. My youngest brother. Only three. "Corren!" I picked him up and hugged him.

"Daman!" he shouted back.

"How are you?" I asked.

"Good!" he was so innocent, too pure for this cold, cold world.

Fawkes spoke up, "I'm not gonna lie, I'm loving this family reunion, but we need to decide what we're going to do next."

"I have an idea," Lawrence announced, "Damon, why don't we show them the surprise who turned up? She's Daman's age. Can't be problematic."

"Are you sure?" Damon looked afraid.

"Certain," Lawrence grinned.

"What surprise? Who is here?" I demanded to know.

"You'll see," Damon told me, "Buckley!"

The stableman came running over, "Yes, my Lord?"

"Find the girl. Bring her here," Damon ordered, and Buckley staggered inside the castle.

Lawrence looked at Fawkes, "You're that disowned Grimm child, right? What's it like for your relatives to not care about you?"

Fawkes was not amused, "You tell me. When did you last see your dad? When you were born?" That wiped the smile off of Lawrence's face.

"We have Aldo, too," Lawrence laughed, "Duke of Guillemin, huh? Interesting. Never heard of Guillemin before."

"It's a nation only for the refined. I doubt they'd let you in," Aldo chuckled.

Lawrence wanted to properly insult one of them, so he looked at Howard, "Howard Barrett. Deceased bride-to-be, correct? I'm sure it was a suicide." Erratically, Howard grabbed Lawrence's throat and put a dagger to it.

"You want to insult me, huh? Then you're asking to die," he warned and pushed Lawrence backwards.

"Daggers are no fun," Lawrence joked.

"Leave off them, Lawrence. I could make fun of your life for an eternity," I warned him.

Buckley came over eventually, "Sylvina Slait, my Lords."

I recognised this girl. Elizella's little sister. One of her greatest enemies, along with Dontin. Like them, she had a tall frame and a slender body. But this girl had blue eyes like the sea and long, wavy blonde hair. She looked like her mother.

"You're Daman, right?" she asked me. We shook hands, "I'm Sylvina."

"It's a pleasure."

"Why am I here?" she asked me.

"Apparently, you know how we can solve this," I answered.

"I don't know who told you that, but I can try to think of something," she took a moment to think and then looked back at me, "Maybe it would help if you could unite the Pargion children. If anyone can convince your mother to reason with your father, it's their children. Send some people to bring

Kristyne and Annyte back here, and send a raven to your parents. They won't deny their children." That was one of the best ideas I've ever heard.

"The Slaits aren't known for their brains. You have a rare intelligence," I told her.

"Dontin is smart. My sisters are idiots," she giggled.

"Well, how do we unite the Pargions?" I asked.

"First," Damon cut in, "Let's wait for Dayron to finish."

'Humans are born to be unique to each other. We specialise ourselves because we live in a society that is complex and has many unique tasks that need to be mastered for us to breathe each day. Only fools make the most unique ones societal outcasts. The intelligent, with our psychological aid, shall deduce how their talents may be an advantage to the greater world and shall learn to welcome them with love.

If you are an heir of an established Lord, the next Emannar Woodgairrd or Simon Pargion, however you feel as if you are an outcast in this Kingdom, know that you are specialised for a different place and function than the rest of your brothers and sisters. If you have your wits about you, then you will follow one of my fine Witanegemotes and unlock your talents to see what it is your master and to learn what skills you will need to preserve the development of your abilities.

So, will you join the Sission Group today, or will you walk away from this letter?'

-Letter from Supreme Witanegemote Gregory, sent to one child from every Great House, asking them to join the Sission Group.

Dayron:

I'm on a road. It stretches outward into the blue sky, as if it longs for oneness. Raindrops come down to bequeath a million sunlit crowns. It was as soothing as the cerulean sky above. Then I looked to the side - the scent of decay. Someone had died here.

I could see the body. Surrounded by fire and the blackest steel a human has ever seen. And the body was horror. Ghostly pale. Bluish lips. His eyes were closed, but he could not be less asleep. There were still tiny movements, a healthy glow to the skin. I can see how his flesh had departed. There was a gash against the monolithic structure before me. The pieces of metal around me must have swept him away, crushed him mercilessly against the monolith. Then I spotted something among the metal. Twenty more bodies, probably more. I looked at one. Clothes I had never seen. They looked advanced for the times. Blood flowed, thick and sluggish, from a slash across her gut, spilling out a nest of glistening grey snakes. A ticket in her hand - 'American Airlines Flight 11.'

A man next to her. Maggots, flecks of doughy white nestled within mangled flesh, feverishly squirming into hunks of gore. This man had an odd white hat and a long black beard than most men I knew. In his hand was an extraordinary contraption, with something that was begging to be pressed. I pressed it and watched a piece of metal fly into the woman's stomach. Interesting.

I looked to the side and saw a dying man, not quite dead but not quite alive. Whimpers. Cries for pain. I reached out to him. Grabbed his hand for support. Pulled him up. Then he sprouted a dagger from his palm and would have cut my abdomen open if he didn't turn to ashes with one touch on the forehead from Morgan.

"You probably want to know what caused this," he stated, "Through the door. Follow me." His soul transformed into a pixie-like state and a beam of yellow light made its way through the door of the monolith. I followed.

Inside the building was a desert. Deserts are part of the golden soul for those who love the big sky and the story of a resilient nature born to survive and thrive, or just a warm and expansive golden brown. And just like most deserts, nobody was here. I just walked, walked, walked...until I saw a sinkhole. I was unable to outrun it and fell in.

There is no wonderland at the end of a fall into a deep hole, especially an endless one. Only the tough climb back to the daylight, regardless of what broke and what hurt. "Breaking is fast. Recovery is slow. Remember that and watch how you go," the bards sing.

I awoke in a room. A lightless room, save for one bulb in a corner. I was on a wooden chair. I could see myself in the wall before me.

"Any questions?" Morgan's voice echoed through the room.

"What happened to those dead people? Was there an accident?" I asked.

"An accident? Good boy, you sound as clinical as their leaders were," Morgan chuckled.

I waited a couple of seconds before I heard a reply.

"These people died from ignorance. Because of their leaders' ignorance. Because of their own ignorance."

The wall before me changed to show another monolith, with smoke emanating from the top.

"How can you have a war on ignorance when war itself is ignorance? You've said that to me," I remembered.

"Good, you remember," his voice laughed, "I would have said it again otherwise. Imagine this happening to your house, Dayron. Imagine being in it as it was brutally destroyed because everything went wrong."

I imagined it. I didn't like what I imagined, "Why do I have to be in it?"

"Some people were in this building when it was destroyed. Remember something, Dayron. One day, you will not be able to breathe. One day, you will not be able to fight the pain. One day, you will not be able to help anyone. You won't talk. You won't laugh. You won't cry. You will never be angry or depressed, or happy again. One day you will lose your chance to save the Earth. One day you will never wake up again. One day you will be beyond repair. But you don't want to be sleeping your entire life, do you? If you don't take action, this will happen. As it did," Morgan lectured me.

"How did this happen? Stormholme doesn't look like this. This looks like a creation, not reality," I questioned.

"My boy, you have no idea," he sighed.

"Besides," I continued, "We must fight our past and never let it control us. You said so yourself."

"This is something we must fight. Otherwise, our past will continue to repeat itself. If our past repeats, we will never truly control our lives," he explained.

"I have never needed to know my past," I argued again.

"Incorrect," he exclaimed, and there was a soul-piercing shriek that shook the room apart. I fell to the ground again and looked up to see a large group of people. Several posters with a man's face - 'George W. Bush, second term!' Elegant clothes I could not recognise as being from my time. I looked at one man there. There is a way people can look dead in the eyes - like their soul is sleeping like they're disconnected from love. It is a 'social infection', as Morgan calls it. To see that in the man before me made me incredibly afraid. Everyone was worshipping this man. They worshipped a corpse of emotion. Why?

"You see these men?" Morgan asked me.

"I do," I replied simply.

"The man at the front speaks the language of money. He uses their power of love to strengthen his love of power," he explained.

"Sounds like the King," I observed.

"For these people, this man is the King," he sighed, "He pledges to be everything to them after the many wars and disasters. He pledges to honour the legacy of those who have fallen. But he fails to truly honour them. He fails to see justice. He barely knows what justice is, for god's sake! These disasters were caused by people. Evil people. He tries to ease their pain but never tries to throw the fist of justice. So, he fails."

"I disagree. Justice doesn't come easy. It takes time," I argue.

"No! This man never made a right move!" he spat.

"How can you know? He could be on the brink of justice. You can't know if you have made the right moves until you have the right outcome," I pointed out.

"Behind you, Dayron," the voice dissipated, and I looked behind me. A door had opened. I walked through to see an astral plane.

"Why am I here?" I could have counted a thousand stars in black space.

"Do you know what a terrorist is, Dayron?" he asked.

"No," I admitted.

"Imagine you are tidying a house by messing up the parts that were tidiest. Are you getting the job done?" he asked.

"No. It doesn't make sense. It makes the house even more untidy," I answered.

"Precisely. That is what the terrorist does," he explained.

"They make houses untidy?" I was confused.

Morgan chuckled, "No, no, that is not what a terrorist does. Instead of finding ways to bring comfort and order to places people are suffering using their ability to love, be logical and speak up, they create more chaos. They double the mess. All they do is make things worse for everyone. They aren't simply bad. They're idiotic."

"That sounds like The Mamba," I mentioned.

"We don't talk about The Mamba. The Mamba is not idiotic. He misuses his gifts, but not on a terrorist scale. The terrorist has a broken logic. The Mamba has none," he explained clearly.

Something appeared in the astral plane. A photo. A man, his wife and daughter.

"What is this?" I asked.

"A photo from before a disaster," he explained, "Not all terrorists are evil men. They're just caught up in the evil. It's inescapable. So they give in, and they lose everything."

"How can we stop innocent people from dying?" I asked.

"We cannot, Dayron. That is the sad truth," he sighed, "Now, what is a terrorist?"

"A terrorist," I summarised, "Is a man who does evil things. They believe they are doing what is right, and the cause may be just, but they carry it out in a manner that just causes unending chaos, and they never realise it. Sometimes, they aren't even evil men, just caught up in the madness."

"Correct," I could hear the sound of a quill scratching on paper, "This session is complete. You shall return to reality shortly."

In a couple of seconds, the astral plane became a vortex of black and white. It was like I had been sucked back into reality in my chair, my head soothed by a bowl of freshwater.

"It's time to wake up, Dayron," Morgan looked at me with a smile, "Damon wants you. Daman is back, and they have a plan."

I pulled my head out of the water and headed over to see my brothers.

Sylvina:

Reunions are always emotional when there is someone you love. An emotional reunion is told in the soul connection of eyes, in the sweet touch of fingers, in the strength of a long-anticipated hug. For that moment is the sweet release, the relief, the chance for joy to take centre stage and dance all night.

Daman. Dayron. Corren. Damon. The Pargions were uniting.

But they were not complete.

Suddenly, another stepped out from the shadows.

Xargaron's night has robbed us of the daytime colours. Ahead of me, Annyte and her friends are no more than silhouettes. I have only their fluid black outlines from which to guess their emotions. Right now, they are relaxed, and that can only mean good things, I suppose. It means that whatever is going on in their heads will not derail the plan, instead helping it a great bunch.

"Daman! Damon! Dayron!" Annyte cried, and they pulled themselves into a tight embrace together.

Daman held the embrace for a moment and then looked at Witanegemote Morgan, "Take Dayron to his chambers. We have business to discuss." He turned back to his sister.

"How are you, sister? Haven't seen you in a while. You've doubled in height!" he laughed.

I decided to speak up, "There is a prophecy that worshippers of some other God shall be the ones to end Xargaron. Perhaps I am looking at these worshippers. What God do you worship?"

"Dayron and I worship The Son," Daman joked, "It's a false religion but more believable than most."

"True," I laughed with him, "Alright, what's the plan? I assume you want to unite your parents before you enact your revenge because, in Stormholme, there are knights and ships by the thousand."

"Speak no more of revenge," Daman waved dismissively, "First, we must complete the Pargions. Who wants to handle Kristyne? Annyte?"

"I've already tried to save her, but she's stubborn. Maybe someone could come with me. Maybe Dayron can help?" she looked helpless.

"Remember Dayron's condition," Daman consoled her, "It's best if he continues his training. Perhaps your friends here can go with you again, and we'll send reinforcements if you need them. Not a lot though. We have greater priorities."

"Alright," Annyte looked disappointed.

"How about mum and dad? What do you think?" Damon asked Daman.

"Dad will be no problem. I doubt he's truly forgiven Emannar, so if we can get someone inside, he'll probably offer support with freeing Kristyne. But mum...perhaps we can make some kind of alliance," Daman suggested.

"Sounds like a plan," I agreed.

Damon looked at Lawrence, "Lawrence, summon Odo or Morgan if he's available. While he's with us, you take care of my little brother."

Lawrence looked annoyed, "What the hell, Damon! I could be doing so much more to help, and you want me to look after a child? I might as well be shining your shoes!"

Daman scowled, "Shut up and do what your Lord tells you to do."

Lawrence looked defeated, "Whatever." He walked off in a sulk to summon one of the two men.

"What are you going to do with them?" I asked.

Daman looked at his brother with approval, "Odo and Morgan are the wisest with words in Bernstaplen right now. If anyone can secure us some alliances, it is them."

"I understand," I smiled at him, and he smiled back.

Eventually, Lawrence returned with Odo Wyne beside him.

"I understand I have been requested?" Odo looked at them with boredom. Odo acted like everything was questionable, and no decision was ever logical to him. People like him are why I prefer the touch of nature.

"Odo, write a letter to Gwendys Wayne asking for an alliance. It is time to end this," Damon looked at him. It was the one time he said something with confidence.

"I shall work on it," he responded.

We waited for a while, remaining in silence (the family reunion was over) until he returned to us with a fully written letter in a half-hour (I suppose he was fond of his work?):

'Dear Gwendys Wayne,

You are either one woman, or you are not.

You are either your husband's wife, or you are not.

You are either the mother of your children, or you are not.

So which are you?

You can either band together with those who love you,

Or you can rebel in a riotous band.

Long-term peace and justice or long-term war and suffering.

Shake hands or shake fists,

Make friends or break wrists,

Sons in your arms or arrows in your arms.

You have the power to make your dreams come true,

You have the power to keep all that you love,

And end all you hate.

Yet you also have the power to make your fears come true,

And to lose all that you love,

And keep what you hate.

There comes a time when a rightful stand against tragedy,

Becomes paranoia and insanity.

Hate is addictive, and it changes the brain,

But love is addictive and ends all the pain.

This is why your children call you to love,

Dream your dream,

What you dream will be.

As ever, your eldest son,

Damon Pargion.'

Gwendys:

"Are you sure about this?" my adviser Kondrad stood by my side. I didn't even want him anymore. He was worthless. He was just a random crook who felt he was up to the task. Unfortunately, he was the only one I could get. He was overpriced and useless as hell.

"My sons are more gentle souls than they'll ever let on," I dismissed him, "Unlike their father, they understand what pride is. Daman is courageous, Damon is astute, and Dayron is wise. Corren too, will be a special soul."

"You gave birth to them," Kondrad looked at me stupidly, "This sounds like bias."

"Shut up, Kondrad," I spat on his eyebrow, "Some may think me bias, but gentle souls they are. If that is a sin, so be it. For now, get out of my sight. I don't need you anymore. Leave my land within 24 hours, or I'll castrate you."

He gulped, "Of course," and left to pack his things.

A knight came into the room, "My lady, the Pargions have been spotted by one of our archers. Come outside and prepare yourself. I can assure you that Simon Pargion is not with them."

"That would be all I need for a ruined day," I sighed.

I got myself dressed and headed downstairs. Just before my sons arrived, I took one last look at my outpost. It was more like a castle now - bold on the blue beyond, standing there as if conjured from the storybook I worked on as a girl. It was perfect, like Bernstaplen without anything that reminded me of him. I used to imagine unicorns in the courtyard, ents for foliage and knights galore because if those towers could exist, why not? Every stone would have been even and square as if those who built it were set on perfection, as if they loved what they made. Walls made to protect a community, to echo with laughter and be the shelter they needed.

It's time to get to business, though. Here they come.

Damon got off his horse and eyed me, "You look a bit older."

"You haven't seen me for weeks, and that is how you respond?" I scowled at him, but my children were laughing, so I decided to join in.

"Mum, don't fake laughter. We've already decided what's going to happen with you, and it's final," Daman looked at me sternly. He was always my least favourite.

"Fine then, tell me," I sighed.

"Let's explain in this way," Damon spoke up, "I speak, and you finish my sentences."

"Sure," I nod.

"The things keeping me stable are..." he stopped, waiting for me to answer.

"My correct point of view, some of my children and the chance to kill him," I smiled. The answer was so easy. I was stable anyway.

"The things that I hate are...," he continued to the next question.

"Everything about him," I scowled. I wanted to start crying at the thought but didn't want them to see my weakness.

"That's the problem," Daman sighed, "We're not choosing between parents. Either you forgive our father for what he did to you in his drunkenness, or you say goodbye. To all of us."

I grimaced, "All of you? Forever?"

"If that's what it's going to come to, then yes. As far as we're concerned, you're both in the wrong here," Daman answered. But...that's not acceptable...

"Sons, if I held this world in one hand and all of you in the other, I'd take you. I know not everything I do makes it look that way, but life is complicated, and it gets complicated as randomly as it gets so quickly. You are my own children, and though I love this world with every fibre of my being, you mean more. Don't let your clouded views of your father get in the-"

"Silence," Daman cut me off, "Don't try it. I wasn't joking." How dare he?

"Shut up, you ignorant child!" I snapped, "You have no idea what happened! You have been misguided by him! Don't let the devil take control!"

An arrow fired right past my throat. I looked back at them, and there he was. The three-year-old Corren Pargion had been taught how to fire a warning shot at his mother.

"As you can see, nobody is on your side, mother. It's time to give this up. This was years ago," Damon and Daman looked at me. I really was powerless...

"Fine. But I draw the line at a conversation with...him. I don't care how much it hurts," I finalised.

"Deal," I shook Damon's hand.

"It's time for us to go, Damon," Daman looked at his brother, but just before they made their way, I grabbed Damon's arm.

"No, wait! I haven't seen you in weeks! Stay a little while longer!" I begged. Daman nodded, and Damon smiled.

"Of course, mother," Damon looked at me.

I welcomed them in for a night of food and entertainment, delight and celebration. What isn't there to celebrate? Children have been reunited with their mother!

It is a joyous day!

'Sometimes, emotionally, it can feel as if there is a sword to your throat. But still, must you think of the world around you? I know how it can feel in your heart. I can sense the invisible arm reaching in and squeezing in. I know the pain you bare. But still, must you pray for joy, even for those who remain oblivious or ignorant to your suffering? Your happiness is mine; I feel the same. I know how much that hand

hurts you. But I don't cry, no, I don't move away. I embrace it. The pain, it gives me a sense of what nobility is.

Learn to be noble. Be noble, take your fears head-on and see how victory comes so swiftly to you.'

-Dialogue from Saede Tanner to her daughter Gwendys Wayne.

Dontin:

"Are you ready?" I asked Tyral.

"Ready," he assured me.

We were ready to go. A legion of Emannar's most idle knights at our humble side, it was time.

We were going to strike a deal with Bernstaplen.

We marched in, horns at the ready, making an entrance as grand as a tyrant, and awaited a response.

There was no response.

There was no response?

"Charge!" Tyral yelled like a toddler, and they broke it down.

There was no response.

There was no response?

Were we alone?

We were.

And it was perfect! The fortress was perfect! There was no dirt, no horses, no people. From the air, it was identical to a smithy's reference drawings, fine blades on a piece of paper. There were chambers and stables, barracks and dungeons galore. A ghost town. A ghost town we could make good use of.

"Nobody is here, I'm certain of it," I told Tyral.

"So that's it then? No fights? No politics? We just get in, and nobody's here?"

"Precisely. I thought this would be far longer than it turned out to be," I sighed.

"I have an idea," he smiled.

"Speak it," I looked at him.

"Let's take this fort for ourselves. Damon probably wants to find Simon, so he's going to attack Stormholme. He can't do that without his castle," he laughed. This was the smartest thing the boy had ever said.

"Wise," I looked at him with pride, "If you expect war, your people will demand a speech. Get up to the keep, now."

Eventually, he made it up there and looked upon his knights with the same pride that I felt when I watched him there.

"Soldiers," he began, "These are dark times. You are about to embark upon a great war. A brutal clash of houses, toward which we have striven many a week. The eyes of the world are upon you. The hope and prayers of all go with you. In the company of our brave allies all across the kingdom, and our brothers in other kingdoms if truly necessary, you will bring about the destruction of a corrupt and misguided ideal, the elimination of all who oppose your great King Emannar Woodgairrd, and security for ourselves in a deadly, deadly world. This will not be an easy task. Despite their corrupt and misguided views, the enemy is well-trained. Well-equipped.

Battle-hardened. She will fight savagely, without morals. But this is the year 2020! Much has happened since the great King Emannar Woodgairrd took the throne. We have inflicted upon many threats great defeats in open battle, man-to-man. Our line of navy defence has seriously reduced their strength on the seas and their capacity to wage war on the ground. Our many fortresses have given us an overwhelming superiority in weapons and manpower and placed at our disposal great reserves of trained fighting men like yourselves. The tide shall never turn! The free men of the Kingdom will march together to victory! I have full confidence in you. I have full confidence in your courage, your devotion to duty and your skill in battle. We shall accept nothing less than full victory!"

"But who says that our war ends with Gwendys Wayne?" he continued, crowds chanting proudly, "We have been swayed from side to side countless times by those careful of our success, our safety in numbers, our lack of treachery. But I assure you, I do not desire to live to distrust my faithful and loving followers. Let the damn King fear! I have always maintained a spirit. I have placed my foremost strength and safeguard in the loyal hearts and wills of my men, and therefore I come, not as your leader but as one of you! I shall be there, in the midst and the heat of the battle, and live and die amongst you all. I shall lay down for whatever god there is, and for my Kingdom, and for my house, and for my people, and for my honour and my blood, no matter how damaged it has become. I know I am a boy. I know I am a weak and feeble boy, but I have the soul of

Emannar Woodgairrd and the wisdom of the Supreme Witanegemote and believe me when I say that when Gwendys, or Emannar, or anyone dares to reprimand me for my beliefs and my success, I myself will take up arms against them. I will be your general. I will be their judge. I will be the prize-giver for every one of your achievements. I will bless the living and honour the dead. I know already, for your work, you have deserved lands and titles and crowns, and your debts shall be paid. In the meantime, we must plead for one last war to end it all. By your obedience to my general Dontin and I, by your conduct in the barracks, by your valour and prowess in the field, we shall, in due time, have a victory for the history books over these enemies of our world, our kingdom, and our people. So, good luck! And let us beseech the blessing of whatever Almighty God there is upon this great undertaking."

Tyral took one last breath before he concluded, "And remember, be noble!"

Kristyne:

I sat down at my seat to watch the latest council meeting.

This was the first court session I had been able to attend since my father's return to Stormholme, so I could only look about nervously as I awaited their next moves. It was my father against my family, which I would not agree to. I could recognise the councillors entering in scrambled groups. Supreme Witanegemote Gregory was seated alone at the council table, seemingly asleep, as Lord Tobas hurried into the hall and Francis Ashford came shortly after with a cynical grin, chatting amiably with Kase and Styve Woodgairrd. Eventually, an announcer came out.

"All hail His Grace, Emannar of House Woodgairrd, First of his Name. All hail his Queen, Elizella of House Slait," he boomed.

Karron Wull, commander of the King's guard, brought in all of his men. Stephyn Tanner escorted the Queen while Auster Magnarok and his wife walked beside Emannar, and they all took their seats. Everyone was wearing their traditional royal garbs - they looked like they always did.

"It is a king's duty to punish the disloyal and reward the rest. Ashford, read the list," Emannar announced.

Francis trembled as he pulled out the list. He cleared his throat and read a list of names, "Styve Woodgairrd, his wife, his sole daughter. Kase Woodgairrd, his wife. Lord Stephyn Tanner. Lord Karron Wull. Lord Simon Pargion, his wife. Lord

Dontin Slait. Jaze Wyne. Damon Pargion, his brothers and sisters, save for Kristyne Pargion..." the list went on. All of these people would be given either rewards or punishments. I was just glad that I wasn't on the list. Francis eventually finished, rolled up the list and mentioned the first matter, "Firstly, we must decide how to punish Stephyn Tanner, sire, for his failure in delivering Sylvina Slait to us. It is the wish of His Grace that Stephyn Tanner be imprisoned swiftly and severely, to be reprimanded for his actions and undergo a slow period of reformation. So the King has wished, with the consent of the council."

Stephyn Tanner got to his knees, "My King, please! Do not do this!" Emannar just waved his palm dismissively, and two members of the King's guard dragged him out as he pleaded for his life.

Francis shook his head and chose to continue, "It is also the wish of His Grace that, as a result of the recent events, Squire Rudd Tymbrenn takes Stephyn Tanner's place on the King's guard. We now request that the Squire come forward to receive his royal plate." Rudd Tymbrenn came forward, looking as smug as a gang leader, and he knelt before Karron as he was given the royal plate. It was just a shoulder-pad with the Woodgairrd insignia.

Francis waited for Rudd to return to his seat and concluded, "Lastly, it is the wish of His Grace that we reveal the plan of the council regarding the recent rebellion of Gwendys Wayne. It has been brought to our attention through ravens that Dontin Slait and Tyral Wayne have been able to claim Bernstaplen without bloodshed, which means that Damon Pargion and his siblings have likely attempted to forge an alliance with Lady Wayne. Simon Pargion shall now be sent to Bernstaplen, supported by several legions of knights, where he shall remain until his children return. We shall give them the choice - submit to His Grace, or die."

There was a collective shudder across the hall.

"If anyone in this hall has other matters to set before the council, speak now or hold your silence," he wrapped up.

"Your Grace," I called out. I rose from my seat and knelt before the King.

"Kristyne," Emannar nodded, "Do you have some business for us?"

"Your Grace, I beg for mercy for my family, even my mother, Gwendys Wayne," I spoke up, on the verge of tears.

"Gwendys Wayne is very much a traitor, Kristyne," he responded, "She has committed unspeakable acts of treason against us."

"I know my mother must be punished. All I want is mercy. I know she must regret what she did. She never intended to offend you, Your Grace. This is just a squabble between my parents taken to the extreme, not a crime against the King. I beg you, mercy."

"Treason is treason," Gregory spoke up.

"And squabbles are squabbles," Auster countered. Out of all of these men, why did the insane one have to support me?

"If Gwendys Wayne confesses her crimes before this council, we shall know that she repents. However, any further 'squabbles' of this extremity and we shall rule with an iron fist," Emannar concluded.

"Your Grace, you do me a kindness," I smiled.

"I know I do," he smiled back, "But you must ensure that there is a confession! I will not accept anything else."

"I know you will not, Your Grace," I smiled more, "I know you will not accept anything but confession. And she shall confess. Thank you."

'The body of Lady Mahald Gwenhevare was found in the middle of the village of Basindale, in her underwear. After Ebon Pargion examined the body and searched her house, he found that she had likely died from hypothermia and was pregnant (the unborn baby, of course, had died with her). Samples of the mind-controlling potion Heartache were found at the scene, and Ebon discovered that the potion had been taken by her lover Umfrey, a new recruit for the Occult terrorists. Umfrey directed Ebon to the Occultists and slaughtered them. How did Ebon deal with the case? He killed Umfrey the same way.'

-Report from a now-deceased knight, Sir Rand.

Byrron:

"The air is getting a bit staler," Garvy Oakley pointed out.

"It's always been hardest to breathe when you're this far away from any fort. For God's sake, out of all the places, why set up camp in the south-east? Because it's the furthest away from Bernstaplen?" Dirron Rygert observed.

"I still can't believe the King wants us to do this. He's lying to our people, and besides, we'll be against the finest knights of Houses Pargion and Wayne. Do we even have a chance, commander?" Duran Durron asked Karron.

"I don't believe in chance, Duran. I know that cooperation equals survival and that death leads to absolution," Karron mused.

"Well, with all due respect, commander, strategically, it doesn't make any sense for all of us to come out of here alive. If I were you, I'd be targeting their weaknesses instead of rushing headfirst. I know you see it as honourable, but..." my brother Briden questioned Karron's methods.

"I'm not sending one or two men to die alone. I value your life more than weakening the lives of the opponents," Karron countered.

"Rushing headfirst is going to cause trouble for us, commander," Briden persisted.

"As expected. When you ask for trouble, you should not be surprised when it finds you," he argued.

"Trouble would find us either way, sir," I spoke up.

"Dang, this is a real mess we've gotten ourselves into, huh?" Garvy joked, and we laughed collectively, except for Karron.

"Your sense of humour is improving, Sir Oakley," Karron observed.

"We need humour in these times. It's not like the King really cares about our fates," Garvy shrugged.

"What do you mean?" Karron asked.

"We get sent to minor battles on a damn daily basis," I looked down, "A member of the King's Guard gets replaced every year. We're just overblown knights, commander. Equally powerful. Equally expendable."

"Expendable? Not to me," Karron smiled, "It's time to go. Charge!"

Suddenly, the carriage door was thrust open like an arrow being freed from the bow, and Karron's war cry queued us for battle.

Sickly blows in sickly dare came to the blades that made cuts in skulls and made bruised blackening skin bleed. For this was combat, bloody and primitive in all the worst ways, something humans can inflict as well as they endure. Each of us stood upon that hallowed ground, the defenders and attackers the same, fighting for survival each in our own way. Time ticked by as time does, neither accelerating nor hesitating, for the allotted moment when combat would commence. And though a watching bard would find noble intent in either battalion, the reality is always pain and excruciating deaths of shrieking souls, of hell made at the hand of man.

I let the bloody lives of three men die at my bloody hands as I turned to Briden, "This ought to be fun. We're bound to die here."

"If we die, I told you so," he joked, and we laughed together.

I watched him quickly fire two brisk arrows at some ballistas Gwendys stole and watched them collapse with agony. But there was no time to admire his handiwork - a brute was coming for me. I had no time to take in the details of his appearance. I just stuck my sword in his fat, bald head and waited for Briden to pierce his iris with an arrow. Eventually, Karron and Garvy broke a man-sized hole in the gates, and we were in.

I definitely killed at least three more men when I heard the voice of Daman Pargion, "The King's guard! Invaders!" Damn right.

We had now all made it through the gatehouse, and the forest of bodies told me that we were occupying the entrance. There was no escape. Now for the barracks.

Fortunately for us, barely anyone occupied the barracks. I supposed that Gwendys was trying to escort her children to safety, except for perhaps Damon and Daman, who may die today. We massacred a couple of men protecting the maids and stableboys. I refused to kill them despite Karron's wishes. I would never kill an innocent.

Speaking of Damon, he was holding a ward for the sickly with four other guards. Gwendys was either unprepared or keeping boyguards for her own protection over the sickly. I expected some kind of fight to be upheld, but after the first three guards were swiftly executed by Briden and I, Damon retreated. He could not retreat forever.

According to Karron, Garvy, Dirron and Duran, they took the courtyard with ease as well. This surprise attack was working well. Too well. What did that woman have planned for us? As I advanced towards the inner sector of the outpost, a man pinned me to the ground and stabbed both of my shoulders with a dagger. I thought I was done until Garvy weakened his legs, deflected an arrow from someone's crossbow and opened the assailant's chest to the cold air.

"Good tactic, though," Garvy observed, "I should try that." He spotted a random archer a couple of steps away and pinned him to the ground, delivering a flurry of dagger strikes to the neck and letting the timid archer bleed out. He came back to me, "Gonna be alright?"

"I've survived worse. I'll be fine," I assured him.

After a large amount of deaths, none on our side, we captured the inner gate. We were nearing the keep, Gwendys's last line.

I despise death. Death is a tragedy for the young and a rite of passage for the old, and so brings different kinds of mourning. Don't they say that none of us will leave this world alive? For my part, I intend to leave the biggest damn footprint I can. Maybe my daughter's footprint will be next to mine, double the size, and we'll walk together. I'd like that.

"Vikarin!" a boy called out. I turned to see Daman Pargion.

"Daman. I don't want to kill you, son. I just have to collect her. It's my duty," I explained.

"You have no duty, just like you have no honour," he spat.

"I don't want to kill you, son, but I will if I have to," I repeated. He drew his sword. Damn it.

He fired two quick jabs to my body, but I parried both with ease and fired counter-strikes. He took a moment to grab his shoulder in pain. He was weak. With my dagger, I cut across his chest and tried to knock him out with the hilt of my rapier. It was unsuccessful. I tried to use Garvy's technique, pinning Daman to the ground and attacking him in a flurry with daggers. I made sure not to hit the bad shoulder. He managed to free himself eventually, and I parried his next attack again, sticking the point of my rapier into his gut. When I pulled it out, he tried to strike me again, which I sidestepped and countered, disarming him.

"I'm not going to kill you, Daman!" I exclaimed for the last time.

"You're going to have to!" he cried, trying to fistfight me. I swept my sword at his legs and made him trip, then punched the back of his head with my right hand to try to knock him out again.

"No!" he persisted and got up again. He tried to pry my sword from my hands. I punched his gut with my free hand and left my sword to lay in his right forearm. He shrieked with pain and fell, and I swear, I was about to decapitate him when I saw Sylvina.

"Byrron!" she cried, "Stop!" I lowered my sword.

"Get out of here, child. You've lost," I told Daman. He spat at me, got up and walked away, with Sylvina tending to his arm, "Sylvina! Where the hell is she? Tell me!"

"I'm not letting you kill her, Byrron!" Sylvina stood before me.

"I don't have a choice!" I shouted back. I was done for today.

But I wasn't, was I? Because Gwendys had anticipated this. And as I heard the chants of many a corrupted man outside the outpost, I realised that we had been outwitted.

We were surrounded.

Gwendys:

It was time. They were here. It was all coming together. I had effectively used my greatest weapon. Chaos.

Chaos brings order when it is infused with love. Then it becomes as orderly as nature. Everything is arranged but fully free, every choice available. Chaos and fear is the problem or order kept by fear that always becomes chaos in the end. So how do you handle the chaos? I think I've cracked it. You need to bring in that chaos slowly, responsibly, a taste at a time, allowing a chosen few to reorientate and crushing the rest. All at once, it is cruelty, for it takes time to learn to change. When a population is deskilled, some will re-skill faster than others, so you select the fastest ones and leave the rest to drown in the dust. The fear dynamic is killing us before we know we're going to die. We need to climb the ladder with caution. It's hard, but the alternative is far worse and far more fun.

The ground glistened like rain had fallen, but rain was not the liquid resting there, not clear but red. The men who died, my pawns, served a greater cause than they knew. I was just considering the numbers, not their skill. Their skill didn't matter. We were going to win regardless. How many had fallen? How many were doing well? That was all I cared about.

"Mother!" I heard and found Damon behind me.

"Yes?"

"You expected this?" he questioned.

"Yes," I nodded. It was good for my son to see my wisdom.

"Please, mother, I know you barely care but don't kill the King's Guard," he pleaded, "They're innocent. They have no choice but to be the King's slaves. Do whatever else you want with them, but don't kill them."

"Damon, these men have committed many an atrocity against everyone in the Kingdom, and, more importantly, Simon favoured them, especially Karron. I have no reason to let them live," I dismissed him.

"Mother...no!" Damon broke, "Don't you see? You're letting your hatred surpass your brain! We might kill one or two of them, but we're going to lose! I'm getting everyone out of here. You tried to get us killed. I'm not dying for you."

"You can't leave," I smiled, "Dontin and Tyral took Bernstaplen while you were here. Morgan saw it in a vision."

"What?" he gasped, "So you've condemned us, then?"

"No, because I'm going to win," I grinned. Damon was about to say something but gave up and walked off. "Where the hell are you going?"

"Away from you," he sighed, "Damn you." Did he just?

"While you're out, summon Priest Narisetti," I instructed him. He scowled, and I heard the door close.

Moments later, Priest Narisetti arrived.

"My lady," he bowed, "What do you request of me?"

"I request a prayer, Narisetti," I looked down at him.

"May I rise?" he looked up like a lost puppy.

"You may rise," I nodded, and he rose. He turned his head skyward, whispering to the wind:

"Of course, there is Rakokh, but it would be better luck to pray to Roxlana, the Goddess of Battle," he spoke first.

"I thought Dohraura was the Goddess of Battle. That's what Ronayne told me."

"Ronayne was wrong," he scowled, "Now, let us pray:

Roxlana, holiest Goddess,

Help us to follow your ways,

Your ways that are victory,

We shall be grateful for our triumph,

We are humbled by your gifts,

We only move our lips in good prayer,

We open our minds to your wisdom,

We understand that you are divine and to be cherished,

We will only serve your power,

We shall work every day to bring your dreams to the world,

We shall revive your children,

We shall treat the natural world as you wish,

Holiest goddess, the keeper of our souls,

The One in Which we Trust.

Amen."

With that, he pulled his cloak around himself tighter to stave off the keen wind. Though spring was coming, the bitter wind still blew. It was times like this I wished for thicker skin, but Narisetti's blessings had gotten me the skin of paper.

"Thank you, Narisetti. You are dismissed," I turned back to the keep, and he walked away.

Let's look at the battle scene again.

Oh my god.

He's here.

I didn't plan for this.

I could not comprehend the man I saw before me, fighting alongside a new legion of knights I had never seen before, with the size of double mine.

He was trying to kill me.

Emannar Woodgairrd wants to kill me himself.

What have I done?

'There is no true remedy for your injuries, I tell you. For some, they may desire Worm Moss. Some may need Heartache to avoid the seething pain. Some just want hugs, affection, laughter and support for the pain to fade away over time. If you can't be emotionally or physically well, you may as well be dead until you are.'

-Sermon from Priest Narisetti.

Daman:

I was bleeding out. Sylvina had treated me to some medicinal herbs, but it would not be enough. I was going to die alone. Mother wouldn't be here. Father wouldn't be here. None of my brothers or sisters. Not Howard, Aldo or Fawkes, who are helping Annyte's crew. Just Sylvina and probably Morgan. They would be the ones at my deathbed.

"Morgan's found some Worm Moss in the orchards. It should act as a bit of a painkiller for you," Sylvina told me.

"Thank you for your help, Sylvina," I looked at her with sincerity.

"I have no interest in watching the battle. I prefer plants," she smiled.

Eventually, Morgan arrived with the Worm Moss. He dabbled it on my chest wound and the pain seared for a moment before dissipating into nothingness.

"How does it feel?" he asked.

"It is not my flesh wounds that concern me," I responded, "It's the injury to the brain that concerns me. My mother has changed everything. I see the world in a different way. I don't trust anyone. Not even my own family."

"I see," he sighed.

"Tell me something, Morgan. Why does my father hate me? He's never called me his són," I looked at him.

"I'm under oath, Daman. I can't tell you." He sighed again, but more sternly this time.

"Then give me an idea, or I'm done with this war," I spat. I'm getting an answer today, whether he will give it to me or not.

He gave up, "Alright. There was an... event. Kept hidden by the history books. You are biologically Simon's son, but there was a... technicality. Complicated things. Not only for you but for every child born the same year."

"Not good enough, Morgan."

"It's the best I can do, Daman," he resigned.

"What would you suggest I do next?" I changed the subject. It was pointless.

"One cannot teach someone the journey when they are at the finish line," he advised me, "The war will be done within...three days, I'd expect."

"It will?"

"It will. This is the climax. For you see, Emannar has been spotted at the gates. Either Gwendys or Emannar will die today, and it will begin the end of the battle," he explained.

"Damn it. My mother is going to die, isn't she? She has no chance against the King! He has everyone! Why can't my father just try to talk to her? It would work eventually!" I screamed.

"It wouldn't. Your mother needs help. She's insane," he countered, "They say we try to exchange beauty for wisdom as we age, and so perhaps that is a root cause of insanity. Not all wisdom is good wisdom, especially when some minds cannot handle it efficiently. In a philosophically-poor Kingdom, we lack what we need to use our wisdom, so we cling to the ephemeral. We stick to what we want to do, not what we should do. 'Tis one of the grandest flaws of humanity, Daman."

"I remember my grandfather," I reminisced, "He would remind me how little I can see with my eyes. How much I could see with my heart. He would say that all the eyes can tell you is a result of what happened, never the reason, the intention, the deep emotions swimming below. "It is only with the heart," he said, "that we can see pain, see the sadness that dwells beneath anger." Perhaps when the heart is our eyes, our eyes show love, and we feel connected within, healed, able to walk with compassion."

Morgan tipped back his round head and chuckled. I looked at him with surprise. My memories weren't funny. "What the hell are you laughing about?" I asked.

"Well, it's ridiculous. You hate your father, but you love the one who truly made your father who he is. Did you never know Ebon Pargion?" he asked me.

"I knew him for ten years. He was a good man. But nothing like my father," I answered.

"Daman, tell me about a time you were happy with your father," he instructed me.

"I've never had a happy moment. He despises speaking with me," I told him.

"Daman, you bold, wonderful, stupid boy. Good things don't always feel good because we don't realise how good they truly are. When it doesn't feel good, it doesn't mean that something is wrong, just that we don't understand it fully. I don't know how angry Simon makes you. Only you do. But these feelings sprout from envy, jealousy, greed, and all of those emotions. We all have them, and they're useful. They let us know when we're on the wrong path. So, determine this: what is the right path for you to take?" he advised me.

"The truth is, Morgan," I told him, "I have absolutely no idea."

Dayron:

She had one. She kept it for me like a cairn. I didn't need anyone anymore. I could do it myself. It was lying right there for me, after all. Nobody was watching. I let my gryphon, Grey, fly freely that morning. He had grown up, and he was too big for my hand or my shoulder. But he would return.

It was time to dive into my next Sission.

Sission. Is that a good word for it? It's just something that came to my mind over time.

I dived in.

It was night. The night expanded as black angel wings do, protecting the earth as she dreams, hugging the stars like a mother to her newborn, making the most innocent of trees tower like colossi as they bathed in the shadows. They were forming the path, the long and winding path. All I could do was follow.

There was a structure in the distance. Is that a building? A circle of neon red encased it. Was it safe? I didn't care to know. Careless rain had formed puddles in proximity, and rain mimics evil. A distant ringing. An unbearable ringing. Eventually, though, it all ended with a single beep.

The raging fires. The sizzle of the fires. Some fascinating creation had caught fire. The death of beauty. Fires have always been societal impurities. One moment life is there, sprawling around with security. The next, there are loud noises, acrid smells and pain that you may or may not recover from. I watched Jaze's horse get struck down by a flaming arrow one time. It always comes as a shock, something the stories and the parents can never truly tell you. It is looking without seeing - emotional blindness.

The fire had torn open a hole in the pathway. A shortcut through the niceties of nature. I took it.

A billion verdant wands of pine waved in the arboreal air; this place was magical, so magical. You could feel it from core to fingertips. From the rich brown earthen hues of the forest ground to the sweetness of the pitch-black sky, the forest is a three-dimensional wonderland for the eyes of those who are willing to absorb the light like they're photosynthesising.

It's a shame there's so much fog.

Then I see the building. A stretched-out row of people wearing clothes I've never seen before. At the front, a man wears eye-patches on both pupils, with rectangles over his ears and between the patches. His shirt, and his trousers too, were blacker than the banners of House Grimm.

I could walk through them like a spectre.

Instantly, I was blinded by a mesmerising flurry of lights. What colour were they? Were they blue? Were they green? Pink? All of the above? I could feel my eyes deteriorating like flesh over hundreds of years, and it wasn't just my eyes burning away - my whole body felt like it had passed the gates of hell.

And my ears, my ears now knew death. It sounded like the end of some kind of song. It was like The Father had composed it. When I was in that pit of multicoloured mayhem, surrounded by drunkards, drug addicts and vagabonds, and the guitars were thumping so hard my bones were vibrating like they were on fire, I could embody my anger, my fear, my frustration, and feel it diffuse out of my body, spreading out in waves. My head went, my arms went, and I sweated like I was still riding a horse. The music was nothing like I had ever heard. It was gorgeous.

Then it changed.

It was something else.

Just one guitar.

'The cuts on my palms beg for your embrace

We bound our destinies, damned the world's jests

Ruptured my soul, pumped it full with grace

Then crying, screaming, whispering last requests

When I wake, I see no angel by my side

Deities die as my soul is purged

No kiss could ever circumvent my crimes

A deceased flame of a passion that once burned

The Lord, I will follow through the fire

To find you drowning one piece at a time

Your heart getting colder to desire

Her lingering scent, bitter sage, weaker thyme

When I wake, I see no angel by my side

Deities die as my soul is purged

No kiss could ever circumvent my crimes

A deceased flame of a passion that once burned

Who can ever know if fate will make me whole?

Or if by some cruel trick you will never come home

My full remorse for my despicable role

Please cast my sins aside so we can see our children grow

When I wake, I see no angel by my side

Deities die as my soul is purged

No kiss could ever circumvent my crimes

A deceased flame of a passion that once burned.'

I knew the voice.

It was John Borrell's voice.

Why was he here?

Everything flashed as some strangers collided with me.

They dropped something.

As I exited the Sission, it was in my hand.

It came with me.

A device. Words sprawled out across the bottom. I pressed a shape with my finger. A song started playing from some buds the same shape as my ears. I put the buds in my ears and lived the mellifluous sound.

I put it in my pocket and walked away.

'You've been alone for a while, Dontin. I know it. You've been trespassing on uncharted grounds for too long. I know you've been crying for help. The thing you've never understood, Dontin, is that if you want to be a warrior, an explorer, a discoverer, you can't rely on others for aid or advice. If anyone tries to, they'll make your job too easy for you. It's better to be in the dark than covered by a false light when you're trying to navigate the stars and develop your instincts. What I can say is this: if someone offers to join you, accept it, but don't take their words to heart. If the right person comes to seek an equal destination, keep them closer than the others, but never let them intercept your soul. The important thing is to ride on, always seeking what makes you stronger.'

-Dialogue from Arvin Slait to Dontin Slait.

Dontin:

Jaron Carner had gone ahead to scout for any Pargion men, and Tyral was collecting a raven, bringing me the word of those around. "I can see banners," Tyral told me, "Yellow banners. I think I see a snake."

Jaze looked at me, "Your sister?"

"Worse," I frowned, "My father."

"Oh dear," Jaze shared my frown. The Slaits truly were the worst of the worst, weren't they?

"Shall I tell the troops to get ready, just in case?" Jaze asked me.

"He won't be a problem today. Killing us will cost him too much," I spat.

Jaron Carner opened the gates. The first men to come through were my uncle Drevyn and his sons Manrel and Dallar. Drevyn's life was a tragedy. He was married to a peasant girl, Palina Oattwright, and they had two sons. When Arvin found out, he declared war. Drevyn only conceded when Arvin sent assassins to Palina's door. His oath now condemns him to servitude until death.

"Uncle Drevyn," I greeted him.

Drevyn lifted his visor, "Dontin," he looked at me with surprise, "You have sided with the Pargions?"

"They weren't here when we came, so we took it," I grinned.

"I can see Jaze Wyne and Tyral Wayne. You're one of the outcasts?" he looked at me with uncertainty.

"They are but acquaintances, friends of mine. Who they are is of no importance to me," I shrugged.

Drevyn sighed, "This might be the most friends you've ever had."

I ignored his statement, "Where the hell is Arvin?"

"Arvin wanted me to strike a deal with the Pargions and send Damon to him to secure it. He's been hiding in a little camp he forced us to construct."

"I'm sure he thinks he's safe there. Take me there. Just me," I laughed.

"As you say," he nodded. I mounted Drevyn's horse, and he rode me to my father.

"How are my cousins?" I asked.

"Still trying to best each other," he laughed.

"People never change," I chuckled.

Drevyn wasn't lying when he called it a little camp. I doubt an estimate of thirty men would be far off. A couple of squires camped out in the open, but the main knights like Drevyn cowered in 5 tents, and Arvin had made himself a tent the size of a commoner house. This was a camp for Arvin's vision of men.

I spoke to Drevyn while I waited for Arvin, "Arvin?"

"He's coming, Dontin."

"My men are hungry. I desire that you go back to them with some meat and ale. We haven't eaten a hearty meal in quite some time," I told him. Drevyn left the tent to carry this out, and there was my father.

Arvin Slait. Lord Arvin Slait. Five-time reject for the role of High Earl. 57 years of Arvin Slait, yet he fought like there had been 22. He was fairly tall, taller than me by a long shot, with shoulders so broad they looked like a child's drawing of a knight. His thin arms exuded muscle, while his hair was long, probably the same length as Elizella's. He never shaved his hair, but his lips and chin had been shaved a good few times. His eyes were the same as all of us, a devilish brown.

"My father. What a pleasure to see you," I bowed.

Arvin sighed, "So you're alive."

"My heart does beat so," I grinned, "Sorry to disappoint you. I know it's a lot of work acting like you care about your own men."

"It is when my son is claiming an empty castle," he replied, "You make the Slaits look like fools."

"The Slaits were already fools," I answered.

"Your sisters have done more manly deeds than you."

"By your definition, yes. That's a way I differ from my many sisters. They're also shorter and female, if you noticed," I replied.

Arvin ignored me, "You went against the King and Queen. You threatened to crush my reputation. Do you have no shame?"

"Don't waste your time talking about your 'reputation,' father," I responded, "When you knew they were coming for Sylvina, you took the first carriage out of Hagueveil. You shamed yourself."

"I am a 57-year-old man," he looked at me sternly, "I have proven myself. You have proven yourself not once. So, don't talk to me about reputation, Dontin."

"Oh, please, I won a battle against Gwendys Wayne. The King's been trying to find a weak spot in her forces for ages, we all know. The King knows that I'm worthy," I fired back.

Arvin ignored me, "I suppose you want something from me. Why else would you come here?"

"To say hello to an old man?" I grinned.

"You want knights?" he insisted on getting me out of here.

"Don't bother. I have enough men for now," I told him.

"Then why the hell are you here?"

"I want to pick apart your brain, father. If the Pargions aren't here, then they're at Gwendys' little fort. Whatever will the outcome be?" I drummed my fingers together like a villain.

"Well, the King likely has double the force. Gwendys has lost everyone she needs. With Jaze Wyne gone, Minbury fell at once into your hands. With Simon Pargion gone, so too did Bernstaplen. It's only a matter of time. Gwendys Wayne will fall today. The real question is, will her children realise this? Or will they die at her side?" he mused.

"By now, they surely realise that this is a lost cause. Their father lives well and good. They wouldn't do something so idiotic," I mentioned.

"I wouldn't be so sure," he continued, "All the youths want is a united family. If they know Simon Pargion is safe, wouldn't they focus on saving the one more likely to die? Doing it could kill them all. It would be Death to the Pargions."

"They'll be forgotten," I sighed.

"But not quietly," Arvin responded, "Simon Pargion only takes the field these days when the scent of vengeance is in the air, and it will be a strong scent tomorrow. But he cannot fight alone. But he will not. One commoner makes little impact, but a thousand? Ten thousand? They could kill the entire King's Guard if they felt like it. Blood and gold shall preserve them all."

"I see..." I couldn't find any issues with his prediction.

"Well, I have learned what I wanted to learn from you, Father. I should be off now. Good day," I got up and started to walk away.

"Wait," he called out. I looked at him.

"Yes, father?"

"When this is all done, I shall have a task for you. If you complete it, it shall mend our reputation," he looked at me sternly.

"Name it."

"Ruger Stunn," he frowned, "His daughter has been imprisoned. The one you were particularly fond of."

"Alarina?" I looked at him with shock.

"Yes, Alarina...they're going to kill her. He wants me to free her, but I will send you," he explained.

"Why does he want our help?" I questioned.

"It's rather simple," he answered, "We'll do the job, and we won't ask questions when he says that he wants to kill her first."

'Dearest Alarina,

Your fire is a thing of beauty. Treasure it as I do. It is eternal, as is my love for you.

Yet such fire belongs in the hands of one who can handle it, who can tame it to a steady flame. One that does your bidding but never becomes your puppet.

I've seen that strength in you more than any other I've met, and knowing how this Kingdom designs my journey to death, I have reason to believe you are uniquely for me. It takes great internal strength to tame such a scorching flame.

So, show me, become my steady light, for one can only lead others out of the darkness when the light is constantly present.

No more teasing. Master yourself so you can master me, and all else will fall into place.'

-Love letter from Dontin to Alarina Stunn.

Gwendys:

I dreamed of a home for my family.

A home for decade upon decade, a small world unto itself. No heads are to be turned when you pass. No names to be called by a million lips. Just space. Your space.

It was nestled in the woodland, as humble as any rock face in this kingdom. Openings in the walls were shy eyes, large to welcome the rays of the sun. Rock walls belonged right where they were - they had grown up on the hallowed ground. It was just a house, but it was a shield. It existed to protect us, those who dwelled within, to quell the elements, and to build a family. My family. I watched it exist. Then Emannar burned it all down.

I rose from the bed. Narisetti was there. "Lady Wayne," he whispered.

"Yes?" I creaked.

"You told me to free Symonnet when the battle was over," Narisetti smiled, "I suppose it is time."

Then I noticed the silence.

"What the hell happened?" I asked urgently, getting up in a rush.

"Some men arrived. They were sent from Tyral Wayne and Dontin Slait. A guild of assassins. One of them fired a stray arrow. It hit Emannar in the eye. Gwendys...the King is dead!" he looked at me with extreme shock.

I won?

I won.

"Find the assassin. Send him here," I commanded him. Narisetti nodded and left the room. He returned with the man, who bowed before me.

"Lady Gwendys Wayne," he spoke, "I am Gyrard, leader of La Perte Inconnue, the guild of assassins. I... I have slain Emannar Woodgairrd in service of youse."

"Rise," I commanded him, and he stood up, "I will not make this long. You have done me a great service. You shall be rewarded appropriately."

"I would like to be rewarded with the freedom of my mate Symonnet. Can youse do me that favour, Wayne?" he smirked.

"I see," I frowned, "That can be arranged. My war is over."

Narisetti came back to me, "Lady Wayne, upon discovering Emannar's death, the King's Guard fled. They are reading his will as we speak. Dontin Slait shall be sending a raven informing us of the decisions made."

"I suppose we must wait for that. But I cannot be excited. Emannar was just an obstacle. I have not yet won my war," I looked at him sternly.

"Your children are returning to Bernstaplen. Dontin and Tyral have kept it safe for them," he informed me.

"Good for them," I nodded.

"You still really want Simon's death, I see," he sighed.

"I want it more than my life," I told him.

Narisetti nodded with understanding and left. I spent about an hour just looking at the marvellous destruction before me when he came back in with the letter.

"The raven has arrived, my lady," he told me, "Should I read it to you privately?"

"Indeed."

His hands rung like bells as he read out the will and testament of Emannar Woodgairrd, kept in his chambers for decades.

Narisetti began reading, *'I, Emannar Woodgairrd, being of full age and a sound mind and memory, do make, publish and declare this to be my Last Will and Testament, hereby revoking and annulling any and all Last Will and Testaments or Codicils at any time heretofore made by me.*

Item I: I direct that all my just debts, secured and unsecured, be paid as soon as reasonable after my death. This may include the completion of any oath I have sworn or any promise I have made to my Kingdom. If they must be completed by man, I place this duty on my kin and my council.

Item 2: All of the rest and residue of my property, real and personal, of every kind and description and whosesoever situate, which I may own or have the right to dispose of at the time of my death, I give, devise, and bequeath in equal shares to my heir, Varn Woodgairrd. Should the preceding person die before me, then I give, devise, and bequeath the said property to Elizella Slait as substitute beneficiary.

Item 3: I direct that my beneficiaries abide by any written statement or list by me directing the disposition of tangible personal property not specifically disposed of by this Last Will and Testament. This directive is mandatory to the extent allowed by law.

Item 4: The word 'Executor' means the same as 'Administrator,' 'Executrix,' or 'Personal Representative' and refers to the person who administers my estate and carries out the terms of this Last Will and Testament. I hereby name, constitute and appoint Styve Woodgairrd as my Executor and direct that my Executor shall serve without bond. Should my Executor be unable or unwilling to serve or continue to serve, then I hereby name, constitute and appoint Kase Woodgairrd as Successor or Substitute Executor. Whenever the word 'Executor' is used in this Last Will and Testament, it shall be taken to include both the singular and the plural, the masculine and the feminine, and shall apply equally to the Executor named herein and to any successor or substitute. Any successor or substitute Executor shall possess all the rights, powers and duties, authority and responsibility conferred upon my Executor named herein.

Item 5: If any beneficiary and I should die under such circumstances as would render it doubtful whether the beneficiary or I died first, then it shall be conclusively presumed for the purposes of this, my Last Will and Testament that said beneficiary predeceased me.

Execution: I, King Emannar Woodgairrd, the Testator, sign my name to this instrument this 3rd of June, and being first duly sworn, do hereby declare to the undersigned witnesses and notary public that I sign and execute this instrument as my Last Will and Testament and that I sign it willingly, that I execute it as my free and voluntary act for the purposes therein expressed, and that I am fifty-three years old, of sound mind, and under no constraint or undue influence.

The signatures of Emannar Woodgairrd, Styve of House Woodgairrd, Elizella of House Slait, and Varn of House Woodgairrd.'

"So Varn is the King?" I asked him.

"Indeed."

"As expected."

"You should be troubled, my Lady," he sighed.

"Why?"

"That first item applies to you. He promised the Kingdom that you would meet your demise. Your fate now lies in the hands of Varn and his council. Varn loves your daughter, he shall be lenient, but the council, they are the true villains. It is never those at the front who you must fear, but those behind the scenes," Narisetti pointed out.

"So, I'm still a threat to the Kingdom?" I realised.

"Indeed. And if I know anything about the council, they will execute the most entertaining option," Narisetti sighed.

All I needed to do was look at Narisetti to work out what he meant.

I was going to achieve my dreams. He was coming.

Weeks of training, and now I could finally slay my goddamn husband.

'He said he would kill us all, women and girls if he found a way to propagandise the extent of our powers. So I let him take me to save my daughters. I let him do what he did to all of us. I buried my magic inside my bones so I could live. He tortured me. He had his way with me. I suffered not because I had sinned but because I am good at what I do, and he

needed coin. We live in a world where any man would hunt us for no other reason than fear. Even though some of us speak of love and of saving nature, people resort to criminal methods to avoid facing comprehension.

Perhaps it was a good thing that he made me suffer. It would teach the girls to hide their powers better.'

-Diary entry from an unknown witch, likely about Matthias Hopkins, the witchfinder general who organised the witch hunts, leading to 500 women of all ages being executed for witchcraft, most falsely.

Dayron:

I read the display on the fabulous machine before me.

'Playlist.'

Then it listed some songs I didn't recognise.

There was a big green triangle next to 'Playlist.' I tapped on it.

The world was a vortex of ash. Then it wasn't.

I was inside something. Something disguised with the aroma of dying flowers. Stone walls captured the warm summer breezes washing over the area, carrying with it a stolen lilac scent and a waft of blossoming magnolias, sickly sweet after baking under the punishing sun and left to die between tyrannical ceilings and frigid floors. It seemed like on the hottest days when the temperatures raced into the forties or fifties, life decayed here, and it was stifling in its absurd persistence to exist. Petals and soft flowers withered to a crisp. All that was left was a pile of insistent ghosts to haunt my nostrils and demand memories of their previous beauty.

There was a man speaking in tongues at the front. A crowd watched him like he was a golden idol. I could see through him. He was an expert in seeing the real person, seeing if they were taking the path of emotional indifference or the path of love. He spoke of love as the supreme first principle, of the right philosophy being the all-important signpost. Thus, instead of giving instructions, he taught folk how to navigate. A flock will always need defence and shepherding, but a pack of good wolves who can keep evil at bay by themselves is strong. After all, if they need teaching all their lives, are they being taught anything at all?

But he was the man who made the world like this. The stench of candied rot penetrated thoughts of golden cups and sipping blood as it mixed with the hazy gloom of burned incense and settled among the worshippers bent forward on wooden benches. Incense to mask the smell of the dead. Incense to encourage devotion. But the purposes of the incense mixed and danced and joined to form a beverage of smoke - sweet and strong enough to manipulate your mind into the correct thoughts.

It was everything, and so was the immense fog. I felt drugged.

"Hallelujah!" they chanted.

The windows were covered by a see-through creation, but despite being transparent, there were reds and blues and hopes and dreams. There was a crescendo of praise and zeal raised by the faith. A cauchemardesque dark room in the back, clouded with wisps of grainy silver cigarette smoke drifting from basement to attic. Dried hydrangea hung in a cross above the centre table, a souvenir of the world to come.

"You have been wondering what the lesson is, haven't you?" the man at the front whispered. His face was covered by a white veil, but his voice was oddly familiar.

I watched the audience nod together.

"You must banish the smoke!" he exclaimed.

"Banish! Banish! Banish!" the mindless worshippers chanted.

"Breathe through the mouth!" he continued.

"Breathe! Breathe! Breathe!"

"Kneel down!"

"Kneel! Kneel! Kneel!"

"And pray. Repeat!" he commanded them.

"Banish! Breathe! Kneel! Pray!" they chanted.

"Listen to your priest. Try to save your soul. Pray!" he demanded.

"Pray!"

"Don't think about your knees, how they ache against the hard church floors. Don't think about the altar, kneeling beneath a crucifix of flowers. Just imagine the Lord. His rough, demanding hands gripped in your hair, his voice grainy and booming like a King's, sliding between his lips, forming the harsh utterance of 'I Am that I Am.' And obey!" the 'priest' tore his veil off now, showing them the true form of obedience. But it was a face I knew well.

It was the face of the Supreme Witanegemote, Gregory.

Annyte:

We found the castle easily enough. A tower of rock amid the jolly green grass, a fine accompaniment to the gorgeous foliage.

They formed a stack and pushed me up and through a window. I was in someone's chambers. Not Kristyne's chambers. I found an escape to the halls and stole out into the darkened labyrinth drawing attention to the throne room, the centre. The ceiling was gaping like an empty void over my head, and the silvery slants of moonlight were piercing through the windows, casting an eerie cross-hatched spotlight on one of the bedrooms. Kristyne always loved moonlight. She was probably in that one. I gave the other rooms no more than a sideward glance to ensure that nobody was there, slipping past with no sound but the whisper of fabric and the slight scuff of a soft shoe on marble.

I peered through the peephole, and Kristyne was there. I opened the door and hushed her.

"As you can see, I'm back again," I whispered to her, "We need to reunite the Pargions, so we're taking you out of here, and that's final."

"Annyte, haven't you heard?" she whispered back, "The King...Emannar's dead. They say Mother killed him."

"Mother killed him? How would she have managed that?" I was shocked.

"Exactly, but they're using it against her. Varn's being crowned tonight," she informed me.

"And you won't be here," I told her.

"I need to be here," she persisted, "Someone needs to be here to listen in. The only options are me and Father, and none of them trust Father."

"You want to be left here?" I realised, my mouth gaping open with shock.

"I need to be left here," she smiled. Then we heard the footsteps.

"Kris-TYNE!" Varn yelled at the top of his lungs. Someone was happy today.

"Yes, Varn?" Kristyne called back and then turned to me, "Hide."

I stood firm, "No. Varn's not gonna lay a finger on me. Not in this mood he's in."

Varn eventually thrust the door open like a horse breaking down a stable door, "How are you?" then he noticed me, "Annyte. How pleasant!"

"Hello, Varn, what a pleasure," I feigned a smile.

"Are you going to be here for my coronation? You always did love festivities," he asked me.

"Only when I'm alone," I replied, "Besides, I'm not going to be here tonight. My family needs me."

"Ah, what a shame," he dismissed me, "Kristyne, I have some news. My mother wants me to select a Queen. I would pick you because you are aware of my...interests, but because of your mother's mishaps in the Kingdom, our marriage is forbidden. I have absolutely no idea who to go with."

"Knowing your mother, she'll pick herself. It'll be some fat and ugly princess from a powerful King, watch," Kristyne sighed.

"You're probably right. My God, you're probably right!" Varn's knees randomly weakened.

"You drunk?" I asked offhandedly.

Kristyne looked at me with disapproval, "You can't ask the King that question, Annyte."

"I just did," I shrugged.

"It's alright. I admit, the council got me a bit tipsy," Varn rose back up, "But I shall be fine for the coronation."

There was a rap on the door, "Varn? It's Francis. The council would like to offer you one last congratulation."

"Come in!" a drunk Varn slurred. I slid over to the corner in an attempt to hide, but it was futile. Francis saw me.

"Annyte," Francis looked at me cynically, with half-shut eyes, "What a surprise."

"Sir Ashford," I acknowledged him. The council eventually diffused, taking up half of the room. I could see Francis, Gregory, Styve and Tobas. Styve came to the front.

"King Varn," he knelt and looked up at his King, "My wife needs me elsewhere tonight. As I cannot be present, I shall now swear my oath."

"Go ahead, good sir," Varn began to cry.

"I pledge my allegiance faithfully to our noble King Varn Woodgairrd, and to the Kingdom under which he stands, one Kingdom under one ruler, indivisible, with liberty and justice for all who dwell in it," Styve swore.

Elizella came in now and chirped with excitement when she saw Styve swearing his oath. Francis closed the door behind her.

"Thank you, Styve," Varn cried.

"Your Grace, it would be a great honour for me if I could serve on the council again during your reign," Styve begged.

"Of course, Styve," Varn assured him, and Styve granted Varn his sword for the proclamation, "I pronounce you, Styve Woodgairrd, my faithful-"

Varn was cut off when Styve's dagger cut his throat open.

Elizella and Kristyne started wailing like sirens. Everything became a blur, audibly and visually. Styve held Varn's corpse in a bear hug. Elizella tried to sprint towards him and beg for his life, but she was grabbed violently by Tobas. "Not now. You cannot," he whispered.

Styve brought Varn's dying head to his mouth and whispered in his ear, "Thanks for the proclamation, but I don't need it. With you dead, I no longer have an opponent to the throne. Your mother broke off her ties to it with the divorce, and your siblings are unwanted outcasts. I'm the logical choice. Glory to the King." With that, he dropped the corpse and let it bleed.

Kristyne stepped forward and looked at the other councillors, "Are you just going to stand there? Arrest him!" Nobody moved.

Gregory spoke up, "Through killing Varn the day before his coronation, Styve has invoked the Law of Succession, making him the rightful ruler. It has been a tradition since before the history books have recorded. Why do you think Emannar was so quick to remove Elizella when he realised that she was untrustworthy?"

Suddenly, Francis grabbed me and put his knife to my throat. If I tried to speak or breathe in too much air, the knife would leave a mark. Gregory did the same to Kristyne.

"Unhand, my sister!" I pleaded.

"Shut up," Francis scowled and struck me on my right cheek.

Styve came forward, "The Law of Succession won't secure my throne. Kase will be after me when he finds out, and the commoners have never been very fond of it," he looked at me, "There's an idea. This girl has many a motive to slay Varn, and we can exploit it. The public shall welcome me with open arms if I slay the slayer..."

Kristyne and I realised what he meant in unison, and Kristyne started screaming, "Leave Annyte alone! Leave her alone!"

Gregory whispered to her, "Child, I'm sorry. If I could prevent this, believe me, I would...it's unjust."

Styve grinned, "Elizella, take your son's body and do whatever the hell you want with it. Maybe you'll find that fabled resurrection pool they tell infants about," he laughed as Elizella grabbed Varn's corpse and left the castle silently, weeping all the way.

"Please, don't do this..." Kristyne begged one final time.

Styve looked at Francis, "If there was any other way to secure my claim to the throne, I would take it. Francis, do it," he commanded.

Then Francis slit my throat.

Dayron:

We didn't know much about the Witanegemotes. Only that the Witanegemotes knew much.

We were now back in Bernstaplen, and I thought it best to present my artefact to Morgan - the object pulled from the Sission. He was issuing commands to Stableman Buckley, and then he came to me, "Dayron, you wanted to see me?"

"I found something," I told him offhandedly. He scratched his head as I presented the device to him. I watched his mouth gape open.

Morgan recollected himself, "You certainly have," and began to inspect the object, "In given time...we shall work out what this is, what this does...where did you find this?"

I stared at him reluctantly for a second before I spoke up, "I pulled it from a Sission. I did a Sission by myself." I looked at the floor to avoid his demeaning gaze, "I know I'm not supposed to do Sissions by myself, but I did. And I found this."

"You...you pulled this from a Sission?" Morgan stared at me with shock, "What was in the Sission?"

Stableman Buckley uttered an inaudible whisper to Morgan. Lots of people uttered inaudible whispers around me, I noticed.

"So Ronayne is back?" Morgan responded, "And John Borrell quit?"

John Borrell quit? The song...it was a depressing song...the Sission was a prophecy. John Borrell was destined to quit.

"I see," Morgan replied, "Carry on with your job, Buckley." Buckley nodded simply and trotted back to the stables, "As I asked, what was in the Sission?"

I stopped to remember for a second before speaking, "It was a room with a lot of bright lights. People were dancing. There was music. First loud music with a lot of screaming, and then...something slow. The voice sounded like John's."

"When did you find this?" he continued asking questions, holding the device up.

"Someone dropped it. When I went to pick it up, the Sission ended."

"Anything else to tell me?"

"One thing," I told him, "I tapped one of the shapes on it, and it transported me into another Sission. It showed a building with about fifty people worshipping one man wearing a veil. Before the Sission ended, the man took the veil off. It was Gregory."

"The Supreme Witanegemote?" he asked me.

"Yes," I told him.

"If the Sissions are getting this useful, then...I suppose it's time for a certain lesson. Follow me, Dayron," he instructed me and took me to the Sission pool.

I dipped my head in, and the Sission began.

I made my way towards a hole in a fence, overgrown with vines and leaves.

"What's this?" I asked Morgan.

"This was one of the many entrances to a building that played a very crucial role in our lives, Dayron," Morgan's voice called out.

An abandoned building located in the middle of the woods? How could that be important?

The path to the structure was laden with brown leaves, and I struggled to keep from slipping as I made my way over. By now, all the trees were leafless, which helped to see further down the path. I approached my destination and sat down on a bench to observe.

The edifice was littered with broken and empty mugs of ale from all the men who came here to sneak a beer. Every few hundred metres, there were poles with thin lines snapped in half, and brown, yellow-green, and blue lines poked out and blew in the wind like weeping willow trees. I sat in the building surrounded by barren trees. It was like a dead jungle - it must have once been teeming with life, but now it was all but empty.

From this spot, I could see every little thing. The roofs of seven abandoned buildings nearby created a skyline from where I sat. A mechanical monolith stood where an inn once did. The sun began to set, and some see-through holes in the walls gave off a powerful glare. The sky was a mix of oranges and crimsons, straight out of someone's masterful artwork. The purple clouds were motionless, waiting endlessly for the sun to set, so they could slumber.

I was sitting in the world of man. The kind of future dreams could only hold.

But was it really my future?

Or was it my past?

A lovely rose garden became a hostile thorn bush. A pleasant swing for the delight of many a child was now creaking in the most haunted way. What terrified me the most was the isolation. The fear. If this wasn't a Sission, I would feel alone. Uncovered. Exposed to everyone who stared at me in return. As I lifted my head to defy an insubstantial stare, something caught my eye. There was no roof to this building. Where had it gone? My fear shifted to curiosity.

I approached the entrance door. From there, everything was monstrously massive. I truly thought I would no longer feel inferior when I entered, but the feeling did not cease. Four endless walls and a staircase leading to the frigid foggy sky. It was like a message telling me that it was all over...but was it?

The dust, cobwebs, and awful artwork on the walls and corners brought me back to reality. I was not the first to experience this unwelcoming, macabre pile of bricks. But yet, the remains of furniture that rested disorderedly, cluttered on the floor, reminded me of death, for this had once been the home of many happy lives and, therefore, full of life itself. And it was all gone. Replaced by rats, spiders, and their cobwebs, dirt, dust, fleece and trash. And trash. How terribly sad to call something great trash. It was ripped, dismantled, stained, abandoned...

Pieces of paper gave the date of a hundred years ago - barely, for they were covered in hurricanes of dust. Containers read 'FRAGILE', where one could identify plenty of broken glass and plates. There were no answers. Just the odour of rot, the sound of creaking, the touch of a rough surface, the sight of a horror scene, and the taste of regurgitated food. For I felt I would certainly die. It was too much to bear.

And, around the corner, the sickly fumes.

As the cold wind rushed against my face, I fled out of that distorted dwelling and decided I would never walk past it again.

"Morgan, what have you just shown me?" I demanded an answer.

"This, my son, is the source," he explained.

"The source of what?"

"The source of the future."

And somewhere, off in the distance, I felt my gryphon chirp.

Kristyne:

There used to be a painting to the left of my chambers. A proud portrait of King Emannar Woodgairrd, displaying his many victories and his grandest tales. It had been stripped bare.

There used to be many people I could trust. There was Ronayne, Alizia, Varn, and Annyte when she was here. Now, Ronayne and Alizia had been sent back to Bernstaplen, Varn and Annyte were dead, and my father had been sent to kill my mother. I am alone here.

This was the first court session of King Styve Woodgairrd's reign (he dismissed the coronation ceremony, never being a fan of the glamour. There was no glamour in being king). I had to attend. I was the only one who knew what Styve did that would be willing to tell others. He wanted to keep me in line. A line of guards stood beneath both sets of windows, some Woodgairrds, some Slaits, as his wife Ashlyh, Elizella's younger sister, was present. No smallfolk. No commoners. Just those who mattered.

I slipped in among them and recognised a couple of faces apart from the councillors. Executioners Bradyn Bulwark and Elden Brune. Kegan Wyne. Even Rabbithead, Emannar's jester, was present.

Nobody here cared for me. I was a ghost, dead before my time.

Supreme Witanegemote Gregory, Tobas and Francis Ashford all sat around their table. Karron was with the King's

Guard, and Auster Magnarok kept Lilyana at his side. It became apparent that Kase was not there.

Eventually, a herald spoke out, "All hail His Grace, Styve of the House Woodgairrd. All hail his lady wife, Ashlyh of House Slait."

Byrron and Briden Vikarin, two members of the King's Guard and brothers, led the King and Queen in, and they took their seats. It was time to begin.

"Cease the applause," Styve commanded, although few were clapping, "I have some announcements to make. Firstly, I would like you all to be aware that not everything has been finalised yet. This has all come so suddenly. Nobody could have expected Annyte Pargion to commit the atrocity of murdering our dear King-to-be Varn Woodgairrd. I can only be glad that I heard the sounds of death and decay and delivered vengeance. Now, firstly, I would like to discuss the council."

The councillors stood up, and Karron Wull came to join them. Styve continued, "A few changes shall be made to my council. Firstly, my brother Kase Woodgairrd has quit upon the knowledge of my coronation. I suspect that he will commit treason and contend with me for the crown. As such, he has been removed from my council. I am glad to announce that my dearest father-in-law, Arvin Slait, shall be filling Kase's seat."

There was healthy applause around the room. Although he was not here, Arvin Slait was known to be a wise man and a strong tactician.

"Secondly, Lord Auster Magnarok has made it clear to me that he no longer has an interest in serving as High Earl. I have chosen to respect his decision, and he shall return to lordship for his House. For his replacement, I have requested Lord Edd Malver of House Malver. Whether he shall accept remains to be seen, but I assure you he will not turn it down lightly," Styve continued. Auster nodded, grabbed Lilyana and ordered her to leave, then turned to us all.

"I would like to leave one last message for you all: be lions," he spoke and then followed his wife.

"Should I escort them out, Your Grace?" Karron asked Styve.

"Don't bother, Karron. You won't have duties like these anymore," Styve replied, "Sir Karron Wull, commander of the King's Guard. You have fought well and hard for our Kingdom, but with your recent failure to defeat Gwendys Wayne, costing us our noble King Emannar, we believe that your days of fighting prowess are over."

Karron looked at him with shock, "My King..."

"Sir Wull, please remove your Woodgairrd-plated armour and give it to your replacement," Styve commanded.

"My replacement?" he asked.

"The King's Guard shall undergo an era of innovation and victory under the leadership of Commander Stephyn Tanner," Styve announced. Stephyn came forward and received his plated armour.

This made Karron snap, "You remove me for weakness...and you replace me with this fool? This man who had sex with a Queen? You shame this Kingdom, Styve Woodgairrd. You are a tyrant. You want to see everything crumble before you!"

Ashlyh decided to speak up, "We do not wish to dishonour you, Sir Wull. Stephyn Tanner is simply the youngest knight with a skill level that could one day match yours."

"You think this...boy can surpass me? You are as big a fool as the rest of them!" he argued back.

"We shall ensure that you possess a satisfying retirement, Sir Wull," Tobas assured him.

"Keep your retirement," Karron spat, "What of my men?"

"That is the next order of business," Styve announced, "I would like Byrron and Briden Vikarin to come forth."

The brothers knelt before their King, "Yes, Your Grace?"

"It has been brought to my attention that you two have proven yourselves intellectually. I have a new role of authority in mind, and I would like you two to be the first ones to undertake this position," Styve told them.

"What is this role, Your Grace?" Byrron asked.

"I would like you two to be my coroners. Solving suspicious murders. If I had not apprehended Annyte Pargion, it would have taken us a while to determine the slayer. You shall reduce the number of instances where this occurs," Styve explained.

The brothers nodded hesitantly and took their plating off. "I shall be holding trials to determine the next knight to join the King's Guard. On that note, I have no interest in these esteemed knights being affiliated with my name. My name is for me and my family only. From now on, the King's Guard shall be recognised as the Royal Guard, to represent not only the monarchy but the upper-class itself."

Randomly, Kegan Wyne darted for the door. "Where the hell are you going, Wyne?" Styve called out.

As he opened the door, Kegan looked back at him, "Away from ye," and headed out.

He carried on with a few other announcements, nothing major. Eventually, it was all done, and I decided to sleep through the day.

In the middle of my sleep, my bed suddenly shook like a silver sword slithering off the rack. I looked through my window to see Annyte's friends from Incognitae, with Jaide Woodgairrd at the front, "Kristyne! We have a request. We want to take you with us."

"I refuse," I shook my head frantically.

"We know you want to leave, but you're afraid of being found. They call us Incognitae for a reason. You shall never be found if you come with us," Jaide offered.

I wanted to reject them. I swore I'd never be like Annyte. But in truth, I had no choice. I needed to accept it for my own safety.

Unfortunately, Tobas entered my room with a knight, and they saw Jaide.

"Intruders!" the knight exclaimed, "Move away, Kristyne, I shall cut them down!" The knight moved his spear towards Jaide's palms, but Tobas grabbed him and repeatedly stabbed his clavicle, eventually dumping the body out the window and looking at me.

"Go. It will be our little secret," he whispered, and I climbed through and down. I was free.

Annyte once said that she'd rather be dead than be royal. She was never righter.

Incognitae.

I was destined to be Incognitae.

'It is said that before King Emannar Woodgairrd finally passed, the death in battle he always desired, an apparition came into view.

The apparition came as an ambassador for a God far away. And once he passed, she spoke of pain unimaginable, a coma the Kingdom was at risk of never breaking free from. For too long, the suffering induced by Grimm Woodgairrd had locked his sons in prison, and while a resurgence of love came through Emannar's perseverance, Styve never had quite the stomach for it all.

It is said that there was no joy evident in her voice nor any hint of a grin on her lips. Only the seriousness of a thief-taker paying their target a visit.

It is said that she said that to take love back to the Kingdom, we needed to heal it first.

Then she left.'

-Extract from the Unitas, added by Priestess Ronayne.

Sylvina:

There had been an avalanche that day. When the sun rose, the forest was snow-white. It had a pristine aura that begged the soul to stop for a moment and let the sight enter your soul. Pink flakes of snow trickled around the atmosphere like they were forged from dreams.

Then the door creaked open, and there was my uncle. Whenever my father had better things to do, he sent uncle Drevyn to deal with me. I wasn't even a month old then. He picked me up and showed me the winter wonderland around me. Being a child, I focused on him and didn't even look at it. I was just happy to be somewhere else.

"Don't like the cold?" he asked me. I just flailed my arms about, so he continued, "I need to be here again today. Your father couldn't come. It's time for your initiation."

Initiation rituals are just making children swear allegiance to their house. Because they cannot do it verbally, they do it physically. Before we went out into the frost, my uncle put the ceremonial necklace on me. I climbed up on my uncle's back, and we went for the trek.

The winter morning was crisp, and there was a frosty chill in the air. Adding to the effect was the sweet surrendering scent of the moist morning dew that cascaded all around. Cool autumn leaves lay scattered on the floor and mixed in with the pleasant wood of the homely cabin and the snow-covered hills camouflaged by the purple horizon. The leaves crunched as he trespassed on that sacred ground.

The trek lasted five days. No food. No water. Just me and my uncle against the world. On our adventure, we encountered a clan of harpies. But he tamed them.

"It is one thing to hunt a beast," he told me, "Another to hunt a species. I will teach you this one day."

Eventually, we arrived at the ritual site, and my head was dipped in the waters of Priest Francis, and he marked me with formaldehyde, the greatest symbol of my initiation. I received his blessing, and I was given one last look at the world before I was dropped off the face of the cliff into Earth.

There was something clear I remembered about that day. The pool I was dipped in. The water had been freshly extracted from The Great Wood.

I was here for a reason.

In the dappled sunlight, amid the boughs and strong-risen roots, I could feel my spirit weave itself into nature as if, for this time, I was one with that place and all the life that was there. It was a celebration of browns and greens. The colours of nature's finest dreams. Eventually, I got deeper into the Wood, and the Wood became a forest.

Upon the forest floor lay trees of yesteryear, fallen in storms long forgotten. The seasons were harsh on it, stripping away the bark and outer layers yet rendering them all the more beautiful.

They bore the appearance of driftwood, twisting in patterns that reminded me of seaside waves; even the colour of the moss was like kelp. They were soft and damp, yet your fingers came away dry. For a moment, I just tilted my head upward and felt my hair tumble further down my back. The shortest trees were still several houses tall, reaching toward the golden rays of spring. Songs of birds came in lullabies and bursts. The silence and the singing worked together as well as any rehearsed melody.

A smile painted itself upon my freckled face, my pink lips illuminated by the overwhelming light. Eventually, my feet began to walk. My soul, body and mind were one. Nobody expected me with them anyway.

I left the Pargions after the battle. They were hopeless. Now one of their parents was going to die, the other would crumble, and they would leave behind a legacy of children to follow their end, except for Daman. He has potential.

It was not a long journey. In time, I found it and dipped my little finger in it, making it bound to me.

A resurrection pool was bound to me.

But who could I use it on?

It was not my decision to make. Eventually, a face would appear in the waters, and they would show me who I should resurrect to best preserve the Kingdom. But a face did not appear.

As I waited there, for many an hour, eventually, one face did appear.

It wasn't a face I liked, especially not one I wanted to revive.

And I didn't even know that he had died.

Dontin:

"I've received a raven from Simon," my father told me, "He doesn't want your help. He's going to face Gwendys alone."

"I see," I nodded, taking a sip of wine. Now that Tyral had given Bernstaplen back to the Pargions, I decided it would be best to return to familiar ground, no matter how much I despised the soil.

"So, I have decided for you that it would be best to deal with Ruger Stunn's request. What say you?" Arvin asked me.

It wasn't like I really had a choice anyway, but I would do it for Alarina.

"I don't see a reason not to help him," I finally succumbed.

"What do you know of Colbagne, where the Stunns reside?" Arvin looked at me sternly.

"I know they're not the friendliest of people," I told him, "And they don't trust easily. I remember how Ruger used to treat me when I saw Alarina."

"Not very well, I remember," he sighed, "We may have our work cut out for us."

"Who took Alarina and how?" I changed the subject.

"House Foler of Lakewell has been engaging in a cold war of sorts with House Stunn for tens of years," Arvin explained, "Lord David Foler finally snapped by abducting his rival's daughter. This cold war is about to warm up."

"And you want a part of it. You want to play both sides, so you'll always end up on top," I realised.

"I've just told you that I'm aligned with House Stunn. How is that playing both sides?" he laughed for a moment, then glared at me seriously.

"If anybody knows what you're truly like, father, it's me," I explained, "You will say that you align with Ruger until he starts to lose. Then you'll turn on him like a seesaw."

"Perhaps I will," Arvin resigned.

"Perhaps," I mocked him, "What's your plan, father?"

"I have already informed Ruger of my battle plans," Arvin seemed eager to share, "Lord Foler splits his men into three separate camps, apart from his main fortress of Lakewell. This may seem like a foolish decision, as there are fewer men in each camp than the present resources provide for, but if you open your eyes when you pass through Lakewell, you would realise how wise it is. The camps roughly form a right-angled triangle, and what do we know about right-angled triangles? The sum of the squares of the two shorter sides adds up to the square of the longest. The camp off in the east is the most fortified, and the castle can easily provide reinforcements to it at any time. In the west, there are two smaller camps, with strength adding up to that of the larger camp, and again, the castle can provide reinforcements. I'm sure Lord Foler has another trick up his sleeve, but who can be sure? I am focusing on the weaknesses of the tactic I am aware of. The weakness I have pinpointed is that the smaller camps are only stronger when they fight together and are supplied with reinforcements. So, I have told Ruger that it would be wisest to send some mercenaries or takers to disable the alarms of the smaller camps, preventing the supply of reinforcemerrd, and then send one-half of his men to one small camp and the other half to another. By taking these smaller camps, we will seize their resources and boost our strength, as well as potential numbers, since not all of them will want to die for House Foler. This should make it more than simple enough to capture the larger camp after the mercenaries disable the alarms. Once we have all three camps, we only have David Foler's fortress itself to ransack. I tell you, he has put most of his forces into his camps. House Foler is not a grand house; it is a proud one. Once we destroy the camps, as I have planned to do, we shall win this war."

I grinned, "It seems you have put a lot of thought into this, so you won't have to betray anyone this time."

"I have seen to it that I will not have to," he frowned.

My cousin Manrel came in now, giving Arvin a report by the look of it, "Uncle Arvin, my father would like to inform you that we are ready for the ride to Colbagne. But there's one more piece of news..."

"What?" Arvin looked impatient.

"King Styve Woodgairrd has elected you for a seat on the council," Manrel explained.

"Damn it," Arvin sighed.

"We have informed him that you are undertaking this quest to conclude this long feud, but he insists on sending a member of his court to assist you."

"Who?" Arvin asked.

Then the man came in. His red fedora-like hat cloaked his ebony eyes, and when he looked up at my father and I, there was an instant look of recognition on our faces. The snake logo on the red bandana he wore. The forbidden weapons were in his hands.

"How do you do, Arvin Slait?" The Mamba spoke up, "They call me Víboro Siniestro."

Daman:

Morgan's herbs were miracles. I could be back on the field in a day. And here I was.

The arid and sunburnt barren land of Novak territory. The eternal desert stretching for kilometres. The sun is intense. It's blazing down on some harsh red rocks, which dot the landscape like freckles. This was a sign of evil. How incredible.

Howard and Fawkes were with me. We were the only hearts beating within miles.

Aldo had chosen to quit the team upon hearing of Styve Woodgairrd's coronation. I remember the moment clearly. He readied his steed and prepared to ride off before we stopped him.

"Aldo, we're returning to the Novaks- "he cut me off.

"Without me. Are you aware, Daman, that I was supposed to betray you?" he questioned.

"Betray me? What for?"

"For gold," he sighed, "After I was exiled from Guillemin, I was nothing. Earning crumbs on my plate and nothing more. I became a thief-taker. Dran Grimm requested your death, Daman."

"The leader of my House," Fawkes frowned, "A cult following Grimm Woodgairrd's tyrannical methods, focusing on us?"

Aldo sighed again, "They don't give the takers the details. I need to return to Guillemin, reclaim my duchy, and save my home. We will meet again, Daman Pargion. Farewell."

He continued to ride away.

The Novak deserts don't change. Never a stronger or weaker wind. Never a drop of rain or a different level of humidity. It's just air. Air and canyons and immense rock structures off in the distance, circling us. It was like a gladiator pit, with stands that exist but are out of each. Every time your eyes wandered back to study the rocks, it seemed like life was on the horizon. We were unreal.

"We haven't got a long way to go," Fawkes informed me, "We're almost there. We can do it."

I looked back at him grimly, "I know we can. But should we?"

It felt like I was walking along a large red scar while the numbing heat hit me. The goldenrod sky watched over us. It was calming, like a summer sea.

I looked up. The sky was the same shade as everything else, yet something was far different. It felt like a separate body.

Eventually, the sun sets on our hopes and dreams. The last rays of light scorch the desert, and the last beams of sunlight break through the horizon. The incredible landscape shifts like a nocturnal animal. The sky was blue no longer. The Sun was no more, yet omnipresent.

We had walked for miles when I eventually decompressed on the rocks.

"Hard to handle?" Fawkes asked.

"I don't want to be here yet," I confessed, "My father has been sent to kill my mother, I know it. I should be there to mourn the one who doesn't walk out."

"Ah, grow up, Daman," Fawkes looked at me with no sympathy, "Look at us. My father cast me out, and I didn't get to say a goddamn word. And Howard, don't get me started on Howard."

I looked at him with disapproval, "You think that's going to help me?"

Fawkes laughed, "I'm not trying to help you. I can't help you. Trying would be a waste."

"He's not wrong, Daman," Howard spoke up, "Nobody can get you through loss. You have to work it out yourself or be stuck in the loop forever."

I didn't bother to respond. I was too angry to respond.

It was better to get some rest.

We were going to end the Novaks.

Then I could finally get some rest.

Simon:

The Sun was bright today. So bright I needed to shade my eyes. It was like the world was overjoyed that I was coming to kill my wife. It was eerily silent too. Perhaps she had lost most of her men in the siege, and the rest followed Damon back to Bernstaplen. Swords did not sing. Metal boots did not clank on the cobblestone floors. Men did not scramble for their lives. Had they left?

No, some of them had not left. I knew it.

I walked down the main entrance to her outpost, sword sheathed.

"How long is this gonna take?" a voice complained. The sound of someone spitting on the floor was present.

"As long as it damn takes," another man answered with frustration.

"How are the horses?" a third asked.

"Calm and saddled. Not going anywhere," the second responded.

"Better keep a good eye on them, Kondrad," the first warned the second.

"Might be a challenge," Kondrad joked, but nobody was laughing, "I'm starving."

"Shut up," the third voice yelled, "He's coming. We've got to get out of here."

"He won't do anything," Kondrad assured him, "We've got a spearman and five swordsmen among us. We'll be good."

I made straight for them, and one man pointed me out, "Curse your mouth. He's here! Get the spears ready!"

One bandit lowered himself and clutched a poison-tipped spear in his palms. He aimed the tip at me and readied himself in a suitable position to throw it straight at me. I kept walking.

"No further, Simon!" the spearman called out.

I stopped to consider reasoning with them.

"Where the hell is my wife?"

"Somewhere around here, Lord Pargion," Kondrad told me, "She'll be here soon. She gave us an order."

"What order?"

"The order was to tell you that she blames you for turning her children against her and keeping them oblivious to all the 'heinous sins' you committed against her during her time as your Lady," the spearman spoke up.

"I can accept that," I told them, resting my hand on my sheathe. Kondrad started laughing.

"Are you gonna attack us? Gwendys told us to carry out another order if you attacked us."

"What would that order be?" I gripped my sword.

The spearman took a step forward, "To put this in your eye."

I resumed walking as he aimed the spear at my pupil. They were quiet.

And then he released it. I rapidly unsheathed my sword and waved it upwards like an elegant baron, just right of where the spear would hit me. It neared its destination eventually, and with one brief flick to the left, I altered its trajectory, and it collapsed to the left of me. I continued walking.

"He...he deflected it..." the spearman exclaimed.

"Get your swords!" Kondrad ordered, and suddenly there were five swords before me while the spearman scrambled for another spear.

Their blades were directed at me as I continued to approach the collection of damaging blades. The spearman found another spear and looked next for the poison coating.

"Get ready!" Kondrad ordered. They spread out at arm's length of each other and readied their swords offensively. They were going to push the line.

Damn it.

One man pushed first. He attached his blade to his right hip and charged at me, hoping I would not react in time. He was stupid, and I held my sword up to cross them. He lost his footing, and I quickly struck his right hip to temporarily immobilise him and leave him shrieking as I dealt with the others.

Two others rushed for me next - hoping for a pincer. I held my sword sideways and blocked the faster man's offence. I grabbed the wrist of the slower man with such force that I gained full control over his sword and inserted it into the other bandit's back. The other lowered his sword, overcome with the shock of his brother's blood on his hands, and I cut his clavicle open.

Behind me, I noticed the immobilised man try to get up and fall.

"Surround him!" Kondrad commanded, unsheathing his sword. It seemed he had finally mustered the courage to duel me.

I slashed another bandit across the backbone. He tried to get one small stab in my leg as he collapsed, but I noticed it and disarmed him with a wave of the sword and ended his misery. Two sirenmen noticed the commotion and entered in an attempt to apprehend me, unaware of my duty, and I kicked a loose cart towards them, sending them tumbling back out of the outpost.

It was just Kondrad and the spearman. One would assume that the spearman failed to collect his tip of poison as he rushed towards me with the spear in his palms and fired a strike. It was parried, but when I tried to land my counter-strike, he did a brief backflip and waved his spear towards me. It was parried again, and when he tried to repeat his backflipping technique, I cut his left leg off. He tried to toss his spear into my chest, but he missed by a great deal, and finally, I ended his life.

Kondrad threw his sword at me idiotically. It didn't even go far enough to pass a metre. I rewarded this lack of skill with a swift and easy decapitation.

Then I saw her.

She was coming slowly, inspecting the bodies with a certain shame. I halted, lowering my sword, as she approached. Eventually, she stopped, and then I realised. She was wearing armour. She had a sword in her hand.

"You killed them all," she called out, "They were pitiful."

"They were under your hire," I responded.

"Do you feel no remorse? Do you not care? Did you ever?" she screamed.

"Whenever I was not sober, I did. Truly. I never wanted this, Gwendys. We've both reacted to this wrongly, it seems," I kept a stern face, avoiding tears because she would probably cut them off me.

"I have never been wrong!" she shrieked, "When have I ever been wrong?"

"You put yourself before your children, Gwendys! You cast them away, your own products! You have listened to no ears but your own! You were destined to fail!" I explained.

She remained silent. "Run away, Gwendys. I don't want to kill you," I warned.

She laughed, "You won't." She unsheathed her sword and directed it at me.

"Gwendys, last chance. Run away," I cautioned her.

"No. You have hurt me enough. Now I shall return the favour."

"Once our blades meet, one of us shall die. Run away now," I repeated.

"When one dies, the other shall shortly. I have struck a deal with His Grace Styve Woodgairrd. If you live, he will decide your fate," she informed me.

She charged at me next, and the sword cut towards me. Her blade pressed backwards as it met my swift parry, and as she advanced again, we collided swords. It was an awful idea, as she pulled out a small dagger and cut across my thigh in a downward motion. I pushed her away, and when she attacked again, I parried again, failing to shove the sword in her gullet when she whirled round and charged at me again. I parried it, but during the parry, she cut across my other thigh. I wanted to give in, but it would cost me our lives. Styve could give me the chance of exile, to run far away, but he would surely kill Gwendys if she was the victor. I turned towards her again and deflected her next attack. In her brief moment of weakness, I stabbed her kneecap. As she collapsed, she sidestepped her merciful end and tried to toss her dagger into my temple. She missed, and I disarmed her.

She said nothing. On the ground, swordless, she clung to her demolished kneecap in defeat. Blood was spurting out - I severed an artery or two. I sheathed my sword.

"Congratulations," she sneered weakly.

I didn't respond.

"It hurts..."

I didn't respond.

"I'm going to die, aren't I?" she asked me.

"Yes," I answered.

She slept on the cold cobble floor and waited to die, curled up like a kitten.

"I'm sorry," I said.

"Don't lie," she whimpered.

"I'm telling the truth, Gwendys. I didn't marry you because I had to. I married you with my eyes and soul. I married you with my heart and a dream of the future. I saw your joys. I saw your sorrows. I knew there was a home with you. And the unfunny part is, I wish I had told you. I should have told you..."

I just watched her for a while, and eventually, Styve arrived with a knight by his side.

"This must have been fun for you," Styve chuckled, "Well done. You killed her." He bent down and looked at her corpse.

"Are you proud?" I asked.

"Lady Gwendys Wayne. Dead," he looked proud of himself.

I didn't respond.

"Well, Simon," he turned to me, "You have done good work here. But you are too much of a threat to keep around."

The knight with him unsheathed his sword.

"Ever met this man, Simon?" Styve looked at the knight, "This is Sir Maximilien Engeramus, Captain of House Baulder's guard. He shall be serving in an interim position while I fill the empty slots. I assure you, he will out-skill you."

"Don't assure me of anything," I warned him.

Styve chuckled again, "Tell you what, I'll make you an offer. Run far away from here, never see any of your family members again, and I'll tell them you died nobly. Do we have a deal?"

I didn't respond. Instead, I unsheathed my sword.

"Don't touch my wife. You've already killed your nephew and my daughter...you're an animal. I... I will skin you alive."

"Right, you don't want me to do my duty! Doesn't matter. Sir Engeramus, show Simon Pargion how we deal with traitors," Styve responded.

"How about you dismiss your bodyguard and fight me yourself," I suggested.

He turned back to me, "A King cannot return to his kingdom with bloody hands. Not unannounced."

"You're afraid. You took all the power from Varn like you were picking plums, and you know that the same could be done to you just as easily. You've succumbed to cowardice."

Styve frowned, "I'm only giving you one more chance before he cuts you down like a fly, Simon. Is your business here done?"

"Yes," I answered with an effort.

"Are you wounded?"

"Not severely."

"Then leave. Now."

It was the only option. I realise that now. I kept standing for a second, avoiding Styve's gaze. I turned to Maximilien Engeramus.

"Knight."

Engeramus looked at me with disdain, "Turn away while you still can."

"You're serving the wrong ruler," I told him.

Engeramus chuckled, "Do not come back. Do not."

I frowned and made my way to the nearest carriage. I mounted Reinhardt, and eventually, I arrived in the sector of the Kingdom Styve no longer owned.

I could no longer serve Styve Woodgairrd.

But I could serve Kase Woodgairrd

Tyral:

It was the funeral day. Everyone's funeral - my father's, my king's, my niece's, my prince's, my sister's. The darkest of October Thursdays.

The clouds were brewing a storm like they were mirroring my mind. A slight breeze stung my neck like a sickening serpent, a common disturbance. Because I was a Lord now, I had to wear these uncomfortable sleeves that kept billowing in the wind. The annoyance it gave me was the most recent emotion I had felt.

I felt dead myself since she died, and it was a couple of days ago that they announced it publicly. My life was grey. And warm. Just like my mind. Up until today, my mind was just a fog, the haziest of fog, and my brain felt like it had been released to bathe in the air. When he died, my days were dim. When she died, my days were dark.

When my grandfather died, we had a funeral far superior to this one. It was just everyone in the home. I remember Gwendys and I cuddling up to our mother before a warm crackling fire where we burned his remains. My father told us stories of his life - his childhood and his greatest victories - and told us that times could only get better. Now it would be my turn, but I would tell them begrudgingly. My father usually ignored me, and he only worked on managing my inheritance. He was the only family member I had that genuinely believed a minor would be plotting to overthrow the King.

It was rather calming, being in a field for corpses. I stumbled and chose to kick my shoes off. I was already drenched in an hour's worth of rain. If they escorted me from the premises for disturbing the sacred ground of the King and Prince, I had nothing left to lose. Wait, I'm going to have to give a speech. How am I going to make a speech? Should I crack a couple of jokes about the cruelty of my dead dad? Maybe about the insanity of my dead sister? No, I'm not going to disrespect Gwendys. Her insanity was genetic.

My mother was not by my side. She had been busy mourning in Minbury since I reclaimed it, cooped up with all the work of House Wayne at her side. No time to go through the stages of grief, only time to sort out the money.

My house is great. Might as well make fun of everything that's wrong with us. Isn't that what the poets do? They always end up making songs and writing stories, and then they get too big for their boots and confuse reality, and get themselves killed. It's comedy! Okay, it's not a comedy. I'm a twisted child, a victim of twisted circumstances.

What is wrong with me?

I'm out of breath. Not sweaty, just dark and cold. My vision is blurry. The pallbearers are bringing in the coffins now. Horns are blowing, and they're ridiculously loud. I can feel my heart rupturing to the blasts.

Many footsteps pattered against the wet stones, making little splashes with every step. There were thousands here, but not one of them truly cared. Not like I did. It was just their duty to mourn.

The losses weren't the only pieces of loneliness I possessed. Dontin was going on a quest with his despicable father, Jaron was returning to court, and Jaze was joining La Perte, with his former prisoner Symonnet who had found his way back to his family.

Everyone was leaving me.

This was the life of a noble, wasn't it?

My loneliness didn't matter to anyone anyway. There was no point in acknowledging my future. Let us focus on the past. Many people paid their respects, but I was barely listening to a word any of them said. Perhaps I should be somewhere else.

Eventually, it was my turn. But they could not find me.

I was Lord Wayne, and I had a house to run.

It wasn't because I was special.

It wasn't because I wanted it.

It was because it was my duty.

'Death is a gateway to rebirth. When someone beloved passes through the gateway, we mourn, but we celebrate. We feel their loss in life and community, but we celebrate their achievements in their first lifetime and all the goodness, love, morality and

445

humanity they displayed in it. It is a time when we are most aware of how sacred it is to be alive, and it makes us appreciate that gift all the more.'

-Priest Narisetti

Sylvina:

She came to me.

She needed me for the first time in her life.

She wanted me to return him to life.

She needed me.

But it was not my decision to make.

It was the pool's decision.

But, alas, they took pity on her.

He was needed to keep the world going round and carry out the best ending.

So, I placed him in that pool.

It was my duty to place him in that pool.

She watched his corpse flutter for a whole day, with nothing to lose.

Eventually, his head came out of the water.

It worked.

He was alive again.

"Hello, Varn," I spoke to him, "It's me, your aunt."

He looked at me, having only just regained his voice, "Sylvina?"

"It's me," I comforted him.

"Where the hell is Styve..." he cried, "Where the hell is Styve!"

**Epilogue: Ronayne**

"I was never treasonous," the knight declared, "I served my Lady proudly while she lived."

There was blood running down his cloak. He had been abused many times on his way here, it seemed. Perhaps he was robbed on the road. Perhaps some hounds tried to eat him alive when he trespassed on their territory. It didn't matter. He had sinned. I tightened my sacred hood, "But you were not by her side when she died, were you?"

"She dismissed us all, Priestess, I swear it!" he begged for the blessing of the gods to obtain their salvation, "How may I repent for my sins against Houses Pargion and Wayne?"

Odo Wyne, the master tactician and new leader of House Pargion's guard, stood with his knights in a single-file line at the west end of the chapel. House Wayne's knights remained at the east end, led by Jaron Carner's daughter Mawdelyn. Their presence spiked the knight's anxiety, as he could be taken away any second with a snap of my fingers. They were not helping.

Narisetti had redesigned this chapel. Everything was flecked with a bright shade of gold; it was like the Sun was inside it. An orange carpet where worshippers prayed led up to the Sceptre of Elatroal, the God of Knowledge and Medicine. The stories say that Elatroal was a deity with ashen skin, flowing black hair and eyes the colour of the stormiest seas. His height and build were human, but something about his appearance made everyone expect him to be a blissful being. He always wore a red-blue-violet cloak that covered him from clavicle to thigh. He would clarify the best solution to your worries, and he would absolve you of shame. He would end all petty brawls, and he would cure you of disease. He was commonly worshipped by men who were assaulted on the roads or parents with sickly children. Temples and chapels have been built dedicated to him at the edge of the Forest of Sanisle in the North, where they tell the famous legends of his competitive relationship with Kash, the ugly God of Alchemy, and how he gave birth to three daughters: Tues, the Goddess of Day, Rosh, the Goddess of the Undead, and Enaendrai, the Goddess of Madness.

Narisetti spoke to the knight, "I'm afraid we have not found a form of repentance for you, knight. You have committed high treason, and this is unforgivable in the eyes of the gods." It seemed cruel, but I knew why Narisetti believed in his inability to repent. "Look at the Sceptre of Elatroal. You see the hole in the centre?"

The knight nodded, "The light through the centre of Elatroal's Sceptre shines on the innocent."

Narisetti observed the Sceptre, "I see no light. Do you?"

The knight looked to the ground, "No, I do not."

"Then you are unable to repent," Narisetti summarised, "The Gods do not want to save you."

Odo Wyne had no problem with that. "Take the knight to our dungeons," he commanded, "And see that he remains there until his corpse begins to rot." The knight began to plead for his life, but his fate had been sealed by the holy gods. He would bleed more in due time.

As the echoes of his footsteps faded away, Witanegemote Morgan shook his head, "He just stood where Gwendys Wayne declared her pledge of marriage to Simon Pargion. What a waste he is."

"That's how it is when your life is on the line," I told him, "How are the Sissions coming along?"

"We've done a hundred and twenty," Morgan told me, "It has gotten to extraordinary levels, I must say. He can now pull objects from the Sissions. He is awfully close to uncovering the mysteries of the Kingdom, and then we can begin his training as the Witanegemote of the House."

"Be careful with how you train him," Narisetti advised him, "We want Dayron to be the Witanegemote of the future. He has the potential to be greater at the role than you have ever been, but you must encourage him to unlock this potential. A dog takes after its master."

"The more you give him, the more he will want," I added, "The Pargions were always fighters, but with Dayron's condition, it's just not possible. This is the best route for him. You must walk him through it in the best possible way. Even if it risks your life."

"Why would it risk my life?" Morgan questioned, "Sissions are not reality. They are visions constructed from past events. I can't die in them...can I?"

"Who knows," Narisetti warned him offhandedly, "We still don't understand why some can access Sissions at differing levels. Is it intelligence-based? Blood-based? Age-based? We are still very unsure."

"Let us move on to a separate matter," I changed the subject, "Damon's parents have left him on a thin line with King Styve. How can we assist him in a way other than prayer?"

Narisetti laid out a list of the members of Styve's council and court. It was not a detailed list, just all the names on a parchment.

'*King Styve Woodgairrd*

Queen Ashlyh Slait

Princess Sarisa Woodgairrd

High Earl Edd Malver

Lord Tobas

Lord Francis Ashford

Commander Stephyn Tanner

Lord Arvin Slait

Supreme Witanegemote Gregory

Lord Dromin Tanner

Sir Jaron Carner

Sir Elden Brune

Sir Bradyn Bulwark

Sir Maximilien Engeramus'

"These are the people we must remove from this list," Narisetti explained, "Firstly, I would like to cross off Supreme Witanegemote Gregory. He does not serve the King, but the realm, and shall soon see the sins of Styve Woodgairrd."

"I would also suggest removing Sir Maximilien Engeramus," I added, "His position in the court and King's Guard is only temporary. He has not sworn any oaths and will not be significant in the grand scheme of things."

Next was Morgan, "All previous members of the council can likely be removed. They do not care for their kings, only for power. Remove Tobas, Ashford, Carner and the executioners."

Narisetti looked at his list now, "This has already been trimmed. I would next suggest Lord Arvin Slait. He has already decided there are better things to do than be a part of the council, and he would likely betray his king easily."

"This is more on a limb," Morgan spoke up, "But Ashlyh Slait is still a 19-year-old girl. She was forced to marry Styve through rise to the ranks of society, and he is double her age. She likely still dreams of romances with some of the knights. If we can set up an affair, Styve will be weakened greatly, and it may also cost him custody of his daughter Sarisa."

Narisetti crossed Ashlyh and Sarisa off the list, "We are left with Dromin Tanner, Edd Malver and Stephyn Tanner. These are the only three that pose a threat to us."

"And they are the ones we shall convince Damon to target first," I continued, "I suggest we all find our own warm fires tonight. I know I will."

I left the chapel and found myself in my pleasant chambers. I hung my hood up, pulled off my shoes and fetched some fresh wood to make a fire. I kept a chalice of mulled wine by my side as I settled by the fireplace. The fire thawed my skin, and the wine warmed me nicely, but it was a sin to drink more than one alcoholic drink on a cold winter's night, so I refrained from having another cup. My time in House Pargion was far from done. I had reports to read, letters to write, and supper with Damon the next day. Damon had been encouraging himself to take more risks now that he was a Lord. I remember when he cried every time Simon refused to bring him along to a battle as if all he desired was to cut his skin open.

When the Pargions most wanted to be united, they were further apart than ever. Daman went off to finish his war with the Novaks to fulfil the vision of some Novak chieftain he befriended, Kristyne has escaped the clutches of Styve Woodgairrd and is in hiding, and her sister is presumed dead. At Bernstaplen, the only Pargions left were Damon, Dayron and Corren. And Corren is a three-year-old, hardly able to lead a House.

So, we had a lot of work to do, the faithful members. Me, Narisetti, and Morgan. The wise ones. I had no reason to feel guilty for plotting out deaths. Those I kill would understand that. I'm just doing my duty. It was Styve who brought shame upon the Kingdom, not House Pargion. What I did, I did for my House. It was not like the council wasn't doing the same thing at the same time.

"They must be," I muttered as I finished my mulled wine.

I looked out the window. The wind was incredibly powerful at this time, ripping through my glass defences like a hurricane outside my door. The chill was fluctuating now. One moment I felt warm as a button. The next, I was an icicle. Black ash and dying embers left by the fireplace were getting darker and then disappearing. A flickering bedside candle cast a pool of dim light in one corner. It was the brightest part of the room that wasn't shrouded in the fire. By the open window, a spray of ice crystals glittered in the light of dusk, some swirling out the window and among the winds. A single raven feather fluttered onto my wooden floorboards. Then I noticed the decapitated head, pinned above my door, dripping with blood.

"Whose head is that?" I questioned myself.

"A traitor's," a familiar voice answered.

He stood in the shadows by my bookcase and approached me, a mace in his hands.

"Narisetti?"

Narisetti lowered his mace and looked at me, "Ronayne. Forgive me for this if you can find it in your heart. I have no quarrel with you. I do this for the preservation of the Witanegemot and the Occult. My superior tells me that you have extended your uses."

"The Occult lives on? I have never been informed of this," I answered, overcome with fear.

"You have never been told for many reasons, I'm afraid. This pains me. You do not deserve to die alone. But you truly believe in those gods. You truly want to support the Pargion children. Gregory and the Occultist simply cannot accept that. So..."

A gust of wind flew through the window, and I shivered.

"Are you cold?" he asked me, "What a shame."

My legs went numb. I wanted to run, but I would surely have my head crushed mercilessly.

"I thought a mace would be a good choice for this. It's embedded with spikes and will enact a slow, painful death. You shall die quickly and effortlessly. You are welcome, Ronayne. You will not have to play a role in the divisions between Styve, Kase and Varn."

"Varn?" for a moment, I didn't understand, then I remembered the report of Elizella running off with his corpse. She must have found a fabled resurrection pool, but whose? "He's dead."

"No," Narisetti answered, "He is alive again, as the Occultist tells me. And he must be preserved. The Sissions say that he could be the victor if we follow our instructions to a tee. May the True God have mercy on our soul."

"The God? Is there a true God? Who is it?" I begged for answers before I died.

"None that you know of. One the children know of," he explained.

I wanted to cry out. To my guards, my children, the Pargions...but the words could not come at a moment that would save me. I just shuddered violently.

"I'm sorry, Ronayne," Narisetti rose the mace again, "You are suffering emotionally with this...outpour of information. Time to end it." Narisetti directed my face towards something he had attached to his mace - a Brimlock, a jewel used to implant images into the mind of the target. He implanted one constant still image into my mind.

The faces of the Occult. There was one for every House, it seemed. They were all different. Some whiter, some darker. Some men, some women. Some thin, some plump. I recognised every face. But which was the leader?

It did not matter, for they had one thing in common. As Narisetti crushed my head open with the mace, I noticed it.

In their hands, they all held daggers.

The Pargions shall return IN

NOBLE: DIVIDED

ACKNOWLEDGEMENTS

Writing this book has taken a year. I didn't imagine I was going to finish it in the first place, but if I did, I wasn't expecting it to take so long. None of this would have been possible without **my dad**. His random obsession with nerdy things like Star Wars and Game of Thrones got me into this fascinating genre in the first place, and now look where it's taken me! Thank you for being such an incredible father, no matter how much you deny that you need glasses.

I would like to share my eternal gratitude to **my mother** for reading every single draft of every single chapter as soon as I was content with the day of work. I truly have no idea how motivated I would be with my life if she hadn't provided me with the drive to succeed.

To **my primary school teachers**, **Mr. Peters** and **Mr. Page**, who constantly encouraged me to pursue and develop my creative writing skills. They never saw my age. They just saw a kid hungry to learn, grow and excel. They never stopped me; they only encouraged me.

I'd like to give a quick mention to all of the boys (and girls) – **Amirreza, Jamts, AmirAli, Fran, Rocco, Stephen, Antonio, Paolo, Zuriel, Lance, Amy, Daniel, Angelo, Dym, Yedidya, Jehremi, Otto, Alexey, Flora and Victoria**. I'd like to give a special mention to **Konrad** for spending six straight hours reading through the first chunk of this book and **Fin** and **Joe** for constantly being a source of inspiration and advice. I'm sure I'm missing someone, and it's probably **David**, so thanks, David. You guys are the best people to grow up with that I could have ever asked for, and I'm so glad I've met all of you.

To **the rest of my family**. To **my aunt Rebeca, her boyfriend Maxi**, and **my cousin Mia**: for always being people I can turn to. **To my Abuela** and **Abuelo**, and **Grandma** and **Grandad**, for always believing in me throughout my life. To **my cousin Patrick**, and to **the late John Brennan**, whose inspirational actions throughout his life have been a tremendous source of motivation.

Finally, I'd like to thank **my deceased bichon Missy** for not sleeping on my lap during the tiring writing process. Thanks for that!

I love you all.

ABOUT THE AUTHOR

During 2020, there was this thing called the COVID-19 Pandemic (heard of it? It feels like a distant memory now), and the extreme levels of boredom said period produced led to Dylan Brennan starting an epic fantasy novel called *Noble: Betrayed*. For years, Dylan dreamed of an entry into the genre that avoided conforming to all the tropes while still being an enjoyable reading experience, leading to the birth of Noble.

Dylan is currently a student and lives in London with his parents. He's an avid reader, musician and gamer but writes a chapter whenever he seizes the chance.

Printed in Great Britain
by Amazon

11000564R00264